A PAT MONTELLA MYSTERY

POISON

to Purge Melancholy

Elena Santangelo

A PAT MONTELLA MYSTERY

POISON

to Purge Melancholy

Elena Santangelo

MIDNIGHT INK
WOODBURY, MINNESOTA

First Edition
First Printing, 2006

Book design by Donna Burch
Cover design by Gavin Dayton Duffy
Cover background image and pattern © Kamil Vojnar/Photonica/Getty Images, bottle © Photodisc

Midnight Ink, an imprint of Llewellyn Publications

Library of Congress Cataloging-in-Publication Data
Santangelo, Elena.
    Poison to purge melancholy : a Pat Montella mystery / Elena Santangelo.—1st ed.
        p. cm.
    ISBN-13: 978-0-7387-0890-4
    ISBN-10: 0-7387-0890-9
    1. Montella, Pat (Fictitious character)—Fiction. 2. Women detectives—Virginia—Fiction. 3. Colonial Williamsburg (Williamsburg, Va.)—Fiction. 4. Psychics—Fiction. 5. Christmas stories. I. Title.

PS3569.A5443P65 2006
813'.54—dc22

2006048244

Midnight Ink
Llewellyn Publications
2143 Wooddale Drive, Dept. 0-7387-0890-9
Woodbury, MN 55125-2989, U.S.A.
www.midnightinkbooks.com

Printed in the United States of America

To
my dear friend,
Polly Whitney

ACKNOWLEDGMENTS

When the Philadelphia Revels centered their December show around Christmas in Colonial Philadelphia, the director, April Woodall, allowed me to help with the research and writing, and so awoke in me a fascination for early American Yuletide customs. Through her, I met Clarissa Dillon, local historian and living history expert on women and cooking of the eighteenth century. I owe Clarissa especially for teaching me about the clothing and foods of the times.

Kris Dippre of Colonial Williamsburg's Apothecary Shop went out of her way to give me an understanding of colonial medical philosophies and medicines, despite my first question to her being about poisons.

One website deserves much recognition: the online diary of Martha Ballard at www.dohistory.org, an awesome searchable primary source from an early medical professional.

On the nonhistoric side, Cynthia Garman gave me her perspective of Williamsburg as a William and Mary alum, Dr. Mathew Beshara answered all my questions gynecological, and Kristin Gagliardi helped me hear Beth Ann's voice clearly. Linda Hanson and Dr. Deb Volker answered my eleventh-hour Virginia questions before a quarter to twelve.

If I got any facts wrong, I don't blame the experts listed above, but my own dense brain.

In *By Blood Possessed*, I thanked Linda Gagliardi for letting me use her computer when mine died in the middle of chapter 13. She did so again with this book. Same chapter. Maybe I'll skip thirteen in the next novel. And thanks to my brother and fellow author, Bob Brooke, who loaned me his laptop so I could keep working until my new PC arrived.

Thanks also goes to my Delaware Valley Sisters In Crime for their support, to Jean Geiger for her second set of eyes, and to Polly Whitney for her hellfire sermon on adverbs.

As always, I thank Linda Gagliardi and my other brother, Tom Santangelo, for being proofreaders, sounding boards, and for listening to me kvetch and moan.

Would ye have a young Virgin of fifteen Years,
You must tickle her Fancy with sweets and dears,
Ever toying, and playing, and sweetly, sweetly,
Sing a Love Sonnet, and charm her Ears . . .

Do ye fancy a Widow well known in a Man?
With a front of Assurance come boldly on,
Let her rest not an Hour, but briskly, briskly,
Put her in mind how her Time steals on . . .

from *Wit & Mirth: Pills to Purge Melancholy*,
—Thomas D'Urfrey, 1719

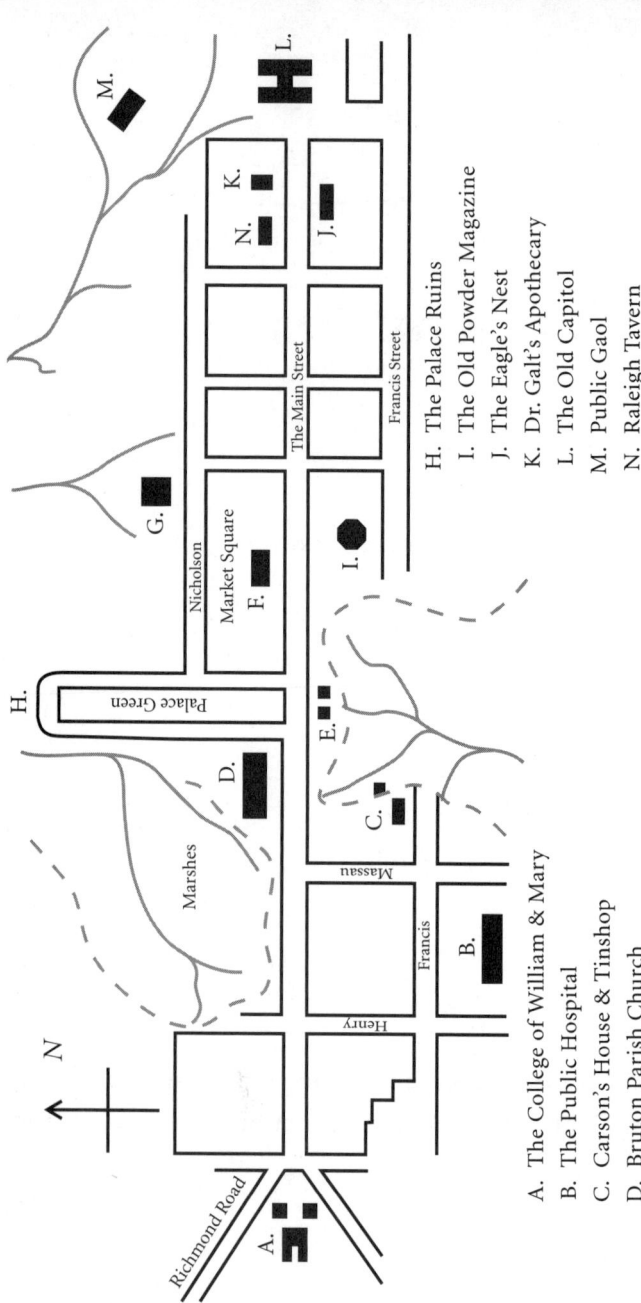

A. The College of William & Mary
B. The Public Hospital
C. Carson's House & Tinshop
D. Bruton Parish Church
E. Greenhow's Store & Lumber House
F. Courthouse
G. Captain Underwood's House

H. The Palace Ruins
I. The Old Powder Magazine
J. The Eagle's Nest
K. Dr. Galt's Apothecary
L. The Old Capitol
M. Public Gaol
N. Raleigh Tavern

ADVENT

December, Present Day

THE FIRST E-MAIL CAME the Sunday morning after Thanksgiving:

"hello how are you in dominion you know me"

The address was one of the free e-mail services with only "CMJSM43" as the name. The subject was simply "Message from the Internet," meaning the sender hadn't typed one.

He often got mail from unfamiliar addresses—the bane of having an e-mail link on an organization's website. Some of the messages were legitimate inquiries, most were junk mail—spam. At least CMJSM43 could spell.

The obvious choice was to hit the delete button. One word stopped him: *Dominion.* Yet he couldn't bring himself to reply, either.

The next Sunday brought another message from the same address:

> "hello how are you we played cards
> hearts with spades remember"

Hearts with spades. He remembered all too well. Can insanity be forgotten? This time, because he needed to know, he *did* reply, "Where are you now?" and typed his initials below.

No answer. A relief. Until Sunday, December twentieth:

> "hello how are you joyce erased your note
> i couldnt read it but Christmas
> i find you play spades"

> *"Strong-Beer, Stout Syder, and a good fire*
> *Are things this season doth require."*

—Titan Leeds, *The American Almanac*, December, 1714

December 3, 1783—The Eagle's Nest, Williamsburg, Virginia

"YE'VE ANGELS DANCIN' ON your fiddle, lad." As John Brennan spoke, he set his pint of beer and his snuffbox upon the table. Every man in the room turned toward him in amazement.

Some twenty of us were gathered in the West Room of Mrs. Vobe's tavern, warmed by fire and drink and the company assembled at the long tables. The oaken panels softened the hearthlight so that our faces glowed the color of fine brandy. Our tall shadows swayed upon the walls not starkly, but as grasses 'neath the water of a millpond. I'd brought my violin and Jim Parker helped himself to one of the house guitars, so the lot of us had been enjoying an evening of song. No one had taken heed of Brennan, sitting quietly by the door, until he spoke of angels.

'Twasn't his praise that drew our notice. Compliments came to Brennan's tongue like mold to cheese. Once there, the flattery was

3

tinted a soft Irish hue and delivered through a generous smile, the effect being that few listeners doubted his sincerity. However, he reserved compliments for his customers, not for poor men such as myself who could ill afford the luxury of snuff, even at Brennan's price.

But no, all eyes viewed his snuffbox. 'Twas never out of his hand in public and that hand never dropped below the plane of his shoulders, except to replenish his box from a cloth pouch in his coat pocket. He kept the snuff at the ready so that when a potential buyer happened within hearing, Brennan could sniff in a dose and remark upon the excellence of the tobacco. Red veins stood out on either side of his nose as testimony to the practice, but I'd seen him sell his wares on the street in this manner, and take away more shillings in an hour than I took in all week.

Now here he was, beer and snuff forgotten, the smile gone from his lips and perplexity in its place, his gaze lingering upon my fiddle, his eyes becoming rounder, as if every host of Heaven now occupied the instrument's curves. All from my rendering of "The Jolly Miller." A common rendering it had been, since my bow was in need of new horsehair and to make it last, I'd been forced to restrain my customary musical vigor.

Sam Walker, the only one of us seemingly unaware of Brennan's unnatural behavior, stood and raised his leather tankard. "A toast, gentlemen."

Everyone laughed, for 'twas Sam's custom to make such a proposal no less than twice with each new round, and to address every man thus, regardless of his birth and status.

I'd first beheld Sam's lean, red face at Germantown in '77. In the thick fog that day, he'd been estranged from his militia and had come upon me, wandering senselessly, knocked on the head by the wayward musket barrel of a less fortunate comrade who'd taken a British ball to his chest. Sam had led me to safety and stayed the bleeding of my skull with a strip of homespun from his own shirt. He'd saved my life thrice more in the next six years, and I his as many times.

"To Mr. Dunbar's angels," he said now. "May they cavort upon his fingerboard for many an evening to come."

"Huzzah!" the company shouted as one, hoisting their cups to their lips.

I bowed deeply. "Your pleasure is my own, good sirs."

"Ah," said Sam. "A wager then."

The men gathered closer, for Sam's wagers were more legendary than his toasts.

"Benjamin Dunbar has delighted us with his fiddle since coming to Williamsburg a month ago." Sam paused to allow the lads to express agreement and, to a man, all did, many pounding the table for punctuation. "From the Eve of All Souls onward, each time we've gathered here, Mr. Dunbar has played every song or dance requested of him, not once claiming unfamiliarity."

Agreement once more, mingled with a bit of wonderment. Sam hushed them by raising a hand. "I propose that, for a stake of tuppence apiece, each man buys the chance to name a tune unknown to Mr. Dunbar. Winner take the pot, or Mr. Dunbar, if he can play all."

Further conditions were set. I was to play each melody through, at which I insisted that, should I fail, my challenger be prepared to sing his own ditty, to prove its existence.

Tucking a wayward lock of my red hair back behind my ear, raising my fiddle to my chin, we began. I played better than three dozen tunes that evening, triumphing until the fourth go-round, when the stake had risen to half a shilling and two, and those wagering had dwindled to four souls.

Then Will Knox asked for a Welsh hymn he'd heard as a boy, of which he recollected not the name, but recited the first couplet. I'd heard the song once, though my memory brought forth only the opening phrase. To resolve the chord, I added the refrain of "Yankee Doodle," which made all laugh.

So ended the wager known ever after as "Walker's Fiddler's Challenge." Though Will took the biggest pot, by the close of our evening amusements, I had in my pocket five shillings four and three bits of a Spanish dollar which had not been there before. Placing my fiddle in its hemp case, I bid the barkeep goodnight and, with Sam at my side, stepped out into the wintry air, both of us buttoning our coats across our chests. The chill penetrated the wool of my stockings. I tilted my tricorn down to shield my face from the wind, saying, "By rights, Sam, you should have half of tonight's purse."

"You earned it, Ben. You're the best fiddler in Williamsburg. Nay, in all Virginia." Yet no smile colored his voice, and he turned not west along the path, but stopped to gaze eastward, toward the end of the street and the old capitol building. 'Twas now a grammar school by day, but after dark it took on a gloomy, forsaken aspect.

"Here are your own wagers, at least," I insisted, holding forth a shilling. "I'll not accept money from a friend."

Sam allowed me to place the coin in his palm, though by his expression, you'd think he'd never before felt silver. His only remark was, "The days grow short, Ben."

Puzzled by his mood, I replied lightly, "That they do, as always in December. 'Tis your favorite time of year, Sam, for the nights are long enough to allow for several trysts."

His mouth twitched into a smile then, but there was no jollity behind it. "I meant for Williamsburg. Not five years ago these windows were ablaze with light each evening."

He gestured along Main Street, where too few lamps twinkled—faint stars through the damp air. The dim flicker of hearthlight shown in both taverns and in one upstairs window of Dr. Galt's apothecary, but no candles at this hour. Candles were conserved in times like this, when money was hard won. Yet—and I thought of the surplus of coin in my pocket—'twas times as this when fools entered most into wagers, in hopes of easy winnings.

Sam turned to view the Eagle behind us. "Williamsburg once had fourteen taverns, Ben. Now two are all that remain. Before the Revolution, this one was called the King's Arms. Only gentry passed through its door. Today I heard that Mrs. Vobe plans to sell."

"What then will you do for venison tarts?" I asked, joking, for Sam had a great appetite for Jane Vobe's meat pies. Yet the news was unsettling, for I was reminded how the citizens of Williamsburg seemed daily to dwindle in number, and that boded ill for my plans to situate myself here.

Sam moved then, turning westward, his feet crunching upon the oyster shells of the path. "The devil of it is that I cannot bear to stay behind Old Man Greenhow's counter much longer." Sam was a clerk in John Greenhow's store and had in the last month often stated his displeasure with the work.

"And yet," he continued, "the import trade is all I know. In truth, I fancy my own establishment." Sam paused, using his hands to outline an imaginary signboard in the air. "'Samuel Walker, Purveyor of Fine Goods.' A fine sound that has to it."

"You need wealth to open a store, purchase inventory, pay the ships—"

"Precisely my point." Sam resumed his walk, jamming his hands into his pockets in frustration. "Even if I had the means, with everyone leaving Williamsburg, who would be my patrons? Greenhow already provides for the gentry still here—"

"And no one else can afford imports of late," I concluded, "with all the embargoes."

Sam agreed. "Still, if I could begin small, offering one item— French wine, perchance—that could be sold from my current lodgings, as Brennan does with his snuff."

I scoffed. "John Brennan's snuff is but the lowest quality tobacco, ground up with dry mint to make it tolerable. He sells for a shilling what costs him less than a penny to produce."

Sam paused, one foot poised in the air. When it came down, he touched his hat to me, saying, "Sir, I bow to your insight." Then he laughed, clapping me upon the back. "Do you see? I need not sell to gentry at all. I can claim as my customers Brennan's patrons—those middling folk who desire the luxuries of the gentry within their own means, and who already frequent Mrs. Carson's to deal with Brennan."

"Those folk can ill afford imported wine, even at cost."

"Imported from France, no. I could do my importing a bit closer to home. York County, say."

"And pass local wine as French? You'd be caught out."

We came even with the old powder magazine, an octagonal building used since the war as a market storehouse. Sam waved me ahead, for the path here was ill kept and it forced us to go Indian file to avoid the worst of the mud, but he carried on his plotting. "I'll call it Rhenish then. And if need be, I could travel farther afield for my stock. See you here, Ben, we've both maintained since the war began that Americans ought to trade more in their own goods. Why, I could make unwitting patriots of the lot of them."

I could but laugh at that and say over my shoulder, "I suppose this is no worse than your last week's scheme to marry a rich widow 'fore the New Year."

"The outcome is more pleasant. The wealthy widows hereabout all long ago lost their comeliness, if indeed they had any to start with. Why should beauty and fortune be so opposed, I wonder?"

"'Tis a device of rich men, to keep Sam Walker from bedding wife and daughter."

"A faulty device, then. A homely lass is often more willing than a pretty one, and the view remedied with ease by blowing out the candle. 'Tis only for the years of marriage that I require a handsome face, to gaze upon across the dinner table each day and not be put off my victuals."

The path widened before Mr. Greenhow's tenement and we walked abreast once more. "Moreover, Sam, no widow would marry you, rich or poor, given your present income."

"Nor you," he returned with a laugh. "None save our landlady, at least, who'd meet you at the altar on the morrow if you showed a willingness. What about it, Ben? Elizabeth Carson owns her house and a half acre, and her Thomas has been in his grave more than two years now. Have the banns announced this month and you could be wed Twelfth Night."

I felt my face grow warm, for in truth, the prospect of marriage was one reason I'd come to Williamsburg. Yet the memory of Thomas Carson, my lieutenant for the late years of the war and as good a man as I'd ever known, could not be so easily dismissed. My reply was, "I'll not marry until I have means enough to improve my intended's circumstances."

"A noble heart, you have, Ben Dunbar. If it's means you want, well . . ." he looked about him, and though no one else occupied the street, brought his voice down almost to a whisper. "A few of us lads go about performing antics on Christmas Eve, and divide equally our take. With your fiddle along, I'll wager we'd double our profits this year."

"Antics? Mummery, you mean?" In the years before the war, bands of masked mummers—sometimes as many as a dozen separate companies an evening—had yearly come to demand entry upon the steps of Mr. Ivey's townhouse in Norfolk, some on Christmas Eve, some New Year's, some Twelfth Night. I'd watch them from the third floor window, until the mistress would send one of her manslaves out to chase them away without recompense. Like as not, they'd fire their pistols and muskets at the house, cursing the master, before moving on.

"In the best tradition," Sam assured me. "St. George and the Dragon. This season our saint shall be Washington and our dragon, George the Third. We'll end the evening at the Eagle and toast the Yule with rum punch. You know all the lads—Jim Parker, Will

Knox, Alex Fisher—and I promised young Tom Carson he could shadow us."

No sooner was the name out of Sam's mouth, than the youth himself came running at us out of the darkness, wearing no coat, nor even his waistcoat. Young Tom was a boy of nine years, tall for his age, with the same broad, kind face as Thomas the elder as I remembered him before he'd died in camp not a week after the surrender. But this night the boy's face was deformed in horror.

"Mr. Dunbar! Mr. Walker!" he called, his voice breaking into its highest falsetto so that he had to swallow hard to gain control of it. He halted, flustered, and performed an awkward bow. "Your pardon, sirs."

As we hurried our steps to meet him, Sam lost his patience. "Manners be damned, boy. Tell us what's the matter!"

Tom straightened, his breath coming fast, one hand quelling a stitch in his side. "Mother says to come at once. Mr. Brennan has took a fit, raving as one mad. Mr. Parker and Doctor Riddick fear they cannot restrain him much longer."

ONE

December 24, Present Day

FIFTEEN MINUTES OUTSIDE OF Richmond, I knew I was insane.

Wistfully, I recalled Christmas Eve last year. I'd goofed off at work until our department potluck began. My tray of chocolate pizzelles had brought kudos from my co-workers—the only time all year, so I'd lapped it up. After work, I'd gone to Uncle Mario's for dinner. Since his wife was second-generation Sicilian, that meant seven fishes on Christmas Eve. I'm not crazy about the smelts or baccalà, but nobody does calamari like my Aunt Philomena. Good squid isn't something I get every day.

This year would have been Aunt Sophie's turn to invite me. Italian sausage and ricotta pie. And after midnight mass, we'd all go back to the house for homemade cannolis sprinkled with powdered sugar and shaved chocolate. Thinking about them now sent my drool glands into overdrive.

So what was I doing instead? I was battling the afternoon traffic on I-64, which was so crowded you couldn't fit a riding mower in the spaces between cars. The sky was that shade of monotonous gray that makes bare tree limbs look the most bleak. Since the temperature was ten degrees above freezing, no pretty Christmas snow would come from those clouds—they existed solely to depress me. Worst of all, my destination was Williamsburg and the home of Gladys Lee, mother of the man I'd been seeing the last eight months.

Seeing? What an understatement. I was, after all, a Montella. Other people have "relationships." Montellas simply rip out their own hearts and give them away. Hugh, as far as my gut was concerned, was It—Mr. Right, Soulmate Central. Why else would I be mentally cursing him out right now?

Not that I *minded* meeting Hugh's family this weekend. I wanted to. Really. But no woman in her sane mind approaches this kind of first contact without her man at her side, right? Better yet, in front of her.

Sure, I understood that Hugh had to put in a full day at the post office—he was a mailman, after all, and up to his well-developed abs in late greeting cards and presents. And no, I hadn't minded driving Miss Maggie to Richmond. Even if I had, I couldn't say no to her.

Nearly eight months ago, Magnolia Shelby had brought me to Virginia because she had decided I should inherit her estate, Bell Run. The whole "why" of that decision would fill a book, so I won't go into it here. Anyway, since I came to Bell Run to live with her, Miss Maggie has become not only my benefactor, but my mentor, housemate, and best friend (I reserved a ventricle for her before handing the rest of my heart over to Hugh). She was pushing ninety-two, and no longer drove a car, so I'd also become her chauffeur. Every Wednesday, I drove her to Richmond to visit her son Frank, who was a psychiatric patient at the VA Hospital. Frank wasn't all that comfortable around me yet, so my routine was to stop in, say hello, then go fill a couple of hours reading in the car or shopping.

Today, though, was Miss Maggie's Christmas visit—she'd stay with her son all afternoon. It was too cold to sit in the car, and shopping on the day before Christmas was my idea of self-inflicted torture. Still, I could have found *some* way to while away the hours. But no, Hugh had come up with a Brilliant Solution. I would drive Miss Maggie to Richmond, taking Hugh's fourteen-year-old daughter Beth Ann with me. I would then drive on to Williamsburg so that Beth Ann could arrive early to help her grandmother with holiday preparations.

Translation: he wanted his moody kid out of his hair for the day.

Hugh would then stop for Miss Maggie on his way down to Williamsburg. She was a family friend of the Lees—practically a surrogate grandmother. Four of the five siblings had been her students back when she taught junior high history. As a teenager, Hugh had come out to Bell Run to do chores for Miss Maggie. After his wife died, and Hugh decided to leave Richmond and all memories of her behind, Miss Maggie helped him get a job at her new post office annex. When Hugh brought Beth Ann—then a toddler—to live in the postal service trailer at Bell Run, Miss Maggie started spending holidays with the Lee family.

So here I was, me and a teenager who'd said nothing since I picked her up this morning except "cheeseburger combo" when we stopped for lunch. The air in my Neon had been replaced with her sulkiness. I couldn't take a breath without being aware of every one of the injustices she felt had been done to her in the last month, all of them somehow my fault.

That wasn't just my normal Italian guilt kicking in. Familiarity *does* breed contempt. The more familiar I got with her father, the more contemptible I became in Beth Ann's eyes. I was okay as a neighbor—she'd even liked me for a few months—but she wanted nothing to do with me as a potential stepmother.

Not that Hugh had ever suggested wedlock. I couldn't blame him—his first marriage had been a nightmare, which is why I hadn't brought up the subject, either. Fear of scaring him off. Problem was, Rule One in the Nice Italian Girl Manual, drilled into me by my mom and aunts, is "No sex until after you dance the Tarantella at your wedding reception." Oh, I was willing to give up my "NIG" status for Hugh—like I said, we Montellas don't have simple love affairs. We mate for life. Emotionally, I'd already taken all the vows.

Well, maybe not obedience.

But the main reason I'd been stalling Hugh off was Beth Ann. First of all, she was always around. Second, if Hugh and I did decide to get away for, say, a romantic weekend, she'd hate me all the more for it. Third, I was a role model. I didn't want Beth Ann coming home pregnant or with AIDS or cervical cancer or even a bad self-image because I'd sent the wrong message.

I couldn't stall much longer, though. Hugh had asked me two months ago what I wanted to do on New Year's Eve. I'd always ushered in the New Year with aunts, uncles, and cousins—playing Michigan rummy until our midnight feast of porchetta and tomato pie—so I was naïve about how far in advance reservations had to be made. The upshot was that Hugh booked us at a swanky hotel in downtown Richmond for their New Year's special, which included dinner, dancing, and a room with a king bed. I was looking forward to that night with an anticipation I hadn't felt since I was ten, when I knew I was getting a five-speed bike for Christmas.

If only I could quiet the voice of my mother in my head ("You're breaking my heart, Patricia Marie!") or keep at bay the image of Beth Ann's face—the betrayal on it when her father finally got around to telling her our plans for next week.

I glanced over at my passenger. Her face was slanted toward the window, and her long, fox-red hair hung down along her cheek so I couldn't see her expression at all. I couldn't picture myself as her stepmother. Or anyone's mother—not yet, anyway, no matter how loud my biological clock was ticking—which was why I'd gone on the Pill two weeks ago (I would have gone on it sooner, but couldn't get a GYN appointment until December).

Thing was, when she wasn't sulking, Beth Ann was a great kid. Less self-centered than most teens. Big heart. Equally big brain that was fascinated by every green thing on the planet. I liked her a lot, and couldn't help feeling that she and I would get along better if Hugh wouldn't push us into mother-daughter situations like this little outing. That scared me, too. As affectionate as Hugh could be—extremely affectionate, in fact—some insecure part of my psyche wondered if he merely wanted me around to give himself a break from parenthood. Especially now that Beth Ann was old enough to ask questions about sex.

Though, come to think of it, even a question about sex would be welcome right now if it would end her silent treatment.

For the umpteenth time, I tried conversation. "Hey, no school until next year."

I got a half grunt, the kind that implied that my comment wasn't worth so much as a condescending roll of her eyes.

Second try: "I liked your band concert last week."

"The drums screwed us up."

"I thought it sounded fine."

"How would *you* know?"

Was she criticizing my lack of musical knowledge? Or had she caught me nodding off during their last number? Not that it was boring—I'd never before heard "Jingle Bell Rock" played quite that slow, with a German oompah beat. I hadn't been sleeping well, though, a combination of holiday stress and leg cramps—rheumatism, I thought, inherited from my mom, or maybe tendinitis from standing so much while I cooked batches of pizzelles to give as gifts. Anyway, for the last week, every night around eight, no matter where I was, my eyelids got heavy.

A change of subject was called for and it occurred to me that I could pump her for information at the same time. "Tell me about your grandmother."

"She's old." No insult intended. A statement of fact, with a silent "duh" for punctuation. Hugh had said his mom was sixty-five. She'd retired this past year from an accounting job she'd held since her divorce, when Hugh was fourteen. Another reason to be intimidated by her—she'd survived an office job well over a decade longer than I had.

"I mean—" I paused to decide what I really did mean. "Tell me what sorts of things she likes."

"Old things."

I gave up on conversation.

* * *

Hugh had written the directions down for me but, of course, I couldn't look at them and drive, too. I managed to remember exit number 238 before having to ask Beth Ann to read the rest. Since she saw the logic in my request, she agreed—one thing about her, no matter how grumpy she is, she stays logical—but between directions, she groused.

"Why'd Grandmom have to move, anyway?" she asked when we were stopped for a light on Route 132. A sign for a hotel sat up on the hill, but otherwise the area was more of a park, all trees and well-tended lawn. "I liked her other house."

"Your father said her new place used to belong to your family. Your grandfather grew up there."

"So it's not a 'new' place. It's *old*."

"Old" was the word of the day. The light changed, I drove on.

"And," Beth Ann continued, bent on proving my total lack of knowledge, "it isn't Grandmom's house. The Foundation owns it."

Miss Maggie told me that the Colonial Williamsburg Foundation owns something like a hundred houses. The little Julia Bell Foundation that Miss Maggie and I dreamed up last May, and had been midwiving through birth pains since, only encompassed a couple hundred acres of mostly forest, which didn't require much upkeep beyond trail maintenance, fire prevention, and discouraging vandals. I couldn't imagine having to take care of a hundred houses, all in need of heating, painting, good roofs, and, worst of all, housecleaning.

"That's probably why she moved," I reasoned aloud. "All her kids are grown and she's retired, so maybe having her own home was too much trouble for her. Now that she's doing volunteer work for the Foundation, she's able to share one of their houses with an employee."

"That's not what Dad said."

To me, Hugh hadn't said much at all, simply that his mom moved less than a month ago and was now sharing her father's childhood home with someone named Evelyn. I knew Hugh wasn't happy about it, but I assumed that had to do with her selling the old house without consulting him or any of his four siblings. Now I wondered. "What did he say?"

That was met with Beth Ann's most profound silence yet, then, "I can't tell you."

I was willing to bet she wouldn't tell me because she'd been eavesdropping—maybe while he was on the phone with one of his brothers—and she didn't want to get caught. Especially since she tried to redirect my attention with, "Three blocks farther, you'll make a left onto Francis Street."

Route 132 was now Henry Street, the road narrowing as the trees gave way to low modern buildings on our right, then again, farther on, as older brick and clapboard shops lined the way. Older, but not very colonial, at least not colonial the way I remembered Old City Philadelphia, which is sort of what I'd expected, since Williamsburg had been the capital of Virginia when Philly was capital of Pennsylvania. Oh, this place was quaint all right, but the quaintness seemed more of a veneer, for the sake of luring shoppers. I was disappointed.

I hung a left where Beth Ann indicated and the scenery changed. On the right, set back across a wide lawn dotted with fat magnolia trees, was a dignified brick building, half a block wide and two stories high, with multi-pane windows and a white, domed cupola flanked by two massive chimneys. At last, architecture that had the same aura as Independence Hall. Was that the old capitol?

"How appropriate that we're spending this Christmas across the street from *that* place," Beth Ann murmured.

Figuring she was baiting me, I snapped, "Just tell me which house is your grandmother's." That shocked both of us. Blatant crankiness wasn't like me—I usually took the barbed sarcasm route.

Beth Ann slouched down in her seat as far as her seat belt would allow. "Next block. Second from the corner." I assumed she meant on the left. The only things on the right were two long-horned cows chewing cud behind a rail fence.

I had to admit, I was impressed by the house, not by its size—on the small side compared to those in modern developments—but by its ambience of solid craftsmanship, especially as I realized it must have been built in an era that had no power tools. The house was white clapboard atop an orange brick foundation, flanked by two bulky brick chimneys. In front, where the weathered wood shakes of the roof continued down at a sharper angle, five dormers stuck out. Instead of a rain gutter, a line of pretty block molding decorated the bottom edge. The window shutters and front door were forest green.

I took in all this detail as I pulled into the drive—a car-wide path of crushed shells—and waited for Beth Ann to open the broad gates in the six-foot wooden fence that surrounded the rear yard of the property. Miss Maggie had said that in Williamsburg's historic section, houses had tall fences or garages disguised as colonial outbuildings, to keep cars hidden from view. Our instructions said to park around back.

Inside the gates, the driveway spread out, but the coating of shells disappeared, revealing a thin layer of gravel pressed into hard-packed dirt. On my left, I saw that the house had a rear wing, forming an "L" with the front. In the crook of the L, a white VW Beetle was parked, so I pulled in beside it.

Beth Ann had closed the gates, and I assumed she'd come back to the car to help me carry in the suitcases and gifts. I got out, slowly, because my legs felt stiff and achy from the long ride, and headed around to my trunk. That's when I heard her knocking at the door.

There were two back doors, actually, one on the wing and one in what would be the center of the main house. Beth Ann was at the latter, a white raised panel door with a black iron handle and latch.

"Hey, come help unload the car first," I called.

"In a minute." She put her hand to the latch, pushed open the door and went inside.

"Beth Ann!" I yelled, pretty sure no one had let her in. Then again, maybe knocking and walking in was standard procedure at her grandmother's house. One thing was certain, I wasn't going to unload the car by myself. I grabbed the fancy-wrapped coffee can of pizzelles I'd made for Mrs. Lee—not about to walk in without my hostess gift at the ready—and went after Beth Ann.

"Grandmom? Hello?" I could hear her calling as I passed through the open door.

Closing it behind me, I let my eyes adjust to the hall, which formed a straight line alongside a stairway to the front door. The transom over that portal let in the gray daylight, showing white plaster, beige-painted wainscoting, wide bare floorboards, and a small colonial-style hurricane lamp on an equally diminutive table. Immediately to my right was a niche with two doors, one open, giving access to a stair down to a dark cellar. But Beth Ann's voice wasn't coming from there.

"Grandmom?" She wandered out of the front room on the left, perplexed, then bellowed up the stairs, as I walked toward her.

"Doesn't sound like anyone's here," I said, thinking it odd—we were expected, after all, and there *was* a car outside. "Maybe we should—"

"Bet she's in the bathroom." Beth Ann bounded up the stairs, calling as she went.

A feeling of uneasiness crept over me. No, not uneasiness. Foreboding? That wasn't right either. Regardless, fear lay at the bottom of it—a cold, clammy paranoia—though I couldn't say what I was afraid of, with the exception of being arrested for breaking and entering because perhaps we'd inadvertently walked into the wrong house.

And suddenly, I knew someone was watching me.

Spinning around, I was startled to see the outline of a man in the shadows by the back door. Startled because he wore britches, buckled shoes, and a long waistcoat over a ruffly white shirt. He was bald on the very front of his head, but the hair that remained was light and long, pulled back at the nape.

> *"If you wou'd have Guests merry with your cheer,*
> *Be so yourself, or so at least appear."*
> —*Poor Richard's Almanac*, December 1734

December 3, 1783—Mrs. Carson's House

"SIRS!"

As we entered the house, we could hear Brennan's voice, trembling, though cocky as ever.

"Sirs, I am indebted to you for your assistance." He stood before the large hearth in our common room, and by the light of its dying fire I saw that he clutched the mantel with one hand, as if to maintain balance. The fingers of his other hand were splayed across his forehead, which evidently pained him. His face was so contorted, I wondered if, a moment previous, he'd retched into Mrs. Carson's stew pot.

Jim Parker stood close by Brennan's side, arms raised, ready to catch hold of the man. Or perhaps having just released him, since a vicious gash spanned the back of Jim's hand. Dr. Riddick, though of small stature, was attempting to block the doorway. Sam touched his shoulder and he stepped aside for us to enter. I set my fiddle case upon the window ledge, so as to have both hands free.

"I assure you, I am quite recovered," Brennan said, sounding far from that state.

Dr. Riddick advanced toward him with care. "You are not well, sir."

"Ah, but I shall be, Doctor." Brennan made a show of it, straightening his posture and lifting his head, his smile quivering, making the shadows upon his face dance. "I do apologize for my behavior—too much drink this night, I fear. I shall—I shall retire to my room. In the morning, I assure you, I shall be myself once more." He walked toward us, determined in his course, but mindful of his steps, as if the floor had become a half-frozen lake.

Before the doctor could protest anew, Sam said, "I too shall retire, for the morrow is no day of rest for Mr. Greenhow. May I offer you an arm up the stairs, Mr. Brennan? I know well what cruel jokes Mrs. Vobe's punch can play upon our eyes and feet."

Brennan at first recoiled from Sam's offered hand, but then nodded, saying, "I thank you, sir," perhaps realizing that Dr. Riddick would not let him leave the room without escort. Or that his legs alone would not carry him much farther.

"A light, if you would, Ben," Sam requested, and I retrieved and lit for him one of the two tin lanterns Mrs. Carson kept by the hearth. Her husband had been a tinsmith before the war. Fine examples of his craft could be found in all corners of the house.

The doctor, Jim, and I watched Brennan and Sam ascend from below, Sam all the while asserting that the quality of rum to be found hereabouts had declined from the British embargoes, and 'twas no wonder a man might suffer ill effects upon the drinking of it.

Once out of sight, we heard a door open above and Sam said, loud enough for all to hear, "There you go, Mr. Brennan. Good night to you."

As we heard the door close, Jim turned back into the common room. There we found young Tom, who I'd quite forgotten, looking relieved. "Go to your mother and sister, lad," Jim said. "Stay all of you together in one room this night, and block the doors."

"Yes, sir." With another awkward bow, the boy left.

"Perhaps we should each take a watch in turn," the doctor suggested.

"Surely that's not necessary," I said. "Brennan was the worse for the rum in him and—"

"He had no rum," Jim said. "Not at the Eagle, at least, for I sat beside him the whole time."

"Aye." Sam had come quietly down the stairs to join us. "He scarcely sipped at his one pint."

Jim nodded. "I tossed it off when he took his leave. 'Twas small beer. Nothing more."

Dr. Riddick gave the table a pat. "Sit here, Jim. Let me see to your hand. Mr. Walker, would you be kind enough to fetch a bit of fresh water? Fill this to half." Taking up one of Mrs. Carson's small iron pots, he passed it to Sam, who took up the lantern once more and left us for the well behind the house.

Jim scoffed. "'Tis but a scratch, Isaac."

"Which I'll wash and dress. The cleanliness of a wound is vital. It promotes the perspiration, which frees the body from superfluous humours that occasion disease." Dr. Riddick had studied in

Philadelphia, had taken his degree just this last year, in fact, and so embraced the scientific methods.

The new practices interested me, though I'll concede my skepticism when they'd been applied to my own person. Still, I was anxious to hear the doctor's views concerning Brennan. I related the odd behavior we'd witnessed at the tavern.

Riddick, in thought, stroked the bristle of his chin. "Unnatural of him. He was raving by the time he entered this house, as Jim will warrant. A mania too pronounced to be afforded to drunkenness. Had he taken any unwholesome food or drink that might account?"

"Not at the Eagle," Jim said once more, and Sam, bringing in the water, concurred.

"Mr. Brennan's not been himself the last fortnight," Dr. Riddick observed with a frown. "Have you noticed? His skin's gone paler, and his voice rough and low. A touch of ague, I thought, nothing more. Now I wonder."

"He's been talking to himself a good bit all week," Jim told us. "I can hear him through the flue, since we share a chimney upstairs. The rumble of his voice, leastways, not the words."

"Were you here tonight, Jim, when Brennan arrived?" I asked.

"I was. I held him while the doctor hastened Mrs. Carson and Polly into their rooms. 'Twas then that I hurt my hand."

Sam took a pipe from the mantel. "But Brennan took his leave of Mrs. Vobe's before any of us."

"Aye," Jim said, "by a quarter hour or more."

As we pondered where Brennan could have passed that quarter hour, Dr. Riddick plunged Jim's hand into the pot. Mr. Parker blasphemed the iciness of the liquid.

TWO

Before I could make a sound, the man said, "Hello." His manner was nervy, on guard, but he had the most disarming Peter O'Toole accent. "I didn't hear you come in."

All I found myself saying was, "The door was unlocked."

He followed the direction of my vague nod to the entrance in question and his eyes grew narrow. "This door? I never disengaged the deadbolt. See, it's still on." He turned the knob of a modern brass lock right above the iron latch, and I heard the bolt snap back.

He had to be mistaken, I told myself. The dead bolt *must* have been open, and when I closed the door, it slipped across. I hadn't even noticed the lock before now, but then, I'd been intent on catching up with Beth Ann.

As soon as I thought of her name, she appeared at my elbow, making me jump. "Who's he?"

His brow cleared, and though his tenseness remained, he smiled. "You're Beth Ann. Your grandmother's shown me photos of you. And so *you*," meaning me, "must be Hugh's friend, Pat." He came forward, hand extended. "So good to meet you both. I'm Ev'lyn Timmons."

"You're Evelyn?" Beth Ann and I exclaimed in unison.

"Not expecting a man?" His smile turned apologetic. "No one ever does."

I shifted my can of cookies so I could shake his hand and say "How d'you do," all the while doing my best not to stare at his clothes and pigtail. Beth Ann, ruder but more honest, left both her hands in her jacket pockets and moved back a step, as if needing the distance to do a complete scientific analysis.

Evelyn didn't seem to notice. "Well, come into the kitchen. You can have a seat while I see if the stove's working yet."

"Stove?" Ah, a piece of equipment I knew something about. "What's wrong with it?"

"Nothing the application of electricity won't fix."

He led the way through the dining room to the right of the hall—a spacious room with a long table in the center and a huge fireplace on the opposite wall. The thick mantel was six feet off the stone hearth and atop its highly polished surface were two identical arrangements of magnolia leaves and large green fruits that resembled oranges. Holiday decorations?

I did a more thorough scan of the entire room. A single, electric candle was centered in each front window, and a small sprig of real mistletoe hung over the doorway we'd just passed through. These were the only Christmas trimmings in sight.

My scan of the room revealed something else. Beth Ann wasn't following us. She was standing under the mistletoe, waiting to be noticed. When I did notice her, she said, "Where's my grandmother?"

Evelyn stopped in the other doorway. "At Greenhow's Lumber House. She wasn't scheduled to work today, but we've had an early flu outbreak and—"

I heard Beth Ann rush down the hall and open the door before I realized she was bolting.

Running after her, I reached the door in time to see her crossing the yard, bound for a gate in the fence. "Beth Ann!"

She turned just enough to yell back, "I know where the lumber house is."

"Help me unload the car first."

"Later." And she was gone through the gate.

I got the urge to scream, "You wait 'til I tell your father," but since I knew I wouldn't—not wanting to admit to Hugh that I couldn't handle his daughter—I settled for mumbling Italian oaths.

"She'll be all right," Evelyn said, right behind me. "The lumber house is a mere half block if she cuts across the back. I'll help you unload. Let me go 'round and open the kitchen door. We can carry everything in that way."

"No. I won't let her off that easy. She'll do the unloading when she gets back." Stated as if I had a terminal case of PMS grouchies—I mean, it was Christmas Eve, for Pete's sake, and Beth Ann was simply in one of her adolescent moods. I sounded like Scrooge cracking the whip over Bob Cratchit. What was wrong with me?

"Right. Well, I do need to get back to the kitchen," Evelyn said. "I'm on my lunch hour and I'm running late as it is."

Lunch hour? Of course, he worked for the Foundation, which explained the costume. I just never pictured living history guides wearing their work clothes around the house. Thing was, I was now loath to follow him back through the dining room—irrationally so. Maybe afraid that if I tried to make small talk, something akin to "So, how long have you and Hugh's mom been shacked up?" would come out of my mouth.

Instead, I said, "That lumber house, it's a half block away? I, uh, I should go after Beth Ann. You know, coax her out of her bad mood before dinner." From Scrooge to *Touched by an Angel* in the blink of an eye. And truth to tell, I was beginning to feel as much a split personality as I was acting.

But Evelyn seemed relieved. "From our gate, you'll spot a high hedge between the houses. There's a garden behind it. You can go 'round it to the street. The lumber house is the second building to the right, with a sign out front about buying tickets. Could you—I mean, while you're there—would you tell Glad I had to pick up more fuses from Maintenance? She'll send someone up to the apothecary to let them know I'll be late."

That explained the source of his relief—he needed someone to run an errand. I still didn't think I could make small talk with him, but I revised my image of him to someone having a job, house woes, and holiday stress all at once and, sympathizing, I agreed to his request.

I was almost off the porch when I remembered the gift I held. I hurried back and shoved the can into Evelyn's hands. "Just some pizzelles. Cookies."

"Lovely. I know the very spot for them."

A curious response, I thought, but then, nothing about this weekend so far seemed normal.

* * *

The garden Evelyn spoke of was in its winter doldrums, though the geometric boxwood borders were green. A brick walk crisscrossed in the middle, and crushed shells provided paths between each section. I could picture it in the summer months, with beds of bright reds and yellows inside the boxwood triangles. At least, that's the way I would've planted it. Since July, gardening had been my job. Granted, I only had two clients with real gardens—everyone else just wanted lawns mowed and leaves raked. Yet those hours I'd spent nurturing flowers and herbs and veggies had been some of the happiest I remembered in the last decade.

But I hadn't stopped at this garden gate for professional reasons. I paused to catch my breath and rest my achy legs. I shouldn't have been out of breath. For the first time in my adult life, I felt I was in half-decent physical shape, because, for the first time in my adult life, I'd been getting some variety of exercise almost every day instead of sitting at a desk. I'd actually lost a little weight over the last few months. Not that I was anywhere near lean, mind you. I mean, there's only so much that could be done with my hips, given my gene pool. But there's no way I should have been winded from the grassy slope I'd had to climb to reach the garden.

Evelyn's words about an early flu outbreak came back to me. Did I have a touch of it? I'd had a flu shot—living with a ninety-one-year-old makes it compulsory—but maybe a different strain was going around. I'd thought about going to the doctor's for my leg cramps. My health insurance, which didn't pay for office visits or prescriptions, had discouraged me. Rheumatism, I'd told myself. Now I wondered. The last thing Miss Maggie needed was for me to be contagious.

Then again, this was Thursday afternoon of a holiday weekend, and Christmas Eve at that. Everyone would be going home early. I couldn't see a doctor before Monday anyway.

"You can't afford to be sick," I told myself aloud. "Not this weekend. It's just rheumatism. And standing out in the cold, damp air isn't doing it any good." Not that the air felt all that cold to me. I was warmer than I should have been, given the mid-fortyish temperature. A fever? I was too young for hot flashes, wasn't I?

Telling myself again that ill health wasn't in the weekend plans, I walked out to the street and paused again at the brick sidewalk, not because I was out of breath this time, but because I suddenly found myself in another era. Sort of. If I ignored the paved street and smattering of tourists—mostly fifty-plus couples dressed as if they were at a fashionable ski resort, with a family here and there done up in Gore-Tex and Timberland boots.

Other than that, though, everything was old bricks, clapboards, weathered shake roofs, and picket fences. Across the street was a stately church of salmon-colored brick. In the street itself was a pile of manure. Authentic enough for me.

Old City Philadelphia had brick townhouses, with a crowded city feeling to it. Williamsburg was more spread out—small town America circa 1776. The houses were set back farther from streets lined with tall trees. Even now, with the trees bare, and the grass between sidewalk and road a dry brown mat, this place had a homey feel that made the day seem less dismal.

I followed Evelyn's directions to the lumber house, a garage-sized building with the gable end to the street. The two windows flanking the door each boasted a holiday wreath of pine, dried flowers, and small slips of brown paper which all seemed to have "Admit

One" written on them in bold script—eighteenth-century ticket stubs, I supposed. A clue to what I'd find inside, in case I missed the big easel placard by the door that said "Tickets Sold Here."

I knew what I'd find inside, though—Hugh's mother. Wishing I had a mirror, I ran both hands over my hair to flatten any stray frizzies. I took a deep breath, mounted the two steps, and opened the door.

My preening was in vain—the room inside was empty. On the left was a counter with computer stations behind it. The rest of the space was taken up by a maze of crowd-control ropes, but no one waited in line.

Then a head popped up over the far computer terminal, or rather, a pair of blue eyes surrounded by liver spots, beneath a brown tweed cap. "Hi, what can I do for you?" said a perky tenor voice.

I walked over to the counter for a better look. The man had been sitting on a stool. Now he stood, though I still looked down on him by an inch. He was elderly, neatly dressed in a sport jacket over a tan cable sweater, and he radiated energy. Change his costume and he'd be perfect as Santa's chief elf. If the elf had one of those mild Virginia drawls. His nametag identified him, appropriately enough, as Nick.

"Is Gladys Lee here?" I asked.

"Popular lady. Someone else was just in looking for her."

"A teenager with red hair? I have to find her, too."

"Well, if the young lady followed my directions, you should find them both at the Governor's Palace. Glad'll be there 'til all the regulars get back from lunch. You can't get in without a pass, though. I tried to tell the young lady that, but—"

"She didn't listen? Yeah, that's the kid I'm looking for."

He nodded. "Had teenagers of my own. Think of it as a disease. She'll eventually develop antibodies and get over it. Someday the fever'll break and you'll have your daughter back."

I didn't correct his assumption—his sympathy was welcome. God knows I didn't get it from Hugh.

"So, want to buy passes?" Nick asked.

Miss Maggie had given me explicit instructions not to purchase tickets of any kind without her, because she was planning to give me her own guided tour of the place. She may have retired from the classroom twenty-odd years ago, but she'd never quit being a history teacher. So I said, "No, thanks, but speaking of lunch hours . . ." and went on to relate Evelyn's request.

"Fuses," the man echoed, shaking his head. "That's the third time this month. We warned them not to move into the Carson house."

Like I said, if you own old houses, you have to fix everything constantly. I now said it aloud.

"Well, sure, that fuse box isn't new," Nick said. "Put in around 1965, I think, but it shouldn't be burning fuses out at the rate it does. Nothing wrong with the wiring." He leaned closer, with the air of one about to impart a juicy scandal. If he hadn't been so short, and the computer not been in the way, I think he would have rested his elbows on the counter. "They told you about that house, didn't they?"

I must have looked as clueless as I felt, because he went on. "Just like Glad not to say anything, but be prepared if anything happens while you're visiting. That place is as haunted as they come. Nothing scary. Ghost plays tricks is all."

"Ghost?" was all I could get out of my throat. Not that I was afraid of spooks. Well, not much anyway. But Hugh—I couldn't blame him really, after those two little incidents during my first months at Bell Run. Okay, maybe not so little. Ghosts threaten Hugh's manly sense of guardianship. He can't protect the women in his life from anything whose solar plexus is made of air, which is why last July I'd promised to go cold turkey on all things Other Worldish. Personally, I'd be happier if Hugh would save his sense of guardianship for when I need to deal with, say, a car mechanic, but we do what we must for love. So being in a haunted house, on the very weekend I was to meet Hugh's family, sounded like a recipe for havoc.

"Oh, you won't *see* the ghost," Nick assured me, sounding disappointed. "Nobody ever has. Just plays tricks—blowing fuses, turning the hot water ice cold. Stuff like that. More of a nuisance than anything."

"You mean all it does is play with the electricity and plumbing?"

"Nothing worse. A nuisance, as I said."

I breathed a sigh of relief. I'd grown up in a hundred-year-old row house outside of Philly. Our fuses blew regularly, and our archaic oil heater never kept up with the hot water demand. The stairs even creaked all by themselves during the hottest and coldest months—a great way to freak out friends during pajama parties. It didn't mean the place was haunted.

"The theory," Nick continued, undaunted by my relief, "is that he's a soldier, which leaves a wide field of possibilities. The British, French, and Americans were all here during the Revolution, and both North and South during the Civil War—"

"Shouldn't you send someone to deliver Evelyn's message?" Rude, yes, but I wasn't sure how else to change the channel.

"Can't. What with Glad up at the Governor's Palace and Clyde—my other cohort—out with a walking tour, I'm here by myself. When Clyde comes back, I'll go, though by then, Evelyn might be back. Let's see, who should I call? The Secretary's Office isn't open today—we're short-handed. Not that it matters. No one's been in here the last hour to buy tickets. Still—"

"I guess I can't get in there either without a pass?" Be faster than waiting for him to explore his options.

"No, but—oh, you mean, you'd go for me? If you wouldn't mind, that would be terrific. You can tell whoever's in front of the door about Evelyn. Do you know how to get there? Here, let me show you."

On the counter was a stack of visitor's newspapers. With a practiced motion, Nick opened the one on top to the centerfold, a map of the surrounding blocks with each building drawn in, all in different colors. Taking an orange highlighter from his breast pocket, he circled the Lumber House Ticket Office, then the Galt Apothecary. They were on the same street, but to my dismay, four blocks stretched between, though two of those blocks were short. Or were the other two long? Still, I said I'd go. I told myself to think of the chore as last-minute Advent penance.

"Say, here's an idea," he said, tapping his highlighter beside another building, colored blue, across the street from the apothecary. "Zela's at the King's Arms this afternoon. She tried living in the Carson house a few years back. Since you're so interested, she could tell you anything you want to know."

I'd come across as interested? As I opened the door, he added, "One last word of advice. Don't call Glad 'Gladys.' She hates it. Goes by Glad Carson-Lee. Adamant about it."

I thanked him, silently cursing Hugh for not warning me.

I opted to walk in the street and avoid the tourists on the brick walks. Instead, I had to avoid the piles of manure, and the occasional horse-drawn carriage that caused those piles, but I could view both sides of the lane better. My pace was a relaxed stroll, to humor my knees, yes, though I found myself enjoying the Christmas decorations. Every building seemed to have garlands or wreaths, most fashioned from natural materials—fruits, vegetables, dried flowers, and all kinds of evergreens. Inside each window, I could see a single candle, of the electric variety, so not quite authentic. I imagined the Foundation's insurance premiums would skyrocket if they used the real thing.

According to the map, which I was carrying folded in half for easy reference, the block that I came to next was Market Square, a field of matted brown grass behind the neat little Courthouse on the left side. The field continued on my right across almost the entire block to an octagonal building labeled "Magazine." For the storage of black powder, I presumed, rather than periodicals, though my imagination conjured for my amusement a colonial newsstand selling copies of *Poor Richard's Almanac*. Perhaps the notion was suggested by the line of rough vendor booths along the road on that same side, each booth occupied by a costumed peddler hawking reproduction souvenirs like tricorn hats and food items like cookies and hot cider. The thought of yummy, warm sweets made me salivate.

To distract my stomach, I tried, as Miss Maggie had taught me, to visualize the scene as it might have appeared on a market day in the 1700s, the open space filled with farmers, merchants, craftsmen, and shoppers. Smells, not only of manure, but of garbage, livestock, cooking aromas, the contents of chamber pots emptied from upper windows of adjoining houses, and the combined body odors of everyone present, perfumed or otherwise. Sounds of talking, shouting, barking dogs, bleating sheep and goats, cackling chickens, and gobbling turkeys. Music? I supposed, though I didn't know enough about the era to invoke more than a fife and drum playing "Yankee Doodle."

Yet, the picture seemed only half complete, and wasn't helped by a bus that pulled behind the magazine over on Francis Street. I gave up and moved on.

Ahead, framed between the bare trees that lined the street, loomed an imposing but graceful brick structure. I flipped over the map to identify it. Ah, so *this* was the capitol. Then what was the building we'd passed on Francis Street? I flipped the map back and located it over on the left side. Public Hospital of 1773, it read.

I was still walking, head bent to the map, trying to puzzle out Beth Ann's comment about the building's location vis-à-vis Christmas, when I plowed right into what felt like a well-padded iron column. My left knee gave out and I suddenly found myself sitting on my tush, looking up at a woman in a black cloak over a red satin dress, complete with a powdered wig and a fake mole drawn on one cheekbone. She carried a bulky cloth sack in each hand. Something about her made me think of a teddy bear in a Marie Antoinette costume.

"Madam," said the woman, raising an eyebrow, but otherwise not changing her perfect posture, "are you much in the habit of charging about our streets like a runaway horse?"

"No, I—" Flustered, I pushed myself to my feet. "I'm sorry. I wasn't watching where I was going."

"Evidently. Your speech is of the northern colonies, which explains your want of manners. Where are you from?"

I wasn't sure if I was supposed to be insulted or charmed by how she stayed in character. Then again, the haughtiness of her words wasn't bolstered by her height, which, subtracting her hair, was only an inch or two above me, and, as I said, she was teddy-bearish. So I laughed instead. "Near Philadelphia—"

"Ah, yes, Philadelphia. Quite the frontier yet, though they pretend otherwise. You'll find gentility here in Virginia, Madam, not unlike that of London. You would do well to learn from it. Good day to you." With a proud curtsy, she sailed off up the street, just in time, too, because I realized that every tourist within earshot had stopped to watch the show. Feeling hot with embarrassment, I hurried on my way.

Galt's Apothecary was a two-story structure with a gray stone block facade, and the first-floor windows stuck out from the walls. Two wide steps led up to the door, beside which stood a young, husky man dressed in britches and a matching waistcoat. No cloak, no topcoat. I felt chilly just looking at him.

He gave me a smile as I approached, but also the kind of eye contact that said he was about to keep a nonpaying customer from the premises. Come to think of it, I'd seen similar "bouncers" in front of most of the houses on my walk, and all the tourists had large badges with conspicuous expiration dates clipped to their outer garments.

I delivered my message and he thanked me, his breath a faint white cloud through the cool air. "Figured it was something to do with that house. Needs new everything in it."

He, at least, didn't mention a ghost. On a whim, I crossed the street to King's Arms Tavern, a Dutch Colonial, like the Carson house, but with an off-center door protected by a small, square porch. Colored blue on the map and therefore a restaurant. Tourists loitered around it, waiting to be seated for a late lunch. On the porch, a petite young woman dressed in colonial garb and holding a tan cloak tight around her arms was manning a podium of sorts. She looked cold.

As I walked up the stairs, she turned toward me. "There's a twenty-five minute wait."

I shook my head. "Are you Zela?"

"No, I'll get her for you." She disappeared inside before I could stop her, probably glad for the excuse to warm up.

A minute later, a statuesque black woman emerged. She had a beautiful face—high cheekbones, compassionate eyes, and a wide smile. Her bearing was noble, though she was dressed like a slave extra from *Roots*.

"I'm Zela. How can I help you?" she said in a low, soothing voice. She must have been curious how I knew her name and why I'd asked for her, but she didn't show it.

In the face of all that calm dignity, I felt silly. "I have a question—it's stupid, really, but—I understand you once lived in the Carson house."

Her smile disappeared. "Yes?"

"I'm staying there for the weekend," I hastened to explain, feeling how lame I must sound, "and I was curious—that is, I heard—" I lowered my voice, so everyone standing around wouldn't peg me for a crackpot. "Someone told me the house was haunted. Not that I believe—I mean, I just wanted—"

"If you want spooky stories, take the *Ghosts and Legends* tour." Zela's voice was surprisingly cold. She turned to the podium and read from the clipboard. "Capp, party of two?"

I recognized the dismissal in her tone, thanked her, and left. But I'd only crossed the sidewalk and stepped back out into the street when she ran up behind me and caught my sleeve.

"Listen," she said, softly and earnestly, "if you feel ill, go to the kitchen. That's all I'll say."

Before I could get a word in, she dashed back to the King's Arms and vanished inside.

"This month the Cooks do very early rise,
To roast their meat, & make their Christmas pies."

—John Tully's Almanac, December 1688

December 4, 1783—Mrs. Carson's House

TAKING TURNS AT WATCH that night proved needless, for Brennan kept us all from sleep with his infernal pacing. His voice could be heard at intervals, carrying on a discourse with himself, though his words could not be distinguished, even by Sam when he boldly put an ear to Brennan's door.

Perhaps an hour before daybreak, Brennan exclaimed, "The devil!" and we heard a scraping sound.

"He's raising a window," Sam said, sitting up in the bed we shared, the wood of it creaking as the ropes strained under the tick, and his shirt a white ghost in the dark of our room.

"Does he mean to hurl himself out?" I wondered.

"With our luck, he'd not achieve more than to break a leg."

But the scraping came once more as the window closed. Brennan's laugh followed, vainglorious and surely mad. Then another scraping noise, more onerous.

"Moving the bed," Sam guessed. "Or perhaps his trunk."

Then all was silence and, at last, I dozed.

At dawn, I was roused by the sound of Sam gasping as he splashed cold water from our washbasin upon his newly-shaven cheeks.

"Can you wake yourself more quietly?" I asked with a yawn.

"Wake myself? I'm yet asleep, and have three cuts upon my chin to prove it. Remember how Lieutenant Carson used to say that if his men would but rise when ordered during the war, he should take us all with him to the Ohio Valley afterward, where the sun would accommodate us with an extra hour's sleep? Days such as this I warm to the notion."

I did indeed remember. "I wonder if he might have. Gone west, I mean. Thomas always spoke of going there in jest, or as a man dreams of boyish adventures, yet perhaps, had he lived—"

"And not had a wife, children, and his father's house to consider. There's a thought. If I'd have that extra hour's sleep, I'd best go before some woman ties me down."

"You'd still rise at dawn, no matter what the o'clock."

"Yes, but to unbar the doors of my own shop, not Greenhow's. I'm off. Go back to sleep, Ben."

I did, and when I next awoke, the south windows of the room were awash in sunlight and the orb of its making, risen more than a quarter arc to its zenith. I dressed in haste, for an appointment awaited me with Mr. Akers in Richmond Road.

Of the doors opposite in the hall, only Brennan's remained closed and no sound issued from within. Jim and the doctor had propped their door open, as was customary, to allow any warmth wafting from the downstairs hearth to enter. They, too, were already off about their business, hurriedly it seemed, for the pallet Jim slept upon by the hearth remained in disarray.

As I descended the stairs, my nostrils detected the spicy staleness of the stewed pumpkin of two days past, warmed over for yet another morning meal. In the common room, I found Dr. Riddick with Mrs. Carson, who stood at her table chopping the pippins which would comprise the bulk of sweetmeats in her Christmas pies. Doubtless the bulk of all the filling, for meat was costly, and since October at least, this house had seen but four paying lodgers. I received my room and board in exchange for the weekly music instruction of the Carson children. A bargain for their mother, for any music master would ask thrice the rate to endure young Tom's playing of the violin.

Elizabeth Carson was a small woman, though not frail. Despite five births—only two of which produced healthy children—and the strain of her widowhood, Elizabeth remained strong and hearty, as well as comely. That, taken with the house and land she owned, brought many hopeful suitors to her door. I knew she favored me above the rest, though I had no illusions that the emotion of love occasioned my standing. 'Twas merely that a music master could introduce her to circles of society not now open to her. Yet, such was her charm that I cannot say I was unaffected by her smile on seeing me enter the room. As was her custom when hard at work, she'd put aside her shortgown to preserve it and wore only a modesty piece about her shoulders, over stays and shift. I found this fashion quite alluring.

"Ah, 'tis only you, Mr. Dunbar." Dr. Riddick breathed out his relief. "I thought perhaps Brennan had heard our talk."

I bowed to them both, my hat to my breast, to which Elizabeth returned a curtsy. "Brennan's not yet left his room?" Odd, I thought, for his custom was to rise early and walk about the grounds of the college, snuffbox in hand, scouting new customers.

"No," came the doctor's reply, "though we've heard him dragging his trunk about all morning. Much as his case interests me, I fear for his actions, and have advised Mrs. Carson to turn him out."

Elizabeth resumed her chopping, her voice unruffled. "And I have informed Dr. Riddick that it's quite impossible. Mr. Brennan has paid his account through to the end of the month—his room and two daily meals—and I have not the means to repay him."

"We shall collect the funds for you," said the doctor. I nodded my agreement, all the while figuring in my head the tally of seven and a half pence for each meal and two shillings a night for a private room.

Elizabeth frowned. "The Public Hospital has been closed these last two years, and no other house would give Mr. Brennan lodging if he truly has become deranged, Doctor. I cannot turn a man out into the street. Not in winter, at least."

"Madam, think of your children."

As if by a conjurer's trick, the back door burst open and the feet of young Tom were heard clambering up the stairs with an exuberance characteristic of his age.

"Thomas!" Elizabeth's usually tranquil voice became that of a sergeant major.

Polly Carson appeared in the room doorway, the blush upon her cheek and nose testimony to the cold without. She was a girl of but fourteen years, and a deformity of her spine caused her left shoulder to slouch a bit—from being put into stays too young, Dr. Riddick maintained. Yet, the promise of her mother's beauty was already evident in Polly's smile, which she unfurled as she curtsied, greeting me and the doctor before saying, "I found him, Mother. He was leading the blacksmith Mr. Draper along Main Street—"

"Mr. Draper?" Elizabeth repeated, as the man entered the house.

"Something about a lock, ma'am." Draper was winded from trying to keep pace with youth, and tugged loose the collar of the heavy wool shirt worn over his smithy's apron. As if to make his meaning clear, he held aloft an iron padlock with key.

"Thomas!" Elizabeth called again.

We heard the lad scurry back down the steps. He thrust his head into the room, nodding in lieu of a bow. "Yes, Mother. Mr. Walker asked me to fetch his powder from the apothecary today, and Mr. Brennan said if I went directly and brought Mr. Draper, I'd earn two bits." Tom held the coin wedges aloft. "I placed Mr. Walker's powder on his mantel, Mother."

"What's this about Mr. Brennan?" Elizabeth set down her knife and, wiping her hands on her apron, hastened into the hall. Riddick and I followed after.

John Brennan stood upon the stair landing, as if 'twere a stage and we his tardy audience. He seemed pale in the stark light of the window above his head, but his deep bow was steady and his eyes rational. "I beg pardon, madam, for borrowing your son for my errand. I am in need of a lock upon my door."

"A lock!" Elizabeth exclaimed.

"At my own expense, I assure you, madam."

"But how shall we sweep your hearth, sir?" she asked. "Or lay your fire, or—"

"I shall happily do for myself," Brennan announced with good cheer, "even in the draining of my chamber pot. I shall also fetch the water I require. As for firewood, Master Tom may place the usual quarter-logs beside my door each day and I shall bring them in. I shall no longer want my meals, though I shall continue to pay the cost to compensate any inconvenience." This notion brought him such jollity that he laughed aloud. "Mr. Draper, if you would, sir?" He made a grand gesture along the stair to complete the invitation.

The blacksmith turned an eye to Mrs. Carson. "Ma'am?"

She gave a sigh and nodded. "Make a tidy job of it, sir. Mind my woodwork."

"Yes, ma'am." And he mounted the stair and both he and Brennan were lost from view.

"Surely, madam," Dr. Riddick whispered, "you cannot mean to keep the man in your house after that?"

Elizabeth spoke to her children first. "Thomas, is the wood split?"

"Nearly all, Mother."

"Polly, help him finish, then bring it in to my hearth."

They each murmured, "Yes, Mother," and with bow and curtsy, turned toward the back door.

Elizabeth returned to her pippins before giving the doctor her reply. "Quite frankly, sir, I cannot afford to lose a lodger right now. Certainly not one who pays for a private room, with an additional shilling and three a day for meals I need not prepare. Mr. Brennan apparently means to lock himself in, Doctor, relieving the worry of my children needing to enter his room. If he becomes a further danger, I shall take action. Now, Mr. Dunbar, will you breakfast before you leave for Master Akers's music lesson?"

I had quite forgotten my appointment. "No, madam, thank you. I'm behind my time as it is." I bid my landlady and Dr. Riddick a good day, took up my fiddle case from where it rested on the sill, and left by the back door.

The morning was chill, with a breeze from the northwest. Polly and Tom were at the chopping stump, white fog escaping their lips as they debated the portioning of the task. All else in the yard— well, privy, refuse pile, and Thomas Carson's now abandoned tin shop—seemed frozen in place by the hoarfrost, thickest to the right where yard bordered marshland.

I paused upon the stoop, setting my violin beside me as I un-buttoned my lapels and drew my coat across my breast. "You look quite well, Mistress Polly," I commented, for she'd had a bad colic not two days previous. "A remarkable recovery. Did Dr. Riddick attend you?"

"Thank you, sir, and no. Mother fed me pepper and a drop of quicksilver."

"Made her puke up a worm, it did," Tom said with enthusiasm.

Polly flushed, but chose to disregard her brother, instead hiding her embarrassment by bending to place the split logs into a leather sling. "So I shall be able to attend my singing lesson today, Mr. Dunbar."

"I shall anticipate the hour." And I would, for distinct from her brother, Polly had a musical ear and pleasing voice.

'Twas then that hammering commenced abovestairs. Glancing toward Brennan's window, wondering what had possessed the man, my gaze fell upon an item on the ground beneath. Even at that distance, I knew it.

Brennan's snuffbox.

THREE

So, THE HOUSE DEFINITELY wasn't haunted, but it might make me hurl. What was up with that?

Zela had returned to the porch of King's Arms and was casting an occasional glance in my direction. A worried glance? Or just annoyed? Did it matter? Here I was, standing in the street, gaping, acting like a stalker.

I began retracing my steps toward the house, wanting to say "Humbug" good and loud, to see if it made me feel better. Unlike Scrooge, though, I already believed in the spirit world.

I reminded myself that I'd only had two run-ins with ghosts in my life. Both had been in the past year and both at Bell Run. Ergo, Bell Run contained some supernatural energy or other that allowed its phantoms to poke through death's curtain and con poor schnooks like me into helping them. Nothing had ever happened anywhere else I'd visited, so nothing would happen here. Period. End of story.

Two blocks farther on, it dawned on me that I might not be able to get back into the house. I cursed myself for not asking Evelyn for a key. I'd have to sit in my car and wait. Ironic, since I'd come to Williamsburg to avoid sitting in a cold car to wait for Miss Maggie. I could turn on the car to get heat, but I'd be wasting gas and polluting the air for no good reason outside of hypothermia.

My fears proved unfounded. When I pushed through the backyard gate, I saw lights in the first floor, rear wing of the house. Parked beside my Neon was a white Miata with a tan leather top.

As I stepped onto the porch, I spied what looked like a playing card on the floorboards by the kitchen door—an Ace of Spades. Picturing someone inside playing solitaire with a deck of fifty-one, I slowly bent to retrieve it. It wasn't a card at all, but a photocopy of one on plain paper, cut to card size. Nothing on the back.

Before I could straighten up, the door swung open and giant-sized running shoes stepped into my field of vision. I moved that field up, over six feet of blue jeans and a double-extra-large ice hockey jersey, to the face of a red-haired Adonis. In build and facial features, he could have passed for Hugh's twin, though he sported no mustache and his hair was a crew cut. Also unlike Hugh, his grin seemed a permanent part of his face.

Flustered, I slid the fake ace into the folds of my map.

"My niece says if I let you in, you'll kill her." His voice was deep like Hugh's, too, but his attitude more carefree.

"I wouldn't kill her *inside* the house."

"Fair enough." He stepped back to let me pass.

Stripping off my gloves, I entered the kitchen, which smelled seductively of roasting poultry. "Friendly" was my first impression of the room, though I couldn't say why. With windows on both side walls, it might be a bright place on a sunny day, but today extra illumination was needed, provided by an overhead brass chandelier (in need of a good polish), and a plug-in fluorescent light that hung over the stove. The stove itself looked to be the first electric one of its kind ever made—chipped white porcelain with black dials above thin-coiled burners that were all the same size. The double sink was about the same era, but the refrigerator was 1960s avocado green. The floor was covered with vinyl red brick squares, nicked and scarred. Mismatched cupboards and hutches filled the spaces between the windows. Beside the stove, a long wooden table served as counter space. On it was the newest thing in the kitchen—a small white microwave.

To my right was a bricked-in hearth, smaller than the one in the dining room but still larger than normal. A cast-iron stove protruded from the bricks. On one side was a picnic table with separate benches. On the other side, what appeared to be a closet jutted into the larger room.

Beth Ann stood by the closet door. "I couldn't unload the car because you had the keys." Her attitude was half-defensive, half-accusing.

Too tired to argue, I took my keys from my pocket and dangled them at arm's length. "Here."

She shifted her gaze from me to her uncle. He turned toward her, so I couldn't see his face, but her lips quivered, trying to hold back a smile, as she came forward to take the keys.

"I'll crack the whip," he said when I started to follow her out. "Go warm yourself by the stove."

He apparently meant the cooking stove, because the other was cold to the touch. Since I wanted to sit more than anything, I set the map on the table and made use of a bench, propping my left leg along its length so I could massage my knee.

Beth Ann and her uncle unloaded the car in one trip, with him lugging two suitcases, a large tote, and a carryall bag stuffed with gifts. He made it look effortless.

Pushing the door shut with one foot, he told Beth Ann to put her own things in her room. "And ask Ma which room she put Miss Maggie and Pat in."

"Your mother's here?" I asked, torn between thinking I should get my foot off the furniture and wanting to continue the massage.

"Upstairs, changing." He set his load by the closet door, then handed me my keys. "What's wrong with your leg?"

"Nothing. My knee hurts a little, that's all. Which brother are you?"

"Lighthorse Harry Lee, at your service."

I laughed, not only because his bow was outlandishly Antebellum, but because when I met Hugh, he'd introduced himself the same way.

"Call me Horse. Everyone else in the family does, except Ma, and Foot, who doesn't do *anything* anyone else does." He meant his brother, whose name was Francis Lightfoot. Horse took my coat, but merely set it atop the suitcases. "Want me to take a look at that knee?"

I felt my jaw drop. Was Hugh's brother hitting on me? Or being a little too brotherly a little too soon? I quickly slid my leg from the bench, which made my knee spasm so that, wincing, my "Uh, no. I'm fine," wasn't very assuring.

"Come on, I promise I won't charge for a house call." Horse was eyeing my leg, but it wasn't an ogle. In fact, he had the exact look

Beth Ann gave Bell Run's chestnut saplings as they succumbed to the blight—one third concern, two thirds scientific observation.

That and his comment made me ask, "Are you a doctor?"

His eyebrows rose. "Hugh didn't tell you?"

Hugh hadn't told me anything about his siblings, other than the fact that his mom had named them all after famous Lees. Then again, I hadn't asked. Not wanting to sound like a total doofus, I said, "I know Ann's a doctor." I'd discovered that on my own, after trying to find a local gynecologist. Miss Maggie's wasn't taking new patients, so Hugh called his sister for me. When he handed me the slip of paper with her recommendation, all he'd said was, "They're right across the hall from her office." It wasn't until I went there and actually saw "A. C. Lee, D.O." rounding off a list of family practitioners on the door opposite that I realized her profession. Anyway, to Horse I said, "I'm just surprised to find two doctors in the same family."

"Two?" Horse hunkered down to give my leg closer scrutiny. "Hugh's the only one of us who can't write prescriptions. Is this where it hurts?" With his large hand, he cupped my left knee, pushing against it with his thumb.

The pain made me jump. "That's the spot. On the other side, too. All four of you are doctors?"

"Yup, we all followed in Daddy's footsteps, though Foot went into psychiatry. Rich would tell you that Acey's Doctor of Osteopathy isn't the same as a bona fide M.D.—she likes to be called Acey, by the way, instead of Ann. We used to call her 'AC/DC' when she was little and it stuck. Foot insists on 'Francis.' We call him Foot anyway." With his other hand, Horse gently lifted and lowered my ankle. "Hurt when I do that?"

"Same places. Not as much as when you pressed on it. No more than the other knee."

"Both knees?"

"The left one's worse."

Removing his hands and standing, he stroked his chin a moment. A bunch of questions followed: Was the pain sharp or dull? Burning? When do I get it most during the day? Anyone else in my family have anything similar?

"That's why I think it's rheumatism. Three of my dad's sisters have it. Poor circulation," I said. Of course, those aunts were also fond of artery-clogging foods like Italian sausage and cream cake, and all defined "aerobic workout" as a good gossip session over coffee and cannoli. I had a healthier lifestyle, didn't I?

Horse nodded to himself. "I want you to lie down up here on the table."

"What? I'm not going to lie down on your mother's kitchen table." Picturing myself prone, with him leaning over me—looking and sounding so much like Hugh—my face heated up, turning, I imagined, a bright poinsettia pink.

He shrugged. "Okay, we can do this upstairs on one of the beds."

"No!" For an instant, I suspected that he wasn't a doctor at all, but was trying to play an elaborate joke on his brother.

Seeing my horror, his grin broadened. He took a wallet from his back pocket and extracted a business card, which he held out for my inspection.

Kratzhower Orthopedic Associates, it read. *L. H. Lee, M.D. Certified in Orthopedic Surgery and Sports Medicine.*

My face must have gone from pink to Santa-suit red. He was a specialist, offering a free examination—no referral, no HMO approval, no appointment, no copays, and no outdated, dog-eared magazines in his waiting room. And here I was, the pro bono patient from hell. "How 'bout if I stretch out on this bench? Will that do?"

"If you think you can keep your balance." A polite way of pointing out that my hips were slightly wider than the seat.

So I became horizontal, with my head toward the back wall. He lifted my ankle again, wrapping one arm around my lower leg, cradling my calf in his palm, and began to move my leg, bending the knee and hip. "Any pain?"

"No more than before," I said. "My knee just feels stiff—*oh!*" Slow and gentle had changed to one swift knee bend and the pain was blinding.

"Where?" he asked.

"From my knee up toward my hip."

"Here?" Still cradling my calf, he used the fingertips of his other hand to trace a path up my thigh.

It tickled, almost sensually, and I was reminded again how much he was like Hugh. I felt every one of my muscles tense and all I could do was nod.

"Lighthorse! What are you doing?" The voice came from the other end of the kitchen. I couldn't see the speaker—Horse was in my way—but since the tone was mature female, I knew it must be Hugh's mom. Panicking, I pushed myself up, wrenching my knee again as I tried to yank my limb free. Horse let go and turned, giving me an unobstructed view.

There, in the kitchen doorway, with Beth Ann gaping over her shoulder, was the Marie Antoinette teddy bear, only now she was wearing a pink sweatsuit that clashed with her short crop of Miss Clairol Spiced Bronze hair. The fake mole was still in place. Or maybe it wasn't fake.

All Horse said was, "Where do you keep your aspirin, Ma?"

Ignoring him, she came forward, her face lighting up in a smile as she recognized me—gracious of her, considering I'd laughed at her when last we met. "Well, look who it is." Gone was the haughty colonial British accent from earlier, and in its place were homey modern Southern inflections. "So, how'd you like Elizabeth?"

"Beg your pardon?" I stood, still in shock enough to think I hadn't heard right.

"Elizabeth Carson. That's who you ran into this afternoon. One of my ancestors. She lived in this very house during the Revolution," she said, as if she thought I'd lose sleep without the knowledge. Then, with the air of someone teaching a less-than-astute tot, she added, "I portray Elizabeth as a living history character, you see."

"Ah." I didn't mean that to come out sounding so relieved. What with her insistence on a theatrical name and her jump into the subject of her latest role, I had an epiphany about the woman. She was an actress greeting fans at the stage door, I thought. Getting on her good side should be easy. "Elizabeth was charming." Offering my hand, I introduced myself.

Her grip was stronger than expected. "Call me Glad. I'm delighted you liked her, Pat. You'll see her again before the weekend's out." Such a twinkle came into her eye that I wondered if my relief was premature.

I glanced at my companions. Beth Ann wore a half smirk that said I deserved this. Horse didn't seem at all perturbed by his mother's behavior, but said, "Ma, the aspirin."

"In the front bathroom upstairs. You can fetch it while I show you all around the house." Still clutching my hand, she turned toward the doorway, so I had no choice but to go with her.

Beth Ann followed on my heels and Horse took up the rear, grinning, but looking less than happy.

"This is the original house," Glad said as we climbed a single uneven step up into a closetlike pantry, its walls lined with shelves stocked with food boxes and cans, "built by Elizabeth's father-in-law, Josiah Carson, sometime before 1750. The kitchen wing was added in 1796."

We passed into the dining room, where she let go of my hand to strike a pose by the hearth. "This would have been the original kitchen. One can imagine Elizabeth here during the war years, cooking, spinning, sewing late into the evening by firelight, keeping her household together, and helping the cause any way she could while her husband Thomas was off with the army."

And so our tour went. We imagined Elizabeth in her parlor, receiving Generals Washington and Rochambeau after the Yorktown campaign. The room now held a worn sofa facing two matching armchairs that flanked either side of the corner fireplace. Framed paintings leaned against the walls where, I presumed, they would eventually be hung.

No Christmas tree, though. The only decorations were single electric candles in the front windows. I told myself that Glad and Evelyn had just moved in and probably hadn't had a chance to decorate. Of course, a poinsettia or two wouldn't have taken any time at all. Then again, some people didn't decorate or even put up their tree until Christmas Eve. Sure, that must be the explanation.

We traipsed down the hall and imagined Elizabeth in the room behind the parlor, which Glad said might have been used for some of the lodgers Elizabeth had taken in to make ends meet during the war. Beth Ann's suitcase was here, on a double sofa bed that had already been made up for the night with a faded, multicolored star quilt. Beside the door, a vanity lamp sat on a bureau. Between the two windows was a pyramid of cardboard moving boxes, with labels like "summer clothes" and "photo albums."

Next we climbed the stairs, imagining Elizabeth doing so to lovingly tuck her children into bed, even while Williamsburg was occupied by Cornwallis's Redcoats. The wood of the treads was two-tone, nearly black with aged varnish on the edges, but worn down into a tan depression in the middle where centuries of feet had stepped.

Glad led us past a small stair that branched off at the landing, dismissing it with a wave. "Leads back to the kitchen wing. Would have been a solid wall there during the war."

We were entering the first room at the top of the stairs when I had what I can only describe as a panic attack. So nasty was the feeling of anxiety that came over me, that I looked around the room for something to be afraid of, real or imagined. Martha Stewart might have been horrified by the mismatched double bed and bureau, 1960s Early American and Danish Modern, but I had no such decor sensitivities.

I controlled my fight-or-flight urge by leaning back against the door, ensuring that no bogeyman could get behind me, but I must have looked pretty wide-eyed, because Horse asked if I felt okay. For the first time, he was frowning.

"Just a headache," I muttered truthfully enough, because the blood pounding in my ears felt like a pneumatic nail gun against my cranium.

"Let's find that aspirin." He wheeled around and I followed him across the top landing to the bathroom—a tiny chamber with tile and fixtures from the early twentieth century, the porcelain chipped and rust-stained.

Horse flicked on the light—a single bulb in a metal wall sconce— and tipped down the toilet seat cover, gesturing that I should sit. When I did, he took my head in his large hands, turning my face toward the light, gently pulling at my lower lids to examine my eyes. The panic departed, along with my headache.

Meanwhile, Glad poked her head into the room and continued her lecture. "My grandparents turned this room into a bath in 1918, but of course, originally, it was no such thing. Since it's so small, Ev says it was probably used for storage. The odd thing is, we found screw holes in an eighteenth century paint layer on the door jamb of the room we were just in, which suggests it may have been kept locked at one time. But if *that* was the storage room, then what was this? A mystery, you see."

"Ma, please," Horse said impatiently, opening the wooden, eggshell-white medicine chest over the sink and taking down the container of Ecotrin that rested between a tall bottle of store-brand antacid and a box of Band-Aids.

Glad blinked, at a loss for words. Hurt by his brusqueness? Or couldn't she imagine Elizabeth taking aspirin?

"Hey," Beth Ann called from the next room. "A cab pulled up out front."

"Who could that be?" Glad headed for the stairs.

Horse glanced through the bathroom window as he reached for a Dixie Cup from the short stack that rested upside down in a little dish on one end of the sill. The other end was occupied by a blue nylon shaving kit and another small bottle of antacid, Mylanta this time. Was Glad's cooking that bad?

"Foot's here," Hugh said. "I wonder where his car is. And his wife, for that matter."

Standing, I craned my neck for a peek out the window. The man getting out of the taxi was tall like his brothers, but thin and dark. A black turtleneck was visible under a long, black overcoat. Black pants and shoes beneath. With one black-gloved hand, he adjusted the black-rimmed glasses on his nose, as if he couldn't quite bring the house into focus. With all that black and his expression, he had the air of someone going to a funeral.

Horse filled the paper cup with water and handed it to me with the bottle of aspirin. "One now, one before bed. We'll see if you feel better tomorrow."

"A variation of 'Take two aspirin and call me in the morning'?" I gulped the orange pill.

Ignoring me, he asked, "How long have you been getting light-headed after climbing stairs?"

"I wasn't lightheaded just now. I had a headache, that's all." Feeling afraid of nothing wasn't a symptom of anything but insanity, so I kept that part to myself. "Though I did get a little winded climbing the hill up to the historic area this afternoon. More than I thought I should have."

"Yeah?" He crossed his arms and gave me that scrutiny-à-la-Beth-Ann again, which I now mentally labeled the "Lee Analytical Gawk." LAG for short. I could use it as a verb, the way my old boss used to make up verbs out of every noun he came across. I remember him saying "We need to incent our employees," meaning "to give them incentives." I pointed out to him that it sounded more like he was going to torch us.

But anyway, with the LAG on me, I imagined myself with all sorts of horrible medical conditions—gangrene, for instance. "Why? What's causing the pain in my knees?"

"Hard to say without some tests. If it has to do with the 'poor circulation' that runs in your family, aspirin ought to help. If it does, I'll let you know what to tell your doctor so he can send you for the right—"

"What's wrong with her?" Beth Ann was back, standing in the doorway, her hands shoved into her sweatshirt pockets, and on her lips, an annoyed pout. A show of concern. I was touched.

"Nothing a little exercise won't cure," Horse said. "Maybe a change of diet, too."

But I *did* exercise, I wanted to say, and my diet was mostly mega-healthy since everything I cooked for Miss Maggie had to be low fat, low cholesterol, and low sodium. He couldn't expect me to give up chocolate, could he?

I didn't have a chance to put the question to him because we all heard raised voices out in the street. We crowded the window for a look.

"Uncle Foot's arguing with the driver," Beth Ann said, needlessly, because we could see both men standing beside the cab. The driver's arms were gesturing his outrage. Foot was composed. One gloved hand gripped the handle of a wheeled suitcase—black, of course. The other hand, closest to us, seemed clenched into a fist. Glad stood on the curb, a light cardigan thrown over her shoulders, talking to each man in turn.

Horse interpreted the commotion. "Foot's come up with a reason not to pay the cabbie. Ma's begging them not to make a scene in the street. Guess I'd better go fix things."

He squeezed by me and Beth Ann backed out to let him into the hall. I'd glanced back out the window a moment, then realized Beth Ann had followed him, leaving me alone.

But I didn't *feel* alone.

Hitting the light switch on my way out, I hurried down the stairs, putting on extra speed as I passed the panic-attack room. I could swear someone was in there. No, some*thing*.

"May grateful omens now appear
To make the New a happy year."

—Carrier verse from the *Massachusetts Spy*, 1771

December 4, 1783—Mr. Akers in Richmond Road

UPON CLOSER INSPECTION, SOME small distance from Brennan's snuffbox, I espied his cloth pouch, still a quarter full of his blend. This I returned to the ground, for as I've said, his snuff was of the poorest tobacco, weakened by the addition of mint, and perhaps other herbs, since fine white particles were mingled into this batch. Moreover, the snuff had been ruined by the damp of the grass. The box, however, I pocketed, thinking it might collect a good price.

Perhaps I should have weighed at greater length why John Brennan discarded his two most constant companions, but my mind soon turned to other concerns. The first was the purchase of a penny loaf from a peddler at the college corner, so that I might break my fast as I walked. Then, afraid the cold air might snap my fiddle strings, I paused to open the case and loosen the pegs. Soon after, my attention was set to keeping my footing upon Richmond Road, still slippery in places with mud from the rain of Friday past. In the best of weather, a swift walk of little more than an hour should bring me to Fair Grove, the Akers' farm. This day my journey would take half again as long.

In the drier spots, the face of Thomas Carson the elder seemed to float before my eyes. His children both favored him. A kind face, as I've said, until contorted in death. A result of cramp colic, so our company doctor had pronounced. Would that it had been so.

Troubled, I bent my musings to the more agreeable matter of which ditty to teach Mistress Polly at her lesson. By the time I'd come to Fair Grove, I'd settled upon "Sweet Is the Budding Spring of Love," as fitting her range and tone, and having a lyric harmonious to her youth.

Noah Akers greeted me at his doorstep, seeming abashed that his garments were finer than my own, though his smile was broad. "Good to see you, Ben. And as usual, never without your fiddle. Beer for you?"

"I'd best take small, thank you. If I down strong beer before we commence, I should make no sense of your ledger." I knew I should address him as "Mr. Akers" now that he'd become my employer, but I could not bring myself to do it. Noah had been one of my messmates during the last campaign, and we'd been through much together. Moreover, at eighteen years of age, he was a half decade my junior. But a fine lad he was—honest, stalwart, and loyal to his friends.

"Here are my sire's papers," he said, bringing me into his dining room, where he had spread the accounts of his estate upon the table. "Sit, Ben. I'll fetch the brew and we'll begin."

Setting my case upon a chair, I surveyed the room while he was gone. The wallpaper, furniture, and draperies were all lesser mimics of those I'd seen in more affluent houses. His mother's hand, no doubt.

While Noah was in the army, his sire had made shrewd gains, not the least of which had brought the family a parcel of land, the recompense of a gambling debt by a Tory departing posthaste for England. The elder Akers had perished during this last month, and his son had become a new, ill-prepared landowner, with a mother and three young sisters to support. Noah was better suited to the plow than the pen, and so had asked my assistance in the sorting out of his father's business.

When he returned with brimming tankards, I asked, "One favor, sir?"

"Name it, Ben."

"The Widow Carson believes I've come here to give you a lesson of introduction upon the violin. As new gentry, she presumes you would be in earnest to learn the arts of music and dance."

He frowned as he set his burden down upon the table. "Mother has said I ought as well, but the price of tobacco was too low this harvest—"

"Yes, I know. The Virginia market is in excess and all export must sell through Robert Morris."

"As you say," he agreed, though in truth, Noah had little understanding of trade. As I said, better suited to the plow. "At present, all else is too costly. I'm sorry, Ben, but perhaps next year I should afford your instruction."

"You mistake my purpose. I am well aware that no music master can now make a living, save among the very rich, who already employ their own masters. I have no intention of starving while trying to pursue an unprofitable trade. Yet, I desire Mrs. Carson to *think* I pursue it."

"Ah." Noah's smile was restored, with a knowing glint in his eye. "I prefer younger maids myself, though for a seasoned woman, the widow is very handsome. All the more so for owning a house, eh?"

"She is, though I fear she abides my company because she believes me to be a music master. A mere clerk is not invited to fancy balls, you see."

Noah sat at the table, slapping a hand upon the documents before him. "Make sense of this, lad—show me profit—and I shall be able to host such affairs and invite you." With a laugh, he took up his own pint and touched the drink to his lips. "So, good sir, shall we commence my music lesson?"

FOUR

Downstairs, I found the front door wide open, left that way by Beth Ann, no doubt. I didn't stop until I was over the threshold and cold air slapped my cheeks, knocking sense into me.

What was I running from?

I looked back over my shoulder, as far up the stairway as I could see from where I stood. Muted gray light from the window above bathed the landing. Nothing there a coat of fresh paint couldn't fix.

I felt like a complete idiot.

Luckily, no one had noticed. Out in the street, Foot was maintaining that a tourist trap like Williamsburg ought to have more than one taxi serving the train station on any given afternoon. And that he should be compensated not only for the half hour he'd waited at the station, but for having to share the cab, wasting yet another fifteen minutes dropping off an elderly couple at a motel way up on Capitol Landing Road.

Horse was paying off the driver, who was whining that he had to get back to the train station. Glad was trying to placate everyone with a lot of "Now, now"s and other useless utterances. Beth Ann stood back from the group a bit, hands still in her pockets. I couldn't see her face, but her body language wasn't happy. Not that I blamed her—Foot *was* putting a damper on the Christmas spirit.

Glancing back into the house, I recalled what I'd heard that afternoon about the place being haunted. Were my panic attacks courtesy of Nick's trick-playing ghost? "Nothing scary," he'd said. Ha! Or is this what Zela meant by "feeling ill"?

At any rate, this wasn't like any haunting I'd ever experienced. My prior spook sessions had never been frightening—at least, never in the sense that I'd felt personal danger.

It dawned on me that settling the question might be as easy as going back inside, up the stairs to that first room, and closing my eyes. This was my way of politely introducing myself to any flesh-less residents. If, in my mind's eye, I "saw" some piece of the past, then yes, I was dealing with a ghost. If not, I had out-of-control hormones.

But I didn't move, thinking instead of my promise to Hugh that I'd say no to the paranormal. I now embraced that promise. With it, I didn't have to admit I was chicken.

I heard footfalls come up the wooden steps behind me and Beth Ann passed by, bound for the doorway.

"Where are you going?" I squeaked out, suddenly afraid for her, too.

She swung her head around, eyebrows rising into that Are-all-adults-this-stupid-or-just-you? look she gets. "Inside. It's, like, *cold* out here?" She rolled her eyes, breathed out a "Duh," and proceeded into the house.

I cast a glance at the street. The taxi was pulling away and Foot was wheeling his suitcase toward the curb. "And if that imbecile cab driver weren't bad enough," he was saying, "all the way up here on the train the woman next to me was jabbering to someone across the aisle. I was trying to speak to my secretary on my cell phone and could barely make myself heard. When I asked the woman to keep her voice down, she said she couldn't hear her friend because of me."

I suppose I should have stayed to be formally introduced to him. Instead, I followed Beth Ann inside, not wanting her to be alone in the house. Sure, she could be exasperating, but I cared about her enough that if the danger I'd sensed upstairs materialized, I'd throw myself between her and it.

To my great relief, Beth Ann headed through the dining room to the kitchen, grabbing a box of Swiss Miss hot chocolate mix off a pantry shelf en route. The smell of roast bird welcomed us, raising my spirits, though the room was dreary because the fluorescent light was out. I assumed Horse had turned it off as we left on our tour, so I tried the wall switch by the door, an antique with two buttons, one out, one already in. I pushed the outtie in, the innie popped out, and the top light went out.

Beth Ann glared at me as I switched the light back on. She started opening cupboards until she found cups. While she filled a mug at the sink, I wandered over to the oven.

"Don't open it," she said, bringing her water to the microwave. "We're not allowed to look until—dammit, the microwave's not working."

Resisting the urge to censor her language, I glanced at the appliance in question, which was when I noticed that the lamp over the stove had a dingy white cord trailing down the wall, behind the long table. I bent over to take a gander below counter level. Sure enough, both the light and microwave were plugged into the same outlet on the baseboard. "Another fuse. At least it's not the stove this time."

"I *hate* this house." Abandoning the cocoa idea, Beth Ann opened the refrigerator and inspected its contents.

I had a good enough view to be scandalized. To me, holiday dinners meant refrigerators so stuffed with food, you had to leap back when you opened the door lest a Cool Whip container full of black olives should fall on your toes. Oh, this fridge wasn't empty by anything but Italian standards, but all I could see were basics like milk, eggs, drinks, and sandwich fixings. Hugh had said his mother would throw two lavish dinners: one tonight, one tomorrow. Before I could stop myself, I blurted out, "Where's the food? For dinner, I mean."

Beth Ann chose a can of Pepsi and closed the door. "Locked up in Grandmom's other fridge, wherever she hides it in this house. We're not allowed to see the contents until dinner. Like the turkey. Although we always have the same things: ham, turkey, yams—"

Glad came back into the room with Foot right behind her. His coat, suitcase, and brother were all missing, but he was still talking. I got the impression he hadn't stopped, nor taken a breath, since he got out of the cab.

". . . the salesgirl was downright rude. Didn't want to answer my questions because other customers were waiting. I asked for her manager and he gave me a run-around about Christmas crowds. I said if they couldn't handle it, they ought to hire more help. God knows they're pulling in enough money . . ."

I guess I could have waited until he was finished, or until Glad found out about the fuse on her own, which would more likely come first. But I grew up in a family where everyone talked at once, and where not interrupting was considered a socialization disorder. Besides, Foot would be turning blue soon, so breaking in was a humanitarian gesture.

With a loud "Excuse me," I told Glad about the microwave.

"Oh, bother. Now where did Ev put the new fuses?" A rhetorical question, because she went straight to the hutch beside the back door, picked up a brown paper bag, peeked inside, and pronounced them found.

Foot shut up as his mother bustled out of the room, Beth Ann in her wake, soda in hand. I thought he'd follow, too, but he didn't. I wondered if *I* should, though by now, the fear I'd felt earlier seemed absurd. Beth Ann wasn't in any danger. And my knees wanted me to sit down.

But first, I introduced myself to this new brother. "Hi, I'm Pat Montella."

Giving me the LAG—his default expression—he took my offered hand in a dry, apathetic grip. "You're Hugh's, er, friend."

Funny how he could make a nice word like "friend" sound so indecent. "Right, and you're his, er, brother." I hadn't spent twelve years in corporate America without learning how to parry.

Horse came through the doorway. "I put your suitcase and coat upstairs in the first bedroom, Foot. Where's Ma?"

"Fixing a fuse." Foot's tone equated that with shoveling manure.

"Apparently the fuses blow out a lot," I said, resuming my seat on the bench. "Evelyn was fixing one when we arrived."

Foot let out a grim sigh. "This place is a dump."

Horse nodded. "Yes, brother, but it's the dump of our ancestors and therefore sacred ground." He crossed to the fridge and, like his niece, scrutinized the contents.

"We need to talk some sense into Mom this weekend," Foot said.

"You always were the optimist." Horse took out a carton of eggnog and, pinching the top shut, shook it. "Where's your wife, by the way?"

"Irene's working late tonight. She'll drive up tomorrow morning and we'll go home together. That's why I took the train."

"I swear, you keep getting married just so you'll have a chauffeur. Be easier to buy a second car for yourself."

"I *have* a car."

"A collector's edition 'Vette that you never take out of your garage." Horse turned to me for an aside. "He never buys anything that depreciates."

"And *he* doesn't know the meaning of the word 'investment.' If he did, he'd be upset about Mom selling the house."

I felt like the little target ball in bocce. Not that I have anything against family bickering. On Grandmom Montella's side of my family, disagreement was an art form and calling a loved one *stupido* was a gesture of affection. But bringing in a third party wasn't kosher. The sport of it was in direct confrontation.

"I never said I wasn't upset." Horse went over to the cupboard Beth Ann had left open and began pulling down punch glasses.

"Knowing our mother, I'll bet she put the money in her *savings* account." Foot shuttered as he said it.

"Calm down. We discussed all this last weekend. As soon as Hugh and Acey get here—"

The fluorescent lamp blinked a dim orange twice, then came on full. Grabbing the excuse to leave, I said, "I'll go tell them they found the right fuse," and hurried out.

Of course, my decision took me through the dining room. I put on the brakes in the hall doorway, realizing that here I was, alone, just beneath where I'd been spooked earlier. And I felt something. I can't describe the feeling other than to say I was loathe to walk past the base of the stairs.

"This is silly," I whispered. Nothing talked back, so my confidence was bolstered. Still, the creepiness remained. Well, I told myself, I'd handled this kind of thing before. And I didn't have much time until Hugh arrived. "Okay," I said, my voice soft so I wouldn't be overheard by any of the Lees I wanted to impress this weekend. "Okay, if you *are* a ghost, give me some idea of who you are and what you want."

I closed my eyes to wait for a vision, which is how it always worked in the past. My lashes were barely together for two seconds when I was kissed. On the mouth. Hard.

Backing away as fast as my feet would carry me—so fast I tripped on a chair leg and ended up sitting on the floor—my eyelids snapped open.

The doorway was empty, except—

Except for the sprig of mistletoe that dangled from the lintel.

Go to the kitchen, Zela had said, and at that moment my one thought was to do just that, and stay there the rest of the weekend.

I would have, too—I was halfway there—when I heard Beth Ann behind me. "What was that noise? Sounded like something fell."

I turned and there she was, in the doorway, right beneath the mistletoe. "Don't stand there."

"Why?" Half inquiry, half defiance. Her specialty.

In lieu of an answer, I went toward her with some notion of pulling her to safety. "Where's your grandmother?"

"Still downstairs. She sent me up to see if the fuse was working." With that, to my relief, Beth Ann moved into the dining room, until she could see through the pantry into the kitchen.

"The light's back on," I said. "I was coming to tell you."

"You were going the other way."

What could I say to that?

Luckily, she was too impatient to wait for an explanation. Spinning around, she said, "I'll go tell her."

"No! I mean, I'll go with you." The last thing I wanted to do was go into the hallway, but I couldn't let Beth Ann cross what I'd begun to think of as "the war zone" by herself. And stranding Glad downstairs by the fuse box didn't seem like a good idea if I wanted her to like me.

But out in the hallway, the creepiness had vanished.

"Grandmom?" Beth Ann called from the top of the cellar steps, which were lit by a bare bulb hanging from the ceiling at the base of the stairs. A full basement opened out to the right, with a dirt floor, but to the left was a dark crawl space, ending less than three feet below the rafters.

Beth Ann repeated her call, louder. Still no response. Glad was either a bit deaf, or something was wrong.

Beth Ann must have thought so, too, because she said, "That's weird," descending enough stairs that, bent over, she could see beneath the level of the ceiling. The stairwell was so narrow, however, that I couldn't see around her.

"Grandmom?" Not a yell this time, but a puzzled question.

"Is it on?" Glad's voice, sounding fine.

"Yeah," said the girl. "Didn't you hear me call you?"

"No." Glad appeared at the base of the stairs and started up, so Beth Ann and I retreated to give her room. "The walls of this house are thick, you see. Ev and I have commented on it often, how sometimes we can't hear each other, even as close as the dining room and kitchen. Far superior to those modern homes with walls so thin you have no privacy whatsoever."

Bag of extra fuses in hand, she led us back around to the kitchen. Again, I felt nothing in the hall or beneath the mistletoe. Except foolish.

* * *

I planned to hide out the rest of the afternoon in the kitchen. Problem was, Glad wanted us all to leave. As Beth Ann had warned, viewing the preparation of the meal was a Lee no-no. Hugh must have known this, so he'd better have a good explanation for not warning me. Something about big Christmas presents with my name on them would be acceptable.

"Why don't you all go up to the Palace Green now?" Glad suggested, standing beside the oven as if guarding a bank vault. "You won't want to miss the Firing of the Christmas Guns."

Christmas Guns? Sounded barbaric. What happened to peace on earth, goodwill toward men?

"It doesn't begin 'til five o'clock, Ma," Horse said.

"Yes, but Beth Ann likes to walk right beside the fife and drum for the Grand Illumination, so you'd better go early."

Beth Ann's face went crimson. "That was when I was little, Grandmom. I haven't done that in years."

Horse carried his empty eggnog glass over to the sink, saying to his niece, "Let's go anyway, Squirt. We can walk up to Greenhow's Store. They're bound to have something that'll ruin our appetites before dinner. Coming Foot?"

He wrinkled his nose. "I have some reading to do. Where did you say you put my bag? First bedroom?"

As Foot left, Horse turned to me. "You'd like the ceremony, I think, but it's a lot of walking. How're your legs?"

"Better." They were, slightly—apparently the aspirin helped— but I wasn't thrilled about the idea of another long walk. Then again, I'd need a bathroom eventually, and no way was I about to go upstairs alone. Though I couldn't run over to the historic area's restrooms every time nature called this weekend.

Instinct was telling me to get in my car and drive back to Bell Run. What with the ghost-abstention promise I made to Hugh, I should do just that. But *because* of Hugh, I couldn't leave.

Common sense was telling me this had to be a bad dream brought on by holiday stress. Any minute now I'd look down, find myself stark naked, then wake up in a cold sweat, vowing never again to eat peanut butter as a bedtime snack.

Horse mistook my indecision. "You should rest those muscles this afternoon. They'll do the Grand Illumination again. You can catch it Sunday."

His "doctor's orders" manner seemed to seal my fate. Glad obliged further with, "Why don't you lie down until dinner, Pat? I put you and Magnolia in the back room, right at the top of those stairs."

She nodded toward the door to my right, which I'd labeled a closet. The bump-out didn't look large enough to contain a stairway. I tried to dwell on that enigma, but kept imagining myself upstairs, alone, prone on a bed, vulnerable. "I'd rather stay here. I . . . I'd like to hear more about Elizabeth Carson." The act of a desperate woman, yes, but I didn't think Glad would let me remain in the kitchen otherwise.

I was right. Her whole face lit up—that one request scored me big points. With Glad, anyway. Horse looked as if he feared for my sanity, and Beth Ann's eyes narrowed, no doubt mentally stamping me "kiss-up."

"Come on, Uncle Horse," the teen said, scowling. "Let's get our coats." She headed for the dining room and he followed.

"So you want to hear all about Elizabeth," Glad gushed, coming to sit beside me, turkey forgotten. "She's such a fascinating person, don't you think? And you can *feel* her in this house."

Not *her*, I wanted to say. Whatever kissed me under the mistletoe, it wasn't a woman. Which, come to think of it, gave me a place to start. "What was her husband like?"

"Thomas?" Annoyance flashed through her hazel irises at me. I'd asked a dumb question. "He was a tinsmith. Left Elizabeth a widow with two children to feed." Her tone made it clear how thoughtless this was of him.

"Did he die in this house?"

Another dumb question. "Died in the war. Right after Yorktown." Glad turned a worried frown on me. "Oh, dear. You aren't afraid to stay in a house where people have died, are you? Because as old as these walls are, of course they've seen their share of death. Elizabeth herself perished here in 1795, only forty-two at the time, but then, women often did die young. She passed peacefully, though, in her own bed, surrounded by her grandchildren."

Sounds of a car on the shell drive reached my ears. I knew it couldn't be Hugh and Miss Maggie so soon.

Glad shuffled over to the door as Beth Ann and Horse returned to the kitchen in their coats. Horse was wearing an extra-large Redskins jacket and announcing, "Acey's here."

I'd already figured that out. Hugh's oldest brother, Rich, wasn't coming—they were doing Christmas with his wife's family instead—and every other sibling was accounted for.

"I saw her pull onto the drive," Horse continued as his mother opened the door. "She got out to open the gates herself. Is she alone?"

"No," Glad said as a red car crossed my line of vision through the doorway. "Her new boyfriend's beside her. She only told me he was coming on Tuesday. What was his name again?"

Horse shrugged, nudging Beth Ann. "Let's help them unload." Glad went out onto the porch.

Curious as to what Hugh's only sister looked like, I grabbed my jacket from atop my suitcase and went outside, too.

The red car was a Toyota hybrid, more in need of a wash than my own, so I felt an immediate kinship toward the owner. Beth Ann barely gave her aunt time to undo her seat belt before opening the driver's door. A sound emerged—a cry of sheer exuberant delight—and a tall woman shot out of the car, wrapping Beth Ann in an intense hug, both of them laughing.

Acey wore a poncho of Southwestern geometric tones that completely hid her niece except for Beth Ann's red mane. The woman's hair was dark blonde, frizzy, and shoulder-length, with long bangs, framing her face like a wig out of ancient Egypt. When she let go of Beth Ann and came up onto the porch to hug her brother and Glad, she had the same easy smile as Horse, under wide blue eyes. She gave off energy without being perky. I knew Acey was the baby of the family, but she looked and acted younger than I expected— almost like a teenager. Yet, with med school and all, she had to be around thirty.

"So you're Pat," she said, coming to me. Clasping my hand, her eyes gave me a once-over, but not a LAG. Then those baby blues reconnected with my own. "We'll talk," she said in a way that made us instant conspirators. I liked her at once.

Turning back to her mom and brother, she said, "And now, the moment you've all been waiting for." She swept back her arm, giving us a view of the man stepping up onto the porch behind her. "Meet Kevie."

And that's when I was *certain* this was all a bad dream, because there stood the one man I least wanted to come face-to-face with in a social situation: my gynecologist.

FIVE

"Dr. Weisel," I said, my mouth being the only part of me that worked when I was in shock. Of course, I was hoping the man would say I had him confused with someone else, that his name was Smith. I mean, I'd seen the doctor for, what? Twenty minutes? More like fifteen. I could be wrong.

I knew I wasn't, though. Oh, his features were average, easy-to-mistake, and yes, he looked different wearing a leather jacket and black cords instead of scrubs and latex gloves, but what made him distinctive was his personality—pleasant and confident, just shy of patronizing and conceited.

"Yes," came his reply, along with a bewildered but friendly smile. "Have we met?"

I told myself doctors see a lot of patients each day. Understandable that he wouldn't remember me. I should have kept my mouth shut. But he was bound to recognize my name, especially since Acey had referred me and I'd only seen him two weeks ago last Friday, so best to get this over with. "Pat Montella."

Still the blank look.

"I'm a patient of yours. I was in your office less than three weeks ago?"

"Ah! Oh, right!" He uttered exclamations while thumbing through mental index cards. "Of course. Nice to see you."

He shook my hand as if he meant it. I was certain he still didn't know me, and I felt like a chassis off his assembly line.

Two beats of awkward silence went by, then Horse said, "Well, let's get your stuff inside. You're coming with us to see the Christmas guns, aren't you?"

Acey, I noticed, was frowning at me, but when I caught her eye, she quickly turned to her brother. "I drove like a bat out of hell to get here in time."

"You always drive like a bat out of hell," said Horse as they headed back to her car. Acey swatted him on the arm, though I doubt he felt it through the lined jacket and massive biceps.

Glad played traffic controller as everything was carried into the kitchen. "Beth Ann, take Ann Carter's bag to your room—"

"Pajama party time!" Acey said to her niece. Beth Ann's face lit up. Taking a large, framed knapsack from Horse, she led her aunt toward the dining room, the two of them whispering and giggling.

"I put, er, Kevin upstairs," Glad said to Horse, heading for the closet. "Second room, next to Magnolia and Pat."

"We'll leave the gifts down here," he replied, placing my carryall and Acey's three boxes wrapped in Sunday comics beside the hearth stove. Then he picked up Miss Maggie's tote and both of our suitcases—all still beside the closet door—and followed his mother. Dr. Weisel waved me in front of him, so I joined the procession.

The mystery of the closet was solved. It contained an enclosed spiral stairway which was so tight, Horse had trouble maneuvering my bags and his bulk up the triangular steps.

At the top, another door opened facing down a narrow hall. The hall ran the length of the outside wall and—owing to the uncovered windows, white plaster, and the fact that we were now above back-yard fence level—was brighter than downstairs, even in the waning winter afternoon. I couldn't quite call it cheery. Some human touch was needed, like throw rugs over the dark red-brown floorboards, or artsy-craftsy wall hangings.

"The bath for this wing is down this hall and around the corner," Glad said, waving Horse and me through the first doorway. Nothing about imagining Elizabeth here, thank goodness. Glad took Dr. Weisel next door to his room, letting me figure out my space without her.

Not much to figure out. The room was squarish, with a small hearth and one window letting in a meager amount of illumination through dark wooden blinds. Horse switched on what was the only light in the room—a floor lamp not far inside the door, at the base of a daybed that hugged the wall. The bulb—no more than a forty, watt-wise—threw a muted glow over the crocheted afghan on the bed. Three small throw pillows huddled in the far corner.

Between window and hearth was the kind of chair that could be folded out to make a thick mattress on the floor, and stacked on its seat were a set of flowered sheets, two anemic-looking pillows, and an Army blanket.

I walked over to the window and raised the blind. The view was of the porch roof, cars, and the rear windows of the main house.

Uphill to the left, in the historic area, lights were beginning to come on.

"Kind of spartan," Horse said, "but then, if you'd come last year, we'd have had to clear floor space for you in the den. This place has enough rooms, at least."

"Was her old house much smaller?" I asked, turning from the window. I slipped out of my jacket and tossed it on the chair.

"Three bedrooms. When Ma moved back to Williamsburg after she and Dad split, Rich and Foot were already in college, so she figured she didn't need anything bigger. Wasn't bad every other Christmas when Rich visited his in-laws, except for Acey, who had to share with Ma—I bet she's thrilled to be in with Beth Ann instead this year. The kids always got the sofabed in the living room, and for the years Hugh was with Tanya, I got the daybed in the den. Then, after Hugh became the postmaster at Bell Run, Miss Maggie started coming. So when Rich and his family showed up, and Acey brought the boyfriend-of-the-month, Hugh and I made do with sleeping bags in the dining room."

Strange to hear him refer to Tanya so casually. Hugh almost never talked about his late wife, and Beth Ann didn't remember much about her mother. I wanted to ask Horse what Tanya was like—in particular, how I compared—but we heard a commotion out in the hall before I had a chance.

"Come on, Kevie," Acey was saying. "Beth Ann and I are ready for our frontal assault on this sleepy little burg. We tried to collect Foot on the way, but he's having too much fun being a curmudgeon. Where's Horse?"

We met Acey and Beth Ann in the hallway and Glad led the way back down the tiny staircase.

Acey waved everyone down ahead of her, except me. "Stay up here a sec," she said in a low voice, pulling me away from the stair door, waiting until the others were out of earshot. "When I gave Hugh the referral, I said you should ask for Dr. Vaughn."

"I did, but she was booked solid for four months, so they asked if I'd see Dr. Weisel instead."

"Oh." Acey looked surprised. Didn't doctors ever have problems making appointments for themselves?

"Does it matter?" I asked. My goal had been to get in to see a gynecologist, and I had, and the exam hadn't been any worse than all the others I'd had in my lifetime. Not better, either, but that's the nature of the ordeal.

"No. I just—I thought you'd like Dr. Vaughn, that's all. See if you can get her for your next annual. In fact, I'll talk to her about you."

I felt a sinking feeling in my stomach. *What's wrong with Dr. Weisel?* I wanted to ask. Then it occurred to me that some kind of jealousy might be involved. Though, if Acey had a problem with her sweetie looking at other women's privates, she was dating a man in the wrong profession.

She was already headed down the steps. And chicken me, not wanting to be alone upstairs, followed her.

* * *

Night came too quickly, as it always does on gloomy winter days. The overhead and fluorescent lamps lit the business part of the kitchen well enough, but left either end in shadow, particularly the pantry and dining room beyond.

"There's a TV up in my bedroom, Pat," Glad said, "if you want to go watch it." Another attempt to get rid of me, though this time it sounded halfhearted. Probably she wanted me to ask about Elizabeth again.

So I did, with a twist. "How did you go about researching your ancestors? You know so much about Elizabeth Carson." Yes, I was brown-nosing. "I've done a little of my family tree, but not in so much detail." Truth was, I'd tried to diagram the Giamo side once, out of self-defense because I had so many second cousins, I couldn't keep straight who was whose kid. The sum total of my footwork involved visiting two cemeteries to find the names and dates of all my great aunts and uncles.

"Oh, I started very young," Glad said. "When I was a girl, every time we drove past this house, my father would tell me how he was born and raised here, and how the place had been in his family from the time it was built until his mother sold it to John D. Rockefeller, Jr., during the Depression. Of course, my father meant Rockefeller's Colonial Williamsburg Foundation, but he always said it like Rockefeller himself sat in at settlement." Distracted, Glad began to open the oven door, then remembering I was still there, hesitated.

"Go ahead, I won't look. Swear to God." I averted my eyes to the opposite wall, hoping the bird wouldn't suffer for my presence. "So your father told you about your ancestors?"

"Heavens, no." The oven door squeaked open and the delectable aroma coming from within quadrupled in intensity. "His parents could trace their roots back to the Civil War, but no further. Wasn't until I had to go to the Foundation library to work on a school paper that I discovered the Carsons."

Out of the corner of my eye, I saw a white flash in the dining room. My heart vaulted up my windpipe. Then I realized the electric candles in the front windows had come on by themselves. On a timer, I guessed, or a light sensor.

As if the candles were a cue, Glad said, "Five o'clock already. Pat, open the porch door a moment. Let's see if we can hear the guns."

I obeyed, wishing I hadn't left my jacket upstairs. Outside, the air seemed damper now, and except for the sounds of traffic out on Francis Street, the night was quiet. "What *are* the Christmas Guns?"

"Back in colonial times," Glad explained, over the crinkle of the aluminum foil she was removing from the roasting pan, "men used to fire their flintlocks on Christmas or New Year's Day, perhaps a carryover from earlier times, when loud noises were thought to keep evil spirits away. Now we do it at night instead of dawn."

A muted *boom-bm* came down the hill, a shot with a half-beat echo.

"There they go," Glad said. "I never could hear them from my old house."

The delight in her voice was so unmistakable, I asked, "How are you adjusting? I mean, you lived in your other house, what—twenty years? And this one, well—"

"Not your idea of how to spend retirement?"

"The place *does* seem to require a lot of attention."

"Exactly why I *should* be here." She closed the oven door. "Since I came back to Williamsburg, I've driven by this house almost every day. More than half the time, it was deserted. I hated seeing it neglected all those years. You can close the door now. Better turn on the porch light, too—the button by the door. Gets awfully dark back there. I should have told them not to take the shortcut.

Though, at least, it's no longer marshland like it was in Elizabeth's day."

I did as asked, pushing the outtie on another antique switchplate. A drab, yellow glow lit up the porch floor and fronts of the cars. "Why was this house deserted? I thought employees of the Foundation live in its buildings."

"They do, for the most part. That's why the structures are so well-preserved, you see. A lived-in house is taken care of." A loud screech sounded from the stove area. I glanced over to see that Glad had opened the drawer under the oven and was removing a rectangular glass baking dish. "And also—I suppose you'll think me silly for saying so, but I think an empty house becomes, well, melancholy. Oh, not in the sense of it having emotions, of course. It's just that," she faced the dining room for a moment, "the walls absorb and radiate back the life within them. That's why old houses have a different feel than new."

"That's not silly at all," I said, thinking of Miss Maggie's cozy Reconstruction-era house that seemed to welcome me from the moment I climbed the porch steps. And my Aunt Sophie's tiny row home, pulsing with the energy of two to four generations under its roof at any given moment through the last century. My former apartment, only a decade old, felt lifeless. Still, as much as I could see that the Carson house had been unloved for quite a while, I knew there was more to its "feel" than simple neglect.

Glad closed the oven drawer, which let out another screech in protest, then considered the dish she held as if at a loss about what to do with it. I was cramping her style again, but I wouldn't be forced from my sanctuary. And anyway, I can't watch someone else cook without wanting to get my hands greasy or floury or whatever. "Can I help? You can swear me to secrecy. I understand, being a cook myself." I didn't, though, firmly believing that good recipes ought to go forth and multiply.

"Oh." The word spoke volumes. Volume one: Glad was a woman who stuck to her traditions. Volume two: no one had ever asked before. Or ever showed interest outside eating the final product.

I pressed my advantage. "Hugh said your Christmas meals are unique." He had, but the tone of his voice equated "unique" with "oddball," which was why Beth Ann's description of usual holiday fare surprised me a bit. "So I'm fascinated. And you shouldn't have to do everything yourself."

"I don't mind. Ev'll be back soon. But, um, perhaps you could help me with the black caps."

Black caps? Sounded like burnt mushrooms to me. "Be happy to. Show me what to do."

Glad set the dish on the long table beside the stove. "The problem is that I've never made this recipe before."

And you're serving it at a dinner party?! I almost shrieked, horrified. Sure, I'd been known to improvise recipes to feed last minute guests, but my meals were always based on time-tested formulas, stretched to go further, or altered to make do with ingredients at hand. New recipes I tried on myself first.

I recalled Beth Ann's "we always have the same things" and wondered why Glad had gone adventuresome all of a sudden. Not on my account, I hoped. But, slapping a smile on my lips, I said, "Let's have a look at it."

Glad crossed to the hutch opposite, slid open a drawer—which was stuffed to the gills with pieces of paper—extracted a standard eight-and-a-half-by-eleven specimen, and brought it back to the table.

The page was a photocopy. "Black Caps" was in italics at the top—innocent enough—but then I read, "Chuse for this Dish a Dozen of large sound Apples." *Whoa!*

"It's from Martha Bradley's *The British Housewife*," Glad explained, "published in London in 1756. Ev found it for me. Let me get the apples. You can halve them." She bustled over to the pantry while I read on.

Understanding the recipe wasn't the problem. Cut the apples in half, core them, place them face down in the dish, dust them with sugar. Easy. The difficulty came where it said to take two "Spoonfuls" (size apparently wasn't an issue back in 1756) of the clear juice of a lemon and "add one Spoonful of Orange-flower Water." Huh?

"I bought Empire apples," Glad said, returning with two clear grocery bags, with a half dozen each. "They have a nice round shape and aren't too big. Eighteenth century fruit was smaller than our modern hybrids, you see."

She headed for the sink, so I went over to help wash the fruit. "What's orange-flower water?"

"Used to be a flavoring liqueur, made by distilling orange blossoms. The closest I could find was orange extract, though I'm sure the taste won't be the same."

I was tempted to point out that since no two-hundred-fifty-year-old food critics would be eating our version, authenticity mattered less than yumminess. I took the tactful route. "Modern extracts are probably a lot stronger. Let's put just a drop or two in a tablespoon of water. Or maybe a drop of the orange with a drop of vanilla extract might be closer to the right taste." Since I defined "right taste" as anything that wouldn't drown the Empire's cidery tang, I added, "Less lemon, too—I assume their lemons were smaller and not as fresh as we're used to?"

"Absolutely. Citrus came by sailing ship from the Mediterranean."

Picturing shriveled, moldy fruit in the stalls of Market Square, I was thankful I lived in this century. Then again, those colonials never had to deal with stubborn produce stickers.

While I halved the apples and arranged them in the baking dish, I asked Glad more questions about eighteenth century foods, not to get on her good side, but because I was genuinely interested. Cooking was my main creative outlet and recipe-collecting my favorite hobby. Here was a new source—the past.

Glad was more than willing to educate me, chattering away as she took a covered bowl from the fridge. Spices, I learned, were in the same boat (so to speak) as non-native fruit. They were shipped from the East Indies, with no tight-closing jars or tins sealed for freshness and tamper-proofing, and so they would have had a weaker taste than we're used to. I also learned that Glad's covered bowl contained fresh pumpkin diced into half-inch cubes, which she put into a frying pan with a pat of margarine.

"Of course," Glad continued, "there were only springhouses and root cellars to keep food fresh. You'd go to market more often— every day in the summer—for your meat and eggs and milk, if you had no cow or chickens of your own. How're the apples coming, Pat?"

Per Martha Bradley's instructions, I'd dribbled the lemon-orange-vanilla concoction onto the apples and sprinkled on a tad more sugar (talk about your sweet tooth!), then set them aside to await their turn in the oven, where they were to "stand Half an Hour in quick Heat." Given the "black" in their name, I guessed that the sugar ought to caramelize (candy apples!) and suggested to Glad that she crank the oven up to 425 F after the bird was done.

Then I asked what else I could do, and Glad, as she slid the now fried pumpkin cubes from the pan to a paper-towel-lined bowl, said, "Let's see. I suppose we could boil the peas for Ev's pudding. I'll fetch them from the pantry."

Pudding? Peas? Two words that, in my opinion, didn't go together. But no sooner was she through the doorway, than I spied lights outside—the headlamps of a car pulling into the yard. Headlamps that I recognized: Hugh's Ford. The porch light picked up the postal insignia on his car door (since he ran a one-man annex, he didn't rate an official postal service Jeep, but the decals on his own car kept him from getting ticketed while delivering mail in our local housing development).

Shouting to Glad as I dashed outside, I was on the porch before he'd come to a stop and beside his driver's door before he'd cut the engine. I could hear the radio through the closed windows. As I opened the door, I was nearly bowled over by Burl Ives singing "Holly, Jolly Christmas." And by Miss Maggie, who was almost drowning him out as she harmonized in her wobbly alto.

The car's dome light backlit the knee-melting grin Hugh gave me as he turned the key. Burl cut off mid-word. Miss Maggie took over the melody without skipping a beat.

Leaning in, I planted a quick smooch on my beloved's cheek, which was fairly smooth and smelling of Old Spice, so I knew he'd shaved before driving down. I craned my head around his bulk to greet Miss Maggie, who had added padded reindeer antlers over her green- and red-striped stocking cap. She wore green stretch pants under a red ski jacket. Christmas Spirit personified.

Since she had her eyes closed as she belted out another verse, and since Hugh had already maneuvered his left hand around to my butt, I took the opportunity to plant more than a quick smooch on him, aiming for mustache and lower lip this time.

His other arm curled around my shoulders, drawing me closer, and though the steering wheel was digging into my ribs, I did my best to oblige, until something—not Hugh's hands, because they were accounted for—slithered across my breasts.

"What the—?" Picturing a large slimy snake, I propelled myself out of the Ford, up against Acey's passenger door. "Something . . . I . . . oh . . . it's your seat belt." I felt my face flush, but told myself, after the day I'd had, I could be excused for being a smidge jumpy.

The strap finished retracting as Hugh exploded into laughter. Shoving the belt aside, he got out, reaching for me again.

Mindful that Glad was watching from within—odd that she hadn't come out, too—I side-stepped. "You're early."

"So make it worth my while." He cornered me at Acey's side mirror—not that I tried hard to get away.

"Hugh, your mom's right inside." The protest was negated by my traitorous hands sliding under his waist-length jacket.

"How'd you two hit it off?" he murmured, mouth brushing against my forehead.

That reminded me that I was mad at him for all the things he hadn't warned me about. "You've got some explaining to do."

"I'm good at explaining." He grazed his lips around my right earlobe, sending a surge of delirium south.

"Save it, lover boy," I managed to breathe out. "Miss Maggie's on her last chorus."

She'd wound into a big finish, but in the middle of the word "Christmas," we heard a window creak open above.

"Hey!" Foot stuck his head out of the first dormer of the original house. Even as a dark silhouette against the dim light of the room behind him, I could tell he was shaking with fury. "I've been yelling for the past half hour. Didn't anyone hear me? The damn door's stuck—I can't get out of this room."

I felt Hugh's laughter boil up inside him again, though he didn't let it out. "I guess we should go rescue him."

"You go. I'll bring Rudolph inside." Yes, I was avoiding the front stairs. But more than that, I had to talk to Miss Maggie alone. Foot was in the first bedroom—my panic-attack room, the room that, according to Glad, probably once had a lock on the hall side. And now Foot couldn't get out.

> *". . . to make Provision for the Support and Maintenance of Idiots, Lunaticks, and other Persons of unsound Minds . . ."*
>
> —Bill to establish the Public Hospital,
> General Assembly of Virginia, 1770

December 24, 1783—The Eagle's Nest

AT FIRST, JOHN BRENNAN carried on his business as usual, though his patrons now were required to knock upon his door. He let in but one at a time, all others tarrying in the hall as if awaiting an audience with Governor Harrison. And when Brennan took his leave, he secured his lock with its heavy key, which he wore on a chain about his neck.

But Brennan's mania increased even as the December sun diminished. He returned to his room at more and more frequent intervals, inspecting the lock each time to ensure its working order, until at last he would leave only to use the privy or bring food from the market or tavern. On those occasions, he became as a man pursued by demons—in truth, he seemed to see such creatures on the street.

His countenance, too, changed. He grew gaunt and ever paler, moving as if his limbs pained him, and the smell of onions followed in his wake from poultices applied to his joints. Around his head, he had tied a compress soaked in feverfew tea. His hands often shook and his teeth began to forsake his mouth, until the top lip curled over his gums. Gone was his cockiness, displaced by dread and a mounting tendency to blame all who lived beneath the Carson roof for his affliction.

On the eve of Christmas, he came to the west room of the Eagle. I'd scarcely settled myself at the hearth, with a gill of stout cider to warm my bones before the evening's mummery in the streets of Williamsburg. Near at hand sat Alex Fisher, Will Knox, and Jim Parker, the latter sipping at a hot whiskey toddy to ease a stubborn croup in his throat. We awaited the arrival of Sam and young Tom to complete our troupe.

The hour being early, only a trio of lads shared the fire with the four of us. Talk was of Brennan's mania.

"He came into the apothecary today," Alex said, "asking after specific cures and the maladies that occasioned their use. I advised him to tell me of his ailment, so I could then say which physics might give him comfort. Comfort, he said, would not help him, but rather, knowing what would make him the worse."

"Mad," Jim coughed out, and all concurred.

"And when I put it to him that he might consult with Dr. Galt or young Riddick," Alex went on, "he said Dr. Riddick might have saved him once, but could no longer be trusted since he took his bed from Widow Carson. 'And *with* her,' he told me. 'The lot of them do.' Brennan's very words."

Will laughed, a deep rumble in his spacious chest. "Your rent is a bargain, sirs, if it includes such service."

The others joined in the mirth, saying, "I shall change my lodgings directly," and "What does Mrs. Carson serve with dinner?" and, from Alex, "Ben certainly wishes it so."

I chose to let them have their jest, to laugh with them and hold my tongue, but Jim spoke out, "Say nothing against the lady." His tone was good-natured, though the firelight brought out the blush of his neck, and he hid his displeasure behind his tankard. "What other matron of this town would take John Brennan into her house and tend him in his illness as if he were kin? None would, that's assured."

"Aye," came a quavering voice at our backs. We turned to behold Brennan standing in the doorway, or rather, leaning his weight upon the jamb. The hearthlight, a jovial gold on our faces, seemed ghostly upon his ill-shaven cheeks, and his eyes were sunken in shadow.

"Aye, she took me in," Brennan said, his brogue bitter as rue. "Took me in when her husband was off in the war. Gave me a warm hearth and victuals while her Tom froze and starved at Valley Forge. Blessed me with her smile, while he could only gaze upon the likes of you." He let forth the cackle of a lunatic. "Took me in, and now I must take myself out. A dollar to any man who assists me in the removal of my belongings from Mrs. Carson's house."

"I should assist you for no pay," Jim said, rising, "and when your possessions are in the street, I shall be pleased to remove your hide as well."

Brennan took a step back, bumping a serving lad passing behind him. "No, Mr. Parker. 'Tis not you I require, nor Mr. Dunbar, nor the others who scheme ag'in me. They come into my room, sirs, and poison my food and drink."

Jim scoffed. "How can we do that? You lock your door always when you leave."

"Perhaps when I sleep then, though I bar the way with my trunk, and place my sacks atop it. Nevertheless, the room is entered each day and I am poisoned, as all who behold me can see. None can be trusted, not even the young mistress and master. So I must take myself away. Who will help?"

"Where will you go, sir?" asked Matthew Hockaday, a quiet, tidy man who clerked at the courthouse.

"Go?" Brennan seemed to cower, as if thoughts of his prospects afrighted him, but then he drew himself up, regaining some of his old conceit. "I shall take up quarters at the Palace, of course."

Brennan seemed to be making a joke, though given his behavior of late, none were certain. "Sir," Alex said, "you recall the Governor's Palace burned two years ago."

"Monday next, to the day," Will added.

"Then I shall not disturb the residents, shall I?" Brennan concluded, as if that be proof of his reason.

"If you have no lodgings, sir," Mr. Hockaday warned, "the court shall declare you vagrant."

Brennan became impassioned. "I'll not have that. John Brennan is no vagrant. My business provides means to buy fine lodgings." He looked to each of our faces for agreement, though, for myself, I could only think how no patrons had come to him since the solstice. His very smile belied his words, for men of means will have their bare gums fitted with teeth of ivory or porcelain. "I have—I've yet to find rooms to suit me, sirs. I assure you, I will."

"The Public Hospital would suit you well," Jim said, breathing in the steam from his cup. "There you'd have a genteel cell indeed, spacious and lavish, with a door locked for you by servants."

The lads had a laugh at that and Will said, "More the pity the place was abandoned."

I'd never seen the inside of Williamsburg's lunatic hospital—'twas, to my thinking, a peculiar notion that a doctor might return a madman to his former reason. Sam had described the house as a fine prison, with large cells and windows for light, and a yard where the deranged might walk about during the day. However, the war had taken money required for maintenance of the hospital, and destitution had caused the closing of its doors two years previously.

"When Dr. de Sequeyra calls upon Dr. Galt," Alex said, "they speak of the hospital opening anew, once repairs have been made."

"Not soon enough," Hockaday stated. "Two lunatics share our jail presently. Mr. Brennan will join them, I have no doubt."

"No!" Brennan exclaimed, fleeing from us, jostling the patrons before the bar who blocked his progress.

"Join them afore the New Year, I'll wager," Hockaday concluded with grim satisfaction, then called out to the boy for another pint.

SIX

"I LOVE BURL IVES's Christmas songs," Miss Maggie sighed, pulling herself gingerly out of Hugh's car. The long ride had stiffened her arthritic knees. "Brings back memories."

Better memories, I gathered, than her afternoon had brought. I knew her regular Wednesday visits with Frank were an emotional drain—having a mentally ill son or daughter is hard on anyone, and Frank had been that way since World War II, more than half Miss Maggie's life. Today must have been especially taxing. Oh, she was cheery enough, yet even in the dim light from the porch, I could see exhaustion in her eyes. I gave her a hug.

But talking to her had to wait. Foot had been rescued by Glad before Hugh stepped up onto the porch, so he returned to get his suitcase and gifts from the car. Then we heard voices coming down the slope behind us as Beth Ann and her entourage returned. After Miss Maggie was warmly hugged by Hugh's siblings, Acey introduced her new beau.

Hugh leaned close to my ear. "Dr. Kevin Weisel? Wasn't that the guy you ended up seeing—"

"Right," I whispered back. "My new GYN."

His eyebrows went up, but since everyone was traipsing inside, he said no more and we followed.

Glad returned to the kitchen with her other son in tow. "I can't imagine why you had so much trouble, Francis. The door opened easily for me."

At the same time, Evelyn walked in, dressed in a plain long brown coat and a round brimmed hat, with musket in hand, looking like he'd just mustered out of the local militia. Glad did the introductions this time. Hugh and Horse each shook the hand Evelyn offered, though with hasty formality. Foot didn't come forward at all. Acey clasped Evelyn's hand as she had mine, gazing at him a moment, then sending her mother a wide grin.

"Now," Glad said firmly, "if you want dinner on time—"

"We know, Ma," said Horse. "Everyone out of the kitchen." He swept an arm toward the dining room, indicating our exodus route.

Wanting to stay, I turned to Glad. "Can I help with anything else?" But she was shaking her head.

Miss Maggie divested herself of her jacket, revealing a red sweatshirt with the words "Reindeer Games Track and Field" on the front and "Dasher" and the number "01" on the back. "Show me where our things are, Pat. And which way to the bathroom."

That, at least, seemed a better alternative than walking under the mistletoe again, so while everyone else followed Horse, I led Miss Maggie to the closet/stairs. Glad followed us as far as the door, touching another two-button switch on the wall.

Up in the hallway, an overhead bulb went on, though it was situated too far from the stairway to illuminate more than the top step. After Miss Maggie and I groped our way to the second floor, I showed her our bedroom, switching on the floor lamp as we entered.

"So, Pat," Miss Maggie said, tossing her handbag onto the day-bed, "what's bugging you?"

She knew me too well. "First promise you won't tell Hugh."

"Oh?" She took off her antlers and knit cap and tried to fluff out her short white hair. "I know you're not pregnant—had your period this month and you're on the pill."

Heat rushed up into my face and neck so fast I longed to yank off my pullover sweater. I hadn't told Miss Maggie anything—she was simply being her super-observant self. I hid my embarrassment by bending over to lift her suitcase onto the bed.

"And," she continued, "I doubt you had a blowup or whatever with a member of Hugh's family already. No tension of that sort in the kitchen just now."

I assured her that I'd been on my best behavior all day.

"So then," she concluded, donning the smug grin of a teacher who, with her face turned to the blackboard, can single out a student passing notes in the back of the room, "this is about ghosts, isn't it?"

I felt a perverse desire to see a glimmer of doubt in her eyes. "How do you know it's not about Beth Ann?"

"Beth Ann makes you crazy. Not fidgety." She pointed to my fingers, which were beating a tattoo on her bag's cloth side. "Besides, Pat, this house always did have a reputation for being haunted. I figured you might run into something today."

"You *knew* it was haunted? Why didn't you tell me before—"

"Don't be silly. You would have had preconceived notions." Unzipping her suitcase, she rummaged for and brought out a hairbrush. "What did you see, Pat?"

"Nothing." With a sigh, I hopped up onto the bed beside her luggage, pushing myself back until I leaned against the throw pillows. As Miss Maggie brushed out her curls, I gave her a rundown of my experiences, out of order—I started with my own, then mentioned Foot being stuck in the panic-attack room, and ended with what Zela had told me. "That's why I spent the last couple hours in the kitchen. Which wasn't easy with Hugh's mom trying to throw me out every ten minutes."

Miss Maggie smiled her sympathy as she tossed her brush back into her suitcase. "Do you feel anything now, Pat? Here?"

I felt exhausted—a nap would have been welcome—but that wasn't what she meant. "Nope. No anxiety. No panic. No reluctance to go anywhere in this room."

"You felt those things only around Foot's bedroom, and at the base of the stairs in the oldest part of the house, correct?"

I nodded, realizing what she was getting at. "You think this newer wing isn't haunted? Just the main house?"

"And maybe only *part* of that. If so, maybe you can avoid further encounters this weekend."

I sat up. "Wait, I don't believe it. Magnolia Shelby *wants* me to avoid ghosts?"

"I thought you were avoiding them anyway, for Hugh."

"I am, but you—"

"Look, I admit, I have a fondness for historical puzzles—"

Fondness? The woman was addicted to them.

"—and the Carson house has plenty of gaps in its record. Oh, the Williamsburg Foundation knows *who* lived here all those years, but not *what happened* beneath this particular roof, especially during the Revolution. If anything. And whoever kissed you beneath the mistletoe this afternoon might have been alive before this wing was built in the 1790s."

An eyewitness, she meant, and as she spoke, Miss Maggie's green eyes grew wide and bright, the way they always did when she got excited. "*But*, this ghost is different from the others you've encountered. You're frightened this time."

True. Other encounters with the Great Beyond had involved fragments of the past so subtle that I hadn't known to be scared until Miss Maggie filled in the historical facts behind my experience. Once she'd educated me, I'd met the disembodied on my own terms, coaxing their stories from them, like I'd tried to do today when I'd closed my eyes. I'd seen things those souls had seen in their lives, even shared thoughts and emotions, yet I could always remain separate, always an observer. None of those previous spooks had ever physically touched me.

Yep, this time I was petrified.

Miss Maggie placed one of her gnarled, arthritic hands over mine. Her fingers were cold. "Leave this one alone, Pat. You're here to enjoy the holiday." She took up her reindeer antlers once more. "I'll go find the bathroom. Be right back."

"There's supposed to be one in this wing, down at the end of the hall. I'll come find it with you." My thought was to test out Miss Maggie's theory while she was with me for support. If I was going to avoid ghosts this weekend, an unhaunted bathroom was a must. Besides, nature was calling.

The hall ran along the outside wall to the front of the wing, then took a left turn. Straight ahead was the bathroom, its entrance almost lost in shadow. At a right angle to it was another doorway, leading into the old part of the house. I could see a faint trickle of light coming up from, I assumed, the opening on the stair landing, and I could hear voices from downstairs.

Miss Maggie nudged me. "Feel anything?"

"No." Only wariness, from the suggestion of what waited beyond that doorway, between me and those voices, or up the stairs in Foot's room.

Miss Maggie hit the light switch in the bathroom, revealing a slightly roomier space than the one in the main house. Another closet, converted, or at least remodeled, in the 1950s I guessed, judging by the dingy pink fixtures and tile, trimmed in black. When I tried to imagine ghosts in that room, I saw Elvis slicking back his hair in front of the wall mirror. That thought was probably suggested by the toiletries case on the shelf behind the toilet. Bigger than a shaving kit, like a women's cosmetic case done in masculine leather. Since Dr. Weisel had the other bedroom in this wing, I assumed the case was his.

"You first, Pat. Call me if you need me."

I didn't need to call her, though I made a mental note to warn her about the faucet knobs—both lifted off easily. Not that it seemed to matter, since only ice water poured forth from each.

But Miss Maggie wasn't in the hall when I opened the bathroom door. She'd been replaced by Hugh, who was leaning against the wall, arms folded, leer on his lips, eyes shining with mischief.

Before I could get a word out, he scooped me off my feet, his burly arms cradling my knees and back. "You can't hide that easily," he said seductively. "Know what's waiting downstairs?" And to my horror, he tramped off through the doorway.

"No!" I flung one arm around his neck, and gripped his flannel shirt, cringing, expecting the panic feeling to hit any moment, and God knew what else. I closed my eyes out of instinct, then realized that's the last thing I should do and opened them wide. "Put me down, please!"

Thinking I was kidding, Hugh let out one of his fake evil laughs as he toted me down a few steps and through the doorway to the stair landing. Then, with the hall light above and table lamp below guiding his footing, he doubled his pace, like Rhett Butler carrying Scarlett, except going down instead of up. He put on his brakes in the worst place imaginable. Under the mistletoe.

"Hugh, please, I—" Further pleas were stopped by his mouth on mine. I took stock of the situation: I didn't feel panic, or more than mild anxiety, or anyone kissing me except Hugh. So I kissed him back. Miss Maggie told me I was here to enjoy the holidays, and this was definitely on my to-do list. But I kept my eyes open a slit.

Thing is, with my defenses still up, the final product was ruined. Hugh sensed something was amiss and pulled away, though he drew in a deep breath as if he needed it.

By way of excuse, I rolled my eyes toward the parlor, where I could see Beth Ann eyeing us from an armchair. "Your daughter's giving us the *malorchi*."

Hugh gave me a blank look.

Okay, I admit my pronunciation isn't high Italian, but that's how all the Montellas say it. My mom's relatives, the Giamos, say "maloik." Though I guessed Hugh might not even recognize the proper "malocchio," so I explained, "the evil eye."

He scowled. "We'll resume this later, in private." Reluctantly, he lowered me to my feet and we turned toward the parlor to join the others.

Horse met us at the doorway. "You're winded, brother. Out of shape."

"Merely out of practice." Hugh laughed again, but his comment had me picturing him doing the same thing with Tanya.

"So how's Manny Ibara's shoulder?" Hugh asked his brother. "Will he pitch this year?"

"Won't make spring training 'til at least March. If he does what I tell him, he'll start the home opener. But Atlanta won't be calling him up this year."

"Good. Richmond needs him."

Hugh had taken me to a couple Richmond Braves games, so I could follow their conversation (though I was still a true-blue Phillies fan at heart). I was impressed by Horse's clientele, but found myself tuning out the sports talk after Miss Maggie came down the stairs and asked Acey about her last vacation: Chaco Canyon, New Mexico on the summer solstice.

"It's one big astronomical calendar, like Stonehenge," Acey rhapsodized. "We watched a shaft of light enter the great kiva and fill a niche opposite. And each night, the North Star is directly above the entrance in the center of the wall. I have a photo of star circles—"

All of a sudden Hugh tugged at my hand, coaxing me toward the door.

"Horse wants to have a word with you."

"Me?" I looked at Horse. "What about?"

"Let's find a place we can talk in private." Hugh's brother led me out into the hall, which didn't feel nearly so cozy as when I'd been snuggled against Hugh. "Mom'll kill us if we go into the dining room while she's setting up. How 'bout the back bedroom?"

I agreed, because I wanted to get out of the hall, and followed him to Beth Ann and Acey's room, where he turned on the vanity lamp. The parchment shade cast an amber glow over everything. I sat on the edge of the sofa bed, facing the doorway, feeling less vulnerable that way, feeling somehow like I'd stepped into the room just in time.

Horse left the door open, but lowered his voice. "How are your knees? The aspirin help any?"

"A little." Very little, but it *had* helped.

"I've been thinking. You said you went to Dr. Weisel, what, three weeks ago?"

I nodded.

"And you started having this pain when?"

"Beginning of last week." What? Did he think Dr. Weisel had done something to my legs during the examination?

"Did he prescribe anything for you at the time?"

Blood rushed up my neck and into my cheekbones like a geyser. No way was I saying "the Pill" to Hugh's brother. Nice Italian Girls are raised by stricter censors than the folks who do Disney cartoons.

"I'm a doctor, Pat. Nothing you tell me will go beyond this room." Then he made it easier for me. "Did Dr. Weisel put you on birth control pills?"

Another nod.

"Ever take them before?"

This time I shook my head.

"How long after you took the first dose did your knees begin hurting?"

I shrugged. "Less than a week. Is that it? Is this just a side effect?"

Horse ignored my question. "This 'bad circulation' in your family—any of your relatives ever have thrombosis? Blood clots? Specifically in their legs?"

Blood clots were serious, weren't they? "I—I don't know—yeah, I think someone mentioned them."

"Anyone you could ask to find out for sure?"

"Aunt Sophie." Keeping track of who died and how was a hobby of hers.

Horse unhooked his cell phone from his belt. "Would she be home now?"

I glanced at my watch. Twenty to seven. "Probably finishing up dinner."

He held out the phone to me. "Go on. Call information if you need the number."

"I know it." Taking the cell, I punched in the digits, wondering why this was so urgent. And feeling my stomach roll over in response to his urgency.

My cousin Lucretia answered. "Yo, Pat! How you doing? Hey, everybody, it's Pat, calling to say Merry Christmas!" She had to yell—the phone was on the kitchen wall, right around the corner from the dining room, but when you stuff a small space with Italian-Americans, all talking at once, it gets loud.

I felt guilty, because I should have *thought* to call and wish them all Merry Christmas. "Lu, can you put your mom on?"

"Hold on—no, wait, she's pouring the coffee. Here, talk to Dad a minute."

Uncle Leo wouldn't get up from his place at the head of the table, I knew, and Aunt Sophie didn't trust portable phones. They had one of those extra long cords, though. I pictured everyone ducking around it to keep from getting strangled as the receiver was passed.

"'Tricia," Uncle Leo said in his raspy voice, a result of smoking too many stogies over more than half a century's time. "You doin' okay? You need anything?"

"No, Uncle Leo. I'm good. *Buona Natale* to you."

"*Buona Natale*. Lemme give you your Aunt Filippa."

So I got handed around the table and had no choice but to wish every aunt, uncle, cousin, and cousin's kid a happy holiday. In my family, you didn't dare snub anyone. Not that I'd want to—if I'd been doing this on my own phone—of course, I couldn't afford the long distance right now. Still, hearing their voices, I realized how much I missed them all.

At last, Aunt Sophie came on. I got the formalities out of the way—wished her *Buona Natale* and asked how her cannolis turned out this year.

"Ah," she sighed, sounding like disaster had hit. "I tried making the shells with those metal cylinders. Next year I'm going back to my corncobs."

I was willing to bet her finished product was flawless. Her cannolis always were, though she always claimed some catastrophe visited annually.

"You know who died?" Aunt Sophie went on. "That Messalina girl from Penn Street."

The name meant squat to me, though I translated "girl" to mean someone Aunt Sophie had gone to school with, and "from" as being before World War II. I tried to break in with my real reason for calling, but she gave me three more obits, then switched gears.

"Did Lu tell you about Marcella? You oughta know, before you call my sister Lydia." She assumed I'd phone all of Dad's surviving siblings, but that, naturally, she'd been first. "Her husband left her."

"Cella's Ron?" My aunt used pronouns freely—"her" might have meant Marcella, Aunt Lydia, or the Messalina girl.

"Yeah, Ronny. Left Marcella for the girl who cut his provolone every week at the Acme Market. Shoulda never let Ronny pick up their order. Marcella coulda done it after work."

Last I heard, Cella not only had a full-time job, on top of raising two kids, but was going to night school for her master's. Regardless, she and Ron had been together since high school (we all graduated in the same class) and, like I said, we Montellas love fiercely. I wanted to ask how Cella was taking it and if her kids were okay. Horse, though, was showing signs of impatience. I vowed to contact Cella soon as I got home, and interrupted Aunt Sophie's litany of "shoulda"s to ask my question.

"Blood clots?" she said. "That's what Pop died of."

"My grandfather?" He'd died before I was born. I'd never thought to ask how.

"Your Uncle Mario had one, too, when he was laid up with his first heart attack. And your cousin Nicola when she was pregnant. Remember? Landed her in the hospital and she almost lost little Joey. Mario's taking blood thinners now. So's Lydia—what's that, 'Lippa? . . . Filippa says she is, too. Me, I just take an aspirin a day."

"So did Dad," I suddenly remembered.

"If you're having trouble, Patricia, you go to a doctor. You want, I'll make you an appointment with Dr. Saluti. Come up on the train and Leo'll meet you at the DeKalb Station."

I spent an extra minute convincing her there were doctors in Virginia. Even if there weren't, Uncle Leo's driving would be worse for my health. Then she wouldn't let me hang up until I promised I'd go to mass for Christmas. Finally, I managed to get off the phone and handed it back to Horse. "Sorry that took so long."

Smiling, he shook his head. "Consider it a Christmas present."

I thanked him, thinking it was the best gift anyone could have given me this year—I was more homesick than I thought. Then I related the family medical woes.

His smile disappeared and, for the first time since we'd met, he actually looked grave. "You shouldn't be on birth control pills with a family history of thrombosis. Didn't you read the warning on the package insert?"

"I didn't see any insert. Dr. Weisel gave me two months worth of sample packs and—"

"Unsealed?"

"Only one card was open, but that's the one I used first." I felt stupid, so I overjustified. "I mean, each pill is individually sealed, and a doctor gave them to me, so I figured they were safe."

"But the insert was missing," he said, disgust in his voice, though it didn't seemed to be aimed at me. "Did Dr. Weisel give you a full examination before prescribing the pills? Did he ask you questions about your medical history and your family?"

"He asked if I smoked and if I had any known medical conditions. Then he gave me a regular check-up." Like I said, I was out of there in fifteen minutes.

Horse scowled, looking very much like Hugh when Beth Ann was being stubborn. "Stop taking the pills immediately. Continue two aspirin a day for at least a week. Drink lots of water. Stay off your feet as much as you can this weekend. You'll need some blood work first thing Monday morning, along with an ultrasound of your legs and a lung scan."

"Lung scan?" Now I was scared.

"A precaution," he hastily assured me. "I don't think you've been taking the pills long enough to do real damage, but we have to check for clots in your lungs and legs to be sure. If I thought you were in real danger, I'd take you to the hospital right now."

Hugh suddenly filled the doorway. "Mom just gave the three-minute warning. Wants us all in the parlor." He saw the grave look on his brother's face, glanced at me, then back at Horse. "She okay?"

Horse relaxed, but still seemed unhappy with the situation. "She'll be fine. Just needs a few tests."

Hugh turned his face back toward me, surveying me head to toe. I usually loved his once overs, but right now I felt like a favorite pet with worms. "Is it what you thought?"

What I thought? I was about to ask him what he meant when I saw Horse nodding.

"What?" I said to Horse, standing. "You discussed this with Hugh? What happened to patient confidentiality? 'Nothing you tell me will go beyond this room,' you said."

"No." Hugh came into the room and took my hand. "Other way around. I consulted Horse. Called him a few days ago, told him you'd been having a lot of pain in your knees and asked if he'd come early today—check you out before everyone else showed up."

"You did that behind my back," I squawked.

"I tried to get you to go to a doctor," Hugh argued.

"After the holidays." I'd told him a dozen times already. Though, really, I'd procrastinated because my health insurance didn't cover office visits.

"I know, but with Horse being an orthopedist—"

"It's a good thing he called me, Pat," Horse put in. "Another week or two taking those pills and—"

"*And*," I added, even madder at Hugh, "you told him I was on the Pill, didn't you?" Because how else would Hugh know what Horse thought?

"I asked him," Horse said, holding up a hand as if he could calm the waters, "after I heard you'd seen a GYN in the past month. But I promise, Pat, from now on I won't talk to Hugh about it unless you're present, and only with your permission. Let's get back to the parlor," he added, dismissing the discussion. "I'm starving."

*"Ladies and gentlemen sitting by the fire,
Put your hands in your pockets and give us our desire."*

—from *Recollections of Samuel Breck*, quoting from a
mummers play he witnessed in America, circa 1780

December 24, 1783—On the Streets of Williamsburg
'Twas Master Tom who fetched us from the Eagle. Some small
bit of reveling had begun in front of the taverns, though the hour
was early and elsewhere the streets were quiet.

Tom led us within the walls of the old capitol, into the shadows
on the north side where, in the dim glow of a hooded lantern, Sam
stood beside a handbarrow piled with the clothes that would be
our costumes. Where he had procured the raiment, he declined to
say. He himself was dressed in a black frock coat and britches, with
a long green waistcoat, all a bit tattered and hanging loose upon
his lean figure.

For Will, who due to his tall stature was our General Washington,
Sam had foraged a moth-eaten blue coat. The wool strained over
Will's broad shoulders, the fabric tearing further to accommodate

his girth. The sleeves were a cuff too short. However, the military trousers fit well enough, if Will remembered not to sit or stoop.

Jim was to be King George, and the red brocade coat Sam handed him seemed tailored to his form. But no sooner was it on, than Jim wrinkled his nose. "What is that stench?" As he moved, I detected the odor myself—both sweet and fetid.

"Some inferior breed of wig perfume," Sam replied, handing Tom a long black cloak to cover his clothes. "Perhaps a bit spoilt with time."

"A bit!" Jim protested.

"'Twill do you no harm," Sam assured him.

"Indeed," Will said, "as King George, sir, you *should* have a stink about you."

We all laughed, Alex the loudest, until Sam presented him with a woman's shift and petticoat, and to go atop, the most homely gown any of us had ever seen.

My own costume was a fringed white hunting frock big enough for Goliath, so its length and girth hid my coat and britches. I tied the excess lengths of sleeve up about my wrists.

Next we took grain sacks with eyeholes cut in them, to place over our heads and tuck into our collars. Masks were a tradition, I knew, but a precaution besides, for other mummers out this night—those with ruffian natures bolstered by excess of drink—might bring trouble. And if trouble brewed, the constable was apt to seize all revelers who'd been recognized.

Beneath the pile of costumes lay two muskets (Sam's and my own) and a pair of fine pistols.

"My grandsire's," Tom said, as Sam gave a hand weapon each to Jim and Will, "and my father's after him."

"We'll take good care of them, lad," Jim said as he primed one pistol with black powder from the horn he'd brought along, and a wad of paper from his pocket. Will did likewise. Sam and Alex took up the muskets, charging them with blank cartridges they'd rolled for the occasion.

"I'll not fire off more than five or six shots all night, sirs," Jim said. "Congress no longer supplies my powder, and money is too scarce these days to send it up in smoke, with no venison or pheasant to be supped upon for the effort."

Alex and Will fervently agreed and, for a moment, Sam was silent—though his face was concealed by his mask, I imagined him crestfallen, so I said, "Then I must play my fiddle all the louder," praying the horsehair would last out the evening.

"So you shall, Ben," Sam laughed, his good cheer restored. "And we shall collect enough coin this night to provide us all ample firepower for the New Year. As I passed the square earlier, I saw guests arriving at Captain Underwood's—gentry in carriages driven by liveried slaves. Enough wealth is enclosed in the captain's house this night that we need only to walk through, and come out the other side with pockets full of gold. We'll begin there."

"Are you mad?" I exclaimed. "Captain Underwood would sooner entertain the devil than invite us into his home. Above all you, Sam." Underwood had overseen our company the last years of the war and a man more drunk of his own power did not exist. Sam, with his free tongue and brash spirit, had oft run ill of the captain, and carried flogging scars to show for it.

"All the more reason to take his coin now, Ben. Think of it as recompense for Monmouth, where his blundering nearly handed all us lads over to the Lobsterbacks."

"Aye," agreed Will. "And for Paulus Hook, when I thought sure he'd ruined the raid by sending us forward too soon."

"And for all his other sins against us." Sam slid a flask from his frock pocket and, after a nip himself, offered it round. "The captain should have donned a redcoat himself, for all the good he did our cause. Besides he shan't know us in our masks. Remember, gentlemen, change your voices, as we rehearsed. Give us a tune as we go along, Ben. 'The World Turned Upside Down' would be fitting, eh?"

Indeed, yet I felt no jollity as I struck up my bow.

SEVEN

We returned to the parlor, Horse in front of me, Hugh behind, one of his big paws on my shoulder, thumb and forefinger kneading my neck muscles. I was still mad at him, but I didn't shrug off the massage; (a) it felt good, (b) it was Hugh's way of making amends, and (c) it seemed to keep the Carson house bogeyman at bay. Whatever the reason, I felt no uneasiness as we walked down the hall.

We'd barely reached the parlor doorway when Glad called everyone into the dining room.

"Supper time," Hugh said with his usual mealtime enthusiasm, and he steered me toward the food. Horse was already heading that way and everyone else followed us from the parlor.

I stopped, stunned, right inside the door, creating a logjam behind me. The room was lit by candles—two tapers on the table, two under hurricane glasses on the mantel, and of course the electric ones in the front windows. Evelyn and Glad stood at the head of the table, both in colonial dress. Evelyn looked as I'd first seen him that afternoon, but now wearing an unadorned brown coat, the kind I'd seen in paintings of Ben Franklin. Glad, rather than wearing her Marie Antoinette gown, had donned more of a Betsy Ross outfit—blue skirt, white apron, peasant blouse with a brown-striped waistcoat over top, and a frilly cap on her head.

But that wasn't why I was stunned. I'd never seen so many dishes of food on a table at one time. Oh, being Italian, I'd seen this kind of quantity, just not the variety. In the center were two large platters of turkey—one with sliced white meat, one with bite-sized dark meat, no whole drumsticks or wings. Both trays were garnished with mushrooms and pickled peppers. In front of the settings at the head and foot were open tureens—a pale yellow soup in one, what looked like stewed cabbage in the other. At the corners were serving dishes of yams, thick sausages, a half-dome of something green (peas pudding?), and a pie of some sort, all elaborately adorned with herbs or slices of citrus fruits. On one side of the table was a pyramid of cornbread squares, on the other, neat slices of bread stuffing. Squeezed in around the edges were place settings of thick maroon dishes, blue and white mugs, and pewter utensils.

"Gather 'round," Glad said, meaning I should quit blocking the door. She began to assign seats. "Ev will sit at the head and I'll sit here." She clutched the chair at Evelyn's right hand. "Then Beth Ann. Where is she?"

She was sulking in the back of the crowd. We let her through, then Hugh went forward, towing me by the hand.

"That's it," Glad said. "Fitzhugh, Pat, then Magnolia at the foot. Francis, Lighthorse, Ann Carter, and, er, Kevin on the other side."

So I ended up right across from Dr. Weisel, which didn't do my appetite any good. Because of him, I'd be having a lung scan next week. I felt Hugh's hand tighten on mine. Glancing up, I expected to see him making eyes at me, but he was looking at Dr. Weisel, too—glaring at him—and his hand had tightened in anger.

Miss Maggie, I noticed, wasn't wearing her reindeer antlers. Not proper dinner attire? More likely she thought they'd get in her way while she was eating. Leaning close to me, she murmured, "What do you think, Pat? *This* is how people in the eighteenth century decorated for the holidays." She waved her arm over the spread on the table. "Note the symmetry of how the dishes are laid out, and the presentation. It was quite an art form."

"I have an announcement to make," Glad said as we took our seats. "Now that I've retired, and with volunteering for the Foundation taking up a lot of my time, Ev suggested that our Christmas Eve dinner this year be somewhat scaled down. We've decided to cut it back to two courses."

Two? Like this?

Miss Maggie grinned at my disbelief. "She usually puts out four, in the eighteenth century tradition—two main courses followed by two dessert courses. Ten to twenty dishes apiece."

"*Madonne!*" I mumbled.

Glad's announcement had been met with silence from her family. She went on. "We've decided to serve this evening a Christmas meal similar to what Elizabeth Carson might have prepared in the leaner years, during and right after the war, when she had to take in lodgers to make ends meet."

Lean? I thought. Ten dishes instead of twenty. Good grief.

"Ev helped me with the menu this year," Glad said. "The pumpkin soup, peas pudding, boiled cabbage, and oyster pie are all from colonial recipes."

"And," Evelyn said as he took up two metal pitchers from the sideboard, "most of the ingredients were easily obtained and affordable in Williamsburg at the time."

Foot looked down his nose at the pie beside him. I wondered which he didn't like: oysters or cheap food.

"We've also decided," Glad added as she began to ladle out the soup and pass small bowls of it down the table, "not to have wine with this meal, but what Elizabeth more likely would have served: beer."

"All right!" said Horse at the same time Beth Ann said, "Oh, gross!"

"Water for you, dear," Glad said to her granddaughter, "and anyone else who prefers it, of course."

"It's brown ale, actually," Evelyn said, bringing his pitchers to our end of the table to pour Miss Maggie's first. "Closer to the English brews served in colonial taverns than modern American beers are."

"In the interests of authenticity," Miss Maggie said, "I'll have a mix of both ale and water. 'Small beer' it was called. The most common drink of the era. Even children drank it. The water wasn't safe by itself." The brew Evelyn poured was a rich red-brown hue and with one sip, Miss Maggie gave it her stamp of approval.

I went with straight water—I'd be getting my usual evening sleepiness soon and didn't want to help it along. Besides, in my opinion, yeast was better off baked into loaves.

I passed a soup bowl to Miss Maggie and she sniffed it appreciatively. "Gladys, you've outdone yourself this year."

Hugh's mother beamed. "You'll want to be careful of the peas pudding, Magnolia. Ev put in a half stick of butter."

"And the oyster pie has ten egg yolks," he admitted. "But we tried to go easy on the fat, cholesterol, and salt in all the other recipes."

The soup was creamy, with Glad's fried diced pumpkin floating in it along with homemade croutons.

Hugh had to surrender my hand so I could eat. Since I was on his left side, he didn't need that hand to slurp soup, so he caressed my thigh under the tablecloth. Beth Ann didn't notice because she was busy scrutinizing each bit of pumpkin—she viewed most vegetables with suspicion. I wasn't sure if Hugh was still apologizing or what, but I didn't discourage him. The moment was short-lived, though. Once Glad began passing the other food, Hugh needed both hands.

Nothing happened until I had a full plate in front of me, a little bit of everything. To satisfy my curiosity, I tasted the peas pudding first. It was a thick paste, but seemed to be no more than peas whipped up with butter. I liked it, though, and for once, no peas rolled off my fork.

I was about to move on to the sausage when a metallic taste seemed to coat my tongue. From the pewter fork? I took a sip of water and that washed the metal flavor all over my mouth. The yams had been cooked with chopped apple and brown sugar—sweet, I thought, that'll kill the taste. No, that made it worse. Starch'll absorb it, I reasoned, so I took a bite of cornbread. Not only was it worse still, I became suddenly thirsty.

While I gulped water, Hugh leaned toward me, his arm nudging mine, and in a low voice said, "You okay?"

The metallic taste disappeared. Totally. Which was when I suspected it hadn't come from the utensils or something I ate. All the shadowy corners of the room seemed to grow darker. "I'm fine," I lied and he went back to eating, his left hand once more finding my thigh.

I glanced at Miss Maggie. She was dragging the morsel of turkey breast on her fork through yam and apple drippings on her plate. As she raised it to her mouth, though, her expression said she hadn't missed my performance.

I did a quick scan of the table. Acey, Horse, and Foot, their faces stark in the wavering candlelight, were discussing anti-inflammatory drug effects on cancer. Horse was shoveling food in, but Foot was barely eating. He was only marginally contributing to the conversation—quite a difference from the talkative whiner of the afternoon.

Glad was asking her granddaughter if she wanted more stuffing—that, yams, and cornbread were all Beth Ann had in her plate. Beth Ann was slouched back in her chair, so I couldn't see more than her arms. The fork in her hand wasn't moving other than to poke at her food. Evelyn was eating quietly, eyes down. No one was paying attention to him—in fact, Foot had his back turned to Evelyn, pointedly, it seemed.

I wasn't even going to look at Dr. Weisel, not caring what, if anything, he'd seen me doing, but as I turned my face back toward Miss Maggie, the rat caught my eye and he leered. No, I didn't misinterpret his grin simply because I wanted another reason to hate him—this was a definite leer. First, I was shocked and shifted my gaze. Acey was sitting right next to him, for Pete's sake. Then I wanted to kick him. I would have if the table hadn't been so wide and my inseam so short.

I tried eating again. The sausage was sausage this time, and the chunks of drumstick, turkey. I'd almost forgotten the metallic taste when a knock sounded at the front door.

A beat of silence went by as everyone looked at each other. Hugh pushed back his chair first. "I'll get it."

No sooner was his hand off my leg than the turkey in my mouth once more tasted like fresh dental fillings.

"No, no," said Evelyn, sliding out of his own chair. "Keep eating. I'll see to the door." He strode into the hall.

Hugh pulled his chair back in, bumping my arm in the process. The bad flavor vanished.

His touch? Was that the off-switch?

"Rich!" Horse exclaimed, and everyone turned toward the hall. First, against the hall light, I saw only a giant silhouette. Then, as he walked into the circle of candlelight, he turned into an older version of Hugh and Horse, though his hair and neat Henry VIII beard were salt and paprika instead of cinnamon red. Under his unbuttoned dress coat, he seemed less muscular and more rounded than his brothers. I got the impression of a man who enjoyed life. I also got the impression he wasn't enjoying it at the moment.

"Am I too late for dinner?" he asked—almost a demand, really— as he set down the kind of gym bag that's carried into upscale health clubs, except this one had the name of a prescription medicine on the side. I'd seen ads for that drug on TV, showing blissful people taking walks at sunset, with no mention of what condition the drug treated. Still, we were told to ask our doctors about it. I wondered what sort of folks did.

Glad seemed stunned by Rich's arrival, but said, "No, no. We've barely started eating—"

"You're just in time," Horse said, standing and crossing the room. "Acey's been arguing that the pharmaceutical companies are the Evil Empire. We need you on our side."

"My car—" Rich gestured outside. "Someone's parked across the street, but I assume the 'no cars' rule is still in effect?"

Horse held out his palm. "Give me your keys. I'll put it around back for you. Have a seat."

"Let me get another place setting." Glad popped up, looking worried, and headed for the kitchen.

Miss Maggie sighed, watching after her. "There goes the symmetry of Glad's table, but it can't be helped. Move your chair over a bit, Pat. I'll squeeze in next to you and give Rich the end."

Made sense, considering his size, and since this gave me an excuse to touch shoulders and hips with Hugh, I didn't mind a bit. Glad returned with the extra setting, while Evelyn made a trip to the closet near the back door to fetch a folding chair. Hugh volunteered Beth Ann to sit on it, which made her brood all the more.

In my family, a newcomer would go around the table, kissing and hugging everyone, or if guy to guy, clapping on the shoulder or shaking hands. Rich took off his coat and sat down, without so much as a "Merry Christmas" to anyone, or a smile for his niece. He also didn't say why he was here, alone, when he should have been at his in-laws with his wife and kids, and no one asked him. The question hung over the room while we ate, like stale cigar smoke, dulling all our appetites. Except for Dr. Weisel, who helped himself to a big second helping of oyster pie and another beer.

I pictured my Aunt Lydia's house tonight, where the main topic of conversation would be what a scumball Ronny was. Candid and emotional, while everyone downed white macaroni with anchovies.

Well, maybe Marcella wouldn't be too hungry, but at least she'd be surrounded by family support.

Here at the Lees, they talked shop. Not that the discussion wasn't impassioned, at least, as far as Acey was concerned. "Physicians who do nothing but reach for their prescription pads are lazy," she maintained. "Patients do better—"

"Doctors of *Medicine*," Rich said, cutting his food into square bites, "are called that for a reason. Patients want prescriptions. They come in saying, 'Doctor, can you give me something for my indigestion?' Sure, I suggest they give up fatty, spicy food, but that's not what they want to hear, so I prescribe a GERD treatment and they go away happy."

Pretty much what I'd done with Dr. Weisel. Asked for the cheapest birth control. Got it. Went away happy.

"Until their condition worsens," Acey argued. "Masking the symptoms instead of finding what—"

"I allow them to feel better until they're ready to make a lifestyle change," Rich countered.

The exchange went back and forth while we all ate, with Glad taking advantage of each little pause to ask if anyone wanted more cabbage or turkey or whatever. Rich and Acey ignored her, the rest of us politely declined.

"Horse," Rich said, enlisting reinforcements, "you see cases like that all the time—ballplayers who come in with the same injury to the same joint. You can't stop them from going right back out and doing it again. Until they're ready to stop playing the sport—"

"But Horse doesn't simply give out drugs," Acey said. "He'll prescribe a brace, or physical therapy, or—"

"Pain killers," Horse put in. "I can't stand to see people wince."

His sister gave him such a black look—a genuine *malorchi*—I knew where Beth Ann had inherited hers.

"My point is," Acey said, "that medication should be indicated only if it improves a condition, and only after bloodwork's done and alternative therapies are—"

"Voodoo," Rich said, his top lip curling.

"Of course you'd say that. Something like osteopathic manipulation doesn't come with a pharmaceutical sales rep who'll take you to dinner and give you gifts." Acey pointed at Rich's gym bag, still on the floor inside the doorway.

"And you never accept giveaways?" Rich asked. "What about the wall charts in your examining rooms?"

"I don't own the practice, so I can't control what goes on the walls, or which pens our nurses use, or—"

"Your prescription pads?"

"They're not from a sales rep—"

"They have pharmaceutical ads on them and you get them free. Same thing."

Acey's face was turning as red as Miss Maggie's sweatshirt. "After my school loans are paid off, I'll be able to have my own printed."

I wondered how, with med school loans, she could afford a vacation to New Mexico. Unless her last beau brought her?

Glad stood, smoothing out her skirt, saying cheerfully, "Well, then, I suppose we're ready for the dessert course. If you'll all go back to the parlor for a few minutes . . ."

* * *

"Kicking the guests out of the dining room between courses," Miss Maggie explained, "was perfectly acceptable in the eighteenth century—they called it "the remove." Guests got to socialize and let their food settle while the table was reset with another harmonious, eye-dazzling layout. Like intermissions between the acts of a play."

We were on the sofa in the parlor: Miss Maggie, Hugh, and me, in that order. My arm was entwined around his—I'd clutched his hand for the procession across the war zone. The result: no bogeymen, just the bare boards creaking beneath our feet. But I couldn't hang on Hugh all weekend. I pictured how I must look, clingy and pathetic. Plus, Beth Ann had gone from evil eye to feigned indifference. Always a bad sign in a teenager.

She was curled up in an armchair, Acey and Horse standing on either side of her as they continued their shop talk with Rich. Foot was leaning against the left wall, listening. Dr. Weisel, I noticed as we left the dining room, had climbed the stairs, all the while pressing his hand to his sternum like he needed to burp something awful. Served him right for making a pig of himself over that rich oyster pie.

"I warned you Ma's Christmas meals were unique," Hugh said.

"If you ask me, that first course was pretty amazing," I said. "You're right, Miss Maggie—like an act of a play. Performance art." And, I thought to myself, Hugh and his siblings sat through it like a rude audience.

"She hasn't always done it this way." Hugh sounded wistful. "We had *normal* holiday dinners when I was a kid."

"And Gladys barely had time for that," Miss Maggie said, "with five children and a husband to look after. Wasn't until her divorce—

Rich was in med school, Foot in college, you and Horse in high school, and only Acey still young—that Gladys could indulge in a hobby."

Hugh rolled his eyes. "Cross-stitch is a hobby."

I shrugged. "*My* hobby's cooking, and you don't seem to mind. And I noticed you didn't leave anything on your plate during the first course."

"It isn't *what* she cooks," Hugh argued. "In fact, until this year, she always made the same things. It's the big production she makes out of her dinners. Just because colonial America did it that way."

"I think it's interesting."

Miss Maggie agreed. "Living history you can eat. The best of both worlds."

"Hugh," Horse butt in, "you ought to be in on this." He looked grave, which was when I realized that their conversation had switched from medicine.

"When are we going to talk to Mom?" Foot asked.

Hugh squirmed—either the topic made him uncomfortable or he was getting ready to stand up. I didn't let go, though, so he stayed seated. "What did you all decide last weekend?"

As I put it together from their ensuing conversation, Rich, Foot, Acey, and Horse had convened last weekend at Rich's shore house to discuss Glad's selling of her house and moving in with Evelyn. Hugh couldn't go because our post office had Saturday hours in December to handle the rush.

Rich wanted to make sure his mother had the money from the house sale invested wisely. Horse agreed, and thought maybe she could be persuaded to move into a cozy, maintenance-free condo.

Foot didn't think Glad should live on her own. "Or invest her own money. She's no longer making sound decisions."

"Oh, come on," Acey said. "She's not senile."

"Impaired judgment can be a warning sign of several geriatric diseases. She ought to have a full physical and neurological exam. And I think she ought to move in with Rich."

"Me?" Rich asked. "You've got more room, with only two of you in that Taj Mahal you live in."

"Yes, but I'm up in Hanover County. You're closest."

"I can't. I'd have to discuss it with Delia first." His tone conveyed the impossibility of that, though he didn't say why. "Besides, having Mom central to all of us is best for her."

"Hanover County isn't central—"

"Foot's afraid he'd have to spend some of his money," Horse said. "You can't take it with you, bro."

"He's *not* taking it with him," Acey put in. "He's willing most of it to cancer research, as he's reminded us a megazillion times. The boy's a saint. Just 'cause none of his dear siblings will ever see a penny—even though an interest-free loan to pay off our med school debts might be brotherly of him—"

"I paid off my own," Foot said. "So did Rich. So can both of you. And that's not why I can't take Mom in—"

"If you want my opinion—" Miss Maggie stood, speaking in a voice she must have honed at school board meetings. The Lees all shut up and turned to her, though none looked deferential.

"You're all too young," Miss Maggie said, "and most of you too male, to know what's best for an older woman."

"We're physicians," Rich replied, his tone capitalizing the P. "Seventy percent of my practice is elderly and at least half of them are women."

"And I've worked with Alzheimer's cases," Foot put in.

"I think Miss Maggie's point," Acey said, "is that Mom needs to be independent. All women do, even though men prefer us helpless." Her eyes shifted toward me, a LAG this time, as if trying to make sense of conflicting data.

I wanted to assure her that I was as liberated as they came, but sitting here, stuck to her brother like a leech, I sure didn't feel independent.

"Which is why," Acey went on in a lowered voice, "we should find out more about Evelyn and how Mom feels about him."

"Feels about him?" Foot looked incredulous. "She doesn't feel anything. She had to latch onto a CW employee to get into this house, and he was the gullible one that won."

Rich agreed. "She's talked about wanting to live here all her life. Too much of a coincidence to believe she fell in love with someone who just happened to be moving in."

"So you're saying Mom's using sex to get what she wants."

"Acey!" Rich, red-faced and indignant, stole a prudent peek at the doorway to make sure his mother hadn't heard.

She hadn't, but Doc Weisel had. He was leaning against the doorjamb, smirking, unaware that a small spot of whitish goo (toothpaste?) clung to his nose, making him look clownlike.

"I expect cynicism from Foot," Acey said, "who brings home a new wife every time he remodels, but not—"

"Dee-sser-hert!" Glad sang from the other room.

The siblings exchanged glances. Rich said, "We'll talk to her after dinner," to which they all nodded.

> *"Just before two of the Clock in the morning,*
> *my house was assaulted by sum Nightwalkers . . .*
> *I cannot see why it was much better than Burglary."*

—John Birge, on wassailing and mummery, 1794

December 24, 1783—Captain Underwood's in the Market Square
THE FIRST FLOOR OF Underwood's house was indeed lit up brightly, hearths and sconces within, and candles at the windows, adding their glow to the lanterns upon the front steps. The steps were of stone, and wide enough for a gentleman and lady to mount them abreast, even though she wear a gown bolstered at the hip in the fashion of the French court.

Underwood's footman, Ezra Lynch, stood before the door, dressed in fine black livery. His shoulders were tense beneath it, from standing long in the cold air. We all knew him—he too had served in our company, a sullen man who'd kept to himself except when bowing and scraping to do Underwood's bidding. He'd risen to sergeant for it, though mercifully, we'd not been in his direct charge.

When we came even with the house, Sam fired off his musket into the air and I ceased my playing. He waited for the echo of the shot to fade, then called out in a voice high and nasal, rolling his R's comically, "Room, room, a gallant room, I say!" As rehearsed, we all bowed low, except Alex, who curtsied with decorum, as if he performed the act daily.

"Ye'll have no room here tonight," Lynch grumbled. "Be off!" The command burst from his lips in a puff of white vapor.

Nonetheless, Sam mounted the steps and with an even grander bow, exclaimed, "Room, a gallant room; pray, give us room to ride, for we've come to show activity this merry Christmastide!"

"I said, 'Be off!'" In the lantern's glow, Lynch's face grew purple.

Sam brought out his flask from his pocket. "First, good sir, will you toast us and the season?"

Lynch's eye settled upon the offered refreshment and his tongue skimmed his bottom lip. He cast a glance through the window, then took the flask. "I could do with a nip. Cold night."

"It is, sir, though your master no doubt brings you in at interval, to warm yourself?"

Lynch's scowl, which told that Underwood had not done so, could not be hidden behind his rather drawn-out nip.

Sam saved him the need to respond. "Have you a Christmas box, sir?"

Lynch smiled, baring the three gaps in his teeth. "I do." He returned Sam's flask, which he might not have done had he not expected the next offer to be coin.

Sam pocketed the flask. "Blessed as you are with an eminent gentleman for a master, who attracts the most prosperous men of

Williamsburg beneath his roof, why, your box must already be full up."

Lynch scowled anew. "I expect the captain's stipend will come at New Year. As for the rest, well, they'll have their own servants to see to."

Sam wagged his head in sympathy. "Yes, they'll all have us believe times are hard." He swept his free arm to include Jim, Will, and the rest. "We all have our boxes as well and our families to feed. And we all have our employers, none generous. Yet, we're all equals now, are we not? We've fought a war to be. And you and I being equal, sir, you deserve a portion of our take, on allowing us entry."

Lynch ran his tongue again over his lips, this time in consideration. "A half dollar for each you collect."

"Half is not equal, sir. We'll give you, let me see—seven portions would come to a shilling on the dollar." It came to more and Sam knew it. He presumed that the footman had no head for numbers.

"I take more than half the risk," Lynch said. "The captain'll go into a proper rage if I let you by."

"And you'll say we held our guns close on you. A shilling and two, sir."

"Two bits or go on your way."

Sam turned his back and trotted down the steps. "So be it. Good night to you, sir."

"Wait. Twenty pence."

"Fifteen."

"Done."

Sam was up the steps, waving us on, before the mist from the footman's lips vanished. "Play for us, fiddler."

First, I touched young Tom's shoulder. "Stay without, lad, and in the shadows. If you see the constable, shout for us. If other trouble brews, run for home."

"Yes, sir." He sounded both disappointed and relieved.

I struck up my bow and played "The Barring of the Door" as I followed the others inside.

EIGHT

The aroma of cinnamon wafted in from the dining room. As we entered, I saw that the tablecloth was gone and the dessert platters were set on the bare wood along with new dishes and pewterware. Two trays of black caps were arranged in a geometric squares, the apples steaming hot and dusted with cinnamon sugar. Two pyramids of dried fruit and two types of cookies—one being a neat stack of my pizzelles—anchored the corners, and small bowls of shelled chestnuts, walnuts, and black-and-white raisins completed the symmetry.

We resumed our seats. With no tablecloth to hide hands under, I had to be content with Hugh's leg touching mine. Still, that seemed to ward off incorporeal practical jokes. Across from us, Acey discreetly let Weisel know about the goo on his nose and he wiped it on his napkin. Too bad. The clown look suited him.

"Again," Glad was saying, "a much simpler dessert course than I usually put out, but a sampling of what the Carson household might have enjoyed during harder times. Except, of course, these anise waffle cookies Pat brought." She pointed to my pizzelles with a slight hint of disapproval. "They're an Italian recipe, I believe."

"We don't know they *weren't* around," said Evelyn. "Besides, Elizabeth would have put out any food brought by guests."

Miss Maggie agreed. "And I can vouch for Pat's pizzelles. They're scrumptious. Everything looks wonderful, Gladys. Is that gingerbread on the other plate?"

Glad beamed at the compliment. "Yes, from the Raleigh Tavern Bake Shop. And these are black caps, from a 1756 cookbook."

The Lees, with the exception of Foot, didn't seem interested in the source or history of the food. They all loaded their plates, replenished their mugs, and dug in. Foot, however, made his mother recite the black cap ingredients. Her litany included a tangent about how I'd prepared the apples and figured out the orange-flower water conversion.

The siblings lowered their forks and stared at me, and Hugh asked, "Mom, you let Pat help you with dinner?"

"Isn't that why you wanted me to come early today?" I countered, feigning innocence.

He gave me a sarcastic sneer confirming both that I'd won this round and that he was the sexiest man on earth. I grinned back and rubbed my ankle against his, to acknowledge each half of the confirmation.

"Pat was so interested, you see," Glad said. *And none of you ever were*, she seemed to want to add.

The black caps were good—oh, the sugar hadn't caramelized, so we were talking more of a simple baked apple, but its flesh had picked up subtle hints of vanilla and citrus, giving it a wonderful light flavor. Recipe-wise, a keeper.

The gingerbread was delicious, too, crumbly and not too sweet, and the chestnuts were still warm from roasting.

The sweets seemed to mellow everyone. Oh, the conversation was still medical, but had shifted to nanotech diagnostics—tiny robots swimming through your innards with a med kit and videocam. Not that I understood half the terminology. Still, I was thankful they weren't discussing something gross, like colonoscopy prep.

When we were all sated, Glad shooed us back to the parlor so the table could be cleared. We all stood up. Doc Weisel sat back down, a puzzled look on his face.

You'd think, with a room full of doctors, someone would have asked him what was wrong. No one did. Not even Acey.

Weisel shook his head as if to clear it. "Feeling a little dizzy."

"Shouldn't have had that third glass," Horse said. "Ale's probably stronger than you're used to." Apparently it wasn't stronger than Horse was used to because he'd had just as much.

"No, I've had it before," Weisel said. "At Legends in Richmond."

Evelyn nodded. "Right. That's where I got it."

"Probably an inner-ear infection," Rich suggested.

Weisel stood again, slower this time, leaning on the table until he was sure of his balance. "Maybe a touch of the flu. I'm feeling chilled, too."

Acey touched the back of her fingers to Weisel's forehead—the first time she'd touched him at all, but this seemed clinical. "No fever. In fact, your skin's cold."

"You should go lie down," Foot said, but with no compassion. I wondered if he wanted to get Weisel out of the way so family business could be discussed. If so, he still had to oust me, Evelyn, and Miss Maggie.

"No," Weisel said. "I'll be all right."

* * *

Back in the parlor, most of us resumed our pre-dessert positions, except now Hugh perched on the side of the sofa, one arm behind his head, his hand resting on my shoulder. I leaned into him, in case he got the notion to move his hand for any reason and break contact. My stomach felt comfortably stuffed and the aftertaste of gingerbread and cinnamon apples lingered. Nap time, my body was saying. I tried to rub the sleepiness out of my eyes.

Miss Maggie sat next to me and Beth Ann next to her, if you could call her nearly horizontal slouch sitting. Weisel occupied one of the armchairs. He seemed paler now, dark eyes wide in their sockets, arms crossed over his chest, and a look of general discomfort on his face. Acey dropped into the other armchair, giving her beloved a disapproving LAG.

Before anyone could say anything, Beth Ann, perhaps to steer her aunt and uncles clear of more depressing conversations about Glad, groused, "I wish Grandmom had a Christmas tree."

My hopes dashed about one being put up later, I turned to Miss Maggie. "No Christmas trees in colonial America?"

She shook her head. "Not until the 1800s. Most of our familiar Christmas traditions come from the Victorians. During the eighteenth century—the Age of Reason, mind you—many ministers held that, if Christ had wanted his birthday celebrated, the Bible would tell us the precise day. On the whole, birthdays weren't considered noteworthy, except for the king's, of course, which was a state holiday."

Miss Maggie shifted her weight forward, gaining energy from talking history. "Christmas was outlawed in early New England—the Puritans didn't believe in it. Neither did the Quakers in Pennsylvania, which caused friction with the Germans and Catholics who didn't show up at Market that day. In fact, the reason many Protestant churches began having Christmas services was to keep their congregants from attending the Catholic churches, who often held special concerts as part of their holy day masses. But rather than preach the Christmas story, ministers more often spent the time sermonizing against revelry and debauchery."

"Mummery," Foot said as an uncharacteristic smile tugged at his lips.

"Mummers?" That caught my ear. I wondered what the New Year's parade in Philly—grown men prancing around in elaborate feathered/sequined costumes—had to do with colonial customs.

"The Philadelphia mummers," Miss Maggie explained, "are only a small remnant of a Christmas tradition that dates back to at least medieval times."

"Not just Christmas," Foot said. "Mummery was part of all the festivals that marked the changing of each season—the superstitious rituals that made the winter days grow longer again, or brought plants back to life each spring. Songs were sung and certain plays performed—like *St. George and the Dragon*." Foot, the whiner and the dinnertime brooder, had been transformed. He obviously loved the topic as much as Miss Maggie. "The first wassails were chanted and danced around apple trees as a wish for a good harvest in the coming year. Mummers began going door-to-door at each holiday, performing their plays and blessing each house in exchange for drinks or money."

Miss Maggie nodded. "Problem was that here in America the practice got out of hand, especially after the Revolution, which changed the economics of the nation. All of a sudden we had nouveau riche and a middle class. Everyone talked of men being equal, but the poor knew better and resented it. Mummers carried flintlocks and *demanded* money. In the early 1800s, mummery was outlawed and it wasn't until mid-century that the law was changed to allow limited activity, like parades. Which is why Philadelphia has their Mummers Parade and New Orleans, Mardi Gras. Otherwise, mummery lives on in Christmas caroling, May Day frolics, and Halloween."

"In regions of Britain," Foot said, "mummers troupes still perform the plays."

"In the U.S., too," Hugh added. "Foot was in a group in D.C. while doing his psych residency. Always played the part of the quack doctor who couldn't bring the hero back to life."

"Typecasting," Rich said.

"He was perfect," Horse maintained. "Doing exaggerated Heimlich maneuvers, using spatulas as defibrillator paddles, pulling things like smoking potions out of his doctor's bag. He was hilarious."

Foot? Making people laugh? I couldn't picture it. Right now he was red-faced, and his smile had disappeared.

"You ought to start a group in Richmond, Foot," Horse told his brother. "Heck, you don't have to go outside the family. I'll be the hero, Hugh can be the villain, and Rich can dress in drag."

"No, thank you," Rich sneered.

"He'd be more appropriate as the guy who collects the money afterward," Acey said, laughing. "Horse, you be the dress-man, I'll be the hero."

"No women allowed," Horse argued. "It's tradition. Isn't that right, Foot?"

"Nonsense," said Miss Maggie. "In the colonies, anyway, there are records of women dressing as men during tavern revelry. Besides, I want a part, too."

Without warning, Doc Weisel slipped to the floor, one arm twitching, but the rest of him dead weight. He landed face down and stayed there, eyes closed, hands still trembling. All four doctors were kneeling beside him the next instant, rolling him to his back.

Hugh sprang to his feet with me, now wide awake, right beside him, but he didn't move beyond that. He knew better than to get in the way of the others.

"Pulse is over a hundred," Rich said, eyeing his watch as he clutched Weisel's wrist.

Acey raced out of the room, calling over her shoulder, "I'll get my bag."

Rich put his ear to Weisel's chest, Foot pushed open each eyelid in turn, Horse reached for his cell phone. Acey came back with one of those ergonomic shoulder bags, purple in color, from which she pulled a stethoscope, a blood pressure wrist cuff, and an ear thermometer.

"I think he took something," Acey said as she fastened the cuff around Weisel's wrist, which was still occasionally twitching, and held that limb across his chest. "His pupils were dilated."

I remembered how wide and dark his eyes looked before our mummers discussion.

Foot grunted his agreement. "Skin's cold. Hand me that thermometer."

"Is he taking any medication?" Rich asked, now using the stethoscope on Weisel's heart, lungs, and the sides of his neck.

"Not that I know of," Acey replied. "He had something on his nose before we went in for dessert—"

The beep sounded on the cuff and Acey checked the numbers. "Low. Ninety-two over sixty-three. But I don't know his baseline."

"Tachycardia with possible hypotension," Horse said into the phone, which is when it occurred to me that he'd called 911.

"Ninety-five point four," Foot reported and Horse added "below normal body temperature" to his litany of symptoms.

I glanced down at the sofa. Miss Maggie was leaning back, observing the drama, worry creases adding to the swarm of wrinkles on her forehead and around her mouth. She held Beth Ann's hand—or I should say, Beth Ann held hers, clutching it so tightly the girl's knuckles were white. The girl had turned her head toward a window, as if the candle, or the blackness outside, fascinated her. She chewed on her bottom lip.

"I'll go watch for the ambulance," I volunteered. "Beth Ann, come keep me company."

She didn't need a second invitation, but beat me to the room doorway. I told her to get her coat, but she said, "I don't need it"—half-defiant, half wanting to escape ASAP. We went out onto the wooden stoop, leaving the door open a crack behind us.

Not until the cold air slapped our faces—the breeze had freshened a bit since the afternoon—did I realize I'd crossed the hall war zone without clutching onto Hugh. I'd been concentrating on getting Beth Ann out of the room and forgot all about the ghost. Nothing had happened. Perhaps the spook had been distracted by Dr. Weisel.

The house had no porch light. Only the glow from the window candles, indoor lamps, and the muted streetlight farther downhill let us see the steps, black patch of front lawn, and white shells of the drive, pale and spooky in darkness. I also couldn't see a house number and no mailbox was perched by the curb. So waiting out here to flag down paramedics proved to be one of my better ideas. I just wished they'd hurry—the damp was already seeping through my sweater. Per doctor's orders to stay off my feet, I sat down on the top step.

Beth Ann sat, too, bundling up her arms between her stomach and knees, either from cold or fright, but all she said was, "That car shouldn't be there." Her gaze was aimed across the street and uphill, where a white BMW was parked.

Behind the car, at the corner, was a stop sign on a little island in the middle of the road, with a warning about driving slow in the historic area. That and the narrower lane here made cars inch forward before passing each other in front of the BMW.

"I hope the ambulance can get through all right," I said.

"Is he going to die?" Beth Ann was still gazing at the BMW, and the question came out terse, as if she regretted asking it before the last word.

I wanted to answer no, to give her reassurance—to give myself reassurance, because besides ruining Christmas, I imagined a death in the house would stir up other-worldly activity. Not that I was an expert on what provokes the spirit realm—most of what I knew about the subject I'd heard from psychics on TV talk shows. But death was the main link, right?

Anyway, I couldn't lie to Beth Ann. "I don't know. I'm not a doctor."

After a few beats of silence, she said, "Uncle Rich wants me to be one. He says I've got the right kind of mind."

Backward logic, I thought. You don't decide what your mind is capable of first. You decide what you want to do, then apply your mind to it. Though, maybe I only believed that because I didn't have the right kind of mind for anything. To Beth Ann I merely said, "I thought you wanted to do something with botany."

She shrugged. "No one cares if you heal a sick plant."

"The plant cares. And whoever eats the plant."

"Or the fruit of the plant. Like chestnuts." She'd eaten a half dozen of the imported variety for dessert.

"Right. *And* whatever's growing next to the plant. I mean, if someone contagious walks into the room, you have the option of leaving, but what's a rhododendron to do?"

That got a laugh from her, but the mirth was short-lived. Evelyn came out of the house just as we heard the ambulance beep its siren through the Henry-Francis Streets intersection.

"I *told* her she couldn't park there," he mumbled, taking off at a trot toward the BMW, which revved up and drove away before Evelyn was off the curb. As the car passed the house and under the streetlamp, I saw a woman at the wheel—blonde, I thought, though that's all I had time to notice.

* * *

"Come inside, you two," Miss Maggie called from behind as the ambulance pulled up. "We'll go in the kitchen where we'll be out of the way and warm at the same time."

Beth Ann didn't protest and I followed her in, leery this time about walking through the hall and dining room.

The hall was quiet enough—no feelings of anxiety other than those trickling from the parlor where I could hear Rich giving orders, Horse still talking on the phone, and Glad uttering faint "oh dear"s. In the dining room, a lamp on the server had been turned on, giving the room a cozy glow. Our dessert plates were still on the table, but the leftovers had been removed. I waved Miss Maggie ahead of me as we went single file toward the kitchen.

Suddenly, I had an upset stomach. Not just mildly upset, either. Pain and nausea. I almost doubled over.

I let out a gasp and Miss Maggie turned around. "Pat?"

"Keep going," I managed to say. My main consideration was getting to the sink in a hurry, though, as I passed over the threshold into the kitchen, the tummy ache disappeared. Oh, my gut still felt packed full, but the cramps and urge to barf were gone, leaving not even a residual belch.

"Pat?" Miss Maggie said again.

"I'm okay. Just . . . just a little indigestion."

"I've got Pepto in my suitcase." She put a hand on my wrist to quiet my protests. "Beth Ann, run upstairs and fetch it, will you? I need it, too. Got what Pat calls *agita*. In the zippered compartment. Pink pills."

Had Beth Ann been seated, I'm sure no force short of an act of God would have moved her. Her whole body conveyed that singular strain of energy deficiency found only in teenagers. Since she was on her feet already, and since Miss Maggie was so darn hard to say no to, she went, albeit not at the requested run.

"Good," Miss Maggie said when she was out of sight. "Now talk fast before she comes back. What happened just now, and at dinner?"

I told her about the stomach ache, and then about the metallic taste and sudden thirst, and how staying in physical contact with Hugh seemed to keep the bogeyman away.

"So that's why you were stuck to him like cat hair on wool. I wondered. Not like you." Miss Maggie pursed her lips. "Weird, though. Almost like you've been experiencing memories of an illness."

"You think that's what it is? The illness that killed the ghost?" Not a notion that appealed to me. I've seen the deaths of the other spirits I'd dealt with through what I can only describe as mediumistic trances (I've been told mine are pretty boring to watch—thank God; they're embarrassing enough). But I'd never *felt* the final moments of those souls. I didn't want to start now.

"It's a theory." She crossed to the table by the stove where, apparently, Glad had been in the process of putting leftover gingerbread in a ceramic cookie jar shaped like a cabbage. Miss Maggie broke off a piece of the gingerbread and nibbled on it. So much for her *agita*. "If we can pinpoint the malady, Pat, we might be able to identify the ghost. And lucky for us, we're in a house chock full of diagnostic wizards."

"Miss Maggie, you can't tell Hugh's siblings—"

"Oh, I won't mention *why* we want to know. Don't worry—"

We heard two sets of feet on the spiral stair. Beth Ann came through the doorway first, then Horse in his Redskins jacket.

"Just take one of them," Horse said to me, indicating the Pepto box in Beth Ann's hand. "No more tonight. They don't mix well with aspirin."

"Yes, sir," I said, not intending to take even one, since my tummy now felt fine.

"I'm driving to the hospital," Horse continued, patting his jacket pockets. "Acey went with the ambulance—I'll bring her back. Now where did I put my keys? Beth Ann, could you run up to the front bedroom and see if I left them on the bureau there?"

"I just climbed the stairs for Miss Maggie." She gave the impression that she could only do this once a day, tops, but she disappeared through the stairway door once more.

Horse swung back to us. "Foot and Hugh are upstairs going through Kevin's luggage, to see if he had any drugs with him that might explain his symptoms. If they find anything, tell them to call my cell—"

Foot came through the dining room doorway, coat over his arm. "I'm coming with you."

"No need," Horse replied. "Besides, there isn't room for all three of us in the Miata—"

"Fine. Just give me a ride to the hospital and I'll get a cab back."

"They wouldn't pick you up after the scene out front this afternoon."

"Then lend me your car. You stay here and I'll drive Acey—"

"Let you drive my Miata? Are you nuts?"

Hugh came into the room via the spiral stair behind Horse. "No drugs, medicines, or controlled substances of any kind in Weisel's bag. And he hadn't unpacked anything yet." Then he noticed the confrontational poses of his brothers. "What's up?"

"Foot's insisting on coming with me," Horse explained. "I keep telling him there's no need for both of us to go—"

"Acey's my little sister, too," Foot persisted.

"There's no room in my car."

Foot appealed to Hugh. "Lend me your Ford, will you? Since Lighthorse is being such a—"

"Wait a second." Hugh could make his voice boom like thunder when he wanted to. His brothers shut up. "I'll need a car in a couple hours to take Pat to midnight mass. If you want to go?" he tacked on, with a glance in my direction.

News to me. How considerate of him to think of it. I'd be able to keep my promise to Aunt Sophie. "Sure," I said, wondering if I could stay awake that long.

He turned back to his brothers. "So, you two can borrow mine, but give me the keys to the Miata, in case you aren't back in time."

"Your Escort?" Horse said.

"Is there anything *wrong* with my car?" Hugh's voice dared Horse to say something about the postal insignia on his doors. For the first time it occurred to me that his being the only non-doc among them might be a sensitive area.

Horse seemed to know better than to go there. Dipping into his jacket pocket, he brought out his wallet with a sigh. "Your Escort's not exactly a chick-mobile, but with Foot along, I won't be cruising anyway."

Beth Ann reentered that instant with the Miata keys.

"How come you'll let Hugh drive the Miata and not me?" Foot asked, whining like his niece.

"If you're coming, let's go." Horse, having swapped registrations with Hugh and taken his Ford keys, headed for the door. Foot followed, shrugging into his coat as he stepped over the threshold.

> *"Poor man at rich men's tables their guts forrage*
> *With roast beef, mince-pies, pudding & plum porridge."*

—John Tully's Almanac, 1688

December 24, 1783—Captain Underwood's in the Market Square
WE MET NO RESISTANCE—the captain had few servants left after Cornwallis set the slaves of patriots free when the Lobsterbacks came through Williamsburg two years ago. Sam claimed some slaves had returned after the surrender, but Underwood's would rather have perished in the marshes than come back to such a master.

We came upon the captain and his guests seated in the dining room before a sumptuous banquet, the flickering light of no less than a dozen costly tapers dancing upon the lavish feast. They were well into the course, but yet remained meat enough on the long table to serve the five of us for a week. The company raised their heads, startled, as we crowded the doorway. No Carters nor Wythes, nor any of Virginia's old families sat here, rather, those for whom the war had brought substance. New gentry. I fancied that in such company, Underwood could claim a seniority denied him elsewhere.

Near the table's foot, I recognized Noah Akers beside a matron who, if looks proved telling, was his mother. As I played my last measure, Noah fixed an eye upon me, then a smile, and I was certain, mask or no, he knew me.

Underwood stood as we entered. "What's this intrusion? Lynch! Lynch!"

"Our compliments of the season, Captain," Sam announced with an elaborate bow. "Pray, sir, give us gallant room tonight, for Virginia's bold champion has come forth to fight. A champion so daring, no foe has yet withstood; step in, our noble knight"—here Sam clapped a hand to Will's shoulder—"Captain Gilbert Underwood!"

Will, flustered by Sam's departure from our rehearsed script, failed to speak his subsequent line.

Underwood, however, gave a scornful laugh. "You'd have us believe that this great oaf shall portray me in your play? And who is your reeking crimson fop? Cornwallis, I suppose."

"No, sir. His Lordship's stink was that of a cornered skunk." Sam won a laugh from the assembly, and two of the gentlemen went so far as to slap their approval upon the white linen tablecloth, though they used only their fingers, not full fists as the lads at the Eagle. To Jim, Sam said, "Step forward, sir, and present yourself."

Jim, his voice so gruff a disguise was needless, said, "In comes I, King George, the British; my colonies have made me skittish. Won't pay their tax, nor drink their tea; I'll send my Regulars 'cross the sea."

Another laugh and one gentleman said that we had "more wit than most of the pirates who go about this season."

Underwood frowned, for I suppose we stole his party's attention from him. "I have no room large enough to accommodate your antics."

"We can perform here, sir," Sam proposed.

"No, my servants are ready for the remove." Underwood gestured for his guests to stand so they might retire from the dining room. I thought how arrogant it was to leave such food upon the table, only to have more put in its place, while so many citizens hereabouts fared poorly this year. Yet I recalled that Mr. Ivey's dinners had been the same—how I'd gorged upon the victuals sent back to the kitchen with no thought to those worse situated.

Lynch pushed his way through us, and Underwood began to question him about how we'd gotten inside, but Lynch silenced the captain with a whispered word in his ear.

Vexed by what he'd heard, Underwood shook his head. That response apparently did not suffice, for Lynch whispered yet again.

The captain's gaze then settled upon Sam and, there fixed, lost some of its annoyance. "Your troupe may perform in front of my house. If any of my guests wish to view your play, they may do so from window or step. Be content with that or the constable shall be summoned and the lot of you arrested for housebreaking."

Sam was not content with that, but before he could say so, Alex curtsied and, in a mocking falsetto, said, "How very kind you are, Captain, as well as handsome. Is he not, ladies?" He tittered girlishly, bringing another laugh from the assembly, then presented his hairy hand to Sam. "Will you escort me, Doctor?"

Sam resigned himself. Performing in the street might still bring recompense, whereas the constable only brought trouble. With a bow, he took Alex's hand. "Play, fiddler."

I set bow to string and "Go to the Devil and Shake Yourself" came forth.

As we quit the house, I scanned the lane for Tom, relieved to see his slight, cloaked figure emerge from behind the tall hedgerow of the next house over. So absorbed was I in seeking him out that I failed at first to notice another caller, seated upon the bottom step: John Brennan.

"Please remove yourself, sir," Sam told him, "for Captain Underwood desires that we should use this space for our stage."

At that, Brennan embraced his knees and over his shoulder said, "I'll not go. If you would have the captain's patronage, so would I."

Sam turned his musket until the muzzle rested upon Brennan's shoulder, close to his neck. "Go, sir, or you shall taste powder."

"Shoot if you mean to. I'll not move."

Whether Brennan was so mad that he no longer held life dear, or whether he'd perhaps seen Sam fire his weapon earlier and knew, as we did, that it held no charge, he clearly meant to stand his ground.

"Commence your scene," Captain Underwood said from his doorstep. "I'll not stand here in the cold all evening."

I began the tune "Lady's Breast Knot," which was Alex's cue. He clutched his skirt and ran down the stair. Swinging around to his audience, giving a splendid curtsy, he announced, "In comes I, old Mother Christmas! Welcome or welcome not, I hope old Mother Christmas will never be for—"

"No, no, no," Underwood cried. "Not this drivel. You promised a fight. Commence the duel."

"Commence!" Brennan echoed with a scowl, rocking himself.

Sam drew in his breath and I felt sure his temper would not hold. In the lull, though, shots sounded, a block or two distant, from over on the Main Street. Brennan cowered at the din.

"Another troupe of players," Underwood observed to his guests behind him. "Perhaps we should send these bumpkins packing and await better diversion."

Sam bowed as if every bone of him were opposed to the motion. "Your duel, Captain." Turning to Jim, said, "'Where is the fool . . . ,' Your Majesty."

And Jim, taking up his cue, recited: "Where is the fool who dares bid me stand? I'll cut him down with my royal hand."

To which Will replied: "In comes I, Gen—er, *Captain* Underwood, who dares to bid thee stand. I come from Virginia, her freedom to demand."

Sam took up a position at my side during the scene, murmuring, "Oh, how I hate that man."

"'Tis his appetite for power," I whispered back. "He wields his authority the way a hungry man wields a fork."

Sam nodded. "And if we would have his coin, or that of his guests, we have no choice but to lie in his dish and be devoured. He'll interrupt again ere long, I'll wager."

I held back a laugh. "During your next line, you mean?"

"If he does, I'll shoot him." The tone of Sam's voice declared his good humor restored as he set to charging his musket once more.

The captain held his peace, though. 'Twas Brennan who cut in, nearly every other line, with ravings of "Long live the King! Death to Tories!" and other such mad declarations, as he persisted in his rocking motion. Jim and Will did their best to ignore him.

Jim: "Come, thou traitorous American dog—"

"Traitorous dog!" Brennan echoed.

Jim: "Pull out thy purse to pay, for recompense will I have, before I send thee on thy way."

"Recompense! Yes, I want recompense!" Brennan cried.

Will: "No recompense shall you have, no taxes shall I pay, but thee and I shall fight it out, before I go away."

Brennan stood at this. Will, diverted, faltered, but Jim provided his cue.

Jim: "Pistols, sir?"

Will: "Er, yes, if you please." This drew a laugh from our audience, for 'twas evident that we carried no swords. "Twenty paces?"

Jim: "Five, sir. I am rather short-sighted." Another laugh, punctuated by two loud "Huzzah!"s.

Sam and Alex moved to the far side of the duelers as Jim and Will paced off the distance, Jim taking comical half steps. Tom came to stand by me.

"Long live the King!" Brennan shouted and I thought he meant to run toward Jim, but after two strides, he held his ground and, for once, his tongue.

Jim and Will turned, took aim, and Jim said, "You may be bold; your blood runs hot, but as King, you see, I claim the first shot."

Will: "At Lexington, you had your shot,"—more huzzahs—"Now taste the lead of this patriot."

My only line: "Together on the count of five, gentlemen. Fire on one."

All six of us slowly counted off. Tom put his hands to his ears on "two" and Jim, as rehearsed, showed the king as coward, cringing and covering his face with his free arm. On "one" there followed a deafening blast as white smoke puffed from all four weapons. Jim clutched his heart and fell to his knees. Before he could issue his ensuing verse, however, Brennan slumped to the ground, blood streaming forth from his chest.

We stood frozen at first—our audience as well. Will held his pistol before him as if afeared of it. Gaining use of his limbs first, Underwood rushed down the steps to Brennan's still form. "They've shot this man! Lynch! Lynch! Sound the bell for the constable!"

Alex cried, "Run, boys!" and, without thought, we did.

NINE

"The toiletries case!" I didn't remember it until Horse and Foot were gone.

"What are you talking about?" Hugh asked, crossing the kitchen to help Miss Maggie graze on the gingerbread.

"A brown leather case, so big," I said, showing the dimensions with my hands. "In the bathroom, upstairs in this wing. Dr. Weisel's shaving kit. Did you search that?"

"His electric razor was still in his suitcase." Then puzzlement changed to amusement. "You mean Foot's vanity bag?"

"Foot? It's his?"

Hugh nodded. "Probably decided to use that bathroom because of the shelf. The front bathroom, with the pedestal sink, doesn't have any place for him to put his stuff except the window sill. I suppose it's too cold there."

"That's not it," said Beth Ann, now perched on a bench beside the table. "He doesn't like sharing a bathroom with you and Uncle Horse. Says you're slobs."

"Next to Foot, everyone's a slob—"

"Of course, there are other possibilities." That was Rich, talking as he entered the room from the dining room. Glad was on his heels and Evelyn, on hers. "The most likely diagnosis, considering the iridic dilation, is a reaction to an outside agent."

Glad wiped her hands on the apron of her costume. "Poor Ann Carter. She has such bad luck with men."

"Bad luck?" Hugh produced a grunt that wasn't quite a laugh. "More like bad taste. This one's the worst yet. What does she see in him? Or any of them?"

I'd heard my aunts voice similar thoughts about every girlfriend my cousin Chenzo ever brought home. Cella and I knew what her brother had seen in them—large bra sizes and low IQs. I guess my aunts had seen this, too, but voicing the question was their way of suggesting Chenzo modify his selection criteria. Anyway, I didn't think Acey had latched onto Dr. Weisel for purely physical reasons. For one thing, I hadn't seen her ogle him even once.

Rich chuckled. "God knows I've gone out of my way to introduce Acey to some of my younger single colleagues. She latches onto losers because she thinks she can redeem them. That one last Easter—what was his name? Bill?—I'd swear he was some drunk she rescued from a gutter the day before. By comparison, Kevin didn't seem so bad. He's a physician, at least."

"A *lousy* physician," Hugh retorted.

Rich was taken aback, as if he thought no doctor could ever be tagged with that adjective. "Why do you say that?"

I shot Hugh a warning glance. My medical predicament was *not* subject to family discussion. He realized his mistake, blinking an apology at me and mumbling, "Horse thinks so."

Rich looked even more displeased. "He shouldn't be saying things like that to you. If he knows of a specific case, we have channels." Translation: doctors should take care of their own.

* * *

Rich left to join Acey and his brothers, explaining that he was the only one of the family who had practicing privileges at Williamsburg Community Hospital. Sounding as if the place couldn't function without him.

Miss Maggie plopped herself down at the kitchen table, showing no inclination to return to the parlor or any other portion of the main house. Following her lead, I volunteered to rinse the dishes. Hugh followed my lead, volunteering Beth Ann and himself to clear the table and load the dishwasher.

When we were done, Glad suggested a game of Goose.

"I'll play," Beth Ann said. "So will Dad."

The six of us settled around the big kitchen table, Hugh in a chair on the end. Goose, I discovered, was an eighteenth-century board game—sort of a gambling version of *Chutes and Ladders*. Instead of a board, it was printed on brown paper. Evelyn unrolled it and we used the sugar bowl, pepper mill, napkin holder, and saltcellar to hold down the corners.

"When this game was played in taverns, each man would bring his own favorite playing piece," Glad explained as she passed around a small Christmas card box filled with random pieces for us to choose from. "Of course, they used real money for betting, but we'll use peanuts like they do in the historic area."

Beth Ann claimed the *Monopoly* dog, and Miss Maggie, the top hat. Hugh took a white chess knight, Evelyn a twenty-sided *Dungeons and Dragons* die, and Glad the *Clue* candlestick. I chose a red convertible from *Life*. I was ready for a midlife crisis.

The evening passed almost pleasantly. No talk of medicine. I didn't have any more weird symptoms. Glad didn't mention Elizabeth. Beth Ann didn't whine. And Hugh *did* play a little footsie under the table.

I say "almost pleasantly" because Evelyn was so jumpy. At first I thought he was keeping a vigilant eye out for the return of the Lee siblings—he glanced at the kitchen door at every little sound outside. Then I realized he was dividing his glances equally between the door, the windows on the opposite wall, and the front of the house through the dining room entry. The sounds outside, as far as I could tell, were nothing more than wind against old wood. They weren't spooky—I'd heard worse creaks and whistles in the house where I'd grown up. And like I said, the sounds were *outside*. The scary stuff, I knew, was inside.

Miss Maggie's long day caught up with her around ten o'clock. Fifteen minutes later, when she couldn't control her yawning any longer, she stood and declared it her bedtime.

Hugh turned to Beth Ann. "You, too, Missy. Off you go."

"Da-a-ad!" A three-syllable moan, reserved for special occasions.

He stood firm. "You have to get up to go to church with Grandmom tomorrow morning—"

"I'm not going to church," Beth Ann countered. "Why should I? *You* aren't going."

"I'm going tonight with Pat," Hugh said, stressing the words to show his irritation.

Beth Ann's jaw gaped. "Why?"

"Because she's Catholic and wants to go to midnight mass."

"I'll come, too."

"No," Hugh affirmed. "You're going to church with your grandmother tomorrow. You need to be up at a decent hour."

Glad said, "The service at Bruton Parish isn't until ten. Let her stay up awhile longer, Hugh."

But Beth Ann held her ground. "I don't want to go to the Episcopal church. I've never been to a Catholic mass."

I thought the argument was silly. "I don't *have* to go tonight. You should all go together, as a family, on Christmas."

"No." Hugh scowled at me, as if I were conspiring against him. "I said I'd take you and I will. And Beth Ann will go tomorrow with her grandmother."

"Fine!" the girl shouted, and fled from the kitchen, through the dining room. I expected to hear her slam a door, but if she did, with the odd acoustics in the older part of the house, the bang didn't make it back to our ears.

* * *

Hugh and I left the house at half past eleven. The treetops were black against an eerie white sky. The wind had crept around the house to the back porch and the chill factor almost made me go back inside for my hat. But Miss Maggie had been sound asleep when I fetched my jacket and I couldn't bring myself to make more noise rifling through my things. Especially since she'd made up the folding mattress into a bed for me and placed a red-foil-wrapped Hershey's kiss on the pillow. All this was visible by the glow of a plug-in Santa night-light stuck into the floor lamp's socket.

Downstairs, Beth Ann hadn't reappeared and from the porch, I could see that her bedroom was dark. I hoped she was sleeping. She wasn't having a very joyous holiday and for some of it, I took the blame.

Hugh's siblings still weren't back, so I suggested we take my car.

"Are you kidding?" he said as he jumped down from the porch in front of his brother's car. "I'm not passing up a chance to drive a Miata. Come on."

The car felt small, even to me. Hugh practically needed a shoe horn to get in. I wondered why the Lee men, big as they were, liked small cars. Well, not *all* the Lee men. The newest addition to the backyard lot was Rich's grey Volvo wagon.

After Hugh was finished fumbling with the stick shift and got us out of the drive, I said, "Tell me about your dad."

He didn't say a thing for a full half block, then, "What do you want to know?"

"I'm assuming, since your mom's small, you've got his looks."

"Rich takes after him most, except he had black hair like Foot. The red comes down on Mom's side."

"And he was a doctor?"

"Still is. Rich sees him at conventions twice a year." Hugh made a big thing of switching gears to cross the Henry Street intersection, but I got the impression it was a diversionary tactic.

"When do *you* see him?" I asked.

Again, we were almost through the next block before he replied. "I haven't seen him since high school, when he and Mom split and she moved us to Williamsburg."

"You never hear from him?"

Hugh hung a right where Francis Street ended, then a quick left. "He sends Christmas and birthday cards, and an annual check for Beth Ann's college fund. That's William and Mary on your right. Behind the brick wall."

I craned my neck to humor him, not that I could see much in the dark, but I stuck to the subject. "So Beth Ann's never seen her grandfather?"

"Sure she has. They send photos to each other over e-mail."

"But she's never met him?"

"He lives in the Southwest. Not exactly a jaunt. What'd you think of Mom?" Brilliant ploy. If I insisted on talking family, he'd steer the conversation to safer ground. "I hope she didn't talk your ear off too much about Elizabeth Carson today."

How much was too much? "It's her pet subject," I said, feeling seasonably charitable. "And I learned a lot about colonial cooking. I had fun helping her."

"You're the first person she's let into her kitchen on Christmas Eve. She must like you." Hugh took his hand off the shift just long enough to give mine a squeeze. We both had gloves on, so the effect was muted, but the sentiment reached my heart.

But that didn't mean I was letting him off easy. "You should have told me she prefers to be called Glad. And that she goes by Carson-Lee. One of her co-workers told me—"

"Carson-Lee?" Puzzled, he took his hand back so he could downshift as St. Agatha's Catholic Church came up on our left. He turned into the lot.

"You mean this is something new? Well, good for her. Lots of women keep their maiden names. I'd do the same—"

"Her maiden name's Hawkins." He pulled into a parking space and cut the engine. What with the scowl he was sporting, I decided not to comment, but as he pried himself from the car, I heard him mumble, "This Elizabeth Carson thing's gone too far."

* * *

"You've done this before!"

I'd said it sotto voce, but Hugh put a finger to his lips to shush me, justifiably, since the priest was starting the gospel. So I waited, my impatience mounting, until the end of mass, watching him more than the priest, or I should say, more than the backs of the couple in front of us. Somewhere a law is written that says if you're short, tall people with big hair will always seek you out and block your view. Tonight was no exception.

The church was a new one, with modern, padded pews forming a semicircle around a raised platform that seemed more like a theatrical stage than an altar. Behind it was a tall stained-glass window, backlit at night so the congregation could still see the abstract pattern. To one side of it, a cross, too small in proportion to the room, hung high on the wall, seeming almost an afterthought. The floor was carpeted in red plush soft enough to sleep on.

I pictured my hometown church this night, with its various shades of pastel marble. The floor would be slippery as people tracked in mud or slush. Full-sized Christmas trees would stand on each side of the main and side altars, and in front of the Sacred Heart altar would be a crèche with foot-high figures dressed in the height of Italian Renaissance style. The statues of Saints Calogero and Emidio and the crucifix above the altar would be blurry from the haze of incense, the smell reeking havoc with everyone's sinuses along with the blend of perfumes, menthol lozenges, and mothballs in the congregation. Kids would make impatient squirmy noises and at least one baby would wail through the readings.

St. Agatha's, in contrast, felt too tidy and too quiet, except when an electric keyboard accompanied the standard carols. Don't get me wrong, I *like* the English carols. But I missed singing "Adeste Fideles" and "Tu Scendi."

Anyway, through mass I kept giving Hugh sidelong glances. I wasn't wrong. He knew most of the responses and all the moves—standing, kneeling, genuflecting (which I kept to a minimum myself, to spare my knees). I had friends back home who were High Episcopal, so I realized there were a lot of similarities, but Hugh seemed the model Catholic, except that he didn't go up for communion. Then again, neither did I, not having seen the inside of a confessional in ages.

As the last note of the recessional, "Hark! The Herald Angels Sing," rang out, I turned to him. "You've been to mass before. You even got the head-lips-heart gesture after the 'Alleluia,' and I forget that half the time."

Hugh grinned, offering me his arm, which I took. "Mind if I stop to light a candle?"

That clinched it. "*Madonne*, you sound like a product of CCD classes. Wait, let me see your knuckles. If a nun's whacked 'em with a ruler, there should be scars."

Hugh let go of my arm so he could pull a buck out of his wallet. "No, we didn't have nuns in Pre-Cana."

"Pre-Cana? You took classes before you got married? Tanya was Catholic?"

The grin faded a bit, but he nodded. "Pretty devout, too. Used to drag me to church every Sunday. Beth Ann was baptized right here at St. Agatha's." Reading the look on my face, he quickly added, "She doesn't know it. She's gone to First Baptist in Stoke with Miss Maggie since we moved to Bell Run, and Bruton Parish when we visit Mom."

We stopped before the votive stand, the electric kind, with a smattering of its candles flickering in predictable patterns. We had electric at home, too. I understood the need—they saved a bundle on insurance, and Aunt Florence no longer had singed cuffs on all her coats. But as a conduit for getting a prayer to heaven, a real flame that wafted heat and smoke upwards still made more sense to me.

Hugh reached up to the top row of candles and switched one on. He didn't kneel or make the sign of the cross or visibly pray— he just stared into the light—but I knew that candle was for Tanya. I hadn't realized until that moment how much he'd loved her. And still did.

Feeling like an intruder, I turned to gaze out at the church, but it was fast emptying out. No one hung around to trade "*Come stai?*"s here.

Light a candle for your brother. That was the voice of my mother in my head, reminding me of protocol and giving me busywork to hide my unease.

I dug out my billfold. No ones.

"Need a dollar?" Hugh reached for his wallet again.

"Can I borrow two? One for my parents and Lou, one for the rest of my dead relatives."

His grin came back. "Can't leave anyone out?"

"Not in my family. Besides, it doesn't hurt to have as many insiders as possible putting in a good word for me with St. Pete."

"Smart. Here." Hugh placed two ones in my palm. "That's from me to your folks for Christmas. And this," his hand disappeared into his jacket pocket this time, "is for you." He brought forth a box covered in midnight blue velvet, about two inches cubed.

My jaw went slack and my brain into denial. Earrings, I told myself. Or a necklace with a small pendant. And I didn't want to open the box and find out I was right.

I didn't have to. Hugh opened it for me and took out a ring. Not your basic diamond, this one had tiny glitters on either side of a small main stone, all set in closer than usual and flanked by gold scrolling. I'd never seen anything like it.

Hugh went down on one knee, which put us almost at eye-level, me having the slight advantage. Then, the magic words: "Will you marry me?"

At first all I could say was "oh my God, oh my God" over and over. I recalled how in junior high Cella and I used to rehearse how we'd react to that question when the time came, though I couldn't for the life of me remember what we'd said. I did finally manage to get a "yes" between my lips. I mean, what woman could have refused that proposal? Ultra-romantic and beside an altar to boot. Not that I'd have said "no" to that man if he'd proposed in a garbage dump.

Hugh had a little trouble getting the ring on—first of all, my shaking hands made a moving target, second, my knuckle seemed to swell on contact. At last, though, the ring was in place, and heavier than I expected. "You like it?" he asked, standing up again. "It's been in my family for four generations."

Which explained the design and richer hue of gold and the size extension underneath. "I love it," I whispered, loving more what it represented.

"I forgot to show you the engraving. It says 'Two hearts beating each to each.' Great-Aunt Priscilla was crazy about Robert Browning's poetry."

"'Two hearts beating each to each,'" I repeated, committing the words to memory. We stood a moment, grinning stupidly at each other.

"Are you going to light those candles?" Hugh asked.

I still had the two ones crushed in my right fist. I smoothed and folded them, then stuffed them into the offering box. Every movement felt different now that I had hardware on my left hand. I was switching on two flames in the front row when my eye stopped on Tanya's candle.

In his family for four generations. That was my inner voice, not my mother's. Suddenly I felt like a bowling ball dropped into my stomach. I had to ask. "Did you give Tanya this ring?"

Hugh turned me to face him. He wore a solemn frown. "Yes. If it bothers you, I'll buy you a new one."

A waste of money. My mother again.

Besides, I didn't want a new one. I wanted the one that went with that awesome proposal.

Then again, now I couldn't help but think of it as a dead woman's ring. Well, Great-Aunt Priscilla was dead, too, I reminded myself. "No, of course not," I said, with a smile big enough to coax another back to his lips.

"Come on," Hugh said, smile mutating into leer. "Let's get outside where I can kiss you the way I want to."

I begged a half-minute to mentally rattle off a *Hail Mary* for each candle. Then added a third, for me and Hugh.

> *"Fear does things so like a witch,*
> *'Tis hard to distinguish which is which."*

—Joseph P. Martin, in his memoirs of Continental Army life

December 24, 1783—On the Streets of Williamsburg

WE FLED BLINDLY FROM Underwood's house, running across the northeast corner of the square, between houses, through gardens, and into the yard behind Mr. Prentis's store. 'Tis there we paused, hiding, behind the woodpile.

"What occurred?" Jim wheezed, his croup and our race laboring his breath. "Who had shot in his weapon?"

All denied, yet none could argue that a man lay bleeding and surely dead.

"We have no leisure to think on this now," Sam hissed. "Ben, Tom, remove your outer garments. You must fetch our clothes for the rest of us."

"I'll go alone," I said, shedding my mask and hunting frock. "Tom, go home, son."

"No, sir." He let his cloak fall to the ground. "You'll need four hands to bring the handbarrow. Moreover, I'll not go home without my father's pistols, nor without one of you to divert Mother's notice while I put them away."

"Right you are, lad," Sam said. "The pistols are engraved with the chariot of the Carson crest. Were they found here, they'd lead the constable straight to our lodgings."

I decided the boy would be safer in my company than left with the others should they be discovered. With reluctance, I left my violin in Sam's care, for carrying the instrument without its hemp sheath might attract suspicion, as it was never my custom.

The number of revelers before the taverns in the Main Street had increased threefold. I whispered to the boy to walk at his usual pace, to mind his manners, bowing or touching his brow to anyone who gave us the same courtesy. I did the same, wishing I had my tricorn to tip, but that I'd left in the capitol yard.

We were nearly through the crowd, most of them too much in their cups to note our passage, when Mr. Draper, tankard in hand, hailed me from the steps of the Eagle. "Mr. Dunbar, the lads inside would have a dance. Come, where is your fiddle? And where is Jim Parker to play guitar? And Sam, for he knows all the ladies' steps to 'Hunt the Squirrel.'"

Breathing an oath, I arranged my lips to a smile and bowed low. "I regret that I am on an errand, sir. I shall return as soon as I may to play whatever your pleasure demands."

"An errand?" Draper said. "What manner of errand is of more consequence on Christmas Eve than passing a bowl of punch among friends?"

"My mother, sir," Tom broke in, "would have me fetch some sewing piecework which she is to do for Mrs. Carlos in Waller Street. I cannot carry it all myself, so Mr. Dunbar has come to lend a hand."

"Ah!" Mr. Draper gave me a knowing wink. "Your errand, then, is to curry favor with the boy's mother." He addressed all men within his hearing. "We've all taken on such commissions for the ladies at one time or another, haven't we lads? In seeking a warm bed of a winter's night?" To which all who'd followed our discourse, and some who had not, gave ready assent. "Good fortune to you, Mr. Dunbar. And if you fail to return here this night"—another wink—"we shall know your errand was profitable."

With that, Tom and I were able to proceed, though we were hardly to the end of the street when I spoke to the boy. "You should not have lied."

He was taken aback at my anger. "But I merely explained our direction, and gave reason for us to carry clothing as we pass the taverns on our return. I thought it clever."

"And what if someone asks Mrs. Carlos of the matter? We shall be caught in your lie, and what then?"

In the darkness, I saw his expression change to fright. "I am sorry, Mr. Dunbar."

His chastened tone in voicing the name rankled me further.

"You should not have spoken at all. I would have dealt with Mr. Draper's inquiry." Deftly, too, I thought, for deceit had been my way of life these last seven years. I saw then that my wrath was for myself, for what I'd become, and that I would not for the world have young Tom follow my example.

I clapped a hand to the lad's shoulder and spoke kindly. "I know you thought only to save our hides, son, but a good man will court

Truth and remain loyal to her always. I want no more lies from you."

"But if I'm asked about this night, about Mr. Brennan? I'll not betray you or—"

"No one will question a boy," I assured him, "except your mother, perhaps, and I shall speak with her myself when I take you home. Carry our secret as close you are able, Tom, until this affair's resolved, but do not lie. Promise me that."

"I will, sir." He squared his shoulders and raised his chin with the air of one who takes on his first trial of manhood.

I prayed that he would fare better than I had.

TEN

HUGH OFFERED TO SHOW me his favorite high school drive-up-make-out place. Reluctantly, I declined. It was past one in the morning, the air had grown considerably colder, we were both exhausted, the Miata would cramp (literally) both our styles, and as we left the church, fat wet snowflakes were coming down in earnest. Being a native Pennsylvanian and therefore more acquainted with snow than Hugh, I knew the flakes would have to get much smaller and drier before they'd accumulate, but I could tell Hugh was a little nervous about driving an unfamiliar car in the squall. So I settled for a few great kisses in the church parking lot.

"I guess you're right," he said as he cleared the Miata's back window of slush with his gloves. "We should get back. Tomorrow's going to be a long day."

At this point I remembered the haunted house, the symptoms I'd had earlier, and the fact that I was to sit through another dinner in that same room tomorrow, and all while keeping him from noticing any supernatural weirdness. He had no idea just how long a day it would be.

I consoled myself on the drive back by watching the streetlights glint off the stones in my ring—*my* ring, I told myself, not Tanya's. This meant not wearing my left glove, so my fingers were frozen by the time we reached the house. On the back porch, Hugh warmed me up with another kiss. We would have made it plural, but the snow was blowing straight at us, and his wet gloves were icing up.

The door was unlocked, and we found Horse sitting at the kitchen table, playing with a Gameboy. Without taking his eyes off his game, he said, "Lock it behind you, will ya?"

While Hugh took care of the door, I crossed to the table—removing my right glove, unzipping my coat—and thanked his brother for waiting up to let us in.

"I had to wait up anyway, for two reasons. One was to see that rock on your finger." Horse looked up then, smiling, ogling my newly adorned hand.

"You knew Hugh was going to propose?"

"Would I have let him borrow my car otherwise?" Leaving the Gameboy on the table, he stood and faced me. "Congrats." And with that, he planted a warm kiss on my cheek.

Hugh, having deposited his wet gloves on the table, draped a possessive arm around my shoulders. "What was the other reason?"

"To warn you about Acey."

"What happened?" Hugh asked. "Did Weisel—?"

"He's alive, though still critical when we left, and they still aren't sure what's wrong with him. But, just after we got to the hospital, his wife showed up."

"Wife!" Hugh and I squawked in unison.

Horse nodded. "The Weasel, as I now think of him, is married, to a hot blonde with the biggest lips I've ever seen on a primate. Acey didn't know—that was obvious from her reaction. If she'd had a scalpel handy, she'd have done some creative surgery on him without the benefit of anesthesia. So, when you see her tomorrow—"

"Hugh, we can't announce our engagement," I said. "Not right now. Your sister'll feel bad enough." I tried to twist the ring off my finger, but couldn't get it past the knuckle.

"No, it's all right." Horse staid my hand with his own. "Acey knew Hugh was going to propose tonight. We all did, as soon as he said he was taking you to midnight mass."

"What, you have a family code?" But as the words left my mouth, it hit me what Horse meant. They all knew it because Hugh had done exactly the same thing before, with Tanya.

Hugh squeezed my shoulders affectionately, which helped allay my feeling of being an understudy. "We ought to get some sleep. Come on, I'll walk you upstairs."

Horse returned to his Gameboy. "When you say goodnight in the hallway, do it in mime. Rich is next door in the Weasel's room and you know how grumpy he is when you wake him."

Hugh turned at the doorway to the stair. "Did he say what's going on to explain why he's here instead of with Delia and the kids?"

Horse shook his head. "You want to ask him?"

"Do I look crazy?" Hugh turned and waved me before him up the stairs.

At my bedroom door, I signaled that he should wait, then ducked into the room, thankful for the night-light so I didn't have to play blindman's bluff. On my mattress, I'd left the long-sleeve tee and light sweatpants I'd brought to sleep in (I made a mental note to invest in some sexier jammies for married life). Atop the clothes were my teeth-cleaning things and the bottle of aspirin. Scooping up the lot, I returned to the hall and let Hugh walk me as far as the bathroom where, farther away from the bedrooms, we could say goodnight good and proper. Well, maybe not proper, but we were good in every sense of the word.

Anyway, Hugh left me at last. I hurried through my ablutions—because I still wasn't convinced the ghost wouldn't bother me in this newer wing—then went to bed. What with the strange mattress, my achy legs, and my imagination dredging up ghosts or, worse yet, fears of my own shortcomings compared to Tanya, I didn't sleep well. Even when I managed to drift off, every time I moved my left hand and the ring pushed against the finger, I woke up.

When I finally fell into REM—a bizarre dream in which Beth Ann, dressed in colonial garb, was politely doing everything asked of her—I was awakened again by what sounded like gunshots.

I was sitting up and listening intently by the time my brain had shaken the sleep out of all its crannies. I didn't think the shots were part of my dream—I could still almost hear their echoes. Several nearly simultaneous shots, like last night's Christmas guns, but this time at varying distances, two being so close that they might have been right outside.

The night-light's dim light was giving way to a faint dawn glow coming through the window. Miss Maggie's breathing was loud, regular, and peaceful, her head no doubt staging a whole ballet of sugarplums. No sound of disturbance from Rich's room, either, and if anyone was stirring in the main house, I had no intention of going to find out.

Instead I wriggled out from under my nice warm blanket—wincing as I bent my achy knees—and crawled across the cold, bare floorboards, over to the window. Frozen condensation—not decorative frost but sheets of ice—covered the inside panes of the bottom sash, so I stood and looked through the slats of the blind. What I could see of the eastern sky was deep red with pink spreading up onto a last strip of clouds. The rest of the sky was deep blue and all the flat surfaces below were white. No more than two inches of snow, though, and it would melt as soon as the sun hit it, but it sure looked pretty.

I heard no more shots. I saw no people who could have produced those shots. Nor did I hear sounds of cars taking those people away. Nor police sirens coming because someone else heard the shots and called 911. Even the silence outside seemed muffled by the snow.

Glad's explanation of the Christmas guns came back to me. "Now we do it at night instead of dawn," she'd said.

I stubbornly went into denial. Those were *not* ghost shots. I'd dreamt them as a result of hearing Glad talk about them yesterday. Yeah, sure, that was the explanation.

And too cold to stand there any longer, I went back to bed. My feet took a long time warming up again, but I must have slept eventually, because the next time I opened my eyes, the sun was streaming in through the window. Miss Maggie was gone, and the daybed was neatly made.

What woke me this time was another commotion outside. Voices. Once again curiosity made me abandon the warm blanket, but the room wasn't as cold this time. The small radiator below the window was warm and the condensation on the panes had melted into little pools of water on the sill.

My corner of the porch roof was sunny and snowless, its wooden shakes glistening as snowmelt trickled down from the roof above. Part of the yard below, however, was still in shadow and covered in white. Hugh was scraping frost off his Escort's side windows, breath puffing from his mouth as he talked to Foot who was using a broom to push snow from the car's roof.

Beth Ann was also helping with snow removal by taking glovefuls off the trunk, one snowball at a time, hurling each missile across the yard at the back gate—not in sheer youthful exhilaration, either. No, she was taking out her frustrations. Had Hugh told her about last night's proposal? Or had she, like the rest of the family, deduced it when Hugh said he was taking me to midnight mass? That would explain her reaction.

I fiddled with the ring. It was looser this morning. So was my confidence. Marriage would come with a teenage daughter. Not only couldn't I picture myself as a mother, at that moment the notion scared the bejeebers out of me. Especially on seeing how much Beth Ann's aim had improved since I first met her.

I heard more voices and the kitchen door slammed. Three more persons appeared from under the porch. Glad was in her Marie Antoinette getup and Evelyn was in an eighteenth century suit of stunning black brocade, both of them wearing gray capes over their costumes. The third figure was Miss Maggie, who I almost didn't recognize. Oh, the ski jacket was hers, and the stocking cap, pulled far down over her ears, but her nose, mouth, and neck were swaddled in a huge green-and-red scarf. Only her eyes showed. If I'd had any doubt, though, she proved her identity when she scooped snow off my car, patted it firm with her red mittens, and launched the finished product at Hugh. She missed, no doubt cursing her arthritis.

Glad and Foot got in the Escort. A slight disagreement followed about whether Evelyn or Miss Maggie would take the remaining seat, each deferring to the other. If I understood all their gestures, Miss Maggie and Beth Ann won out by declaring their intention of leaving together by the back gate. Which was when it hit me that they were all going to church. Hugh had apparently changed his mind.

Were Hugh's other siblings going too? Would I be left in this house by myself? I decided to grab a quick shower and dress, then hole up in the kitchen.

Fifteen minutes later (my shower was quicker than planned due to lukewarm water), dressed in jeans and a bulky pullover, I descended the spiral stairs to the kitchen.

The light over the stove was on. I realized that even a sunny day couldn't brighten this room, at least not in winter—the wing pointed north, the east windows shadowed by the main house, the west windows by the high yard fence.

Acey was sitting at the table. She was dressed in a gorgeous copper-colored caftan covered with African tribal motifs. On her feet were baby blue bear claw slippers with painted toenails. A magazine was open in front of her and beside it, a spoon rested on a folded paper napkin. One hand caressed a coffee mug, the other cradled a cell phone against her ear.

As I came through the door, her voice was soft but insistent. ". . . No, I told you, he's stable, just not conscious. I called the hospital this morn—hold on a sec." Acey faced the phone away from her mouth and her eyes met mine. Hers had dark circles under them. "Coffee's on the stove," she said, "and hot water in the teapot. Help yourself."

Real coffee was a treat. Miss Maggie wasn't supposed to have caffeine, so we only brewed decaf (remembering the chocolate kiss on my pillow, I made a mental note to find her stash so I could regulate her intake). When I felt the need for a morning catalyst, I usually had a can of Diet Pepsi.

On the long table next to the stove were mugs, spoons, tea bags, sugar, napkins, and a glass-covered plate of leftover cornbread. As I fixed my coffee, Acey continued her conversation, but her tone had become resigned. "Listen, I have to go . . . yeah, I wish that, too . . . um-hum . . ." She repeated the affirmative murmur twice more. "Merry Christmas yourself . . ."

It *was* Christmas. Without the tree, stockings, and other visual clues, I'd almost forgotten.

Acey's holiday wish had been tinted with a hint of sarcasm, but her gentle voice returned. ". . . Me, too . . . Bye." Then to me she said, "Bring that cornbread over. I'll get the blackberry preserves." She crossed to the fridge. "Milk in your coffee?"

"No, thanks." On the way to the table—mug in one hand, plate of cornbread and a few napkins in the other—I glanced out the window. The Escort was parked in its spot. "I thought Hugh went to church with his mother."

"He did." Acey set a jar of preserves and two butter knives between us and sat down again, elbows resting on the table, forearms spread in welcoming body language. "There's no parking near Bruton Parish so he brought his car back here after dropping them off, then walked. It's only a half block. Ma just didn't want to get her dress wet."

I settled opposite her. "Did your brothers go, too?"

"Foot did. Horse is still sleeping. Rich is in the living room, reading his *JAMA* there so it won't get contaminated by my alternative medicine ideas." Her grin turned wicked. "I read the mainstream rags, too, but I always bring fringe journals to these gatherings." She patted her magazine, which was cracked open to an article titled *The Effects of Magnetic Sleep Therapy on Aging Rats.* "I have my reputation as a witch doctor to maintain."

As I was reaching for a piece of cornbread, she intercepted my hand, her fingers cold against mine. She surveyed the ring, saying, "Did you ask Santa for this or was it a surprise?"

"A complete shock," I replied. "We hadn't talked about marriage yet."

"I suppose Hugh thought he couldn't wait until next Christmas to propose."

"He wouldn't have to. Any other day of the year would do." It came out impassioned. Embarrassed, I took my hand back, but then I told myself I'd better find out the truth now. "Why Christmas?"

Acey picked up her mug and walked over to the stove. From a side seam pocket in her caftan, she took a foil-wrapped tea bag. "I guess he thinks it's romantic."

"So's Valentine's Day. Why did you all know he was going to propose when he took me to midnight mass?"

"That's his M.O." She poured steamy water into her mug.

"He proposed to Tanya the same way?"

Acey brought her mug back to the table. The tag hanging over the side said it was green tea. The delicate fragrance reminded me of Asian restaurant teas, but the color of it wasn't appetizing. "Men are creatures of habit. How many times have you heard the same old pick-up lines in bars? They find what works and stick to it."

The sarcasm that tinged her "Merry Christmas" earlier was back. Thinking about Dr. Weisel? I hunted around for something compassionate to say.

She spoke first. "You don't *look* like Tanya—except for your dark hair and eyes—and you seem a lot more down to earth than she ever was. Something about you, though, is like her. Maybe it's just because you're both Italian-American—"

"Tanya was Italian?"

"Half, I think."

No matter. If she'd had one drop of Italian blood in her veins, she was a *paesan'*. That made it worse somehow.

"What I'm trying to say . . ." Acey wrapped her hands around her mug and I got a good look at a ring on the forefinger of her left hand—plain gold with a small red stone. I wondered if Weisel had given it to her. "My experience with men is that they all seem more concerned with what I can do for them—sex, cooking, cleaning—than with who I am as an individual."

"All humans do that to some extent." I wasn't a seasoned veteran, lovelife-wise, but office politics were founded on the same principle.

"Not all humans." She got up again, to dispose of her tea bag in the can under the sink. "Maybe Hugh doesn't. I don't know. I've never figured him out like our older brothers." When she turned, the wicked grin was back. "I know exactly which buttons to push for them."

I'd seen a version of that grin on Hugh's lips during his occasional roguish moods—which I found extremely sexy—but I had this epiphany of Acey as the Lee family devil. If I'd been the much younger sister of four brothers, particularly ones as easy to torment as Rich and Foot, possibly I'd have developed a similar defense mechanism. Come to think of it, I had. When I worked in corporate America, no obnoxious co-worker had been immune to my voicemail pranks.

Acey crossed the kitchen to retrieve the sugar bowl, but no sooner was it in hand than her grin vanished, replaced by puzzlement. She was gazing through the window, toward the back of the yard. "Someone just went out the gate."

"One of your brothers?"

"Too thin." Setting her mug down on the stove, she opened the door and stepped outside, letting the cold air rush in. The snow on the porch had been swept, but the floorboards were still wet, so I stayed put.

Yet I spied something else on those floorboards, right at Acey's feet. Something that looked like a playing card.

Scooping it up, she brought it inside, fetching her tea and sugar en route to the table, before setting the paper between us.

"Photocopy of the King of Spades," I observed, trying to remember where I'd left the street map with the ace inside.

"No knock on the door," Acey mused, "and I didn't see anyone climb the hill to DOG Street—uh, that's Duke of Gloucester for you nonlocals. The bearer didn't want to be seen. So, was this dropped or left on purpose?"

"Left, I think." I told her about the card I found yesterday.

She raised her brows. "Odd. Who's it for, I wonder? Ma or Evelyn? Because why would someone follow any of the rest of us here? Though I suppose one of Foot's psychos might—meaning his patients, not his ex-wives—oh, wait!" Frowning, Acey picked up the copy and LAGged it.

"What? You think it's for Foot?"

"I was thinking of Kevie's wife. She's thin—that is, those parts of her free of collagen and silicone—"

"I found the ace before you arrived yesterday."

"Oh, right. But why would—"

We heard voices in the yard and through the window I saw Miss Maggie, Hugh, and Beth Ann. I went over to the kitchen door and opened it for them, but only Miss Maggie and Beth Ann mounted the porch. Hugh went straight to his car.

"Have to go pick up the rest of 'em," he called. The rat. He was leaving me to face his daughter alone for the first time with his ring on my finger.

Miss Maggie didn't give things a chance to get awkward. Pulling off her scarf, she whispered, "Quick, while Hugh's out. Beth Ann needs to tell you something."

Beth Ann didn't look like she needed to do anything but escape. Not an option—Miss Maggie had a vise grip on her hand.

"Come on," Miss Maggie continued, beckoning both of us toward the dining room. "Beth Ann's room."

She wanted me to go into the main house? Was she nuts? "Why can't you tell me here?"

"Go ahead," Acey said, standing up. "I need to go get dressed anyway."

But Miss Maggie waved her back down. "No, no. You finish your tea. We won't be long and the bedroom's a better place. Christmas secrets, you know." She had an elfin beam on her face, but I was sure this had nothing to do with gifts. "Beth Ann, grab Pat's hand. Time's a-wasting."

I expected the girl to balk at that order considering the profound scowl on her lips, but she offered a hand. Figuring I'd better not miss a bonding opportunity, I gave her mine—my right one so the ring wouldn't draw attention. Miss Maggie pulled Beth Ann along and I followed.

We passed through the dining room, around the stairs—Rich glowered at us from the living room—down the hall, and into the back bedroom. Without incident.

Miss Maggie shut the door and slid out of her coat. Today's sweatshirt was green with the caption "Rudolph at his beach house," and sported a picture of the reindeer in a lighthouse, guiding ships into harbor with his nose beacon, a battery-operated red light that blinked on and off. I wondered if she'd kept her coat on in church. "Keep holding hands, you two," she said. "Pat, any problems between the kitchen and here?"

I shook my head which made her nod. "My theory is, if you're in contact with anyone in the Lee family, the ghost doesn't bother you."

"Miss Maggie!" My jaw dropped and I glanced, mortified, at Beth Ann beside me.

"I told her," Miss Maggie said. "Had to. She saw the ghost last night."

"What?!"

Beth Ann, who was trying to unzip her jacket one-handed, went red to the roots of her hair. "It was just a dream."

"Tell Pat what you told me on the way to church." Miss Maggie motioned us both to sit on the bed. "I want to hear it again anyway, so I can picture it in this room. Quick, before your dad gets back."

That was all the warning Beth Ann needed. "I woke up when Aunt Acey came in last night. She didn't turn on the light and after a minute, she went out again, onto the porch right outside our room. I think she was talking on her phone. Anyway, I felt someone sit on the bed and when I rolled over, there was this girl, looking at me. She seemed absolutely real, but then she . . . she faded away."

"Tell Pat what she was wearing," Miss Maggie prompted.

"A long skirt and white blouse, and a white triangle tied around her neck. With an apron and a white cap."

"A girl?" No way, I thought. The spook kissed like a man.

"A teen," Beth Ann amended. "She had freckles like me."

My dream came back to me, in which Beth Ann had been wearing clothes like those she'd described. Since my REM sleep has been a tourist spot for Other Siders before, I wondered if I'd seen Beth Ann's apparition.

"She didn't sit quite straight," Beth Ann went on, "like something was wrong with her spine. But I *must* have imagined her. I mean, I wasn't scared. If she'd been a—"

"One way to find out." I let go of Beth Ann's hand and waited. Nothing happened. Not that I expected anything—I'd been in this room with Horse last night, not touching him, and no spirits bothered me. Except Tanya, that is.

With a deep breath I said, "One other way to find out." I closed my eyes.

I heard Miss Maggie say, "Pat, be careful," but the sound grew muffled, as if by the last word, she spoke into a pillow.

Still, no visions of dead people danced in my head. Remembering that the last time I did this, it helped to have an antenna of sorts, I said, "Beth Ann, give me both your hands." My own voice sounded far away, but I felt her hands take mine in a grip so tight, you'd think one of us was in danger of drowning.

My clothes suddenly reeked of wood smoke and body odor and cooking smells. I felt like I needed another shower. The room grew cold. The bedspread I sat on became a scratchy wool blanket. My eyes seemed to adjust to the dark. A faint glow came from the direction of the parlor—there was an open doorway in that wall. And I heard voices.

December 24, 1783—Polly's Room

"Mrs. Carson!" Dr. Riddick had burst into our house and pounded upon the door to Mother's room. "Mrs. Carson, please, I must speak to you."

I heard Mother hasten from her chair by the hearth where she'd been trimming her shortgown in some few ribbons as decoration for the Christmas devotion on the morrow. "Hush, Doctor," she said as she entered the hall. "You'll wake Polly."

This he could not do, for though I'd been abed for an hour, sleep would not come, not with my brother yet running abroad. Mr. Walker had told Mother that he and our other lodgers—Mr. Dunbar and Mr. Parker—wished to take Tom for his first taste of Mrs. Vobe's rum punch, but Tom had told me their true purpose. I comforted myself that he was safe with Mr. Dunbar, yet I worried for the latter as well. I blushed to think how greatly I'd come to anticipate each singing lesson.

Wondering if the doctor's tidings concerned Tom, I tiptoed to my door, listening, then entered the dark hall. Mother had led Dr. Riddick to the dining room, as she called it, though we cooked there as well. I felt my way along the wall until their words were clear. They lit no candle, though their forms blocked some of the moonlight coming through the windows to the hall.

"I bring dire news, Madame," the doctor was saying. "John Brennan is dead."

I stifled my gasp lest I should be discovered, yet I was not grieved by the news. In the years that Mr. Brennan had been our lodger, I'd loathed the man. At first I feared he would supplant Father, for he was too bold toward Mother and, in my youthful naïveté, I thought her too taken with his charm. I saw now 'twas him that was taken— so she'd persuaded him that keeping a private room might serve him well. "'Tis a man's world," she often told me, "yet we are their weakness, Polly. If you would better your station, you must learn to beguile." I felt, though, that I should never acquire the art.

Now Mother was saying, "Poor man. 'Tis a blessing, I suppose, yet his infirmity did not seem so grave—"

"He did not die of illness, Madame. He was shot."

This time I could not stifle my surprise, though neither could Mother, and so I was not heard.

"As you know, Mrs. Carson," Dr. Riddick continued, "I have taken great interest in his recent derangement. Indeed, when my time has been my own, I have followed him about to observe his state of lunacy more closely. I was about the business this evening, and trailed Brennan to Captain Underwood's house—"

"Captain Underwood?" Mother exclaimed.

"Yes. Brennan went there often, thrice in the last week alone, to appeal to the captain for alms. He was given them at the door, but never admitted. This night some revelers were there performing on the steps. Brennan somehow got between their action and when they discharged their flintlocks, he fell, shot in the chest."

Revelers! I thought, and prayed God not Tom's troupe.

"An accident, then?" Mother said.

"Negligence, like as not. One of the actors presumably failed to remember he'd put a ball in his gun, no doubt due to the excess of drink that this season inspires in such men. The fellows ran away in fear and the constable searches for them this instant. As I was close at hand, I saw to Mr. Brennan myself, but he was past aid."

I heard the loose floorboard near the windows creak, as if the doctor or Mother now stood looking out.

"I took the liberty, Madame," Dr. Riddick continued, "of arranging for Brennan's burial in the potter's field. He was not a member of Bruton Parish and I believe has no family close by—"

"None at all, that I know."

"As you say. I thought you would not want a wake here? Few mourners would come, at any rate, save the curious."

"You did quite right, Doctor. I can ill afford the expense. And I suppose the burial fee—"

"Settled, Madame," said Dr. Riddick, "by recalling one of my old debts. In fact, I ask you not to mention the matter about town, lest it cause embarrassment to a certain party."

Mother, relieved to be spared any expenditure at all, readily agreed.

ELEVEN

FIRST THING I SAW when I opened my eyes was Rudolph's nose blinking on and off.

Beth Ann's hands still gripped mine. Turning my head to look at her, I saw her gaze, troubled, focused down on the ring. When she realized I was back from wherever it is I go during these episodes, she let go and with a scowl, jammed her fists into her jacket pockets.

Miss Maggie pursed her lips. "Did you see the girl Beth Ann saw?"

"Not exactly. I saw out of her eyes. At least, I assume it was her. She felt like a teenager—all hormones. Her name was Polly Carson. This is the room she slept in."

"Polly. I should have known." Miss Maggie nodded to herself. "She was the only girl to grow up in this house during that era. Josiah Carson, her grandfather, had only boys, as did Polly herself—"

"Wait, wasn't Josiah Carson Elizabeth's father-in-law?"

"Right."

"So Elizabeth was Polly's mother? *That* was Elizabeth?"

"You saw her?"

"I heard her." I related the scene to Miss Maggie and Beth Ann, the kid doing her darnedest to seem apathetic.

Miss Maggie rubbed her hands together like a miser with a new shipment of gold. "First thing is to write down those names before you forget them."

"I have my notebook," Beth Ann volunteered. Sort of. She didn't actually move to retrieve it until Miss Maggie waved her arms wildly in encouragement. She pulled from her suitcase a blue spiral-bound.

"Give it to Pat," Miss Maggie said. "I don't have my reading glasses."

Beth Ann took out a box of colored pencils and selected the brown one, saying, "I'll write." Message: the book was her territory. She flipped through it, past her many sketches of wild plants, looking for a blank page.

"Let's see." Miss Maggie paced in the small space. "The doctor's name was Riddick—spell it the same as that real estate firm in Stoke for now. And the dead man was John Brennan. Spell it how it sounds. And Dunbar—did you say he taught Polly singing? Beth Ann, write 'music master' next to his name."

"Walker was another," I said, "and Parker."

"No further clues about them, though," Miss Maggie mused, "other than that they'd taken Polly's brother out mummering. So they were probably in the working classes."

"And Captain Underwood." Good name for a character from a Saturday morning cartoon, if you asked me.

"Him I've heard of," Miss Maggie said. "Gilbert Underwood was an officer in the Revolution. He moved west sometime in the 1780s, I believe, to seek his fortune in the Ohio Valley. We should be able to narrow down the year by finding out when he left versus when Polly was in her teens."

A knock came at the door, making us all jump. "Beth Ann?" Hugh called. "Come on, we're opening presents in the parlor."

"We're coming!" Miss Maggie hollered back, reaching over to tear the page from Beth Ann's notebook. "I'll hold onto this." She folded it three times and stuffed it in her stretch pants pocket. "Let's go."

As we got up to leave, Beth Ann hooked a hand into the crook of my arm. I glanced back but she was doggedly not making eye contact. She was, I realized, touching me, reluctantly, to protect me from demons. I kept my trap shut, so as not to dissuade her.

Miss Maggie intercepted Horse in the hallway and sent him to the kitchen to fetch our bag of gifts. Glad, already changed into a powder blue sweatsuit, and Evelyn, now in chinos and a flannel shirt, were carrying presents down from upstairs. In the parlor, Miss Maggie, Beth Ann, and I were waved toward the sofa by Glad, who sat down in one of the chairs, looking worried and mumbling things about having to get dinner under way. Evelyn went off to bring extra chairs from the dining room.

Acey came in after us with her three gifts. Rich wasn't overcome by Southern chivalry enough to offer her the other armchair. In fact, since no one had expected him, and gifts to and from him had already been sent and received by mail last week, Rich rudely continued to read his medical journal and ignore the gathering horde.

Acey seemed more at ease sitting on the floor anyway, cross-legged beneath her African caftan.

Hugh also settled to the floor beside Beth Ann's end of the sofa. Today he wore a navy pullover of ultra soft fleece—the kind that begs to be touched. Not that I needed encouragement.

Miss Maggie turned to Rich and asked him if he had this year's school photos of his kids yet. He laid aside his journal and pulled out his wallet. His three boys—ages seventeen, twelve, and ten—all had the Lee red hair. The youngest two, he bragged, were on the honor roll. The eldest had failed math his first term, simply because he hadn't done his homework, not that it mattered (according to Rich) since he intended to major in theater arts instead of pre-med. Said with a sneer.

Hugh rolled his eyes. "Bob's a good actor. I've seen him in his school plays."

"He could do it as a hobby," Rich maintained, "the way Foot used to. He should have a real career."

"He doesn't *have* to be a doctor—"

"Where *is* Francis?" Glad asked, anxious to avert an argument between her sons.

"In the kitchen," Acey replied, "on his cell with Irene. Maybe she's blowing us off again today. Foot must have told her about us and she's running scared. Not like Pat here. She's got guts. Has to if she's marrying Hugh."

I felt Beth Ann's arm go tense beside mine, but at least she didn't pull away. So far, I wasn't having the weird symptoms of the night before and I didn't want to start. Time to change the subject before Beth Ann stomped out of the room. "Foot mentioned his wife working late yesterday. What does she do?"

"Department store clerk," Acey said, "and that's about all we know of her. None of us have met the little gold digger."

"Now, Acey—" Glad began.

"Really, Ma, why else would anyone marry a curmudgeon like Foot except for his money? Though I guess I could say that about all his wives."

"Not Katharine," Hugh murmured.

Acey agreed with a nod. "No, Foot was up to his ears in debt then. They were both young—must have been all hormones—"

"Acey—" Glad's tone was less tolerant this time.

Hugh broke in. "His loan was paid off by the time he married Rita, but you couldn't call him well off."

"Rita felt sorry for him," Acey maintained. "She was one of those women who prey exclusively on widowers. Like the one who chased after you when Tanya died. What was her name?"

"Ann Carter, stop it now!" Glad exclaimed, though she didn't possess a voice that could sound threatening. Had my mom uttered those words, I'd have hidden under a table for an hour.

Acey smiled. "Ma, be realistic. You have to admit Rita got a great divorce settlement by the time she and Foot split up. So did Leslie, although she didn't last half as long. And now we have Irene, four years younger than me. People must think she's Foot's daught—" She broke off, her smile widening, and I realized she'd been watching the doorway in case the brother in question showed up, which he had. "Pull up a piece of floor, Foot."

His smirk said he didn't do floors. He held four presents, all wrapped in non-Christmas paper that boasted the names of the dot-coms where he'd purchased them online.

Horse came in with our presents, yawning like he'd just pulled himself out of bed, though his hair was combed, his chin shaved, and his hooded sweatshirt wrinkle-free.

I didn't have much to contribute to the proceedings, outside of a wrapped can of biscotti and sesame seed cookies for Hugh's mom and a small gift for Beth Ann. Since my budget was tight this year and the kitchen was where I felt most competent gift-wise, I'd gone the food route. For Miss Maggie, I'd made low-fat, no-cholesterol pizzelles and oat bread. Hugh and Beth Ann got three kinds of cookies, including chocolate pizzelles. All these were presented the night before we left for Williamsburg so they wouldn't turn to crumbs during the trip. I'd also given Hugh an IOU for one homemade and very romantic dinner per month for a year, not something I wanted him to open and read aloud in front of his whole family. Miss Maggie, too, opted to give me her gift in private: a check for a whole lot of money.

"It's what you need most right now," she'd said. "Your health insurance alone's eating all your earnings from the fall."

Thinking about that, I wondered what percentage I'd have to shell out for Monday's blood tests and lung scan.

Anyway, I didn't have much to do after I unwrapped my two gifts—one, a pretty purple sweater from Hugh and Beth Ann. The other was from Glad: two pounds of flour and a pound of Scotch oatmeal from the Raleigh Tavern Bake Shop, "stone ground in the same manner as it was in 1740." Hugh told her I liked to cook, she explained. Odd, but at least useful.

Everyone opened gifts at the same time. Oh, we Montellas do the same thing, with all of us thanking each other, craning our necks to see what everyone else got, commenting, laughing, teasing, then more laughing. That is, all of us talking at once and delighting in each other's delight. Here with the Lees, gift-opening seemed like a chore. The mood was subdued, the remarks, polite. Except for Miss Maggie, no one's face lit up. LAGs abounded.

Beth Ann analyzed the little plastic greenhouse plant starter kit I gave her a bit longer than the Christmas socks she got from her Uncle Horse, but not as long as the meditation crystal from her aunt. I couldn't tell if she liked any of them.

The gifts seemed to fall into predictable patterns. Horse gave funny presents, Foot's were straitlaced and expensive, like the tie he gave Hugh (though Hugh hardly ever wore ties). Glad's were purchased at the shops of Colonial Williamsburg, all evoking the eighteenth century in some way.

Acey's offerings were meant to improve physical and spiritual existence. For instance, she gave her mother a tabletop electric water fountain with a Japanese garden design, to "help relieve stress" and "make you sleep better."

Among themselves, the siblings did a rotating gift exchange. Hugh had Acey this year, and I'd helped him pick out a sweater for her (not unlike the one he'd bought for me—men can be so unimaginative). Had I known her then, I'd have suggested a sari instead.

Horse gave Foot a genuine whoopie cushion, which evoked the first emotional response—the laugh Horse got from seeing his brother's appalled face.

Acey nudged Rich hard on his leg. "Did you get my present?"

He didn't look up from the article he was reading. "It arrived."

"Did you open it?"

He grunted.

She took that to mean "yes," and turned to the rest of us. "I sent him an aromatherapy heating pad. Thought it might warm his disposition."

Rich closed his journal. "You could have picked a better scent than eucalyptus."

"I tried, but they don't make them in *eau de old fart*."

I bit my lip to keep from laughing aloud, but Foot, of all people, let out what could only be called a guffaw. To everyone's surprised look, he said, "Oh, come on. It's the funniest thing Acey's said in ten years."

"More like twenty," Rich said, but his habitual scowl had softened.

And suddenly the mood in the room relaxed to the point where, for the first time, I could almost picture this crew growing up together.

"Your turn, Horse," Acey said. "Tell us what Rich sent you. A white lab coat like the one I got last year? Even though he knows neither of us wears them."

Horse hesitated enough, glancing at Rich, that Foot suggested, "A rectal thermometer?"

"Actually, uh—" Horse began.

"He didn't get anything." Rich surveyed the faces around him as if judging whether he should say more. Then he reached into his cardigan pocket and took out a flat object wrapped in green foil. "It—I didn't put it in the mail soon enough, so I brought it along instead. I'm sorry it's not much this year."

"A CD," Acey guessed as Rich handed the gift to Horse.

"Music?" Beth Ann said, as if questioning her Uncle Rich's taste in such things.

Foot shook his head. "More like the Physician's Desk Reference on CD-ROM. Pirated, of course, or it'd be in a nice box."

"You're all wrong. It bends." Horse flexed the item a few times, then tore the paper off. Inside was a plastic sandwich bag and inside that, something that made Horse's jaw drop in shock. "My God, I haven't seen one of these in thirty years."

"Last weekend at my place, you mentioned that you still had your collection." Rich seemed embarrassed by his gift. "Though you probably already have this one."

"I do, but mine's faded and chewed up around the edges. This one's in mint condition." Horse, beaming his pleasure, held up his prize at last so we could all see it—a gold-on-black Pittsburgh Pirates patch, pirate in the center with the name of the team, the words "My Favorite Team" above, and "Bazooka—BLONY" below. "I collected 1950s *Bazooka Blony* patches in high school," Horse explained to those of us not in the loop. "Man, this is the *best* present. Thanks, Rich." He returned the patch into its bag, then slipped it into his sweatshirt's pouch pocket.

Rich reddened further and sought refuge in his journal, but Glad said, "You visited your brother last weekend, Lighthorse? Why didn't you stop by?"

The mood in the room turned awkward as Horse glanced around at his siblings for help. "I wasn't in town, Ma. We were at the shore house. So were Acey and Foot."

"We got together"—Foot had lost his humor and was all business—"to discuss your selling the house and moving here. We think—" A sound like a cat purring came from his torso. He reached inside his jacket and brought forth a small cell phone. "Probably

Irene," he mumbled as he flipped it open. "Dr. Lee speaking . . ." His face turned grave. "Just a moment." He went out into the hall.

Glad took advantage of the interruption and stood. "I need to get to the kitchen or we'll never eat today." She bustled out and Evelyn followed.

"Guess that leaves us to clean up," Horse said, seeming relieved that the confrontation had been avoided. He began balling up the used wrapping paper around his chair.

"Don't, Uncle Horse," Beth Ann cried. "That can be sorted and recycled." An environmentalist after my own heart.

"Okay," Horse replied, smoothing out the paper. "Go ask your grandma for some bags."

Beth Ann glanced at me, then down to where our legs were touching, and didn't move.

"You heard your uncle," Hugh said to his daughter. "Go on."

"I'll go," Miss Maggie cut in. "I need to stretch my legs anyway or my arthritis'll freeze 'em right up." She handed me the pile of gifts on her lap, slowly rose to her feet—her joints were already stiff—and shuffled out.

Hugh scowled at Beth Ann and was about to reprimand her when Foot came back into the room looking, I thought, pale.

"Irene's not coming?" Acey asked, trying to shift attention away from her niece. "What's her excuse this time?"

"That wasn't Irene." Foot returned his phone to his jacket pocket. "It was the hospital. They found an antidepressant in Dr. Weisel's stomach contents. A tricyclic."

"Explains his symptoms," Rich said. "He should've known better than to drink alcohol when he was taking—"

"Why'd they call you and not me?" Acey broke in.

Foot shrugged. "I gave them my number as a backup."

Acey pulled her phone from the pocket of her caftan. "It's still on. And no messages."

"What kind of tricyclic?" Rich asked impatiently.

"Protriptyline." Foot sat down in the chair Glad had vacated and when he spoke again, there was compassion in his tone. "It can cause delayed cardiac complications, Acey, so they've changed his condition back to guarded. He's half-conscious, but delusional."

I remembered the glob on Weisel's nose. "Is protrip—whatever—is it a white liquid?"

I got two condescending doctor-sneers (from Rich and Foot) that said laypersons shouldn't butt into medical discussions. Horse's grin wasn't condescending, but conveyed the same message.

Only Acey knew what I meant. "The stuff on Kevin's nose last night? I've never prescribed protriptyline, but I think it comes in pill form. Foot, you're the shrink. What about it?"

"No, it's not a liquid," he replied grudgingly. "I have two patients on it. Five or ten milligram tablets. I remember because I just had to cut a dosage two weeks ago—one patient started having delusions that his ex was stealing his pills."

"*Dosage.*" Rich pounced on the word. "That's what's important. Did Weisel's normal dose react with the ale he drank, or did he deliberately try to OD?"

"Hugh didn't find any medication in his bag," Foot pointed out. "If he was on protriptyline, he'd have to take it at least three times a day. He would have packed enough to last him the weekend. Excuse me." He left the room and I heard him climb the stairs.

"So"—Rich placed his fingertips together—"if he brought only a single dose with him, an attempted suicide is indicated. Is that likely, Acey?"

"I don't know," she said, dazed, but then her jawline stiffened and her sarcasm returned. "Obviously, he didn't tell me everything." Her gaze fell on the phone in her hand and her devil-smile appeared. "Seems a shame his wife has to spend Christmas day at the hospital. I think I'll ask Ma if she can come to dinner." Acey jumped to her feet and ran out of the parlor before her brothers could object.

"She's up to something," Rich said.

"As always," Hugh mumbled.

> *"Do not let your Children and Servants run*
> *too much abroad at Nights."*

—December page of Nathaniel Whittemore's 1719 Almanac

December 24, 1783—The Streets of Williamsburg

YOUNG TOM AND I retrieved the handbarrow and brought it to Mr. Prentis's yard without further delay. In our absence, the others had settled upon a plan of action.

"Alex and I will dispose of the costumes," Sam said as he removed his black breeches, "and we'll hide the firearms and powder in the Carson tin shop, where all will be at hand for our customary Christmas volley at dawn. Then we shall carry our guns inside with no one the wiser."

The tin shop was a small wooden building standing at the edge of the Carson yard. During the war a storm had changed the course of a neighboring creek and the shop now sat on the brink of marshland, and so had remained vacant. The stain of spring floods marked its walls.

"The rest of you," Sam concluded, "will follow our original scheme and proceed to Mrs. Vobe's tavern, where we shall join you as soon as we may."

I agreed, though I yearned to bring Tom home straightway. Still, 'twas better that the boy be prepared to answer his mother's queries about his first taste of rum punch. Also, if I did not return to the Eagle, no doubt the lads we'd met earlier would spread rumor of a liaison between myself and the Widow Carson. I wished to avoid that, if only to prevent such rumors from reaching Elizabeth's ear, along with reports of false errands to retrieve piecework.

Sam and Alex made a quick job of their part—precisely the time it took me to instruct Tom how to sip at his half-gill of punch, to nip thrice at my own gill, and to play five repeats of "Successful Campaign." Their work was perhaps too quick, for when they entered the crowded oaken room of the Eagle, Sam's shoes, stockings, and the knees of his breeches were wet through and caked with mud.

"Gentlemen," he announced with his usual bravado, "I must claim a place by the fire. As you see, I've had a dispute with a puddle."

"Puddle?" said Mr. Draper, his eyes glinting in the firelight. "The James River, more like." To which the assembly added such comments as "Bit cold for a swim," and "A woman's to blame, I'll warrant."

Only Mr. Hockaday gave serious thought to the matter, saying, "'Tis dangerous to cut across the marshes these dark nights. The water's high, with all the rain this last month." But Mr. Hockaday, to my relief, was ignored in favor of jest.

They made room for Sam at the hearth, and were encouraging him to remove his stockings lest he court a chill, when who should come into the room, and straight to my side, but Lynch.

Sam took the situation in hand. "Sergeant Lynch! Good of the captain to let you come tonight and toast the Yule with us. Call for the boy, lads. More punch is needed."

"I'm on the captain's business." Lynch drew himself up a half inch taller and raised his voice. "Helping the constable search for some nightwalkers what done murder in front of Captain Underwood's house."

The room fell silent.

"Murder!" Sam exclaimed, sounding as shocked as anyone present. "Come, Sergeant, tell us this news."

Lynch needed no goading, though in his story, the marauders held their guns to his head to gain entry to the house, and when "poor Mr. Brennan" interrupted their play, all four with weapons turned and shot him.

"All four, you say?" Sam slipped his feet from his shoes and held his toes nearer the flames. "Mr. Brennan took four balls?"

Lynch scowled. "No, only one in the breast. The others missed."

"Or had no ordinance in their weapons, perhaps?"

"Still," Lynch insisted, "one of the villains done murder. He'll hang for it, as will the others, for helping him. And anyone else who hides him."

"What did they look like?" Mr. Hockaday asked.

Lynch gave a fair description of our costumes and to my dismay, ended with, "The one in the hunting frock played the fiddle, quite well, in truth." And his gaze settled upon the instrument in my hands.

"Half of Williamsburg can fiddle," Sam stated, "and half of those are fairly skilled. A shame none played the glass 'armonica. That would narrow the field." Which brought a laugh from the company.

"I might have seen your nightwalkers," Mr. Draper cut in. "Early in the evening. Perhaps two hours ago—perhaps more. I was coming 'round the capitol on my way to the Eagle. They were prancing up the Main Street ahead of me. 'Twas too dark to make out their dress, but one was a fiddler, quite good, though not as masterful as, say, our Mr. Dunbar."

I was thankful now for the difficulties in playing while walking and with cold fingers.

"Interesting, that," Lynch said. "One of the captain's house-guests—a Mr. Tyler of Norfolk—claimed he'd heard only one man better on the fiddle and that was a Norfolk music master, now deceased, name of Edward Dunbar."

"Your father, Ben. What a coincidence." Sam's voice was light, but he eyed me, wondering, as I did, if this man from Norfolk knew me. I recalled no Mr. Tyler among Mr. Ivey's associates. Indeed, all those men, like Mr. Ivey, had removed themselves to England early in the war, rather than be imprisoned as Tories. I strove to remember the faces gathered around Underwood's table, yet with the limited vision of my mask, and the fact that some diners had their backs to us, I could take no comfort from my memory.

"We'll join in your search, Sergeant Lynch," Will said, downing the rest of his punch. "If all us lads have a hand, we'll make short work of it." Those of the company not already sluggish with drink, agreed. In truth, rum made them so bold that Lynch could not refuse them.

I reached for my violin case. "I shall see Master Tom home."

"I, too," said Sam, more for Lynch's benefit. "I shall fetch dry stockings and, at any rate, we should inform Mrs. Carson of her tenant's death. Mr. Parker, your croup is worse. Come home, sir, and place a poultice upon your chest."

Jim's cough was, on the whole, much improved, though he yet carried a dull, damning trace of stale perfume about him.

When Will and Alex had led Lynch and much of the assembly away, Sam said, "Go on. I shall follow as soon as my feet regain some warmth. Perhaps a bit of your punch might spur the process from the inside." He nodded at my half-drunk gill.

"Take it," I said, wondering what he meant to do after we left, for I could always tell when Sam spoke less than truth.

Jim, Tom, and I took our leave then, the boy nearly dozing as he walked. We passed bands of revelers along the Main Street—some masked, some not—greeting those we knew, touching our hats in courtesy to those we did not.

But when we'd rounded the corner of Nassau, and no one was near, Jim said, "You both must have seen who shot Brennan."

"No," I said, and Tom echoed with, "Nor I. You drew all eyes to yourself at that moment, Mr. Parker, with your antics."

"Then you know I'm without blame. You saw me put only powder in my pistol, Ben, and precious little of it."

I nodded, all the while wondering if a wad and ball might have been left in the weapon, overlooked as Jim primed it.

But surely Sam would have cleaned the pistols?

I said nothing of my musings, resolving to question Sam on the morrow.

TWELVE

Miss Maggie returned with a handful of grocery bags. "Here, Hugh, you sort the paper. I need to take Pat and Beth Ann back to the kitchen."

"Me?" Beth Ann asked with her usual what-am-I-being-volunteered-for-now misgivings.

Hugh got to his feet. "This time you're going if I have to carry you."

"She'll come." I grabbed Beth Ann's hand as I stood, gently squeezing it. She got the message—I needed her to get out of the old part of the house. Hugh might have paused to wonder why his daughter didn't give me a hard time as I towed her from the room, but he merely smiled paternally at both of us. Poor naïve man.

Miss Maggie led us back through the dining room, where Acey swept past us, cell phone to her ear, saying "W-E-I-S-E-L. Better yet, give me his nurses' station . . ."

Beth Ann squirmed out of my grip as soon as we crossed the kitchen threshold and hung back, alert for a chance to escape, but Miss Maggie said to her, "Stick around. This may interest you."

The breakfast things had been cleared away and now half the room's horizontal surfaces were covered with bowls, plastic food containers, and bags. Evelyn was placing two flat roasting pans inside the oven. Glad was nowhere in sight, but as I opened my mouth to ask what was going on, she came back into the room via the spiral stair, carrying a large scrapbook.

"Here you are," she said when she saw us. "Magnolia thought you'd like to see my copies of the house documentation, Pat."

Beth Ann let out a quiet groan, but Miss Maggie caught her by the elbow, saying, "'Bout time you got to know your ancestors, missy. Besides, I don't have my reading glasses, so you'll have to read for me."

Beth Ann, I could tell, was all set to ask why I couldn't read instead, so she could go off and sulk as she pleased. The glint in Miss Maggie's green eyes stopped her. We were hot on the trail of our ghosts, her expression said. Beth Ann sucked in her breath, "Is Polly Carson in that book?"

"No," Glad replied. "Her records, and her husband's, are in the next volume, which begins in 1795 after her mother's death. This one covers 1750 through 1783. I'll go fetch the other—"

"Don't bother yet," Miss Maggie said. "We can start with this one. We'll sit at one end of this table, if that's all right, Gladys? I'm sure we'll have questions for you."

"Oh, well . . ." Glad looked torn, wanting her dinner to be a complete surprise, yet wanting to talk about Elizabeth. Her pet topic won out. Glad set the scrapbook at the far end of the table, saying, "Yes, let's sit here. I'll get the beets."

While we gathered around the scrapbook, Glad fetched a plate, knife, and blue bowl, then joined us. From the bowl she took a cooked, peeled beet and sliced it down the middle.

"I could do that for you," I volunteered. Like I said, I can't watch someone else cook.

Miss Maggie agreed. "Let Pat give you a hand, Gladys. That way you can get on with dinner. You can answer our questions as easily from the stove or sink, or wherever you need to be."

Glad hesitated. "Most of today's dishes are already prepared, and only need to be warmed up at the proper time. Except for the meat, of course, and well, I suppose I *could* mix the spoonbread while you slice the beets?"

I assured her that beet-slicing was a specialty of mine.

She eyed me dubiously. "But you see, they must be sliced longways, a third of an inch thick, and in the shape of a fish—a sole, actually."

I was intrigued. "Sure. I can do that." I went over to the sink to wash my hands.

"Ev," Glad said, "maybe you should bring the rest of the food up from the cellar?"

Evelyn turned from the window by the stove. "Oh, yes. Yes, of course." Seeming flustered, he went out through the dining room.

Drying my hands on a paper towel, I returned to the table where Beth Ann was already browsing through the scrapbook with fascination. I glanced over her shoulder before sitting down. The book had plastic sleeve pages and the photocopies inside seemed to be lists of things like furniture and cooking utensils.

"Household inventory," Miss Maggie explained. "Done by Thomas Carson when his father died in 1766."

"Thomas Senior kept very detailed accounts," Glad said as she popped the lid loose on a plastic bowl and carried it to the microwave. "Wrote down every sale of his tinwork and every expense for his house and family. Most of that book is his records."

Miss Maggie nodded. "But I seem to remember seeing ledgers that Elizabeth wrote, too, after her husband went to war."

Glad beamed at our interest in her favorite subject and, setting the bowl in the microwave, came over to Beth Ann. "Toward the back of the book." She flipped the pages. "Here you go. August of 1777. That's when Thomas purchased a lieutenant's commission and mustered in."

"Purchased?" I echoed, taking my seat and pulling the beets closer.

"Not unusual," Miss Maggie commented. "One of the earlier verses of 'Yankee Doodle' goes," and she sang out,

"'There is a man in our town;
I'll tell you his condition,
He sold his oxen and a cow
To buy him a commission.'"

Glad, ignoring the recital, returned to her job. "Thomas no doubt heard of the British sailing up the Chesapeake that summer. The war came much closer to home, you see—"

Beth Ann broke in, tapping the first ledger page. "These numbers don't add up."

"Yes, well," Glad hit the nuke button, "Elizabeth had little schooling, but her math did improve with practice."

"Her detail suffers, though," Miss Maggie observed, turning the pages, leaning back to bring them into focus. "The first two months she copied Thomas's format, then she starts using more and more abbreviations and, as the years go on, she makes entries less and less often."

Something in the ledger caught Beth Ann's eye—she stopped Miss Maggie's hand. I tried to get a look, but the handwriting was too difficult to decipher at a distance. Miss Maggie couldn't make it out either and told Beth Ann to read it aloud.

The girl wrinkled her nose in concentration. "Looks like '*J-dot-B-R-E-N-dot, room and—mealf?*' Then a word spelled '*y-s*' and '*week*' and the entry is '*6s*-comma-*3p*'."

"'J. Bren., room and meals this week,'" Miss Maggie translated. "'6 shillings, 3 pence.' Gladys, did you ever find out who Elizabeth's lodgers were?"

"Not all, and nothing conclusive." Glad, bottle of white wine in one hand and butter dish atop of a carton of eggs in the other, closed the fridge door with her foot. "The entry you just read—made in January of 1778—was Elizabeth's first lodger." She set her load on the worktable by the stove. "In December of 1777, the *Virginia Gazette* carried an advertisement for 'fine snuff and other genteel accoutrements' sold by a John Brennan, 'late of Norfolk and now situated at Mrs. Vobe's'—the King's Arms Tavern, he meant." The microwave beeped and Glad removed the bowl as she talked. "If 'J. Bren.' is the same man, perhaps he moved to this house the next month because it was more private. You see, as Elizabeth took in more lodgers, this 'J. Bren.' paid more, probably to retain a single room."

"Or at least a single bed," Miss Maggie said. "Beds were expensive, so lodgers had to share—sometimes three grown men to a twin-sized frame. If you wanted personal space, you either paid more or slept on the floor." She tapped the plastic page and mused, "So, John Brennan was a traveling salesman."

"Not in the way we think of them, of course," Glad said.

Miss Maggie agreed, explaining to me and Beth Ann, "A young tradesman would go from town to town, selling his wares from his room, testing the waters, so to speak. Once he found a promising clientele, he'd settle down and open his own shop, or at least arrange to share space with an established merchant. Did John Brennan stay in Williamsburg?"

Glad put a half stick of butter in her bowl. "There's no other mention of Brennan in the *Gazette*, but 'J. Bren.' paid Elizabeth room and board through October 1781. Must have been a hard time for her. Her Thomas died about that time, and with the capitol no longer in town, she didn't have many other boarders."

"When was Polly born?" Beth Ann blurted out of the blue.

Glad, perhaps used to rapid changes of subject while giving tours, answered smoothly. "She was christened at Bruton Parish in September of 1769, and her father wrote that he paid a midwife five shillings on the last day of August—oh, Ev, let me give you a hand."

Evelyn had returned with two heavy-looking grocery sacks dangling from one hand, and his other arm wrapped around a precarious stack of plastic containers and large Ziploc bags. He managed to control the load until he tried to set them down on the table where Glad was working. The stack toppled, three Ziploc bags hit the floor, but the seals held.

"No harm done," said Evelyn. "I'll get them."

But Glad helped anyway and I saw the smiles they exchanged. Whatever Hugh and his siblings thought, I knew Glad hadn't simply "latched onto" Evelyn to get into this house.

Glad straightened up. "They've been asking about Elizabeth's lodgers, Ev. Tell them about Dr. Riddick."

"Dr. Riddick!" Miss Maggie exclaimed, then to hide her excitement, she added, "I think I've heard of him."

"Elizabeth's ledger lists a 'Dr. R.,'" Glad said.

"And Dr. Isaac Riddick was in Williamsburg for those months," Evelyn concluded. "Dr. Galt wrote of him seeing patients at the apothecary."

"When was this?" Miss Maggie asked.

"1783," Evelyn said, "between June and December. Riddick left Williamsburg rather abruptly and Galt hints of some scandal, but doesn't go into detail. The bigger mystery may be why Riddick came here in the first place. He'd only just finished his studies in Philadelphia, a city that offered favorable opportunities for him to set up a practice."

"While Williamsburg," Miss Maggie said, "turned into a sleepy country village after the capitol left in 1780."

Evelyn nodded. "There were quite enough doctors in town to tend the people who remained here. Galt does make one brief mention of Riddick's interest in mental illness—"

"He came to study at the Public Hospital?" Miss Maggie suggested, to which I asked, "The building across the street?"

"Yes," Evelyn replied. "The Public Hospital of 1773 was the first hospital for the insane in North America."

"Little more than a jail," Miss Maggie put in, "but it represented the new theory that the mentally ill could possibly be cured."

Evelyn crossed to the hutch beside the stove. "The hospital closed during the war for want of funding, and didn't reopen until 1786. Riddick may have come to Williamsburg to meet Dr. John de Sequeyra, the hospital's attending physician, but it's odd that he stayed more than six months with the facility closed." Evelyn opened the lower cabinet and took out a large stock pot.

"How are the beets coming, Pat?" Glad asked.

I'd been so absorbed in the discussion, I only had two sliced. I started hacking away and assured her they'd be ready in a minute.

Beth Ann, I noticed, had turned to the last page of the scrapbook, pointing and whispering as Evelyn poured water into the pot.

Miss Maggie asked aloud, "What about the other lodgers? For instance, this December 1783 entry lists 'S.W.' and 'J.P.'"

"We don't know for sure," Glad said. "They both took rooms in late spring, right after the army had been sent home, so it's likely they were soldiers rather than students."

"And," Evelyn said as he carried the pot to the stove, "they both stayed here at least seven months, so one would assume they had jobs. Among the employers who kept good records, nearly a dozen men with the initials 'J.P.' are listed."

"But only two with the initials 'S.W.'" Glad opened one plastic bag, lifted out something heavy wrapped in greasy white cloth, and put it in the stock pot, cloth and all. "Silas Wilson, who worked at the courthouse, and Samuel Walker, employed by John Greenhow."

Miss Maggie's eyebrows did their "pay dirt" dance. "You said they stayed 'at least' seven months. They moved out of the Carson house in 1784?"

"We don't know that either," Glad replied, heading for the sink to wash her hands. "That's the last ledger we have of Elizabeth's. The records for the years 1784 through 1795 are missing."

* * *

Sculpting the beet slices didn't take long. Beets cut longways already sort of resemble a flat round sole fish. I just had to carve a tail. It reminded me of my Great-Aunt Isabella (on the Giamo side), making biscotti that looked like fishes and birds and wreaths for Advent. *This* felt like Christmas, more than anything else I'd encountered in this house.

Anyway, Miss Maggie begged a potty break, I said it sounded like a good idea, and she said, "Come help an old lady up these stairs." That's when I knew she had more in mind than a break. She never called herself an old lady without ulterior motives.

Glad, interestingly enough, seemed sorry to see us go. I think she was starting to *like* having visitors while she cooked. Good, I thought, because the kitchen is where I feel most at home, and if I was going to be her daughter-in-law—

"You take our bathroom," Miss Maggie said as we reached the top of the stairs. "I'll use the other, and we'll rendezvous in our bedroom."

Five minutes later, I was sitting on the daybed, my mentor standing by the window. On her sweatshirt, Rudolph seemed to be blinking more slowly now. I remembered that Miss Maggie had not been present for the news about Dr. Weisel, so I filled her in, though I couldn't remember the name of the drug in his system.

"Protriptyline," Beth Ann said as she came in, carrying her notebook and brown pencil. "It's an antidepressant."

"*Pills to Purge Melancholy*," Miss Maggie said with a grim nod. When I raised my eyebrows in question, she explained, "An eighteenth century songbook—the whole title was *Wit and Mirth: Pills to Purge Melancholy*. Now, instead of wit and mirth, we have real pills. More effective, maybe, but singing has no harmful side effects."

Beth Ann plopped down on the other end of the daybed. "I just checked the bathrooms for antacid. Thing is—"

"Antacid?" I echoed.

"That's what was on Dr. Weisel's nose last night. Liquid antacid."

I remembered how he'd held a fist to his sternum before going upstairs. "I saw two bottles in the front bathroom yesterday."

Beth Ann rolled her eyes in exasperation, like she was dealing with a young child. "I've been trying to tell you, Grandmom's and Uncle Horse's bottles are both gone from the front bathroom, and Uncle Foot's isn't in his bag in the back bathroom. And no empties in any of the upstairs trashcans. I looked in Dad's suitcase, too, but he packed tablets instead of liquid."

"Hugh takes antacid?" I asked, surprised. "He has a cast iron stomach."

"Not when he eats something with nutmeg in it. My uncles and granddad are the same way. They all have an intolerance."

I mentally reviewed every recipe I'd ever cooked for Hugh, sure I had put nutmeg in something. Or mace, the outer shell of the nutmeg. When was he going to tell me? After I made him sick?

"I knew about Hugh," Miss Maggie said, "but not the rest of them. Rich has this intolerance, too? But not Acey?"

Beth Ann nodded. "I don't know if Uncle Rich or Uncle Foot even brought any, and Uncle Horse might have repacked his. But isn't it weird that Grandmom's bottle's missing? We both saw it in the cabinet yesterday."

"Glad might have moved it," Miss Maggie suggested.

"Or Evelyn," I mused. "Might have put the bottle in his room, or carried it down to the kitchen."

Beth Ann shrugged and made a noise like "I don't know" with her mouth closed. Then, bored with nonmysterious explanations, she said, "Shouldn't we write down what we learned from Grandmom's scrapbook before we forget it?"

Miss Maggie took the paper from her pocket and handed it to Beth Ann. "And we'd better be quick about it, before Gladys wonders where we got to. Let's see, next to 'John Brennan' put 'snuff salesman' and put 'Samuel' in front of 'Walker' and—"

"Wait." I pointed out that I might have heard the names in my vision wrong, or that "J. Bren." probably wasn't the same man as John Brennan. "After all, there's a two-year discrepancy between when 'J. Bren.' left the Carson house and when Dr. Riddick and Samuel Walker lived here."

"No," said Miss Maggie, "there's a discrepancy between when John Brennan stopped paying Elizabeth money for his room and board, and when the other two men started. Doesn't prove Brennan stopped living here. Bartering used to be common. Why, I remember Stoke county doctors taking chickens and bushels of vegetables in exchange for care right up through the 1950s."

I sat up straighter—my legs were getting stiff with all this sitting. "You think Elizabeth Carson let John Brennan pay her in—in what? Snuff?"

"I don't know. Snuff isn't as unlikely as you think. It's as addictive as cigarettes—"

"Brennan was a drug dealer," Beth Ann blurted out, a look of enlightenment on her face.

"Yes, he was, in a way." Rudolph stopped blinking at that moment and Miss Maggie looked down in disgust. "Drat, and I didn't pack a spare battery. What was I saying? Oh, right. Elizabeth must have used bartering with both John Brennan and Mr. Dunbar, the music master. You'll recall we didn't find his initials with the others, yet Polly said he gave her singing lessons. Earned his keep that way, I'll bet."

Miss Maggie always took my visions for gospel truth. To me, they felt no different from a daydream—a product of my overactive imagination.

I was about to remind her of this when Beth Ann sat up, alert, asking, "Is there a car pulling in?" she asked.

I heard it then—car wheels on what was left of the snow in the backyard.

Miss Maggie glanced out the window. "Two cars. Anyone else comes, they'll have to park on the roof."

Beth Ann lunged for the window. "One must be my Aunt Irene. I've never seen her before."

Curious, I joined the two at the window, peeking over Miss Maggie's shoulder. She was right about the parking. The front newcomer, a white BMW, pulled in alongside the fence, blocking in the Escort, Miata, and Rich's Volvo. The second driver stopped even with the house, so only part of a green bumper was showing. Probably assessing the parking situation.

"That's the car that was parked across the street last night," Beth Ann said, her forefinger smudging the window as she pointed to the BMW.

She was right. Getting out of the driver's seat was a tall blonde woman dressed in form-fitting leather—jacket, pants, and high heels. The form they fitted was Barbie-ish and, with the heels in the inch of snow left on the ground, she moved like a marionette, hands hanging in midair for balance. I heard the kitchen door open and the woman glanced up at the porch. That's when I got a good view of her face, which was maybe thirty percent lips. Mrs. Kevie.

"Doctor Weisel's wife," I said. "Acey invited her to dinner."

"How interesting," Miss Maggie observed, "that she left her husband's sickbed to dash right over here."

The driver of the second car—a thin Asian woman—got out and poked her head shyly around the corner of the house. By her gestures, she seemed to be asking where she should park.

"Think that's Aunt Irene?" Miss Maggie asked, but she didn't wait for Beth Ann's reply. "Let's go find out."

She snatched up our paper of names from the bed, Beth Ann took up her notebook, and we all paraded down the spiral stairs.

Evelyn and Horse were on the back porch directing traffic. Standing sideways in the open doorway was Hugh, letting the cold air in. At the window, Foot stood by his mother whining that Irene wouldn't have a place to park when she arrived.

Since that answered Miss Maggie's question, she asked Glad who the second newcomer was.

"A friend of Acey's, named Sachiko. Apparently Acey had called her and told her what had happened to Dr. Weisel, and this friend was worried and drove down from Richmond." Glad didn't look at all happy to have two extra dinner guests, though if this dinner was anything like last night's, she'd have more than enough food.

"Aunt Acey's in the shower," Beth Ann said. "I passed her going in on my way to Miss Maggie's room. I'll go tell her." And she disappeared back up the steps.

Hugh stepped into the room and shut the door. "Let me get my coat and keys. I'll park the Escort over at Merchants Square and walk back."

"Why don't I move my car instead?" I volunteered. "You're already blocked in."

That amorous leer of his materialized. "Better yet, you follow me and give me a ride back. If I can't find a spot at Merchants Square, who knows where I'll end up?" Made sense, though his expression was saying that we hadn't had a moment to ourselves all day. Seize the day and all that. Which made even better sense.

Hugh said he'd fetch my coat and keys along with his own and went up the stairs just as Weisel's wife came inside.

She gave us a collective once-over, then centered her gaze between Miss Maggie and Glad, unsure who her host was. "Hi, I'm Cherry Weisel. So nice of you to invite me to dinner."

Cherry? I told myself it could be short for Cheryl or Cerise, but I got the impression she'd handpicked it herself, so to speak. Cosmetically, she seemed a perpetual twenty-three, but considering her attitude, I was willing to bet she was no more than two years younger than me. Maybe older. And without the heels, no more than two inches taller than me. Bust-wise, I had the advantage, but her Scarlett O'Hara waist showed hers off better.

Evelyn and Horse led our second arrival into the kitchen. In complete contrast to Cherry, she had a boyish figure and was naturally twenty-something. Her delicate features, though anxious and uncertain, were makeup-free and framed by short, silky black hair. She wore jeans and high-top sneakers under a navy pea jacket, with blue driving gloves on her hands.

The first words out of her mouth, addressed to Glad, were, "I'm sorry to barge in on your dinner. I won't stay. I just—Acey called and sounded so—"

"Sachi!" Acey had come down the stairs behind us. She'd thrown her caftan back on, but her hair was wrapped in a towel and her feet were bare. Besides surprise, I could have sworn I saw a tinge of fear in her eyes. "You shouldn't have come."

A half beat of silence followed, which Glad broke with, "Ann Carter, don't be a fool. Of course you're welcome, Sachi, and you'll stay for dinner." A gentle but firm order. For the first time since I'd arrived, Gladys Lee sounded like the head of the family.

"This cold uncomfortable Weather,
Make Jack and Jill lie close together."

—Nathanael Ames's Almanac, December, 1749

December 25, 1783—Mrs. Carson's House

DARKNESS STILL PRESSED AT the windows when Sam woke me. He was dressed, his coat buttoned across his breast, and if not for his white shirt and stockings, I should never have seen him in the blackness of our room.

"The sun will be up soon, Ben. Hurry. I'll go wake Jim and fetch our muskets. We'll meet beside the woodpile."

My head and limbs felt yet asleep. I'd lain awake late, my thoughts taken up with planning how I should avoid this Mr. Tyler of Norfolk, as well as pondering the puzzle of Brennan's death, alarmed further by what Elizabeth had told us. Dr. Riddick had been following Brennan about, observing his condition, and had seen the shooting. Had he, I wondered, recognized us? He'd gone out again, Elizabeth said, to tend to a patient, and had not returned when I retired. Sam had also come in after I slept, so I hadn't the chance to question him.

Our room was very cold this morning, the bare floorboards chill against my feet. In haste, I tugged on my wool stockings and britches, and blew upon my fingers as I buttoned my waist- and topcoats. Having no time to shave or tie back my hair, I pulled my duffel from under the bed, rolling it out until my hands came upon my red Liberty cap. The moths had made several meals of it since I'd worn it first at Morristown, but the cap would do this morn to keep my hair from my eyes and my ears warm beneath my tricorn.

'Twas then I heard a light foot upon the stair, and as I left my room, the furtive opening and closing of the front door. Jim, I thought, and laughed at his care in not waking the household when in a few moments, we'd be firing charges at the rising sun, waking the entire town. I thought also how lost in sleep he must have been to miss Sam's direction to meet at the woodpile. Thinking to collect him, I followed him below, feeling for the steps in the darkness, and pulled open the front door.

The air was damp and the ground white with hoarfrost. At the top of the block, a man crossed the street at a run. Though only a faint blush of dawn touched the eastern sky and I saw naught but his silhouette, I knew the build to be Dr. Riddick's.

"Ben!" came Sam's hoarse whisper from behind. He was at the back door, beckoning me. Closing the front, I hurried down the hall to join him.

Once outside, he gestured to my musket, leaning against the side of the house. "Primed and loaded for you."

I took it up, wincing because it was so cold. "The metal feels like ice."

"Made worse, I'm sure, by the uphill window of the tin shop being propped wide open 'neath its shutter, and that fastened but loosely, with the turn of a bent nail, from the outside. 'Tis the only way in, now that the creek is risen nearly to the top step in front of the door. Fortuitous for me, or I'd have had two cold swims last night and another this morning."

"What of last night? How did you get wet?"

"An error in judgment as to the sinking of our costumes. Nothing for it but to wade out as far as I could with yet another brick, to send Will's britches to the bottom. Come, let's go 'round by the chimney, where we can see the sunrise."

"Where's Jim?" I asked as I followed him.

"Still abed and resolved to stay there another half hour. 'Tis the first night he's slept through since that croup came upon him, so I had no heart to insist."

"Dr. Riddick was up when you looked in?"

"Riddick? No. I couldn't see his bed in the dark, but I heard the ropes of it creak with his weight. Why do you ask?"

I told him what I'd just seen.

Sam leaned his back against the brickwork of the east chimney. "He's out earlier this time. I suppose I woke him."

"This time?"

"If you rose at daybreak, Ben, like those of us who work for our bread"—Sam elbowed my arm to show his jest—"and dressing, looked out from our bedroom window, you too would have seen the doctor's last foray. Since he's come to Williamsburg, perhaps once each month, though heeding no schedule, he rushes off at dawn, and always to the hospital."

"The hospital? I thought it closed."

"It is, but that's where he goes. He follows a pattern—comes in very late the night before, leaves at dawn and is not seen all the day, then returns late again, with a story of some patient in a far corner of the county. My curiosity got the best of me on the third instance—I trailed him and saw him enter through the hospital's yard. I'm convinced he uses the place for trysting." Sam shivered, but not from cold. "What woman would agree to such surroundings? The building's layered in filth, and on my oath, the wraiths of lunatics still pace the cells."

'Twas my turn to shudder. Sam noticed and laughed. "At any rate, I'll wager no woman meets Riddick there twice. As I said, his visits are infrequent, with three to eight weeks between. It takes him that long to woo each—" A shot sounded across town. "Damnation! Someone's beat us to the punch. A shilling says Will Knox was the man."

Sam raised his musket and sent back an answering blast, as did I, just as the sun set its first rays upon the pastureland across the creek and marsh to the southeast. Four more shots came in response as other men fired off their Christmas guns.

Sam brought from his pocket two more cartridges. "Fire a second, for good measure. To keep the Devil away all the New Year long."

A waste of powder, as Jim said the night before, but I took the cartridge and charged my musket. In Norfolk, I'd never been permitted to engage in the practice—nor keep a weapon, for that matter. I'd listen each Christmas morn from the window of Mr. Ivey's front attic, where I'd shared sleeping space on the floor with a stocky, bewhiskered servant named Evans. Not 'til after I'd met

Sam—at Valley Forge, our first Yuletide—did I salute the Nativity thus.

Despite it, the Devil yet pursued me.

Still, I raised my musket, pulled the flint to full cock, and fired. Sam followed suit, and in the calm that ensued, we heard a thumping on the sill above our heads.

"Do another!" young Tom cried with delight, his cheeks flushed as he leaned out of the open window. His waistcoat, not yet buttoned, hung on his shoulders.

"Tom, close that!" his sister commanded from inside, "and go fetch the water before Mother comes back down." Taking Tom's place at the window as she tied the last knot to her modesty scarf, she curtsied. "Good day, Mr. Dunbar, Mr. Walker."

We both bowed, I with tricorn in hand, too late thinking how moth-eaten my cap, and how rough the bristles upon my chin. Polly merely smiled as she lowered the sash.

Sam turned to me. "Here, take my musket in with yours. I must be off to Greenhow's, for Mrs. Tucker will no doubt come in before devotions, seeking pins or bayberry candles or some such, and would be most disappointed to miss my charming attendance." He took off at a run straight up the hill, and so I missed my chance to question him.

At the door, I passed Master Tom, buckets in hand, headed for the well at a run. As I turned up the stair, I could hear the welcoming crackle of the fire in the common room hearth and Polly singing snatches of "Sweet Is the Budding Spring of Love" as she warmed last night's mutton broth for our breakfast. But I would make myself presentable first.

Jim's door was open and the man himself was slipping into his short coat.

"I thought you'd still be abed," I said from the doorway.

"With all the household plotting against me?" His voice was clearer than I'd heard it in a week, and his protests evidence that he felt better. "First Sam, then Isaac, then you clodding down the stairs after Isaac, then Widow Carson moving around the next room. And the house has a bad draft this morning and, top it all, I've had to borrow a shirt from Isaac for mine yet reeks of that retched perfume—"

"Wait. Mrs. Carson? In Brennan's room?" I remembered Polly saying, "*. . . before Mother comes back down . . .*" and glanced at the door beside Jim's. Closed, but the lock was undone.

"She's in there now," Jim said. "Why cleaning it couldn't wait until we'd all gone to work . . . I haven't time to wait for breakfast before—"

"Mistress Polly has broth ready. I smelled it as I climbed the steps. Leave enough for me."

Jim smiled. "I'll not swear to it. I'm hungry as an ox." Taking up his tricorn, he passed me and took the steps by twos.

I brought the muskets to my room, hastily tied back my hair, then crossed the hall and opened Brennan's door. Air as cold as outdoors hit my face.

The room was not tidy—the bed unmade and moldy crusts of bread lay upon the small table. Brennan's spare shirt and stockings were on the floor by the bed, and his second waistcoat and britches were draped across the single chair. Still, considering a madman had confined himself here nearly a month, it might have been worse.

Elizabeth, with blanket thrown over her shoulders, was on her knees at the fireplace, using a hearth shovel to move the ashes to a tin pail. "Oh, good day, Mr. Dunbar." She stood to greet me with curtsy and gracious smile, despite the shovel in her hand and smudge of soot on her nose. "You've—you've forgotten to shave, sir."

"I thought I felt a draft." I nodded to the windows of the room, the sashes of which were both raised.

"I'm sorry for that. I opened them last night, fearing miasma. I'd not have my children, nor the rest of you, becoming lunatic as Mr. Brennan did. I'll close them as soon as I've finished cleaning."

I nodded, now seeing the reason in her action. "So you believe his derangement was caused by unhealthful vapors?"

Elizabeth came around the bed, letting her blanket fall upon it, and stepped out into the hall beside me, closing the door to keep the cold air at bay. "All illness is, else why would so many people become sick in winter, when no fresh air can enter a house, and in summer, when a stink rises from the marshes?" She lowered her eyelids, hesitant. "I daresay Dr. Riddick would call me old-fashioned, with all his talk of body humours and such."

"I too hold little faith in scientific medicine, madam." She stood close enough to disconcert me and I fumbled for words. "Someone thought to give you the key to the lock, I see."

"The doctor, when he brought me the news last night."

"I should be pleased to help you sort through Mr. Brennan's belongings and carry them below for you."

"And I should be glad of your help. I hope to be done with cleaning the room before devotions—will you escort me, sir?"

I rarely missed the chance to hear Mr. Pelham play the organ at Bruton Parish Church, but today I feared Mr. Tyler might also be in attendance. "I deeply regret, madam, that I have an appointment this morning. However, I shall return in time for dinner, for I would not miss your Christmas pies for the world."

Her sweet smile once more appeared. "Then I shall let you be on your way. But do not forget"—she reached up, stroking her palm along my cheek—"to see to your beard, sir." With a soft laugh, she let herself back into Brennan's room, leaving me in the hall with the memory of her hand upon my face.

THIRTEEN

The day was cold and crisp, so I was shivering as I followed Hugh's car out of the drive and left onto Francis Street. Evelyn was behind us in his Beetle, but he turned right. Acey's friend Sachi had backed her car out into the street so we could get out. A red SUV pulled up behind her, the woman behind the wheel signaling her intention of also turning into the drive. Irene? If so, Foot preferred his blonde and young-looking. Typical man.

I set the fan on my heater up a notch and tested the result by holding my bare left fingers up to the vent, since with the ring, I'd found I couldn't get my glove on. The vent's air was still cold, so I put my hand in my coat pocket.

All I knew was that we were headed toward "Tavern Parking," where Evelyn thought Hugh would have the best luck finding a space. We were also headed in the same direction I'd walked yesterday one block over on Duke of Gloucester Street. In fact, after about two tenths of a mile, I spied the octagonal magazine set back a little ways on my left, with the courthouse a half block behind it.

Fewer tourists were mulling around the Market Green than yesterday. I wondered if the holiday or the cold kept the rest away.

Houses dotted the street, but on my left I mostly saw white picket fences and hedges, which I realized were the backyards of the shops over on the main drag. A shingle on one white outbuilding showed where the King's Arms was. I thought of Zela and suddenly wanted to compare notes with her.

My beloved turned right between a break in tall evergreens. I followed, surprised to find a large parking lot hidden from the street. Hugh drove to the rear, choosing a space away from other cars in a fairly empty row. I pulled in on his driver's side.

No sooner was he in my passenger seat than I blurted out, "Can we get away for dinner tomorrow night?"

He put on his roguish grin as he shut the door. "You asking me on a date?"

"Sure. You're easy. See, I already picked you up."

"Okay, I'll play hard to get. Let me think, do I want to spend a Saturday night alone with you or eating leftovers with my weird family? Hmmm." He was looking out the window with feigned nonchalance, but his left hand crept—*very* chalantly—onto my thigh.

I resisted the urge to climb all over him, figuring I'd get stuck on the parking brake. "I want to go to the King's Arms Tavern."

Hugh looked at me then, and I hoped he wouldn't see ulterior motives in my face, but all he said was, "Oh."

"You've eaten there and the food's lousy?"

"No. I've eaten there, and the food's great. You'd love it." His expression went all romantic on me, making me picture him taking Tanya to eat there.

Was I paranoid or what?

Hugh massaged my leg. "I just don't think I'll get reservations for tomorrow. You usually have to make them two, three days in advance." Seeing my disappointment, he added, "I'll call when we get back to the house. Maybe we'll luck out."

In response, I leaned over and kissed him.

His fingers probed their way up under my jacket and his other hand took over thigh duty. "Turn off the car," he murmured. "We'll be here a while."

"But the heat finally kicked in."

"You've got me to keep you warm." He almost took back his words after my frozen left hand met his cheek, but I had to admit, the man was an efficient and eco-friendly space heater.

Unfortunately, Hugh blew it during the first breath break, saying, "I knew Beth Ann would be okay as soon as we were engaged."

"Say what?" I sat back, the better to look him in the eye without crossing mine.

"You know, my daughter?" Moving his hands to my waist, he tried to coax me back toward him. "She's been following you around like a puppy today."

"That isn't—" I caught myself before mentioning anything about ghosts. But I somehow had to correct his misconceptions. I pushed at his arms to ward off his distractions. "Wait. What did she say when you told her?"

I got a blank look back, confirming my suspicions. "All right, so you didn't tell her this morning, but you discussed this with her before this weekend, right? She knew you were going to ask me?"

Scowling, he withdrew his hands. "I needed Beth Ann's permission to propose to you?"

"Not her permission, just—" We were both still in emotion-mode, and his scowls always brought out the stubborn, combative Italian in me. I tried sucking in a cold breath to clear my thoughts. Problem was, we'd done too good a job making the car's air steamy, as evidenced by my fogged-up windshield. "She's only fourteen, Hugh, and our getting married will be a major change in her life. She needs to feel like she's in on the plan."

"Okay, okay. We'll talk to her when we get home." His tone declared the break over and he reached for me once more.

I pushed him away again. "We? No way. You've got to talk to her alone. You're her father."

"And you're going to be her mother."

"No!" I sounded vehement, like I was in total denial. I hunted around my head for why I'd said it, and remembered Beth Ann's face as she held my hand that morning and stared at the ring. "Hugh, that's what your daughter's scared of. Even though Beth Ann can't remember Tanya, the title of 'Mother' is reserved. Seeing this ring on my finger makes her feel like you've gone out and found a replacement, the way you would if your TV broke." That was unfair and I knew it—from what Miss Maggie told me, I was the first woman Hugh dated since Tanya's death and we're talking more than ten years. Beth Ann would see that, too, because, as I've said, she's logical. Was the replacement theory her feeling? Or mine?

"I told you," Hugh said, "if you don't want that ring, I'll buy you another one." The tone of that offer last night had been "I'd do anything for you." Now it sounded like "I'd do anything to end this conversation and get back to making out."

Which got my dander up even further. "That's not the point. Putting another ring on my finger isn't going to fix everything." As soon as the sentence left my mouth, I knew I didn't mean Beth Ann any longer. "You proposed to me the same way you did to Tanya. I bet you even kissed me under the mistletoe the same way, didn't you?"

His scowl deepened until his eyebrows nearly touched. "So now you don't like the way I kiss."

"That's not what I meant."

"It sure sounded like it."

"Don't be such a *stu-NAHD*. I only—"

"Don't curse at me in Italian."

"That wasn't cursing. If I wanted to curse—oh, forget it." I started the engine, so mad I could barely think to crank up the defrosts before trying to drive anywhere.

"Oh, come on, Pat." He put one of his big paws on my shifting arm, not rough, but not tender either. "What the hell are we fighting about?"

"If you don't know—"

"I *don't* know."

I wanted to curse him out then, for not being able to read my mind when I myself couldn't put into words what I meant. And for being the only person on earth who could make me cry during an argument. Instead, I bit my lip to cork the tears, then said, "Take your hand off my arm so I can drive." My voice shook.

He let go, with a testy sigh.

I backed my Neon out of the space, thankful for the stripes of clear glass on the rear window. The front windshield wasn't as accommodating—I swiped off the condensation with my gloved hand. I could feel Hugh's eyes on me, until I pulled out of the lot, then he turned to look out the window. Neither of us spoke all the way back, me because opening my mouth would uncork my tear ducts.

While Hugh was closing the gates, I parked alongside the fence and ran for the house. The kitchen door was open and the room empty—I caught a glimpse of Glad setting the table in the dining room. She was back in her Marie Antoinette dress, with a fancy bonnet in place of the powdered wig. I dashed for the stairs and was near the top of them when the kitchen door slammed below. *Please don't let him follow me*, I prayed. All I wanted was a good cry.

Closing the bedroom door behind me, I fell onto my floor mattress and let the sobs come, realizing too late that there wasn't a box of tissues in the room. I was a few minutes into my orgy of self-pity—done calling myself a complete idiot but just starting where I gave myself a failing grade in Life 101—when I heard the door open and close softly. I glanced over my shoulder, ready to ream out Hugh in a fit of hysterics.

Miss Maggie stood there, looking worried. "Did you tell Hugh about the ghost, Pat?"

"No!" I blubbered.

She sighed, but not, I thought, with relief. "Let me get you some tissues. Here, help me put my suitcase on the bed. And take off your coat."

Sniffling, I got up to do her bidding, dropping my jacket on the mattress.

As a reward, Miss Maggie gave me a full purse pack of Kleenex. "Hmm. Hugh came in looking like a totem pole and went straight up to his room, and you're here doing a fair impression of Niagara Falls. If this isn't about ghosts, then it must have to do with that ring on your finger." She took hold of my left hand, pack of Kleenex and all, and held the ring close to her eyes. "A real beaut. Old, too. Reminds me of my mother's."

"It belonged to Hugh's Great-Aunt Priscilla." I felt a lump form in my throat again and more tears streamed down my cheeks. "And to Tanya."

I was too watery-eyed, and too absorbed in my own misery, to note her reaction, but after a moment she patted the daybed. "Have a seat, Pat."

I did, hugging my knees in front of me, until my muscles twinged and I had to straighten my legs.

Miss Maggie sat beside me. "Since you're too sensible to get all het up over a little hunk of metal and stone, I'm guessing this is the tip of the iceberg."

"He's been treating me like Tanya," I blurted out. "Like he doesn't care that I'm different. Like"—I suddenly recalled Acey's comments about men—"like he doesn't care about who I am, as an individual."

"Oh, I wouldn't say that. He doesn't *know* much about who you are, any more than you know him all that well yet. Takes more than a few months to figure out a person."

Was that the whole problem? Did Hugh and I simply need to get to know each other better before rushing into marriage? I voiced the question aloud, more to see how it sounded to myself than to bounce it off Miss Maggie.

Of course, she told me her opinion anyway. "Pshaw! No one would get married in that case. Even after fifty years with Jake, when I thought I had him pegged, he'd up and surprise me, and not always in a way I liked. But that's one of the things that made marriage interesting."

"So you think we should just go for it and everything'll work itself out?"

"Nothing ever works itself out, Pat." She put her gnarled hands around my left one, which hid the ring. Intentional? Or simply a gesture of comfort and affection? "I won't say *what* I think you should do—my own selfish motives are bound to creep in—but let me give you a few things to think on. First off, your life changed for the better last May when you came to Virginia. Made you feel good about yourself, maybe for the first time. Part of you, though, is defined by that big Italian family of yours, and you've been missing them."

That scored a bull's-eye. Right this minute my cousins would all be gathering at their parents' houses, everyone kissing and hugging. There would be Christmas trees and Nativities lit up, tables set, stereos blaring Perry Como carols, football games on TV, and drool-inducing aromas wafting from the kitchens. Babies crying while the older grandkids try to snitch butter cookies from heaping trays on dining room sideboards. Uncle Mario snitching black olives from the plastic-wrapped antipasto dish. I would have given anything to be there. A few more tears escaped.

"On Hugh's side of it, well . . ." Miss Maggie let nostalgia glaze over her eyes a moment. "You know he was in my history class in junior high. I had Horse the year before. They looked liked twins back then, so I suppose I expected Hugh to take after his outgoing, class-clown brother. Nope, he was quiet and serious as can be. That was the same year Jake first got sick. I ended up hiring

Hugh to come mow the lawn and do some work around Bell Run that summer. He was the only student willing to ride his bike out from town. Came every Saturday during the fall, too, until Gladys moved down here to Williamsburg. Never thought to see him again. But I got an invitation to his wedding, which is when I met Tanya." Miss Maggie stole a peek in my direction.

"Keep going," I said impatiently. "Tell me about her."

She shook her head. "This story's about Hugh, not Tanya. I only saw him with his wife twice, at the wedding and at Beth Ann's christening. He had this look in his eyes, Pat. I can't describe it—I just know it hasn't been there since Tanya died. I don't mean love—when he looks at Beth Ann, you can see he cares about her more than anything. Not passion either, though just as potent. Anyhow, since you showed up, I've started seeing little glimmers of that look now and again."

Maybe I couldn't see the ring, but I could feel it, tight on my finger. Crying had made me puffy, I told myself. Still, a noose came to mind. "The look's not for me, Miss Maggie. He's dredging up memories of Tanya."

"Oh, very likely."

"If you're trying to make me feel better, that didn't help."

"Like I said, I'm giving you a few things to think on. For instance, the fact that until now, he was dead set on letting those memories lie." Miss Maggie pursed her lips in thought. "You ought to talk to Beth Ann."

"Not you, too. That's what started the whole argument." I recounted the gist of it.

"So don't talk to her about your engagement. Talk to her about her father. After all, she's known him fourteen years and she's a bright kid. Bound to have an opinion worth hearing. Wouldn't hurt for you two to compare notes."

I suspected ulterior motives, but trusted Miss Maggie's wisdom, so I agreed to have a chat with Beth Ann.

"Good. Now go wash your face and come right back. I've got news about your 'old house' symptoms." Her green eyes were sparkling.

"Miss Maggie, you didn't tell—"

"No, no. I just played Name-That-Ailment with our panel of experts downstairs. Go on, wash your eyes. You'll feel better."

The woman was a master of suspense. I hurried off down the hall. I was closing the bathroom door behind me when Cherry Weisel came barreling through the doorway from the main house. I hadn't heard her approach. Darned weird acoustics.

She pulled herself up. "Oh!"

"Be right out." Embarrassed by my red eyes, I hid behind the door. "Or, there's another bathroom. Keep going up the stairs and across the hall."

"Right. Thanks." And she was gone back through the doorway.

Minutes later, when I was halfway back to the room, I heard a board creak behind me. Glancing over my shoulder, I caught a glimpse of black leather around the corner. Cherry? The other bathroom must have been occupied.

As I entered our room, Miss Maggie said, "Ah, now you look human again." She was standing by the window and swung around to look outside. "I'm watching Evelyn. He's come back from moving his car, but he's still outside the gate, like he's hunting for something on the ground. And I just recalled that when we walked back from church, we saw footprints in the snow there. Beth Ann pointed them out."

"Probably made by the person who left the cards." I told Miss Maggie about it.

"Ace and King of Spades? How interesting."

I wondered if "ace" translated to "Acey." She *was* the family prankster, and I had only her word for it that she'd seen someone going through the gate. Acey might have planted the card herself. Had she made the footprints? Not in bear-claw slippers. Besides, the ace had arrived before her.

Miss Maggie didn't give me time to muse further. She waved me to the bed, indicating that I should be seated. I complied. "Heavy metal poisoning."

"What?"

"Heavy metals. Lead or mercury, most likely. That was the consensus on hearing the symptoms. The metallic taste clinched it, they said."

"Metal poisoning? That sounds so Industrial-Age. Not colonial."

Miss Maggie shook her head. "Lead and mercury were much easier to get hold of in the eighteenth century, Pat. Musket balls were lead—all ammo was. Blacksmith's were exposed to lead all the time. Or someone with shot left in him from an old wound could have it leech into his system and poison him eventually. And mercury was a common medicine."

"The silver stuff that used to be in thermometers?" I pictured someone downing a spoonful of it like cough syrup. Yuck. "Wouldn't that kill a person outright?"

"Not in small doses. Taken over enough time, though—Andrew Jackson took mercury pills. So did Abe Lincoln. A toxic dose, too, from what I've heard. He stopped 'cause he thought they made him grumpy. Good thing—he might not have been around to run for president. Or he might have gone insane. Heavy metal poisoning can do that. Remember the 'mad hatters' of the nineteenth century, who went nuts from sniffing mercury fumes as they molded top hats."

"Insane?" I echoed.

"Exactly. You said Riddick talked of Brennan's 'lunacy' and 'derangement.' Lead or mercury poisoning would be a dandy explanation."

"So you think I've been experiencing Brennan's symptoms? Shouldn't I have felt crazy?"

"Delirium is a symptom of long-term exposure. Maybe you just haven't been in the old house long enough."

I thought about that, and didn't like my conclusions. "If that's why—okay, let's say Brennan had an old war wound that—"

"He didn't fight in the Revolution. Lived here the whole time."

"A hunting accident, then. Or he was taking doses of mercury for too long. Whatever. Don't you see? If Polly Carson's the ghost that Beth Ann saw, and the symptoms *don't* belong to Polly, then—"

"Right. The house has *two* ghosts." Miss Maggie grinned from ear to ear, delighted by the prospect. "Furthermore, I believe Brennan's exposure to heavy metals wasn't accidental, and that his death wasn't a shooting mishap. Because why else would he be trying to get your attention, Pat? Ghosts don't walk for nothing. Bet on it, he was murdered."

> *"See, there he lies,*
> *But ere he dies*
> *A doctor must be had."*

—from *Recollections of Samuel Breck*, quoting from a mummer's play he witnessed in America, circa 1780

December 25, 1783—The Public Hospital

AN HOUR LATER, SHAVED and fed, I left the house for my "appointment." I'd said that merely to avoid attending devotions and meeting Mr. Tyler, yet I saw an opportunity—once Elizabeth and her children were at church, with Jim and Sam at their trades, and the doctor otherwise occupied—to return to the house and search Brennan's room. At last, my quest here in Williamsburg might prove fruitful.

Until then, I should have liked to pass the time at the Eagle with a pint, but last night's antics had put no coin in my pocket and this year I had no master to furnish my Christmas box (though Mr. Ivey had never been generous). So I contented myself to look in at shop windows. In Norfolk, some few merchants—Catholics, for the most part—refused to unlock their doors Christmas Day or Twelfth Night, but on Williamsburg's Main Street, all were open.

Yet as I strolled along, my thoughts played through the murder of John Brennan, now picturing Dr. Riddick watching from the darkness of the Market Square at our backs, perhaps seeing what we were too close to observe. Or perhaps raising a gun himself, firing in unison with the others. He owned no weapon as far as I knew, but might have taken Jim's musket. Yet the finest marksman could not be certain of accuracy with such a gun at such a distance. Unless his aim was not for Brennan, but for another.

No, I thought. Doctors knew other means of ending life, more assured. Means that might not be questioned. I found I'd turned my steps back toward the college. I walked a block farther, to Henry Street, where I'd not be seen from the Carson house as I made my way to the hospital.

Williamsburg boasted fine public buildings. The hospital did not number among them. 'Twas large—situated alone in a square block, occupying half its width—but the structure had none of the grace of the capitol or college buildings, nor even of the small town hall. Moreover, the roof was in need of new shakes and many of the window panes were broken or missing altogether. Paint flaked from sill and jamb. Sheep often grazed upon the front green, yet near the edifice bramble and thistle grew high amidst the grasses. Their thorns pierced the wool of my stockings and caught hold of my britches and coat as I made my way along the rear of the building. I might be seen from perhaps three houses here, far fewer than in front, and I hoped these residents would be too occupied to gaze from their windows.

For the same reason, I thought, the doctor would chose a room on this side. The first course of windows were too high for me to look in, so I scanned the ground for small stones, tossing them through the openings, calling his name softly as I walked along. Often the stones rebounded with a metallic sound. I glimpsed black iron bars inside the sills.

At the window by the east yard, Riddick's head and shoulders appeared to one side. "Mr. Dunbar? What is it, sir? Does someone require a doctor?"

"No, sir, but I require a word with you, regarding what you saw last night at Mr. Underwood's."

No reply came at first, so I wondered if he'd heard me. Then, "Come over to the yard. I'll meet you there." Annoyance colored his tone.

The yard was surrounded by a tall wooden fence with little space between its planking and no gate, to discourage the deranged from wandering off while taking the outside air, I supposed. I was puzzling how Riddick had gotten in when the two planks nearest the bricks swung out from the bottom. The doctor, behind them, beckoned to me. I was larger of frame than he, and 'twas with difficulty that I squeezed through the opening.

The yard was wide as the building, the ground muddy and uneven at this end. A forest of weeds hid the far corners. When I stood straight and faced the doctor, I was taken aback by his raiment. He wore not his coat, but a large wool overshirt, as a common laborer might wear on a cold day. 'Twas chestnut brown in color, but a good portion stained darker, and it gave off a repelling odor.

"What is your query, sir?" he asked in a low voice, peevish and impatient.

"Mrs. Carson said that you'd witnessed Mr. Brennan's murder last evening."

"And yourself as well, Mr. Dunbar, eh?" He nodded. "Jim practiced his speeches in our room the last week, and hearing them last night, delivered with his particular cough—"

"Did you see who shot John Brennan, Doctor?"

He stroked his chin with a frown. "I did not. My attention was for Brennan alone. His reactions to your play aroused my deepest interest. I can, however, absolve Jim of the murder, as well as the other man who fired a pistol."

This told me that Riddick could not identify those in our troupe other than Jim and myself, and possibly Sam. I vowed to give none away. "But sir, if you didn't see who—"

"The ball that killed Mr. Brennan was too large for a pistol. 'Twas from musket or rifle." The doctor smiled with conceit. "Science, sir, can show us what is missed by the human eye. I can also tell you that the ball entered Brennan's chest here." He placed his fingers above his right breast. "It broke the top rib, pushing that broken piece left, into the bronchi, that is, the windpipe leading into the lungs. This may indicate that he was shot by the man on his right side—the one in the long black coat. Mr. Walker, I believe. Yet, Brennan was moving about, and may have turned the instant he was shot, so—"

"You performed surgery? Was he alive after—" I nearly said "after we left" but caught the admission before it reached my lips.

"Would that it were so and I could have saved the man. But no, he was dead when I first examined him on Captain Underwood's steps."

"*First* examined?" I'd put importance to the phrase only because I'd put memory to the fetor of his garment. 'Twas a smell I'd met on battlefield and in camp, and more to the point, in the elder Thomas Carson's tent two years past: the smell of death. "You're examining him now—performing surgery on his corpse. Here. This morning. And this is not the first time you've—"

Riddick hushed me with a finger to his lips, glancing at the high fence as if it could hear. "Come, let us discuss this inside, Mr. Dunbar." When I made no move to follow, he said, "Please, sir. I would not have you think ill of me. I'm a doctor, and want nothing more than to save the lives of others with Brennan's affliction. What I learn may cure derangement someday. And if the ailment ever besets a child of yours, sir, you'll thank me. But I'll not speak of this in the open."

I hesitated, my curiosity warring with my aversion. "This, er, examination—will it tell you why Brennan turned lunatic?"

Riddick, nervous at the delay, nodded. "Quite possibly. That is, I've found signs on the corpse that I've seen in similar cases. And I believe his madness may be related to his murder."

Curiosity won out. I told the doctor to lead on. We went through the side door. He set the rusty bolt after us.

The hall smelled of old urine and filth. Lining the passage were doors, their small square windows allowing scant sunlight through. Dust swarmed in the rays like bees.

Riddick opened the first door to our left. The room was larger and brighter than any jail cell I'd seen, yet with barred window, it reminded me of such. The walls had been whitewashed, though some past resident had covered the bricks with drawings in charcoal, some quite good, some grotesque and horrifying. The space was cold as outdoors, owing to the broken panes, yet I was glad of the air, for the cell reeked of death. Brennan lay in the center of the floor, with no pallet between him and the rough boards. His britches were the only clothing on him.

During the war, I'd seen the chests of men ripped asunder by musket balls, yet I'd never grown numb to the sight, nor had I any desire to observe Dr. Riddick's further violations of the man. My gaze did not tarry. I crossed to the window, to take more wholesome breaths.

"Before beginning my dissection," the doctor said, "I thoroughly examined Brennan's skin and orifices. He'd been losing teeth this last month, you'll remember. Those remaining in his mouth are loose, and his gums marked with blue lines. I've seen this evidence twice before with my own eyes, and read of a similar case in London. All three persons showed signs of derangement. I believe all three were poisoned."

"Poison!" I faced the doctor then. "Cassava?"

"Cassava?" His echo showed his confusion, but then he seemed to gain enlightenment and murmured to himself, "Could it be? How odd." Aloud he said, "No, no, Mr. Dunbar. Do not mistake my reaction. The poison of the cassava root is quick, killing within the hour. John Brennan's mania was not brought on by cassava. But why ask? The plant's not native to Virginia. In truth, since the British embargoes, even the cassava meal—the tapioca—is too costly for all save the gentry."

"I knew of a man poisoned with it," I said cautiously. "The word came to mind."

Dr. Riddick stroked his chin once more, surveying my face as if I were one of his lunatic subjects. Then he turned to where he'd stacked Brennan's jacket, waistcoat, and shirt, all in a neat pile against the wall. Lifting the coat free, he plunged his hand into a pocket and brought forth a leather pouch, smaller than the one Brennan had used for his snuff, yet I presumed it served the same purpose.

The doctor offered the pouch to me. "I think, sir, that you should look inside."

I still thought to find snuff, doctored, perhaps, by the addition of a poison. I remembered the fine white particles that had been in Brennan's pouch and box when I'd discovered them outside his window.

In this small bag was a piece of brownish-black tuber. 'Twas much dried out, and flaked as I moved it about, but I knew what I held. I'd come to Williamsburg to find just such proof.

"Cassava root, is it not?" Dr. Riddick asked. "Until you made mention of it, I'd not realized. Now sir, as I do not believe in coincidence, pray tell of the man you knew poisoned by this substance, and how you came to live in the same house with a fellow who carried about a bit of the root in his pocket."

I was in debt to the doctor for completing one of my tasks, yet, though I resolved to answer his queries, I could not tell all. "The man was Lieutenant Thomas Carson. His death was thought to be from cramp colic. On bringing Mrs. Carson news of her husband's death, I met John Brennan. He seemed familiar, but I'd returned to camp before I remembered seeing a soldier who resembled Brennan passing our tents on the morn of Tom's death. I deemed it nothing more than resemblance, until I found shavings of this root within the lieutenant's canteen, and a small lump of it on the ground where his tent had stood. Still, I did not know what I'd found, and no man in my company could put a name to it. We thought it a purge that Tom had taken when he'd first become ill. For the next year, I showed it, I think, to every doctor in the army. One from Connecticut had suspicions of its true nature, and brought me to the Rhode Island regiments, to a Negro soldier who'd been raised in Jamaica. He knew it straight'way."

Frowning, the doctor gazed from the window a moment. "I'd not swear that shavings of cassava in a canteen could kill a man. Still, his food may have been poisoned as well. So, you knew of this, and suspected Mr. Brennan. What did you do?"

"Quite properly, I reported to my captain." The memory brought a bitter laugh. "Captain Underwood, of course. He thought it impossible that one of his officers might have been murdered, moreover, with a poison procured only in the tropics. Yet, he said he would take the affair in hand. I inquired after the matter thrice more, and was at last told that Underwood's superiors ordered that, with no sound evidence against Brennan, and with the company surgeon swearing to cramp colic, the business should be dismissed. The war was over, Underwood explained, and officers were more concerned with petitioning for their pensions than with an *imagined* case of murder. We were furloughed out less than a month after, so no action was taken."

"Yet you came to Williamsburg."

I merely nodded. Williamsburg had not been my choice—'twas too near Norfolk. I'd meant to head west, start life anew in the mountains, but the memory of Elizabeth, and John Brennan in the same house, and the innocent faces of Polly and young Tom—I'd vowed to find the truth. And now I held a bit of it in my hand. John Brennan *had* been Thomas Carson's murderer. Yet, who'd been Brennan's? And why? "What poisoned Brennan, Doctor?"

Riddick came out of his reverie. "Of the two men I've seen with similar signs—one worked with quicksilver daily in his trade, and the other frequently took a powder of mercuric salts to treat syphilis."

"Quicksilver is no poison—"

"Ah, but it is, if taken in sufficient quantity. Indeed, many physics turn poison in quantity. But there is another theory as well involving quicksilver. Neither of the men showed corruption of the intestines, yet both had much liquid in their lungs. Both exhibited increasing mania before death. The physician attending the London case surmised that breathing mercuric powder may bring about derangement. I would go further to say that breathing the steam of heated quicksilver might produce the same result, though in Mr. Brennan's case, the powder is most likely. Either he took it himself, mistakenly sniffing in a bit with each dose, or someone put it in his snuff. Perhaps the same man who fired the killing shot last night."

I said nothing, thinking instead of the one man I knew who took powder each day for a case of French disease gotten during the war. Sam Walker.

FOURTEEN

Beth Ann came to tell us dinner was almost ready. "Grandmom wants everyone in the parlor again." As she delivered the message, her gaze sought out my ring finger. She must have noticed her dad's mood when he came back, and no doubt my eyes were still a bit red—they felt totally wrung-out. Like Miss Maggie said, Beth Ann was a bright kid, capable of putting two and two together. I wondered how she felt, seeing the ring, realizing the engagement wasn't off. Yet.

That "yet" had popped into my head way too easily, I decided. I shoved it back into my subconscious, not wanting to deal with it. At least, not on an empty stomach.

We headed down the hall, Miss Maggie making a pit stop at the bathroom while Beth Ann and I waited for her in awkward silence. Then, as we were about to step through the doorway into the main house, Beth Ann said, "If we hold hands as we go downstairs, and all through dinner, someone's bound to ask why."

Before Miss Maggie could protest, I cut in with, "She's right." I wasn't anxious to relive the symptoms, especially now that I knew I could go Looney-Tunes from them, but keeping Hugh from discovering that I was in touch with the Other Side was still a priority, now more than ever. And I couldn't put Beth Ann in any position where she'd have to lie to her father for me.

"Here's what we'll do," I announced. "Beth Ann, can you stay within arm's reach? If I start feeling sick, I'll find some reason to touch you that won't look too weird. Okay?"

She nodded, relieved to be free of embarrassment.

So we trooped downstairs, me slightly behind Beth Ann so I could slap a hand on her shoulder at a nanosecond's notice. Oddly enough, though, I didn't have to touch her once, not even in the evil front hall, where we lingered because Cherry was blocking the parlor doorway. Sans leather jacket, she wore a tight V-necked red sweater that showed off breasts nearly as impressive as her lips.

I told myself to be compassionate. Her hubby was in intensive care, and here she was, spending Christmas with the family of his girlfriend. I imagined she felt more like an outsider than I had in that room with the Lees last night.

I heard heavy feet on the stairs and glanced up. Hugh was coming down, hands in his pants pockets, looking like a forlorn puppy who's had his nose rubbed in a paper-training mistake. Like a puppy, I found it impossible to stay mad at him. Then again, also like a puppy, I couldn't help wondering if he had any idea what part he played in the smelly stuff on his nose.

As he looked down on us, seeing me next to his daughter, his paternal smile curved up the ends of his mustache. At the bottom of the steps, he draped an arm over each of our shoulders and said, "How're my girls?"

I glanced at Beth Ann, to find her glancing at me the same instant. She rolled her eyes. I laughed.

"Is the other man still up there?" Cherry interrupted.

"You mean Evelyn?" Hugh asked. "Yeah. He's changing. What do you need him for?"

"Oh, nothing. Never mind." With that she swung around and went into the parlor. With a frown, Miss Maggie watched her go.

"Is Sunday okay?" That was Hugh, talking to me.

"Sunday?" I echoed, confused.

"For the King's Arms. I couldn't get us in tomorrow, but they had a five-thirty opening on Sunday."

"Oh. Sure, that's fine." At least it gave me time to think how to talk to Zela with Hugh breathing down my neck.

"If you're going to the King's Arms, Pat," Miss Maggie said, "you should try the game pie. And the peanut soup—"

"That's my favorite," Hugh said.

Miss Maggie agreed with a nod. "And you'll love the Sally Lunn bread. I'll have to take you to one of the other taverns for lunch."

While she was rhapsodizing about tavern meals—did I mention that, next to history, food is her pet topic? Or ahead of history?—anyway, while she was salivating, I saw Evelyn above on the stair landing, slipping through the opening to the rear hall. He was back in britches—the elegant black brocade he'd worn to church. His jacket hung over his arm as he buttoned a gold waistcoat.

I decided not to tell Cherry he was headed for the kitchen. This close to dinner, she wouldn't be welcome there anyway.

Five minutes later, we were all called into the dining room, and not a moment too soon. Hugh and Miss Maggie had gone through all the tavern menus, giving their opinion of each item saying things like, "The sweet potato muffins and cheddar biscuits at Christiana Campbell's are so good, I could fill up on them and skip the entree," until I was so hungry, I was ready to eat gruel. Cold gruel.

Glad and Evelyn stood by the table in their finery, Glad looking as Christmassy as Miss Maggie's sweatshirt, with her red dress, silver jewelry, and sprig of evergreen pinned to her white bonnet.

I gave them extra credit for food presentation again. The table was decked out in fine china, with a handpainted soup tureen in the center. At the top and bottom were platters of chicken cutlets and fish filets, decorated with green leaf lettuce and red peppers. In a square around the tureen were bowls of spoonbread, baked beans with bacon, cooked spinach, and the beet-fishes I'd carved, breaded and deep-fried, all garnished with fresh lemon, orange, and herbs. Only seven offerings instead of ten like last night—a sensible cutback in my opinion, and still more than enough food.

Glad waved her hand toward a card table that had been set up near the windows. Sunlight streamed over a white tablecloth and three settings, though not fine china like the main table. I supposed they only had twelve settings and we now had—I counted places: thirteen. Thirteen? Aunt Sophie would have pulled someone in off the street to avoid that number.

"We had to add a second table," Glad said. "Since the men wouldn't fit well, and I wouldn't want to split a couple, I thought perhaps Beth Ann, Miss Maggie, and, er, Cherry could sit there."

"No!" Beth Ann cried, then, when everyone stared at her, she added, "I want to sit with Pat—and Dad."

Luckily, Hugh was too busy being a father to note the hesitation. "Beth Ann, don't act like a baby."

"Chill, bro." Acey came forward, looking casual in faded jeans and maroon turtleneck under a woven hooded pullover. The design looked South American, though I couldn't say which country. "Sachi and I can sit with Cherry. I know how much Miss Maggie likes to be near the food."

"And how!" She was already leaning over the table, sniffing the aromas and smacking her lips. Only Cherry looked less than thrilled with the seating arrangement.

So we settled in—Evelyn and Rich at either end of the big table, Glad, Beth Ann, me, and Hugh on one side, and Miss Maggie, Horse, Foot, and Irene on the other. Thus, I got my first good view of the newest arrival.

Irene was supposed to be three years younger than Acey. She looked more like eighteen. Her long dark blonde hair was pulled back into a braid and rampant freckles gave her face a clean-cut farm girl look. She was my height (short, that is), though her slim build made her seem taller, as did her choice of wardrobe—black tights under a longish sparkly blue sweater that hung straight over her small hips. Her wide blue eyes seemed to carry a permanent expression of incomprehension, making her look the quintessential dumb blonde. I wondered how much of it was real and how much put on to lure rich doctors like Foot.

Glad, still standing, smoothed the satin of her dress. "We'll start with a turkey pottage. More of a stew than a soup, really." She recited the ingredients, looking at Foot as if to let him know she did it for his sake. "Pat, would you mind serving, since you're closest?"

Hugh had rested his hand on my leg when we sat down and now let go to help pass the cup-sized servings. No symptoms hit. While I dispensed the pottage, Evelyn filled glasses with white wine or water. The satin of Glad's dress rustled as she took her seat.

The pottage was delicious, though very filling. Doling it out in cups was smart. I vowed to take tiny portions of everything else, so as to pace myself to get through the next three courses. Not easy with the spoonbread, a cornmeal pudding that had become my favorite Southern food in the last year.

As everyone satisfied initial hunger pangs, the only sounds were spoons brushing against china and the slurping of pottage. Then Horse—first one done—set down his spoon and said, "All right, Magnolia. Now that we've got you where you won't run away, you have to tell us how we did on your little medical quiz. Was it lead poisoning or mercury, or were we off base entirely?"

"Lead poisoning?" Evelyn echoed, interested but out of the loop.

Miss Maggie dabbed at her mouth with her napkin. "A little game of Name-That-Diagnosis we were playing earlier. Truth is, I don't know. A friend of mine had those symptoms for a while." Her eyes twinkled over the table at me. "I was simply curious."

"If your friend consulted a physician—" Rich began.

"She couldn't at the time. However, I don't think she's had the symptoms since." A questioning glance in my direction. I returned a minuscule shake of the head.

"Odd you should mention the subject," Evelyn said as we commenced filling our plates. "Last October, when I began work on this house—several things needed mending before Glad and I could move in—well, anyway, my assistant became ill and lead poisoning was suspected. His symptoms were always at their worst while he was here, yet all sources of lead had been removed from this building during the last four decades. Then his blood tests came back normal, so we never did find out what had made him sick."

"No one else fell ill?" Rich asked.

"No," Evelyn replied, "and neither Glad nor I have had problems since."

"What exactly are these symptoms?" Sachi asked, with an attitude projecting both intelligence and common sense, and a voice projecting a personal interest.

Rich turned in his chair to answer. "Depends on how the substance is introduced—ingestion or inhalation—and whether the case is chronic or acute. Generally, the patient will have a metallic taste in the mouth, headache, abdominal pain—"

"And others that shouldn't be mentioned at the dinner table," Horse cut in delicately. "Why do you ask, Sachi?"

"Oh, I—" She gave us all a shrug as if to apologize for bringing up the subject. "When I first arrived, I went upstairs to use the bathroom, and I felt really sick when I was in the upstairs hall."

"You didn't tell me," Acey said.

"I didn't want you playing doctor," Sachi replied. "I only felt sick in the hall, not in the bathroom or down here. It was weird. I didn't have a metallic taste, or even a stomach ache, but I *did* have a bad headache, and a feeling like—panic."

"Anxiety attack," Foot pronounced. "You were nervous about coming here uninvit—that is, without calling first."

Sachi nodded. "That's what I thought, until you started talking about people getting lead poisoning in this house."

"You wouldn't have severe symptoms right away in a chronic case." Horse reached for more baked beans. "But, I wonder—Pat got a nasty headache up there yesterday afternoon, right outside Foot's room."

Hugh raised his eyebrows at me. "Yeah?"

"Wasn't so bad," I murmured. "Forgotten by the time you arrived. Or I *would* have let you play doctor." I was hoping to divert him from my poisoning symptoms. It worked better than I thought. Under the tablecloth, he ran his fingers along my thigh, sending pleasurable little spasms up my body. I sent my free left hand on a seek-and-postpone mission, before I was tempted to excuse myself and drag Romeo upstairs to a bedroom.

"Headaches brought on by holiday stress," Foot mumbled while cutting his fish filet into bite-sized squares.

"Maybe not," Acey said. "When I was at William and Mary, they rented this place to college students. One guy kept getting sick, until he finally had to go home for the semester. This might be a case of Sick Building Syndrome."

I almost laughed out loud. If only they knew how sick this building was, and why. I did feel comforted that I wasn't the sole victim. Odd, though, that the symptoms didn't hit everyone. I leaned forward so I could see around Hugh and past Rich's shoulder to where Sachi sat, wondering what we had in common outside of double-X chromosomes. We were different ages and ethnicity. Or was that the reason she *wasn't* having any of the same symptoms I'd had during dinner last night?

Her fork was in her left hand, I noticed, yet she handled it awkwardly. Her right hand was under the tablecloth, as was Acey's left. Aha! Sachi had figured out the Lee-touch antidote.

I got a glimpse of Sachi's left forefinger and the ring it bore: gold with a red stone.

Cherry spoke up, interrupting my speculations. "To tell the truth, I haven't been feeling so hot since I got here. In fact, if you'll excuse me, I'm going to pay your bathroom another visit." She made a hasty exit, high heels clopping up the stairs to the second floor.

"Anxiety-related," Foot diagnosed, "what with her husband and all."

"I hope so." Evelyn stood to retrieve the wine bottle and water decanter from the sideboard and began refilling glasses. "I've checked everything I could think of. Had the furnace cleaned, chimneys swept, and all the vents vacuumed. Made them test for radon and had carbon monoxide detectors put on all the floors—"

"From what I know of the Colonial Williamsburg Foundation," Miss Maggie said through a mouthful of beets, "they don't let just anyone make maintenance decisions. So, Evelyn, what do you do when you aren't wearing britches?"

Everyone laughed, even Evelyn, though he went crimson to his ears.

Glad answered for him, with pride in her voice. "Ev's a historical restoration architect for the Foundation. He only fills in as an interpreter if he's needed. Like this week when half the staff was down with the flu."

"Right." Evelyn topped off Foot's water glass. "That's how I met Glad. The day after she became a volunteer, she came into the housing office to ask why the Carson house was vacant and could she arrange to live there. I was within earshot and heard her say she was a direct descendant of Elizabeth Carson. Gave me an excuse to call her and invite her out for coffee to discuss her genealogy. In the name of research, of course." His eyes twinkled as he gazed across the table at Glad. She smiled back. I sighed as I do when romantic movies have happy endings.

Rich ruined the moment. "Lucky for you, Mom. If not for that chance meeting, you'd never have moved here."

"Nonsense." Evelyn replenished Rich's wine. "The Foundation would have let Glad rent the house, and at a reasonable rate. Better to have the place occupied than sitting empty. No, I'm the lucky one." He turned back toward Glad. "Well? We might not get a more appropriate cue."

She nodded, pushing back her chair to stand, smoothing her satin overskirt. Evelyn set down decanter and bottle and went to stand by her side. Glad cleared her throat. "We have an announcement." Superfluous, but it gave her time to lick her lips and swallow, and glance at Evelyn. By the time she spoke, everyone knew what was coming. "We're going to be married."

I opened my mouth to congratulate them, but Glad didn't give me a chance.

"January sixth, actually. Twelfth night. In keeping with the colonial custom." As an afterthought, she added, "You're all invited, of course."

Miss Maggie broke the shocked silence by raising her wine glass. "To Gladys and Evelyn: happiness and a long life together." Then she sent one of her teacher-warning looks around the room.

"I'll second that," Acey said as she and Sachi hoisted their glasses in unison. "We'll be there, Mom."

I nudged Hugh with one arm while joining the toast with the other. He followed suit, but didn't open his mouth, so I said, "We will, too. Congrats."

Beth Ann lifted her water as Horse voiced a deep, "Huzzah!" and downed his wine in a gulp. With a sigh, Rich jumped on the bandwagon.

All eyes went to Foot, including Irene, who was fingering her glass stem, waiting for his cue. He scowled and pushed back his chair. "I've had my fill of this meal." He left the room and we heard him take the stairs two at a time.

Before awkwardness set in, though, we heard two cries from above—a masculine "Hey!" followed by a feminine "Let go!" This last was repeated twice more amid sounds of scuffling.

Hugh was out of the room a second before Horse, and both were up to the stair landing by the time Acey, Beth Ann, and I entered the hall.

"Stop her!" Foot yelled from above. "She's a thief!"

You'd think two men the size of pro linebackers could stop one woman. Problem was, Cherry used her teeth, fingernails, and high heels to full advantage, kicking Hugh hard on the shin as she pushed past him. Horse held onto her for a few seconds longer, but she managed to squirm around and knee him in the groin. He went down and she disappeared into the rear hallway.

"Go after her!" Acey called. "I'll head her off in the kitchen."

Foot and Hugh took up the chase. Beth Ann ran after her aunt. I felt immediately ill and clutched my stomach.

Miss Maggie was beside me, whispering in my ear. "Hurry, get to the kitchen."

I obeyed, pushing past Rich, Evelyn, and Glad as they tried to see what was going on. Beyond them, Irene stood by her place, not sure what to do. Sachi stood by Beth Ann's, holding the chair for support, obviously feeling as awful as I did.

I hooked my hand around her upper arm. "Come with me. Quick!"

She responded to the urgency in my voice, letting me pull her through the pantry and into the kitchen. My nausea vanished the moment I crossed the threshold and I turned to Sachi. "Do you feel better?"

She nodded, amazed, but said only, "I have to help Acey."

We heard feet thumping down the circular stair. Acey crouched, waiting for the door to open. When it did, she launched herself in such a beautiful flying tackle, I pictured her playing football with her brothers, and beating them. Cherry sprawled face down, arms flailing. Sachi grabbed one wrist, I took the other, and Beth Ann sat on the woman's feet.

By the time Foot and Hugh came through the door, Cherry had given up struggling.

All of them were breathing hard, but Foot managed to bellow, "Someone call the police!"

"Go ahead, call them!" Cherry shouted. "Wait 'til I show them what I found in your luggage. I *knew* one of you tried to kill Kevin. Now I have proof."

Acey sat back, taking her weight off Cherry. "What are you talking about?" Then to Foot, "What does she mean?"

Cherry answered. "Get everyone off me and I'll show you."

"Let go of her," Acey said. We did, though Hugh moved himself between Cherry and the outside door. Having seen what she did to Horse, I moved to Hugh's side.

Cherry stood, running her hands down her leather pants to get the kinks out. Then, with a grin, she reached down her sweater and from her cleavage brought out a small brown prescription bottle.

Foot made a grab for it, but Cherry yanked it away. "They're antidepressants," she said. "Like what poisoned Kevin."

"Now some with Feasts do crown the Day,
Whilst others loose their Coyn in play."

—Titan Leeds, *The American Almanac*, December 1714

December 25, 1783—The Hunt

I RETURNED TO MRS. Carson's house, still intent on examining Brennan's room while my landlady and her children were at Christmas devotions.

Brennan's room was still cold, one window yet open a crack. His bed had been stripped of blanket and ticking, and his spare shirt, waistcoat, and britches were laid out to air upon the ropes. His trunk stood empty.

I no longer needed proof of Brennan's role in the death of Thomas Carson, nor did I hope to find written evidence of the act. I now sought some clue as to how Brennan had been driven to lunacy, and why, if the poison would have killed him eventually, he'd been shot instead.

If Riddick was correct, then Brennan's first signs of madness were from mercuric salts mixed into his snuff. Indeed, 'twas likely the very reason he discarded the items, seeing them tainted. I presumed that he'd found no fault with the snuff, mint, and stores of tobacco remaining in his room, or he'd have thrown them out as well. Yet, I scanned these sacks first, as best I could without spilling out the contents. No contaminant was evident.

Nevertheless, after Brennan had the lock put on his door, his lunacy had progressed. How had the quicksilver been given him? He'd fetched his own water and food, and kept his new snuff pouch close to his person, as well as the key to his room.

His few possessions provided no answers, and I soon gave up the hunt in favor of another errand—paying a call on Alex at Dr. Galt's Apothecary.

When I arrived, the sole patron was Mrs. Hockaday, the young, proud wife of Matthew. She was saying, "Mary claims her monthly pain is so great, she cannot stand to cook or do her chores. I've given her sanicle root and some burnet—of course, one can't find balm flowers or shepherd's sprouts this time of year—"

Alex made sympathetic noises.

"She said they made her worse. Not that I believe it—sanicle has always worked for me. Matthew says she's lying—all slaves do when opportunity affords, he says. Yet, Mary does seem greatly pained, Mr. Fisher."

Alex nodded his understanding of her predicament. "Perhaps a different physic? Rue, I'd say, to loose the menses, with a bit of rhubarb, in case a costive bowel is to blame."

She frowned in doubt. "English rhubarb? The price has risen so since the embargoes."

"Anise, then? I can give you an ounce at four pence."

To this she agreed. Alex weighed the seed and dried rue, and when she'd gone, turned to me. "What will you have, Ben? A remedy for rum punch headache? Half the town's come in for such a cure this morn."

Assuring him to the contrary, I leaned across the counter and lowered my voice, lest Dr. Galt hear from his back room. "Do you remember the first day I came here, Alex?"

"I should say so. Asking after poisons. Had I not known you since Brandywine, I'd have called the constable straightway. As it were, I knew you to be the only man in Williamsburg who could fashion a decent toddy from army rations. Playing fiddle all the while."

"The poison I inquired about—cassava root. A piece of it was found in Brennan's pocket."

Alex let go a low whistle. "Not happenstance, I take it?"

Shaking my head, I asked, "You sell physics from the Indies. Do you obtain them all through the importers? Greenhow? Tarply?"

"Yes, of course. They employ the ships, after all." Alex rubbed his chin. "Though, if a man wished to avoid a documented transaction, he might pay a sailor to procure his desire."

"What about during the war?"

"Trade with the British islands was trickier, but from what I've heard, many a merchant vessel carried a variety of flags, depending on which ports they sailed for. Or, for all we know of Brennan, he might have come from the Indies himself and brought the root with him."

I conceded the point. "Another query for you: quicksilver. If taken in large quantity, will it turn poison?"

"Poisons again?" Alex's brow ascended a good half inch. "Nearly every medicine on these shelves will turn poison in quantity, quicksilver included. 'Tis sometimes a very fine line between cure and kill. Why do you ask?"

I spoke with care, so as not to betray the doctor. "I've heard that quicksilver can drive a man to lunacy if the powders are breathed in."

But Alex laughed. "Heard from Dr. Riddick, no doubt. His pet subject."

"Do you believe it?"

He gave a shrug of the shoulders. "I've not decided. Yet, I'll admit that I've begun telling my patrons to hold their breath when swallowing the powders, and to keep the liquid from candle and hearth lest it steam. No harm in caution. But if you're thinking Brennan's lunacy was brought on by quicksilver, well, he got it elsewhere. I sold him nothing."

"What of the others in our house?" I asked. "Jim and the doctor? Have they purchased it?"

"Ah, you think Brennan might have stolen it. Let me think." Alex took a scrap of homespun from beneath the counter and wiped the scale. "Doctor Riddick, of course, takes a small case of physics with him when he makes his calls. If used, he brings back payment from his patient. I believe quicksilver is one of his staples."

"Does he help himself to your stores?"

"When I'm not about. Many's the time he or Dr. Galt are called to a sickbed when the shop's closed."

"And Jim?"

"Bought an ounce of quicksilver not two months ago for a purge. As for the others, I know Mrs. Carson keeps the physic on hand for herself and children. And Sam, as you know, takes the salts regularly." Alex slapped the counter. "I forgot until this instant. Beginning of December, young Tom came in with the instruction that Mr. Walker had misplaced his powders and would like a new supply for the coming fortnight, which I sent along with the boy. There's your answer. Brennan must have taken Sam's powders."

FIFTEEN

Foot made another grab for the pill bottle, but Cherry stretched her arm away from him, holding him off with her other hand. She didn't realize she was putting the bottle right in front of Beth Ann, who snatched it out of Cherry's fingers, then retreated to her aunt's side.

At that moment, Miss Maggie led the rest of the troops in from the dining room. Horse was limping, but okay.

Acey, relishing the idea of an audience, crossed her arms across her chest as she took a step toward Cherry. "You weren't trying to *find* proof upstairs. You were *planting* it. Because if Kevin dies and it looks like suicide, you won't get his insurance money."

The accusation hit a nerve. Cherry's eyes practically flashed fire back at her. "He *didn't* try to kill himself."

"No? Well maybe *you* did. You've got the motive, honey."

"Uh, Aunt Acey?" Beth Ann interrupted. "This has Uncle Foot's name on it."

Acey took the bottle from her niece and read the label. "Wait, this isn't protriptyline."

"It's an antidepressant," Cherry maintained. "It says so on one of those little warning stickers on the side. I think. I mean, it says not to take it with *other* antidepressants, so I—"

"This is an MAO inhibitor," Acey said, as if that made everything clear, which I'm sure it did to the doctors present. For the rest of us, Acey added, "It's a different class of antidepressant entirely. Couldn't be mistaken for protriptyline in Kevin's blood." A classic LAG took over her face, aimed at Foot.

His response was to scowl and hold his hand out for the bottle. When Acey gave it to him, he fled through the open stairway door, slamming it behind him.

Acey turned to Rich and Horse. "Why's Foot taking MAO inhibitors?"

Horse shrugged. "He never told me about it."

"Me neither," Irene piped in.

Rich said nothing at first, but when everyone stared at him and Acey said "Out with it," he admitted he'd known.

"Last weekend, when we were down at the shore house, I walked into his room as he was packing the bottle Sunday afternoon. He tried to hide it, but I—"

"Why didn't you tell the rest of us?" Acey demanded.

"It was a matter of confidentiality and—"

"He consulted you professionally?"

"No. I—"

"Then you aren't his doctor. You're his brother. I'm his sister, who has a right to know he's taking a dangerous drug."

"Calm down, Acey." Rich ran a hand through his graying hair. "Foot assured me he's being careful—watching what he eats, self-monitoring his blood pressure, getting liver scans every other month. He'd been taking milder antidepressants, on and off since Katharine died, but they became ineffective, and he's intolerant of the other classes. This is the only medication that works for him—"

The beepy ringtone of a cell phone butt in. Six hands went to various pockets, six heads bent to check cellular screens.

Cherry was the one who called out, "Mine," reaching to unhook a tiny phone from her belt. She listened to the caller a moment, said "uh-huh" twice, then turned her back on the rest of us and walked over to the hearth. A few seconds later, she hung up and swung around, her face defiant once more. "I have to go back to the hospital. Kevin had a heart attack."

* * *

The next fifteen minutes were spent getting jackets and keys and moving cars. Hugh chivalrously volunteered to move mine for me. Or maybe he was still kissing up after the argument.

Perhaps on a similar guilt trip, Rich offered to take Acey to the hospital.

"No, thanks," she said. "I'm staying here."

Rich decided to go anyway, to find out what was happening on her behalf, he said. He left right after Cherry.

Glad shooed the rest of us from the kitchen and dining room, so she could get the second course out.

"I'll be right with you," Miss Maggie told me. "I've got a quick question for Evelyn first."

Irene announced her intention of trying to rout Foot from his hole and went upstairs. Acey said that she, too, was going up to the bathroom. Sachi followed her. Which left Beth Ann, Horse, and me to settle in the parlor, Horse leaning against the wall by the mantel, Beth Ann and me on the sofa.

Miss Maggie and Hugh joined us less than a minute later. Still wearing his jacket, Hugh came to stand behind the sofa, giving my neck a massage with one hand while returning my car keys with the other. The man had his priorities straight. So did I let myself wallow in the attention? No, I glanced to my right for Beth Ann's reaction, expecting to see her usual resentment.

Instead, she was staring at the fireplace, her thoughts obviously far away. Because of her Uncle Foot? Then again, except for the pill bottle episode, she hadn't uttered a word since we sat down to dinner. In fact, I recalled that she'd barely touched the chicken and spoonbread on her plate.

I'd promised Miss Maggie I'd talk to Beth Ann. I was debating if I should do it now when Irene walked in, once more full of doubt. The expression seemed wrong for her, maybe because it implied thought on her part.

"Francis says his door's stuck again," she announced. "I couldn't push it open. He told me to send Hugh up."

"I'll go, too," Horse said, heading for the door.

"He doesn't want you." Irene sat in one of the armchairs. "Or Rich or Acey. That's what he said. Just Hugh."

Maybe because they're both widowers, I thought, watching Hugh leave. Maybe Foot wanted to talk about his first wife. Problem was, another possibility occurred to me. One I didn't like at all.

I turned to the remaining sibling. "Horse, can I ask you a medical question?"

"Shoot," he said, resuming his pose near the hearth.

"Rich said Foot was intolerant of other classes of antidepressants. What does that mean?"

Horse put his hands in his pockets. "Drug intolerance can mean different things. Technically 'intolerance' means the body treats a substance as foreign and toxic. I knew of one patient who had such an intolerance to milk that sipping it would bring pain to the tissues in her mouth. But intolerance can also mean a medication's side effects are too hard for a patient to endure. Or the drug might cause an allergic reaction, like itchy eyes or a rash. Or an adverse physiological reaction." He grinned. "For instance, someone with a history of, say, thrombosis, might develop blood clots from certain medications. That's an intolerance."

He thought I was asking with my own case in mind, so I clarified my next question. "Can intolerance make a drug fatal? I mean, in one dose?"

"Oh. Well, assuming the prescribing physician performed a thorough examination, reviewing the patient's medical history, family, allergies, and other medications taken, including vitamins and herbals, *and* assuming the patient follows his doctor's and the pharmaceutical instructions regarding dosage, time of day and interaction precautions, then I'd say the chance of a reaction that severe is almost nil. Though not impossible. Of course, some patients never follow instructions. They take the doses wrong, or drink alcohol with their meds—"

"Like Dr. Weisel," Beth Ann broke in.

Horse nodded. "He should have known better. Alcohol with an antidepressant is a nasty combination."

"Uncle Foot didn't have ale last night or wine today," Beth Ann said.

"Right, and he didn't have caffeine. He also asked Ma the ingredients of everything she served, because he can't eat certain foods while taking MAO inhibitors."

"Sounds like they react with everything," I said. "I guess he'd have to watch what other drugs he took, too."

"Oh, sure, Foot knows all that." Horse came over to the sofa and hunkered down in front of his niece. "Don't worry about your Uncle Foot, Beth Ann. He's always been super-careful. And now that the rest of us know, we can help him."

* * *

Glad called us in to the second course. I paused in the hall near the stairs, signaling Beth Ann to wait with me. Hugh was on his way down, but my eye was on Sachi, two steps from the bottom, looking woozy, in pain, and about ready to hurl.

"Grab her arm," I whispered to Beth Ann, but she already had her hand on Sachi's wrist. I asked the latter if she felt okay. Her expression said Beth Ann had worked a miracle cure and she was opening her mouth to ask how. I interrupted with, "Where's Acey?"

"Taking a nap. Said she was up late last night." Her gaze, though, flickered not down the hall to Acey's room, but back up the stairs.

I had no time to question her. Beth Ann, talking fast and low so her father wouldn't hear, said, "Stay close to me and you won't feel sick. We'll explain later." And she pulled Sachi toward the dining room.

As soon as Sachi got between us, I felt sick again. I ran up four steps to intercept Hugh, hiding my obvious relief as I touched him by asking, "How's Foot?"

"All right." Hugh's furrowed brow belied his reply.

"He's not coming down?"

"He's better off alone." Hugh slipped his arm around my waist. "Come on. I'm hungry." As we passed beneath the mistletoe, he paused to plant a kiss on my forehead. Nothing passionate, just an I'm-glad-you-came-this-weekend kind of smooch. More sexy than he realized. Yet, I knew something was bugging him.

The table had the same layout as before—seven dishes—only this time slices of roast beef and ham sat where the fish and chicken had been earlier. In the center was a pyramid of small tarts, surrounded by plates of fritters, stewed apples, a high, round loaf of bread, and what seemed to be eggs cooked in brown gravy. I knew the look since my mom used to cook eggs in tomato sauce as a wintertime lunch for me.

Beth Ann put Sachi next to her grandmother—"so she doesn't have to sit at the card table by herself," she explained to Glad—and took my chair. I sat beside her, steering Hugh into Rich's seat. Everyone else settled down where they'd been before, leaving Foot's chair vacant.

Without him there, Glad gave a more abbreviated description of the foods, but I learned that the tarts were mince pies, the fritters were potato, and the bread was the infamous Sally Lunn. "From

Raleigh Tavern Bake Shop," Glad added. "I don't have the patience to make it right. Be careful, Magnolia. You know it's loaded with butter and eggs."

Miss Maggie had sliced off a thick slab, but innocently passed it to Horse beside her as if that's what she intended all along, saying, "Who else wants some?"

Once I'd tasted it, I understood. Sweet and rich, but light. Easy to pig out on. However, as Evelyn went around, pouring red wine, I again took tiny portions of each dish, telling myself there were two dessert courses to come.

Beth Ann, I noticed, took only ham, bread, and a fritter (I *had* to work on that kid's gastronomic courage). Hugh took everything, but wasn't shoveling it down as usual. I reached under the table-cloth and tickled his knee. It got a smile out of him, though no more than a two-point-four on the Mirth Scale.

"So, Sachi and Irene," Glad said, "it's so nice you could both come today. Tell us something about yourselves, won't you? Sachi, how long have you known Ann Carter?"

Sachi sent a hesitant glance around the table. "Six years. We met at a seminar on homeopathic medicine."

"You're a doctor, too?" Horse asked.

"Oh, no. I manage a pharmacy. Chain store. Though I'd like to own a little independent someday."

"Six years," Glad echoed. "What a shame Ann Carter never brought you down here before. Irene, dear, what about yourself?"

She blinked twice, as if it took that long to understand the question. "Oh, I work in a department store. That's why I couldn't come last night. We were open 'til midnight."

Glad cut her roast beef. "That's what Francis told us. How did you meet him? You've only known each other a few months, haven't you?"

"We didn't start dating until September, but I met him . . . let's see . . ."

"Last spring," Horse offered. "When Foot hired his new receptionist. He said you two were friends."

"Right." Irene stabbed a bite-sized piece of ham. "I used to stop by his office on my days off so Marcy and I could do lunch. Then he asked me out and, well, here I am."

Horse dunked his bread in his gravy. "Foot said Marcy played matchmaker. Set you and him up."

"She did?" Irene's wide eyes widened impossibly further as she sipped her wine. "She never told me that."

Miss Maggie, meanwhile, was staring through the pantry to the kitchen. She leaned forward, then back, as if to get a better angle. "Gladys, I believe someone's at your back door. Could've sworn I saw a shadow."

Evelyn nearly tipped over his chair as he dashed out. Miss Maggie followed him, and Glad stood, watching after them from the pantry doorway. I couldn't hear Evelyn and Miss Maggie after they passed into the kitchen and once more, I marveled at the house's weird acoustics.

Miss Maggie returned after a moment, carrying a small piece of paper. "Not the back door. The window across from it. I should have known—the sun's coming in on the west side, which is why I saw a shadow. Anyway, someone jammed this under the wood on one of the panes, on the outside facing in."

As she held it up, I exclaimed, "Another card! The Queen of Spades this time."

Evelyn came in, out of breath, his face grim.

"Did you see who left it?" I asked.

He looked at Glad, blinking nervously. "Just someone playing a prank—a child, that's all." He reached for the wine decanter. "While I'm up, more wine anyone?"

We settled back down to finish dinner, everyone's nerves frayed, with the possible exception of Horse, who helped himself to thirds on everything. I asked Glad a few questions about colonial Christmas foods, which she answered eagerly. Evelyn and Miss Maggie joined in, providing a comparison of traditional English fare (roast beef and mince pie) versus traditional Virginia fare (ham and apples). At Miss Maggie's urging, I gave them a rundown of traditional Italian menus and Sachi, traditional Japanese.

We at last pushed away from the table and filed back toward the parlor. Hugh headed for the stairs, but I grabbed his hand. "Hey, I want to talk to you."

"First let me check on Foot, okay?"

"Take your time," Miss Maggie told him. "I need Pat for a little while. And Hugh, send Acey down. Tell her we'll be in her room. Sachiko included."

"Will do." He squeezed my hand before letting go, then took the steps two at a time.

Since I didn't feel like puking, I knew I'd find Beth Ann at my side. Sure enough. Sachi was right behind her. Horse was already in the parlor, but Irene was still in the hall, chewing her bottom lip as she gazed up the stairs after Hugh, so I couldn't ask Miss Maggie what she had in mind.

"Come on," she urged, herding us along the hall to the back room. "Time's a-wasting."

With the afternoon waning and the remaining sunlight coming in the opposite side of the house, this room seemed downright gloomy. I switched on the vanity lamp. The sofabed, I noticed, hadn't been made—just the sheets yanked up over the pillows and the quilt straightened.

We waited for Acey, who came in a few seconds later, looking wide awake and not at all in need of a rest. I wondered what she'd been up to while we were snarfing down course two.

Miss Maggie shut the door and waved toward the bed. "Have a seat, all of you. I want to explain to Sachi why this house is making her sick."

With a sinking feeling in my stomach, I plopped down near the pillow end, next to Beth Ann.

"Sick?" Acey echoed, turning to her friend as they sat side by side at the bottom. "How sick?"

"Not in any way you could cure," Miss Maggie said. "Pat and Sachi have been experiencing the symptoms of heavy metal poisoning we talked about at dinner, but theirs are ghost-induced."

Acey opened her mouth, then seemed to change her mind.

Miss Maggie described my symptoms, telling how they go away in the newer part of the house, and whenever I touch a Lee.

"That's why you were all over Hugh last night," Acey said. "I didn't figure you for the clingy type."

I nodded. "I don't seem to have to touch Beth Ann like I do Hugh. I only have to be beside her, with no one in between."

"Women are better healers," Acey quipped. "You say this ghost doesn't bother anyone with Lee blood? Or do I mean Carson blood? What about Cherry and Irene? I'll bet good money Cherry didn't go upstairs because she was feeling sick. She just wanted to snoop. And I don't think Irene's felt ill since she got here—hard to say, though, with that dumb blonde act of hers."

"I have a theory." Miss Maggie paused for dramatic effect. She learned that teaching thirteen-year-olds. "I asked Evelyn about his assistant. The man's African-American."

"Like Zela," I exclaimed, then told Acey, Sachi, and Beth Ann who Zela was.

"That student I mentioned at dinner," Acey said. "He was black, too. And Sachi's Japanese-American. So we have a bigoted ghost?"

"A ghost reflecting the beliefs of the age," Miss Maggie said. "Remember, most blacks living in Williamsburg in the 1700s were slaves. Free blacks wouldn't have been treated better. And probably no one in this household had ever seen an Asian."

Acey nudged her chin towards me. "What about Pat? Your ghost has something against Italians?"

"Possibly." Miss Maggie gave me a once over. "Possibly something else altogether. I'll get to that in a minute."

I shook my head at her—a silent plea for her not to tell Acey about my Other World run-ins.

"I might have seen this ghost," Acey said. "If she's a teenager with scoliosis. Curvature of the spine."

"Aunt Acey," Beth Ann cried, "you saw Polly? Me, too."

Acey raised her eyebrows. "So she *wasn't* a figment of that brown ale I had as a nightcap? I saw her, all right. Right after I turned out the light and got into bed last night. She was standing in the doorway there—I could just see her in the moonlight coming down the hall. Which is why I thought it was a hallucination. I knew I'd closed the door. Her name's Polly?"

"Polly Carson," Miss Maggie explained. "Elizabeth's daughter. Was she doing anything?"

"She glanced down the hall, then back at me. Twice." Acey wrinkled up her nose as she tried to remember. "It was like she wanted to tell me something was happening, or someone was coming. The whole thing lasted all of three seconds, if that. Then she was gone, and I diagnosed her as a hypnagogic dream, brought on by stress. Or Evelyn's oyster pie."

"I didn't have the pie or the ale," Beth Ann pointed out. "We both saw her, Aunt Acey."

"Okay, we saw her." Acey pulled her legs up onto the bed and crossed them. "If I remember what Ma's told me, Polly didn't die until she was something like sixty. Why would she haunt this house as a teenager? And why is she making people sick?"

"She isn't," Miss Maggie said. "John Brennan is. The other ghost." She told who he was, how he died, and what she suspected about his poisoning.

"Wow. Two ghosts." Acey turned to Sachi. "We never had this much fun in Ma's other house. Well, if we want Brennan to leave you guys alone, we need to avenge his murder. How hard can that be? We'll hire a medium, have a seance, and ask Brennan who killed him. Then we impose the death penalty, which should be easy, since the culprit's already dead."

"Don't make fun, Aunt Acey. Just 'cause you don't believe in ghosts—"

"I do, Squirt. At least, I'm open to the possibility. I believe in a lot more things in heaven and earth than my brothers ever will.

But what can we do about it? Nothing I learned in med school prepared me to treat a poisoning-slash-shooting victim who's been dead more than two centuries."

Beth Ann frowned, then looked at me. "You can do something, can't you, Pat?"

"Like what?" Acey asked.

I was at a loss for words. Miss Maggie replied for me. "Pat has some special skills in this area. But I won't say anything more. It's up to her."

"Please?" Beth Ann said. "Before he makes you and Sachi seriously ill?"

I scanned the faces around me—concerned, curious, genuinely pleading. This last got me in the gut. Saying no to Beth Ann when she looked like that wasn't an option. "Okay, I'll try." To Acey, I said, "You can't tell Hugh about this."

"He'd freak," Beth Ann assured her aunt.

Acey crossed her heart, holding up her hand. "He won't hear a word from me. What are you going to do?"

"Beth Ann, give me your hands," I said.

"Aunt Acey, too. She might help."

"She might at that." I held out my left hand to Acey. "Make a circle with me and Beth Ann."

"Wait," Miss Maggie said to me. "I told Acey all this for a reason—so you'd have a doctor present if you decided to try another trance. I want Acey's hands free, in case you need help."

"You're sneaky, Miss Maggie."

I let go, but Acey merely switched her grip from my hand to my wrist, saying, "I can maintain contact and monitor your pulse at the same time. Trance, huh? Sachi, get my bag. Over on the floor there. Let me take Pat's vitals before she starts."

So I had my temperature, pulse, and blood pressure taken. Ninety-seven-point-four, seventy-nine, and one-thirty-five-over-seventy-two, respectively.

"A tad high," Acey commented. "Nervous?"

"Antsy," I replied. "Let's get this over with before Hugh comes looking for me."

We made our little circle and I closed my eyes.

Almost immediately I smelled wood smoke and the aromas of cooking food. I felt warmth on my face, cold air on the back of my neck, and something thin and heavy in my hands. The visuals formed more slowly, but when all was clear, I found myself before the dining room hearth, using my apron as a potholder to lift a cast iron kettle, about two gallons in size, filled with some kind of stew. Setting the pot beside me, I turned back to the tall trivet that had supported it, with the intention of stoking the fire beneath.

> *"O blessed Season! lov'd by Saints and Sinners,*
> *For long Devotions, or for longer Dinners."*
>
> —from *Poor Richard's Almanac*, December 1739

December 25, 1783—Home

'TWAS MOTHER'S CUSTOM AFTER devotions to linger in the church vestibule, greeting reverend, gentry, and the wealthier merchants. "My mother did the same," she once told me, "and thus made a good marriage for me. So shall I for you and Thomas." She felt, however, that children were best not present at such exchanges, and so my brother and I were always sent home ahead of her, to see to our chores.

Mother had planned an elaborate Christmas feast—twenty receipts to each course. Yet, with our small table and but one large serving platter, the bounty of each offering would be compromised. No matter, for only Mr. Dunbar was expected to partake with us. I feared more that our receipts should lack in other respects. We could afford little meat: three pigeons, a rasher of bacon, a leg of mutton—rather old and fatty—and a squirrel Tom had killed in our yard yesterday morn. All else needed to be fashioned from flour, sugar, suet, turnips, onions, potatoes, apples, and some few eggs.

I set to work at the hearth. From the squirrel, Mother had made a pottage, which was simmering over glowing embers and needed only to have the fire stoked beneath it, as did the pudding. Yet, when I reached for fuel, I found but two quarter logs beside the hearth.

"Tom, did you bring in wood this morning?"

He did not pause as he dragged a sack of potatoes to the table. "I did indeed. Four quarters."

"Four? Only four?"

"None of the rooms upstairs required more firewood and Mr. Brennan no longer has need of it. Mother brought three logs down from his room and set them there at hearthside. Two and a half, anyway. One was part burned."

"They're not there now."

"One of the lodgers must have carried them to his room." Tom made no move to find out, but settled himself at the table with a paring knife.

"Well, we haven't enough wood for dinner," I said. "You should have known we'd need more today. Go bring some in. At least another six."

He shook his head. "Mother told me to skin these potatoes and I mean to have half of them done when she walks through the door."

"So that you might get permission to go out with Mr. Walker on the eve of New Year, I suppose."

Tom smiled but did not move from his post. I might have mentioned that a shortage of firewood would earn Mother's anger as easily as a shortage of pared potatoes, but to save time, I went out to the woodpile myself.

Upon my return from church, I'd removed my gown and donned my apron, so to keep my best clothes from soiling. Now the wind on my arms made me shiver, and thus I ran from door to woodpile, cursing my brother when I found no split logs.

"Mistress, you shall catch your death on such a day." Mr. Dunbar was at the very end of the yard, beside the pile on which we discarded our ash, meat bones, and rubbish.

The unheralded sight of him made me first speechless, then as I noticed the half-burned log in his hand, curious. "Sir? Did you take that from the dining room hearth?"

"No, mistress." He came across the yard to the chopping stump. "I found it buried 'neath the ashes and garbage, as you can see from my appearance." The arms of his coat were indeed the worse for ash. He set the log upon the block and removed his outer garment, shaking and brushing it clean, then draped the coat about my shoulders. I no longer felt cold, but not for use of the raiment.

"Do you know, mistress, who might have hidden this wood where I found it?"

"No, sir. If that log is from Mr. Brennan's room—"

"It is. I saw your mother remove it this morning."

"Tom said that Mother placed it and two others beside the dining room hearth before church. They are not there now—the reason I've come out for more wood. I presumed one of the lodgers must have taken them to his room. Perhaps this was discarded for being half-burned." Poor excuse, I thought, for the waste of good fuel.

"No," Mr. Dunbar said. "I imagine we should find this fellow's two brothers deep within the ashes as well."

"But why?"

"Might I have the use of your hand ax, mistress?"

"I shall fetch it for you, sir." Gathering my skirts, I ran lightly to the door, and retrieved the hatchet from the closet beneath the stairs. I found Mr. Dunbar waiting for me just outside. He took the ax, offered his arm, and escorted me back to the stump.

"Stand clear." Wedging the blade into the burned end of the log, he gently tapped it upon the block until the length of wood split. From each half, forth from two places in the grain, silver liquid emerged, beading, as if the log bled from its wound.

"Quicksilver!" I cried, amazed.

"Aye." He stooped to inspect each wedge. "This was drilled, then the mercury poured in and the holes stopped with some brown substance." With one finger, he poked at the plug.

"Why?" I said again.

Mr. Dunbar sighed, musing, "To drive a man mad. Perchance, given time, to kill him. Once the lock was upon his door and his snuff could not be poisoned, this way was found."

My gasp brought him from his reflections. He stood and faced me. "Mistress Polly, who placed John Brennan's wood beside his door each day?"

"'Twas Tom's chore, though when he was off on some errand, I brought it up, or Mother, if I was needed elsewhere. Sometimes if Dr. Riddick was about, he carried it above stairs for us."

"How soon after the chopping was this done?"

"We swept the hearthstones first, and on market days, Mother had no time to attend to the wood until after the midday meal. She chooses which logs to place in each room, keeping the fattest downstairs for cooking. You and Mr. Walker get the next best, because Mother favors you, sir—" I felt a new blush and wished I could speak with more eloquence. "Then Mr. Parker and the doctor, and Mr. Brennan would get the worst."

Mr. Dunbar raised his brow. "Your mother did not favor Mr. Brennan?"

I remembered my silly fear when Mother first took him in, that she favored Mr. Brennan over much, but on reflection, I said, "No, on the whole, I believe not. He always got the worst of the wood, I know, even when officers from the army lodged with us, and Mother only charged them half."

"Is that so?" He seemed struck by the notion. "You mean after the surrender? American and French officers?"

"French then, sir. Americans before, for two weeks in September when the army was encamped nearby."

"And when Cornwallis occupied the town in June, did your mother lodge any of the Redcoats?"

"They gave us no choice. Five officers were assigned to us. Mother charged them each a shilling more for the week they stayed."

"Did Brennan consort with those officers, mistress?"

"Consort? He spoke with them, certainly. Sometimes late into the night. I could hear the murmur of voices, though not words. I recall him conversing with the Americans and Frenchmen in the same manner. He was friendly to all who slept beneath our roof."

"Between June and October of that year, mistress, was Brennan absent from town for any length of time?"

I thought back to the time. "Twice that I recall. Over one night both times. Seeking out a cheaper source of tobacco, he told us."

"Back to the logs—where are they kept until their apportionment?"

"Beside the dining room hearth, sir."

He frowned. "Once placed beside Brennan's door, did his wood remain long in the hall?"

"At times. Mr. Brennan was not always in his room. Even when he was, Mother told us never to knock upon his door to let him know. She said if he would make our work difficult, and not pay for the convenience, then he would reap no special courtesy from us. For myself, I think she might have been afraid of him after he became mad, and wished to protect us. You could ask Mr. Walker what he thought. He was in the dining room when she spoke. As was Mr. Parker, I believe."

"Ah." Mr. Dunbar's hands, I noted, were red from the cold. "Let us put this log back beneath the ashes for now. Promise me you will never burn it, or the two others, if you find them."

I promised, then watched him push the two wedges beneath the pile with the hatchet, after which, he said, "I shall split new wood for you, mistress."

"You needn't trouble, sir. I—"

"My pleasure, I assure you." With that, he bowed.

I thanked him with a curtsy, yet could not meet his gaze.

"However," he said gravely, "with this favor I wish to purchase your silence. Will you say naught of this to anyone? Even your family?"

I assured him that I would keep our secret.

SIXTEEN

First thing I heard was a whispered "Damn, we woke her." I had something like an ice cube against my neck and both my wrists were confined—Acey's fingers on my left wrist, something soft and tight on my right.

I opened my lids and saw Beth Ann's blue digital watch maybe three inches away. The blinking colon between the numbers made my eyes cross, so I looked at her hand instead. She still had a grip on me, in fact, was holding my arm across my chest. On my wrist, Acey's little blood pressure cuff beeped and deflated.

"Amazing!" Acey exclaimed. "One-ten over seventy. And your pulse came down to sixty-five. Temperature didn't budge. Whatever you're doing, Pat, it's better than meditation." Breaking the circle, she reached to pull her stethoscope from her ears. Sachi moved the business end of it—the ice cube—from my jugular, or whatever that pulse on the neck is called. Beth Ann let go and slouched back against the pillows.

Miss Maggie cut to the chase. "What did you see, Pat?"

She had me trained to start from the beginning and give minute details. I only editorialized on two points: "Dunbar looks familiar somehow, but I can't place him," and "Mercury in firewood? Would that work?"

Sachi fielded my last question. "Mercury vaporizes at a fairly low temperature—"

"She was a chem major," said Acey.

"Just having a leaky thermometer around on a hot summer's day could be dangerous," Sachi continued. "The fumes are heavier than air, so they wouldn't go up the chimney."

Miss Maggie added, "Fireplaces back then didn't have glass doors or metal curtains. In the winter, with no central heating or energy-efficient windows, I bet Brennan sat as close to the blaze as he could."

"What doesn't make sense here," Acey said, "is that none of this was common knowledge in the eighteenth century. Who would have known mercury fumes were poisonous?"

"There was a doctor living in this house," Beth Ann suggested.

"Not only that," Miss Maggie said, "he had an interest in mental illness."

"If he knew of the link between mercury and mania, that's your murderer." Acey laughed. "Rich would say all physicians are above suspicion, by virtue of their oath. I say always suspect doctors first, by virtue of their egos."

"Dr. Riddick may be the poisoner," Miss Maggie said. "He might even have fired the shot that killed Brennan. But how do we put the victim to rest so he'll stop bugging Pat and Sachi?"

I shrugged. "I didn't do much good. I couldn't find out enough."

"That was our fault," Acey said. "The pressure cuff woke you. Though you didn't flinch when Sachi put the thermometer in your ear."

"No." I took off the cuff and handed it to her. "I think, well, Polly seemed reluctant to tell me everything."

"Because of the promise she made to Mr. Dunbar?" Another Beth Ann suggestion.

I nodded. "Possibly. Her crush seemed strong enough that she might have held that promise sacred."

A knock came at the door, along with Horse's voice. "Ladies! Dessert's on."

Miss Maggie's ears perked up. "We'll continue this later." She bustled out.

I stood to leave, too, but Acey said, "I need a quick word with Pat. Beth Ann, stay close to Sachi, okay?"

Sachi closed the door behind them on the way out and Acey faced me. "Look, I know you don't want Hugh to find out any of this—and he won't hear it from me. After all, I was your attending physician—but you need to tell him yourself."

I shook my head, vehemently, as if to ward off the notion. "I can't. He hates when I—"

"He's afraid of the unknown. Big deal. Aren't we all? Why should he be pampered?"

"That's not—I promised him, last summer when we first started going out, that I wouldn't do the ghost thing anymore—"

"A promise you broke this weekend."

"Not my fault. I didn't *ask* for poisoning symptoms."

"I know." Those two words held all kinds of compassion. She sighed. "Listen, Pat. You've got a gift, on many levels. You can tap a part of your brain so off-limits to most people that quote-unquote modern science pretends it doesn't exist at all. And from a physiological point of view, you've got a method for dealing with stress that hypertension patients would kill for. Trust me, when perimenopause shit comes your way, if it hasn't already, using this natural tool you've got will save you tons of unpleasantness."

Acey hesitated, seeing if I wanted to respond. When I didn't—we Italians can be *molto* stubborn—she gently took my left hand and held it up between us. "Are you ready for what this ring represents?"

"What? You mean—?" I couldn't say Tanya's name aloud.

"I mean the whole 'til-death-do-us-part thing."

"Oh. Yeah, I'm ready." Despite my argument with Hugh, no second thoughts lurked in my mind about the actual commitment.

Acey laughed. "I think you are. If wearing Tanya's ring's a problem, better tell Hugh you want Great-Aunt Mildred's. No strings attached to that one." She released my hand. "My point here is, if you're heading into marriage, you want to avoid two things. Lying is one. You're going to have to lie if you keep secrets. The other is giving up any part of yourself for Hugh. Don't give up your gift for a mere man." She turned to leave. "Having planted that evil thought, I'm off to nosh sugar."

"Wait, I have a question for you."

Acey stopped with her hand on the door. "Fair enough."

"You and Sachi—you have matching rings."

Holding her fingers up, all bare, she said, "Me? I'm not wearing a ring."

"You were this morning."

Acey lowered her hands. "I could say you're mistaken. Or that I'd borrowed Sachi's ring and gave it back to her when she showed up—"

"Her fingers are thinner."

"Okay, here's a good one: Sachi and I are members of a secret cult that uses decoder rings."

"Are you gay?" I blurted out.

Acey blinked, swallowed, then let her smile return. "I was right. You've got guts. Most folks would go with 'Don't ask, don't tell' as being proper and not liable to get their tush burned. Not you. You came right out with the G-word."

"I'm not trying to pry. I'm only asking because—"

"You're wondering why, if I'm happily involved, married, or whatever term you prefer for the arrangement, I not only brought along a boyfriend this weekend, but one as scummy as Kevin Weisel?"

"Who ended up in intensive care within a few hours of his arrival."

That made her lose the smile and the attitude. Acey wearily leaned against the door, her face rife with conflicting emotions. "I wish I hadn't brought him. His own gluttony was to blame, but he shouldn't die because of it. Though, considering how else this *could* have played out, I won't say I'm completely sorry."

I wanted to ask her what she meant. She didn't give me a chance.

"It started as a joke. Of course. Lots of tragedies do. A month after I graduated from college, Rich tried to set me up with a doctor friend of his. I said no thanks, not interested, I'm headed for med school. Rich didn't take that threat seriously. I'm not sure any of my brothers did, but Rich was the worst. Understand, he'd been playing sitcom-dad to the rest of us since Ma got divorced. He figured I'd wimp out halfway through my first semester and want a hand-picked Prince Charming waiting in the wings to whisk me off to the land of babies and minivans. Rich's paternal skills at work." Acey drew in a deep breath. "Sorry, tangent city. Back to the story."

I sat down. My legs were starting to ache. Way too much stress, I decided.

Acey continued, "For our Labor Day cookout that year, Ma, bless her soul, called to warn me that Rich wanted to invite his doctor friend to dinner. I said, 'Tell him I'm bringing a date.' A male friend of mine from school went in on the joke with me. Unfortunately, John was too nice and a med student to boot. Rich approved. I craved a higher annoyance factor. So there was my challenge: for every family gathering I had to suffer through with Rich, I vowed to find a totally obnoxious date. And the finding has actually proved easier than dumping each guy the day after. Have I shocked you yet?"

I ignored the question, saying, "Rich wasn't supposed to be here this year."

"Right. Which is why I didn't have a date as of last weekend when we all met at the shore house summit, which I attended only because I felt Ma needed a woman there defending her sudden declaration of independence. Anyway, Rich wanted to know what sort of loser I was seeing lately and well, one good taunt led to another. In the end, I said I was bringing an honest-to-Pete M.D. to dinner. Foot and Horse were there, so I had to pull it off. Piece of cake. Kevin had been hitting on me since I joined the practice across the hall. When I suggested Christmas weekend away, he jumped at it. I wonder what excuse he gave his wife."

"He didn't balk when you told him you were going to your mom's house?"

"I didn't tell him until we were on the road yesterday."

"What about Sachi? What does she think of this?"

Acey didn't respond right away. She strolled over to the end table, reaching out to brush a speck of fuzz from the lampshade, leaving the shade slightly lopsided. Her face was more brightly lit now, and I saw lines of anxiety.

"Sachi was supposed to have dinner today with some friends of ours. She'd rather have gone home this weekend to see her parents and two younger sisters, but a year and a half ago she made the mistake of telling her family she was gay. Her father told her not to show her face again." Acey swung toward me, her hands finding her jeans pockets. "She won't hear of me staying with her on holidays. Knowing that I can still come home is important to her. If I have to dredge up fake boyfriends to perpetuate the myth that *allows* me to come home, well, that's cool with her."

I had a feeling that this was the heart of the matter, more than just playing an elaborate joke on Rich. Acey was afraid of her family finding out. I reran Glad's reaction to Sachi in my brain and said, "I'm pretty sure your mom knows."

"Does she?" Acey cocked her head as she considered the idea. "Ma's been a big surprise lately. I don't know if it's retirement or Evelyn or maybe even this house. Something's changed her."

A sticky silence settled between us. I was wondering what I'd do if she'd ask me to keep her secret. Not that I'd tell Hugh under normal circumstances, but if she had anything to do with slipping Dr. Weisel the protriptyline—Did I really think she had?

Through the Venetian blind slats, I saw a flash of lights, and grasped the diversion. "Something's going on outside."

Acey yanked on the cord to raise the blind and give us a clear view. The yard was dim in the late afternoon twilight, but the back fence was lit by headlights. Rich, I presumed. Then the porch light came on, and I saw a minivan docking alongside the fence. Glad appeared on the porch, wringing her hands.

"The plot thickens," Acey said. "Rich's truelove Delia's here." She headed for the hall, with me close behind, and there we found Evelyn unbolting the outside door while Horse, Beth Ann, and Sachi waited nearby. Like the rest of us, the newcomer wasn't allowed to view the dining room until the next grand unveiling, so Glad directed her daughter-in-law our way.

Delia stepped over the threshold—a big woman, seeming more in scale to a Lee man than me or Irene. She wore a bulky zip-up cardigan for a coat, over a denim overall dress, kneesocks and black sneaks, showing a preference for comfort over fashion. She also wore an aura of world-weary resolve, as if to say, "Bring on the next crisis. What's one more?" I'd seen the look before, always on the moms of teenagers.

The first words out of her mouth were, "He *was* here, right?"

"If you mean your dear hubby," Horse replied, "absolutely. He just went—"

"Wait," Delia interrupted. "Let me guess. He's at the hospital."

"You've got Rich pegged, Del," Acey said.

"Some wives worry about the other woman. With me, it's the other HMO." It came out glib, like Delia had said it dozens, no, *hundreds* of times before. "Guess I should go hunt him down." Though she looked less than thrilled with the notion.

Evelyn spoke up, "We were about to sit down to dessert. Won't you join us?"

Acey agreed. "I don't know what's up between you and my bro, but it's bound to be Rich's fault. Sit and eat with us. I'll buzz him and tell him to get his fat ass back here." She reached for her cell, but before she could punch the on-button, Delia stayed her hand.

"No. Not yet." I got the impression, whatever she intended to say to Rich, she didn't want an audience. In the end, though, she agreed to stay awhile.

Evelyn closed the door and we all walked toward the dining room where we found Glad blocking the doorway. "Beth Ann, go ask your father and uncle if they're coming down, so I know how many plates to put out this time."

Beth Ann frowned at me and Miss Maggie hastily volunteered to go fetch Hugh herself. Guiltily remembering her arthritis, I shook my head. "The kid and I'll go root him out together."

So Beth Ann and I climbed the steps, my knees protesting each riser. I was tired—my usual late afternoon slump—and also hadn't been drinking as much water as Horse had prescribed. I vowed to down a quart of it with dessert.

Upstairs at Foot's door, I let Beth Ann do the knocking and summoning ("Dad! Grandmom wants to know if you and Uncle Foot are eating dessert with us!") while I inspected the door jamb by the light of the single electric wall sconce in the hall. A shallow indentation was still visible where the lock had been—the lock Dunbar said Brennan had put on his door, proving this to be the salesman's room, where mercury-tainted logs had burned in the fireplace.

With Beth Ann right beside me, I didn't get the headache or panic attack I'd experienced yesterday, but I felt *something*. Worry? Mild anxiety? Like the hint of fear I'd felt at the bottom of the stairs after we first arrived.

The door shook as someone tried to open it. My eyes were focused on where the lock had been, and I saw the door stick right at that spot. On the other side of the wood, I heard Hugh curse loudly. Remembering how Glad had let Foot out yesterday, I told Beth Ann to try opening the door.

She turned the knob, pushing, and the door swung in without effort.

"Evelyn's got to get this door fixed," Hugh groused. "I had a heck of a time getting in, and Acey had to let me out earlier."

I heard Foot behind him. "That's why I didn't close it all the way last night."

A door that only opened from the outside? And that only Carson women descendants could open easily? Added to the fact that Carson women descendants kept the bogeyman away better than anyone else in the house. I got the feeling someone was trying to tell us something. Thing was, if this ghost was playing charades, I couldn't get past "First syllable, sounds like . . . ?"

"Aunt Delia's here," Beth Ann announced. "Will you come down, Uncle Foot? Please?"

Foot was stretched out on the bed, hands behind his head. He pushed himself up on one elbow to gaze at his niece. He must have had as hard a time saying no to her pleading look as I did, because after half a moment he took a steadying breath and said, "Yeah, I'll come down."

Beth Ann turned to me. "We have to go tell Grandmom."

I reached over for Hugh's hand—I still needed to talk to him. "You go ahead. I'll come down with your dad."

Her eyes went to our entwined fingers, but she didn't scowl this time. "Come on, Uncle Foot. I'll race you."

With an abrupt burst of energy, Foot launched himself off the bed and out the door. We heard Beth Ann shriek, "You cheat!" as they clamored down the steps.

Hugh pulled me farther into the room and, cradling my face in his free hand, kissed me. I kissed back. He wrapped his arms around me. I reached up to run my fingers through his hair. The interlude could have been wonderful—better than dessert—except dummy-me forgot to keep my eyes open.

Suddenly I felt someone else kissing me, roughly. Holding me too tight. I caught a glimpse of red cloth as I pushed away.

"You're still mad at me?" Hugh had let go and was studying me through narrowed eye slits.

Thank God I still had my hands on his chest, so I felt nothing worse than embarrassment. "No, I—" Acey was right. I'd have to lie to him if I didn't tell him about the ghost. Then again, I didn't have time now. "I'm sorry. I'll explain later." I stood on tiptoe to smooch him, my lids open.

He wasn't convinced. "We ought to get downstairs."

"Wait. I have to know something first. Why did Foot ask for you specifically? Because you were the only sibling not at the shore house last weekend?"

Hugh's jaw dropped a half inch. Pay dirt.

"And what does Foot think?" I asked. "That the drug they found in Dr. Weisel was mixed into a bottle of antacid?"

"Yes, but how did you—"

"Your observant daughter told me the white glop on Weisel's nose was antacid. I figured he was self-absorbed enough that if he got *agita*, and remembered seeing antacid in the bathroom, he'd just go take a swig, without benefit of spoon or dosage cup. And if he didn't take the protrip—whatever, himself—"

"Foot thought it was his own Mylanta," Hugh said. "He's always been paranoid, thinking everyone's out to pick on him, but this time, well, if you mix the medicine Foot takes with the type of antidepressant they found in Weisel, it's likely to be fatal. So Foot took the bottle from his vanity bag and brought it to the hospital last night—"

"He made them test it, and told them what to look for in Weisel's system, right? That's why he insisted on going. But Foot's antacid must have tested clean."

"How do you know that?" Hugh was starting to look peeved at my deductions.

I still had my hands on his chest. I moved them around his waist, and my breasts up against his abs to placate him. "Because the other bottles in the front bathroom disappeared. When the hospital called this morning, they must have given Foot the lab report."

Hugh nodded. "He said they found antacid in Weisel's stomach last night, so a toxicologist was called in to test the bottle, in case it was deliberate poisoning. She was really pissed to be up all night Christmas Eve on a wild goose chase."

"So your brother decided one of the other bottles must be tainted instead and he confiscated them?"

"Foot says they're in a safe place. Wouldn't tell me where." Hugh absently slipped his arms around my back.

The sensation distracted me, but I kept my mind on business. "One bottle was Horse's, wasn't it? I saw it next to a shaving kit in the bathroom. He was the only one of you here at the time."

"Right, that was his. Foot said Horse had it sitting out like that last weekend, next to Acey's stuff on the counter in the bathroom the three of them shared."

"So Foot thinks what? That Acey or Rich put the antidepressant into Horse's antacid?"

Hugh shrugged, dazed, like he was in total disbelief himself. "They had the opportunity, and either of them could write a prescription for the stuff."

"What about the other bottle? The one in the medicine chest? Weisel might have chugged that one instead."

Hugh sighed. "Ma's. She always keeps a supply handy."

"Evelyn might take it, too."

"Maybe." Hugh pulled me closer, touching his cheek to the top of my head, probably so I wouldn't see how troubled he was. "Jesus, Pat. Who'd want to harm any of them?"

December 25, 1783—Market Green

HAVING NO WISH TO be seen from Captain Underwood's windows, I situated myself farther along Nicholson Street, behind a large oak that stood on the green across from the Randolph house. What I hoped to learn from viewing the scene in the noonday light, I had little notion. Yet, here Brennan was slain.

No blood was now apparent upon Underwood's steps. They'd been scrubbed clean. The house, too, looked stark and empty this noon, with no fine horses beside the curb and no footman at the door, though smoke rose from three chimneys.

"Benjamin!"

I started, swinging around, to find Noah Akers beaming at me, his nose red from the cold. Flustered, I nearly forgot to bow and touch my hat.

"Delighted to see you," he said, with a hearty clap to my shoulder. "I've just left Mother visiting with old Mrs. Withers. While those two hens cackle together, I thought I'd walk about for health, as the modern doctors advise. I'll wager they deliver such advice from comfortable chairs by their fires." He nodded toward the Underwood house. "Shocking what happened last eve. I dined there, you know. Mother and I."

Noah studied my reaction as he spoke. 'Twas with caution, I asked, "You saw Brennan murdered?"

"That I did, from the window right of the steps. Mother sat there to watch the antics, and I stood behind her, so my view was not good. We heard little of the play, for the sash was closed against the cold. Yet, I thought I'd have another look today, for Mother claims that after the shot, she saw smoke beside the hedgerow."

The hedge alongside the next house, Noah meant, where young Tom hid himself while we'd been inside. I surveyed the row now. 'Twas tall as a man. Taller, perhaps. I pictured a musket barrel, forced through its greenery. "A bit far to assure a true aim," I said with doubt.

"For a musket, yes, but not a rifle."

A rifle? Musket shot fired through a rifled barrel, spinning the ball to its target with greater accuracy? Yes, possible. In the army, only sharpshooters wielded such arms—rifles took too long to load when a company faced a line of Brown Bess muzzles. Also, rifles cost more, so men like me relied more on luck and less on aim when coney hunting.

Noah seemed to read my thoughts. "Rich men can afford to amass a show of fine weaponry. The captain displays his collection upon the south wall of his rear parlor. No less than six rifles hang there, fancily inlaid and carved. I admired them before dinner—"

"And after Brennan was shot?"

"I regret that I did not think to view them again. Indeed, we were given no opportunity before the second course was served. And Mother made no mention of the smoke until this morn."

I considered the idea. Was it happenstance that the murderer of Thomas Carson should himself be killed at the house of Carson's commanding officer? Had Underwood perhaps never reported my suspicions to his superiors? Had there been some link 'twixt him and John Brennan before the war's end? I was beginning to form a notion what that link might be.

But no, Brennan did not die at Underwood's hand. The captain watched our play from his door, in my constant view. "Who, sir," I asked, "do you presume fired the fatal shot?"

Noah placed the fingers of one hand between the breast buttons of his coat for warmth. "My sire was a great one for antics. He went about reveling each year, always as St. George's dragon. As a boy, I shadowed him, much as that young lad did last night. The last two years before I joined the army, Father let me play the part of Molly Muggins. I wore Mother's skirts." He laughed, his eyes shining, as if seeing anew a happy time past. "But I cannot recall playing at a single house of gentry where a footman or two—or every manslave in the place—did not stand at the ready, in case our antics turned rough and troublesome."

I saw his point. No liveried servant had been in attendance of our play. "Was Lynch inside?"

"I did not see the man, nor any other servant. Possibly they were all required for the remove in the dining room." Noah seemed to think it unlikely. "Moreover, after Brennan fell, 'twas some minutes before Sergeant Lynch rang the bell for the constable. Though, with Dr. Riddick appearing from the shadows to tend the victim, perhaps Underwood first wished to see if Brennan could be saved before calling for Lynch once more."

I could tell from Noah's manner that this supposition did less than satisfy him, so I asked, "Now that you view the scene by day, sir, what is your opinion?"

"I believe I may seek out the constable myself and just mention Mother's smoke to him. Give him something to ponder besides the whereabouts of those revelers." Noah removed his hand from his coat and undid the lower buttons, the better to reach into his waistcoat pocket. He brought forth a small purse. "I meant to bless your Christmas box this Tuesday, when you come to do my accounts, but today is as well. And here is a bit more for—well, I don't imagine you collected much fiddling last evening."

He knew of my part for certain. However, I merely accepted and expressed my deepest gratitude for his gift—three dollars and six bits, more coins than I'd rubbed together at one time in four months.

"You deserve it, Ben, for all you've helped me this month." Smiling, he added in lowered voice, "Though, if you hear of any future plans for mummery, you might mention that you know of a lad who cuts quite a figure in a skirt."

"That I will, Noah. And, if you would, I know of a part you might play sooner."

SEVENTEEN

Everyone was already in the dining room when Hugh and I went downstairs. The room was now candlelit, as I'd seen it last night, with the addition of a single taper with a hurricane glass cover on the small table where Acey and Sachi sat. "'Far from the madding crowd,'" Acey explained, "though they aren't so 'madding' without Rich here."

At the main table, Horse sat at the foot and Delia next to Miss Maggie, opposite the two empty chairs left for me and Hugh. It might have made more sense for me to sit between the two big men, but I plopped myself down next to Beth Ann, leaving Hugh and Horse to bump knees. If I lost contact with Hugh, I still had his daughter for backup health insurance.

Glad hadn't allowed anyone to dig in until we arrived. Justifiably, too, because this was her most amazing layout yet. Like last night, the tablecloth had been removed and the desserts were set out on the bare wood. At the head and foot of the table were upside-down cones made from raspberries and cherries, respectively, both with sugar glazes to hold them together, each summit capped by a holly leaf. Shelled nuts made a nest around each base.

Of the four dishes surrounding the center, two opposite diagonals displayed dried fruit: apples and apricots, pears and pineapple, all garnished with colorful hard candies.

Glad pointed to one of the other two platters. "Apple tansey," which was a sweet omelette fried over slices of apple, then flipped out so the apples were on top.

Opposite that was a plate of what Glad called "ratafia biscuits, flavored with almonds," which reminded me of the lighter-than-air Stella Doro Anginetti egg-white cookies my Aunt Lydia buys by the carload. Around the pile of biscuits were star-shaped purplish-blue flowers.

"Borage flowers," Glad replied when I asked. "They're candied and perfectly good to eat."

The *pièce de résistance* was center stage. "A Floating Island," Glad explained. "The whipped cream in the bowl has lemon and sack mixed into it—"

"Sack," Evelyn interjected as he reached for a bottle of white wine and the water pitcher, "was the name given to fortified Spanish wine or, more commonly in the eighteenth century, an English honey-wine, spiced with rue and fennel root. I used mead, though I couldn't find fennel root this time of year, so I substituted a few of the seeds—"

"The Italian Market," I broke in. "In South Philly. They have fennel root in December. My cousin Tutti brings it to every Montella New Year's party. Let me know next time you want it and I'll call Tutti."

Evelyn sent me a smile from over Delia's shoulder, his face ruddy in the candlelight. "Thanks. I'll do that."

"As I was saying," Glad continued, "floating on the whipped cream is an island made from thin slices of French roll, which back then meant a hard crusty bread. It's layered with two kinds of jelly: currant and hartshorn."

"We fudged here as well," Evelyn apologized as he poured Acey's wine. "Hartshorn jelly was made from ground deer antlers—"

"Eewww!" Beth Ann exclaimed, wrinkling up her nose.

Evelyn laughed. "That's what made it set up, you see."

"Ev used ordinary gelatin," Glad assured her.

The finished product *did* look like an island, with more whipped cream on top—the real stuff, not the aerosol—like snow on a mountain. The rim of the bowl was garnished with dabs of different colored jellies and slices of orange. Miss Maggie gushed her praise and so did I. Even Delia said, "Wow, Mom. Very ambitious this year."

Horse asked impatiently, "Can we eat now?"

Glad looked surprised, as if eating these creations hadn't occurred to her. I personally thought it a shame to ruin them, especially since I was still stuffed with pottage, spoonbread, and Sally Lunn and wasn't sure where I'd put dessert anyway.

"Forget about your stomach for once, Horse," Acey said. "Some of us want to hear what Ma has to say."

"No, it's all right." Glad resumed her seat. "I'm quite finished."

No sooner were the words out of her mouth than the ambient light coming from the kitchen went out.

"Blast!" Evelyn exclaimed. "Another fuse."

"Only the overhead lamp." Glad patted the table near Evelyn's place. "Sit and leave it until after the course."

"No, I should check." He set his pitcher and bottle on the sideboard. Lifting the candlestick from his end of the table, he went off through the pantry, the candle's circle of wavering light making an eerie silhouette of his head and shoulders.

The kitchen wasn't an absolute black hole, I noticed. Glad had left the porch light on and if I leaned forward, I could see the glare from outside casting windowpane-shaped rectangles on the kitchen's vinyl bricks. But sans candle, the darker end of the dining room and pantry seemed extra creepy. I was twice as aware of our shadows high on the surrounding walls, seeming to have a life of their own every time someone passed a dessert plate. Thank goodness we still had light filtering in from the lamp in the front hall.

Evelyn returned and restored the candlestick. "Whole kitchen's off. Stove and fridge. I'll go change the fuses before our next course is ruined. Won't be a minute."

"Wait, I'm coming with you," Miss Maggie announced, pushing her chair back from the table. I raised my eyebrows at her—Magnolia Shelby never abandons a full dish of food without good reason. She winked at me and shuffled off after Evelyn.

"That's the third time this weekend." Foot's tone was steeped with I-told-you-so superiority.

"Fourth," said Glad, oblivious to his disapproval. "The stove was out when I got up this morning. Odd. Usually doesn't happen so often. Elizabeth must be restless this weekend."

Beth Ann froze with a ratafia biscuit between her teeth. "You mean Elizabeth Carson?"

"Of course." Glad beamed as she cut a slice of tansey for Evelyn. "I've felt her in this house since we moved in. Ev says I'm being silly, but I know she's here. I wonder if the authenticity of these dinners stirred her curiosity—"

"Stop it!"

We all stared at Hugh, who hardly ever raised his voice in anger. Oh, I'd heard him bellow halfway across Bell Run's acreage, threatening to ground Beth Ann, but that was all dramatic license. When he's intensely angry, he holds it in.

"Take it easy, bro," Horse said, setting his fork down.

"No." Hugh was mortified by his reaction, I could tell, but he went on anyway. "This Elizabeth Carson crap has to stop. I swear, next thing Mom'll start believing she *is* Elizabeth." He glanced from Horse to Foot. "Do you know she's changed her name to Carson-Lee?"

Glad sat up a tad straighter. Not that she could slouch in the stays she wore. "I see nothing wrong with being proud of our blood ties to a fine old Virginia family. Especially now that I've moved back into the very house where—"

"You are *not* a Carson," Hugh seethed. "None of us are Carsons. There haven't *been* Carsons in Williamsburg in more than two centuries."

"We don't know that," Glad said. "Elizabeth's son Thomas might have—"

"You were born plain Gladys Hawkins, Mom." Hugh's rage seemed to deflate all at once and the next words came out more like a plea. "What's wrong with that? Ever since I can remember, you've been trying to be someone you're not."

"Like every other human being on the planet," Acey piped up. "Including you, Fitzhugh Lee, with your going to the woods for a life of quiet desperation à la Thoreau. At least Ma's aspirations aren't self-defeating."

"Aren't they?" Foot asked. "We have clinical terms for folks who believe ghosts come to their dinner parties."

The kitchen light came back on and Glad jumped to her feet. "I'll just go see if the refrigerator's working." She practically ran out through the pantry.

"Nice move, Sigmund," Acey said to Foot.

Miss Maggie bustled in all excited. "I love old cellars. They can tell so much about a building." She resumed her seat and began filling the thumbprint of a ratafia biscuit with glazed raspberries. "For instance, this house originally had only a crawl space beneath it. Makes sense. The land around Williamsburg was always swampy, which was one of the reasons they moved the capitol to Richmond. The summers here were thought to be unhealthy. They knew nothing of mosquito-born diseases, of course—they thought the illnesses came from inhaling the stench of pond scum. Anyway, back at the time of the Yorktown campaign, a French officer made a map of this area, and if I remember right, it showed a stream running by this house."

"Absolutely right." Evelyn had come back during her lecture. He set the bag of fuses on the sideboard. "The basement wasn't dug out until the 1940s, after the Williamsburg Tunnel segment of the Colonial Parkway was completed. They'd re-engineered the landscape for the project, draining the marshes, so it made a basement feasible. That's when the first restoration of the house was done:

a new heater put in, and visible pipes and wires moved below the floors."

Glad re-entered, assuring Evelyn that the appliances were once more working in the kitchen. He held her chair as she sat down, then took his own.

"What I thought was interesting"—Miss Maggie paused to chew a piece of fruit-ladened biscuit—"is that the fuse box for the kitchen wing is mounted on the original brick foundation, whereas the box for this part of the house is mounted below the other, on the 1940s cinder block foundation. And according to Evelyn, the electricity in this wing never goes off."

"Then all you need to do is replace the kitchen fuse box." Delia made it sound as if home improvement projects were in the same league as grocery shopping and laundry for her.

"In the decade after the restoration, the Foundation tried changing the box several times with no luck," Evelyn explained. "I've put in for a circuit breaker box, but I don't know—"

"Mount it on the cinder block," Miss Maggie insisted. "That'll solve your problems."

"I'm willing to try anything." Evelyn looked at his guests. "I apologize. This isn't a common occurrence. I don't know why it's happening so much this weekend—"

"Ma knows," Acey broke in. "It's the ghost."

"Don't start," Foot warned his sister.

Acey ignored him. "Oh, I believe her. See, I saw one of the resident specters myself." She paused to increase the shock value, grinning at the disbelief on her brothers' faces.

"Please, Acey," Foot said. "Why must you—"

"Because it's true." Acey stuck her tongue out at him. "I saw a ghost in my room last night. Sorry, Ma, it wasn't Elizabeth Carson. I saw her daughter, Polly."

"Polly?" Glad seemed both fascinated and confused. "I suppose she must have stayed to look after her mother, as she did through the last years of Elizabeth's life—"

"No," Hugh said, loud and firm. "There *are no ghosts* in this house."

"Yeah-there-are." Beth Ann made one word out of three as she glanced around me at her dad. "I saw Polly, too. In the same room."

Everyone went silent. They might all assume Acey was lying, but Beth Ann was different, though Foot went so far as to ask, "Did your aunt put you up to this?"

"No!" Beth Ann let out one of her grown-ups-are-such-a-pain sighs. "I saw the ghost before Aunt Acey. And we didn't tell each other until a little while ago."

During the general outcry that followed, Hugh scowled not at his daughter, but at me, like this was all my doing.

Need I say that this annoyed me a smidge? "Hey, don't look at me. Polly's *your* ancestor."

"So you saw her, too?" he murmured, not pleased.

"Not—uh, not in the same way." Problem was, he knew which way I meant. I could see my betrayal on his face—I'd broken my promise. And maybe he was wondering if this was an indication of how I'd treat other vows between us.

Obey. I *knew* that one would be the real bugger. Love and honor were easy by comparison.

My first instinct was to make excuses. Plead self-defense. This ghost was trying to poison me, after all. Or I could say, when I found out Beth Ann had seen Polly, I wanted to make sure she was in no danger. Hugh *did* want me to act maternal, right?

But long before Beth Ann mentioned her sighting, and before I'd felt a twinge of nausea or taste of metal, I'd closed my eyes beneath the mistletoe, trying to start a conversation with someone two centuries dead, in direct violation of my promise. Worse yet, guilt-wise, I'd been kissed by someone other than Hugh—twice—and hadn't told him, so I felt like I was running around behind his back. Not that I'd asked for or enjoyed either experience.

I abruptly remembered the first ghost I'd met at Bell Run. I was kissed then, too, and *thoroughly* enjoyed it. And didn't feel guilty in the least. Why? Because (a) the episode led to my first kiss with Hugh, and (b) I'd known at the time that I was experiencing someone else's memories. This last phantom smooch *interrupted* a kiss with Hugh and—

Hold the phone. I was *still* experiencing someone else's memories, wasn't I?

Someone else's memories?

It hit me like the smell of a rotten tomato what that had to mean, and a soft "*Madonne!*" escaped my lips.

"What?" Hugh said.

Across the table, Miss Maggie was asking me questions with her scanty white eyebrows. Beth Ann, I saw, wore her "Please don't embarrass me" look.

She and Miss Maggie could wait. I reached for Hugh's hand, leaning closer to whisper, "Can we talk after this course?"

Without losing the scowl, he nodded, but he squeezed my hand, which I took as a good omen. Then again, the squeeze made me feel the ring, like Tanya was putting her two cents in.

Meanwhile, Hugh's siblings hadn't noticed any of this exchange because they hadn't stopped arguing since Acey and Beth Ann made their pronouncements.

"Ghosts *do not exist*," Foot was maintaining. "They are hallucinations created by the subconscious, sometimes by stress. Such visions occur in the early stages of sleep, as yours did—"

"I wasn't asleep yet," Acey countered.

"You weren't fully awake either," Horse said. "Not after that big glass of ale you had with me before turning in."

"I was *not* drunk—"

A loud banging at the back door made us all jump.

"Rich," said Delia, starting to rise. "I recognize the impatience."

Horse stood, waving her back down. "Sit. I'll fetch him."

A moment after he went out, we heard Rich bellow, "I've been knocking at the kitchen door. Didn't anyone hear me?"

"The walls are very thick," Glad explained for the umpteenth time. "Ev and I often comment on it."

We waited in silence. I heard the outside door close and the rumble of low voices in the hall, but Rich and Horse didn't appear. It dawned on me that Rich would have seen his wife's van in the yard.

Acey had the same thought, yelling, "Yes, Richie-dear, Delia's here. Come on in, ya big chicken."

Delia grinned at her sister-in-law and sat down, slouching casually to give the impression that she didn't care whether her hubby was here or not.

Rich showed his face at last, pausing just inside the glow of the candlelight, the shadows enhancing his pout.

Miss Maggie stood, taking up her plate. "Rich can sit here. I'll join Acey and Sachiko."

"Please do, Magnolia," Acey said. "Save us from certain indigestion."

Rich held his ground, making brief eye contact with his wife, then addressing his sister. "Are you at all interested in Dr. Weisel's prognosis?"

Acey went serious, though strictly clinical. "He survived the attack?"

Rich nodded. "Fortunately he was in good physical condition. However, he can't remember anything after a golf game he played in college. Other brain damage can be expected."

"So," Horse said, coming into the room in time to hear this last speech, "the Weasel will never practice medicine again?"

"Probably not." An expression of pity crossed Rich's face.

Horse came straight over to Hugh and whispered in his ear. I caught the word "Come." They both went out into the hall.

"What's going on?" Beth Ann asked, voicing my thoughts.

Hugh and Horse only conversed a few seconds before we all heard the front door open and close. Hugh returned alone.

"Where's Lighthorse?" Glad asked. "Is he outside without his coat?"

"He'll be back," Hugh said, bypassing the table, heading for the pantry. "So will I." The kitchen light went out again, this time because Hugh switched it off as he entered that room.

Evelyn had twisted around to watch Hugh leave. "Perhaps, er, excuse me, won't you?" He hurried off into the kitchen.

"Come on, Sach," Acey said, standing. "Time to be nosy." They joined the exodus.

Beth Ann turned toward me, saying in a low voice, "Can we go, too?" Meaning she intended to, and if I didn't want to get sick, I should abandon my dessert.

But I was just as curious. "'Scuze us," I said to those left, and followed Beth Ann out.

Hugh had switched off the porch light, so I could barely see the step down into the kitchen. I felt my way with my feet, then walked as fast as I dared in the dark. Over in the vicinity of the door, I heard Hugh telling Evelyn and Acey, "Horse saw someone looking over the back fence when he let Rich in. He went around to Nassau Street." The plan, as I understood it, was that Horse would cut between the houses to the fence while Hugh did a frontal assault from the house.

Acey's opinion was the same as mine. "How quaintly macho. You'd think you two would know better after your run-in with Cherry."

"She caught us by surprise," Hugh grumbled.

"Right, whatever," Acey sighed. "This time I'm sticking with my baby brother to watch his ass for him."

"You stay here," Hugh commanded.

"Make me. I've got eight years on you, old man, and I can run faster—"

"Listen," Evelyn broke in, "whoever's outside isn't harming anyone. I don't think—"

"This person," Acey said, "is probably the same one leaving playing cards. Aren't you at least curious?"

"No, I—" Evelyn seemed flustered. "Let's just forget the whole thing and return to dinn—"

I felt a rush of cold air and knew Hugh, or more likely Acey, had gone through the door. Instinct made me follow. Sachi got to the door at the same time; as we bumped she mumbled, "Sorry," and lunged ahead.

The porch light came on—Evelyn's doing, I presumed, until I noticed he was beside me as we left the porch. Hugh was a step behind Acey at the back gate, Sachi, not far behind. Beth Ann passed us the next second.

Something heavy slammed against the other side of the fence, near the northwest corner. Grunts ensued, then Horse cried, "Got him!" I saw the top of Hugh's head disappear below the fence, and a frail tenor voice shrieked, "Get off me!"

As I went through the gate, the shadows on the other side of the fence prevented me from seeing the action, but the voice shrieked again, desperate this time, "Let me go! Please, please, please, please!"

Acey, clasping another photocopy, scrambled uphill into the light. "Jack of Spades this time."

"That's mine! My calling card! Give it back! Make her give it back! Get off me!"

Horse and Hugh, holding each of the intruder's arms, lifted him, maneuvering him into the light until we could see his face. Gray beard stubble clung to his too-gaunt cheeks. Sixtyish, I estimated. And absolutely horror-stricken. He was trying to make himself smaller, pleading all the while. "Let go! Evie, please make them let go! Please!"

Evelyn, I realized, had been saying just that. "Let him go. You're hurting him. He can't stand being touched."

Exchanging glances, Horse and Hugh let go.

The man fell to his knees, curling himself up. "Didn't mean anything, Evie. Only your old buddy, Spade. Just wanted to . . . wanted to . . . to . . ."

"You wanted to visit," Evelyn said quietly. "I know, Spade. I wish you could. Were I here alone . . . Where's your sister?"

"I didn't want to come to Williamsburg, Evie. Joyce made me. Her husband wanted a vacation . . . but I can't . . . can't . . . can't . . . all the people . . . can't go to restaurants . . . can't . . . like when we were in Dominion and they tried to make me—"

"Dominion?" Horse cut in. "Dominion Hospital? Up in northern Virginia?"

"That's a psychiatric hospital," Acey said.

"Right!" Spade seemed thrilled that he'd communicated. Something he apparently didn't do often. "Evie and me were there . . . he . . . he helped me . . ."

"You worked there?" Acey asked Evelyn.

He shook his head. "They don't employ restoration architects." Scanning the faces of each future in-law before him, he sighed. "No, I was a patient."

"Extravagancies bring Sickness."

—Nathaniel Whittemore's Almanac, December, 1729

December 25, 1783—Mr. Greenhow's Shop

HAD THEY NOT BEEN secured in their sockets, I believe Sam's eyes would have forsaken his head when I entered Greenhow's shop. He stood behind the side counter, telling Mrs. Blair of the virtues of Philadelphia dishes over Delftware. Leaving her with instruction to study the glaze for herself, he hurried over to stay my course before I could gain two feet inside the door.

"Are you mad?" he whispered. "The old man will return any moment. He knows you've no hope of being a patron. I could lose my post."

"Mr. Greenhow's in his lumber house," I replied in a low voice, "showing Noah Akers a chest of drawers."

"Yes, I know, but—"

"Noah will keep him there until I've had a word with you."

"Ah." Sam cast a hasty glance at Mrs. Blair, who'd brought one of the plates close to the window, so as to gain light for her careful inspection. In a loud voice, Sam said, "Soap? Yes, sir, we have quite a fine selection of imported soaps there in the far corner of the shop, if you'd care to look."

I thanked him with a curt bow and proceeded to the rear wall, to a shelf of paper-wrapped soap balls with perfumes so intoxicating as to make my nose itch.

Sam, meanwhile, was assuring Mrs. Blair that no less than service for twelve would suffice. Had I not been waiting, I'm sure he'd have convinced her to take fourteen, with a full compliment of salt cellars, serving platters, and tea service. As it were, he let her compromise at ten, with no accompaniments. Promising delivery within the hour, Sam had her sign on account, walked her to the door, and bid her good day in a speech so pretty, the matron left in a fit of giggles.

Sam closed the door and ran to my side. "Quick, before someone else comes in."

"The other clerk?"

"Off on a delivery, but he shan't be long."

I related Noah's suspicion that one of Underwood's servants had shot Brennan from the hedgerow.

Sam seemed not the least surprised. "I knew none of our weapons done the deed. I'd cleaned them all myself just before we met at the capitol and we all saw them charged. Then, while watching our duel, I heard a rustling in the bushes behind me. A dog, I thought. 'Twas after, as Alex and I sunk our costumes in the marsh, that I remembered the rustling, and with it, the absence of servants during our play. That's why I got home late last night. I went back to Market Green and tarried in the shadows until Lynch returned from his search, so I might have a brief word with him. He's the bla'guard, mark my word."

"You accused him?"

"No, not that. And not to worry, for I spoke no hint of our part in the mummery. Indeed, I told the sergeant very little—merely that, like Riddick, I'd been traversing the green and saw all events. But Ben, a guilty conscience will make much of little."

"He confessed?"

Sam laughed. "Not Lynch! Yet he was shaken by my description of movement in the hedge, and this morning, when one of the captain's maids came in to purchase coffee for today's dinner, she told me that Mr. Lynch had gone off at daybreak on an errand for their master. All the way to Richmond."

"Richmond? Far enough that he'll not be questioned in the matter."

"Precisely. And I'll wager he stays away until foul weather blows over."

So, I thought, if Lynch shot Brennan, the poisoner of Thomas Carson, was there a link between the two murders? Aloud I said, "Dr. Riddick claimed that in the last month, Brennan begged at Underwood's door often. Yet only there and at no other house."

"Did he now?" Sam, mindless of his actions, shifted the soaps to a more pleasing arrangement. "Did Mr. Brennan receive alms from the good captain?"

"Until last evening."

"Sounds less like alms and more like recompense."

"My thought, as well."

"Payment for holding his tongue? *There*'s reason for shooting a man, if Brennan possessed proof of Underwood's treason during the war."

"You still believe the captain turned traitor?"

"I've always maintained it, have I not? As turncoat as Benedict Arnold himself. No man could blunder as much in battle unless he planned to do so." Sam's eyes shone with sudden hope. "Perhaps the proof's yet in Brennan's room."

"No, I went through his things this morning."

"Blast. I'd dearly love to see Underwood writhe."

"What if—that is, the evidence may yet exist—"

The shop door swung to and in walked Mr. Greenhow. Noah was on his heels like a hound at his master's boots, saying, "I'm not certain of the chest, sir. I shall have to bring Mother along—"

"Quite all right, Mr. Akers. For now, I'll write up the purchase of—" Greenhow's eyes had sought out his clerk and settled on me the same instant.

". . . and these soaps are favorites with the ladies, Mr. Dunbar," Sam was saying, as if he'd been hard upon a sale the last minute. "French perfume, of the finest quality, and not simply around the outside. No, the redolence will last as long as the soap—Ah, Mr. Akers, sir! I hope you found what you wanted?"

Noah nodded, more in apology to me than in answer to the question. "A small table." He stressed "small" for I'd told him a fortnight ago not to put any luxuries on account until at least the New Year. I should have known he'd be no match for a skilled merchant like Greenhow. This purchase was my fault, so I vowed to find Noah greater profit in the months ahead.

To assuage Sam's employer, and satisfy a new whim of my own, I said I'd take one of the soaps.

Greenhow smiled his disbelief. "Those are three shillings apiece, Mr. Dunbar."

I almost cried aloud. Three shillings? For soap?

"I believe Mr. Dunbar meant one of these." Sam bent over to the bottom shelf, to retrieve a smaller ball, unwrapped and brown in hue, with but a faint hint of lavender about it. "At nine pence."

Even at nine pence—but, I agreed. Sam was never wrong in the matter of ladies' favorites.

EIGHTEEN

"BETH ANN, RUN AND fetch your Uncle Francis." A firm order, issued from behind us. The figure beside the gate was wrapped in a dark cloak with only a white cap to make her visible. I could have sworn for a second that Elizabeth Carson stood there. But, no, the voice was Glad's. "Go *now*."

Beth Ann came out of her shock and took off at a run, sliding on the wet grass as she went through the gate.

Glad walked toward Evelyn, forgetting even to lift her skirts off the damp ground. "Relax, Mr., er, is it Spade?"

The man now stood, his Southern manners ingrained enough to supersede his psychosis. "S-S-Spading, ma'am. Spade for short."

"My son Francis is a psychiatrist. He'll know what to do."

"Foot's awesome." Acey sounded sincere. "Our screwy family taught him everything he knows."

"The rest of you, go inside," Glad said with a hint of impatience. "Ev and I can handle this. *Go*."

Hugh moved first, pushing Horse toward the gate. Acey, Sachi, and I followed. We passed Foot, bundled up in his long black coat and scarf, in the yard.

Miss Maggie was waiting for us on the back porch.

"No big news," Acey told her. "Only that Evelyn did time in a looney bin. I wonder if this'll change Ma's wedding plans."

Beth Ann met us right inside the door. "Steer clear of the dining room."

Even with the dim candlelight and bad acoustics, we could tell at a glance that Rich and Delia were in the midst of an argument.

"I need to change," Horse said, heading for the back stairs. He wasn't making excuses—his shirt and pants were streaked with grass and mud stains.

"Me, too," said Hugh, following his brother. Sure, the knees of his jeans were a little wet, but that was a definite wimp out.

"And I'm an old lady who hasn't had a potty break in too long." Miss Maggie waggled her eyebrows at me. Our secret code: conference time.

"Ditto thirty-something me," I said.

"Ditto the teen," echoed Beth Ann.

So the three of us climbed the spiral stair. I noticed as we left, Acey and Sachi settling at the kitchen table, right where Acey had a good view of the dining room.

"I wasn't kidding about the potty break," Miss Maggie told me in the upstairs hall. "But afterwards, I want to hear about that epiphany you had during dinner."

We all used the facilities. During my turn, I paused while drying my hands, my gaze falling on Foot's bag, picturing it last weekend on a shelf beside Horse's shaving kit and whatever Acey's toiletries consisted of (I guessed baking soda for toothpaste and an herbal cleansing solution). Could I picture Acey or Rich slipping something into Horse's antacid bottle? Acey was better cast than Rich in the role, but the "something" would be of a practical joke nature. For instance, salt. Not a potent and potentially deadly drug.

We reconvened back in our bedroom. I sat immediately on the daybed—my knees hadn't appreciated their recent foray out into the cold air. Beth Ann hopped up on the other end of the bed, kicking her feet as they dangled.

"Out with it, Pat." Miss Maggie crossed her arms over Rudolf.

"Hugh and I were in Foot's room, and I had another vision." I was loathe to say, in front of Beth Ann, that I'd been smooching her dad at the time. "Another kiss, like downstairs, only this time, I got a glimpse of red cloth."

"Red cloth?" Miss Maggie's arms came down and she stepped closer. "What about your other senses, Pat? Hearing, smell?"

Then I remembered—my hands on Hugh's chest hadn't felt his soft fleece sweater. "The cloth was rough, like—like wool. And there was a faint smell, like a sweaty jock wearing a cheap Jean Naté knockoff."

"You're sure the wool was red?"

I closed my eyes. No vision came, but I got a clearer view of my memory banks. "Sort of dirty red, with tiny white specs."

"Dandruff," Beth Ann concluded.

"No," I said. "More like powder."

"Wig powder." Miss Maggie was beside herself with excitement. "We might be able to get confirmation in Glad's documentation downstairs."

"Confirmation of what?"

"You don't know? I thought that's what your epiphany was all about."

"No, what I realized at dinner was that, if I'm experiencing memories from the past, then the memory of being kissed by a man would belong to a woman. That ghost is female."

"Of course." Miss Maggie looked as if she wanted to slap her forehead for not thinking of it sooner, but she didn't. "Well, we know of two females in this house at the time."

"Polly?" Beth Ann ventured.

"I hope not." I shuddered at the idea of a young girl being handled like that. "When I—shared Polly memories, I didn't sense any experience like that, so unless it happened after—"

Miss Maggie shook her head. "If I don't miss my guess, that last kiss occurred in the summer of 1781."

"Summer?" I echoed. "Couldn't be. Polly's memories took place in wintertime."

"Nevertheless—"

"Excuse me?" Sachi stood in the doorway. "Acey wants to know if you're all done with the first dessert. She and Delia are going to put the food away for Acey's mom."

I assured her I was stuffed. "But I'll come help," I added, conditioned by my mother and aunts to feel guilt at such times. I stood, shaking the stiffness out of my knees.

"We'll all go," Miss Maggie declared and led the way back down the stairs.

Delia and Acey were bringing the remains of the floating island and apple tansey into the kitchen as we arrived. Delia looked less laid-back than before, as if she'd wanted to dump the bowl of whipped cream she toted over someone's head. The someone in particular, Rich, was nowhere in sight. I pictured him hiding behind his *JAMA* somewhere.

"Set the food on the table," Miss Maggie directed. "Pat, get the plastic wrap. Sachi, you're in charge of rinsing dishes. Beth Ann, help your aunt." Like any good general, she sat herself down at the table to oversee her troops.

I found the plastic wrap in the bottom of the hutch near the sink along with a box of Ziplocs, and settled at the table to work on the leftovers.

By that time, Miss Maggie had one of Glad's scrapbooks open in front of her. "Drat. Left my reading glasses upstairs again."

"Have you ever considered wearing them on a chain around your neck?" I asked, sealing a skin of plastic over the floating island bowl.

"Tried it once. Ruined the cool young chick image I was going for." Chuckling, she lifted the last ratafia biscuit from the plate Beth Ann set on the table.

We all heard heavy feet on the stairs. The door swung open and Horse entered, now wearing warmup pants and a Team USA hockey jersey. "Perfect!" he exclaimed, pouncing on the box of Ziploc bags. "I need one of these for my Pirates patch."

Acey, just coming in with a plate of dried fruit in each hand, said, "You dope! Did you still have the patch in your sweatshirt pocket when you tackled Spade?"

"The patch survived, thank God." Horse took a dried apple slice from the dish. "The plastic bag ripped, that's all."

"So, you liked the patch?" Delia asked.

"Like it? Best gift Rich ever gave me. In fact, in view of my brother's usual taste in presents, I'd say I was pleasantly floored by it." He popped the apple slice into his mouth whole.

"Oh?" Delia set the plate of glazed cherries on the table. "And what did Rich say about why he bought that patch?"

Horse noticed, as I did, the anger under the surface of her question. He glanced at his sister, who'd paused in her commute back and forth from the dining room to listen in on their conversation. "Rich said he heard me mention last weekend that I still had my collection—"

"*He* heard you?!" Delia exploded. "*I'm* the one who heard you say that."

"Take it easy," Horse soothed. "I believe you."

"Yeah? Do you also believe that I do all of Rich's Christmas shopping and wrapping for him? Even the stupid gifts he insists I get for your gift exchange every year. Which is how I knew he still didn't have anything for you as of last weekend. He'd been so busy at work, he couldn't take two seconds to give me a clue what to buy. So I went on eBay last Saturday while you were all sitting around whining about Ma. That Bazooka Blony patch was going off at auction Monday night. I stayed up 'til midnight to make sure I won the bid, then had the patch FedExed to me so I'd have time to wrap it and overnight it before Christmas. And do you think Rich appreciated it?"

"Sounds just like Big Bro," Acey said. "Let me guess, he didn't let you send the patch because he didn't think it was up to his usual brilliant standards in gift-giving, right?"

"That was his excuse," Delia said. "His real problem was that I got it on eBay, which he refers to as my 'extramarital affair.' Fine for him to spend every waking hour at his office and the hospital, but let me get a hobby and—"

"Pretty expensive hobby, isn't it?" Horse said, reaching for another apple slice, seeing I'd already bagged the dried fruit, plucking a cherry from the cone instead. "I mean, I guess it depends what you buy, but—"

"I made three hundred bucks just selling the clothes the boys grew out of."

"Bingo." Acey moved closer to the table. "Rich is afraid you'll get too independent, Delia. You'll realize you don't need him or his paycheck anymore, then Sayonara City."

Delia shook her head. "With a son going off to college next year, two others outgrowing shoes faster than I can buy them, and a zillion repairs needed around the house, Rich's paycheck can't cut it alone." She turned to me. "Your mom ever tell you to marry a rich doctor?"

"Oh, yeah, all the time. My aunts, too."

"It's a myth. There *are* no rich doctors."

Horse took another cherry. "Foot would argue with that. Then again, he's two-thirds investment banker."

"Foot doesn't have kids."

Hugh came in from the dining room. "So *here*'s where everyone is."

"Except Ma, Evelyn, and Herr Freud," Acey said. "They're still outside."

"And Rich," Delia said, "who's off licking his wounds."

"I saw him in the parlor." Hugh came over to join the grazing at the leftovers. "Where's Irene?"

"She went upstairs after Foot left." Delia headed for the dining room once more.

"I didn't see her up there," Hugh said.

Horse sucked the glaze from his fingers. "The back bathroom door was closed when I went passed it. Hope Irene's not sick. Some of Ma's dishes were on the weird side today."

"Some?" Hugh murmured, moving out of the way to let Delia put the raspberry cone on the table.

"You didn't have trouble making a pig of yourself." Acey turned to follow Delia back into the dining room.

"A man's gotta eat," Horse said. "And there's not much he can do when his sister acts immature and hides his antacid."

Acey swung around, puzzlement on her face. "Hide?"

"It's not where I left it, and on account of your past record, you're suspect number one."

Hugh and I exchanged glances, but he didn't tell them Foot took the bottle, so I didn't either.

"Though," Horse continued, "I can't think why you would, unless you were having an attack of conscience about tampering with it last weekend at Rich's. Knowing I still haven't forgiven you for the time you put Tabasco in it."

Acey grinned at that. "If you didn't have that disgusting habit of chugging your Mylanta straight from the bottle, you'd have noticed the color difference."

"So, what was it this time?" Horse asked. "Cayenne pepper? Horseradish? Laxative?"

"Nothing. Honest." She tried to look innocent. Her devilish smile negated her halo.

Horse took another cherry. "I can prove you're lying. Last weekend I placed a hair so it just stuck out of the bottle cap. It wasn't there when I packed to leave Sunday afternoon."

Acey burst into a laugh. "I know. I saw the hair. And I'm still telling the truth. I put nothing in your Mylanta."

"Did you check the contents of the bottle?" Hugh asked his brother.

Horse shook his head. "Forgot. Didn't have time at Rich's. Then I left my bathroom stuff packed for this weekend. Didn't remember until I unpacked yesterday. Figured I'd wait for an opportune moment to get my loving sis to confess before trying to use the antacid again. Anyone got thumbscrews I can borrow?"

Acey raised her right hand. "I, Ann Carter Lee, do solemnly swear that I did *not* place any substance whatsoever inside the Mylanta bottle belonging to Lighthorse Harry Lee—or anyone else's for that matter—within the last, say, six months." It didn't help her case that she was still laughing, or that she added, "This I swear on my father's grave."

"Dad isn't dead yet," Horse pointed out.

"Clinically, no," Acey said, "but, I ask you, does he live on in our hearts?"

The kitchen door opened, bringing in a cold draft along with Evelyn, Glad, and Foot.

"Francis persuaded Mr. Spading to tell us which restaurant his sister was at," Glad explained. "He called on his cell phone and she came."

"I told her to take the poor man home," Foot grumbled. "He hasn't been taking his medication regularly. Then to bring him to a tourist trap and expect him to stay in a claustrophobic motel room while she's out enjoying herself—if she did that with children, she'd get arrested."

"I wish I could have done something," Evelyn said quietly.

Foot shook his head. "You did right not inviting him in, not with all of us here and his socialization disorder. You say you've received e-mail from him? If you keep up a correspondence with him . . . Come up to my room with me while I hang up my coat and I'll tell you some things you can do."

Evelyn and Foot climbed the back stairs.

"Well, Foot's converted," Acey said. "Now he likes Evelyn. As a patient, anyway."

"Ann Carter," her mother admonished, this time sounding as if the day's events were wearing on her. "Ev was ill more than forty years ago. He's been fine since."

"Ma, you knew about his history?" Horse asked.

"He told me the first week I met him." Glad took off her cloak. "I don't know why—he wasn't compelled to mention every virus he'd ever had. But, you see, he was in the London Blitz as a child. Apparently, after coming to America, he experienced a delayed form of what we today call acute posttraumatic stress. He committed himself to Dominion and made a full recovery. My response to him was that I started having kids about the same time, and I *still* wasn't over that. Now, what are you all doing in my kitchen?"

"Clearing the table for you." Delia had returned with a stack of dishes, setting them beside Sachi. "Don't argue, we're almost done. Horse, bring over that empty biscuit plate."

For a few moments, we all bustled around. Hugh went to help Delia in the dining room, persuading Horse to join them. Acey gave Sachi a hand at the sink. And as fast as I could wrap leftovers, Glad had Beth Ann either put them away or set them on the table near the stove, to be transferred to the basement fridge later.

Miss Maggie, the only one exempt from chores, asked Glad, "Elizabeth lodged British officers during their occupation of Williamsburg, didn't she?"

"Sad to say, yes." Glad set the dried fruit on the hutch by the stove. "She needed the extra money, I suppose."

"Did she list those lodgers in this journal?" Miss Maggie tapped the scrapbook in front of her.

"Under 1781, end of June, beginning of July. The entries are hard to decipher—all abbreviations. She lists one major, three aides-de-camp, and a company surgeon. For just a week."

Miss Maggie nodded, explaining to the rest of us, "The British hung around about nine days before heading off toward Yorktown." I saw her logic now. "Red wool" equals "Redcoat." I didn't get a chance to quiz her further because, when Evelyn and Foot returned, Glad finally shooed us from her kitchen. On the way to the parlor, Hugh hijacked me, leading me by the hand to the back of the hall, to the little alcove created by the cellar door.

Romantic, I thought, though a poor choice of trysting place because, almost immediately, Evelyn came along. He was balancing the floating island bowl and three Ziplocs of various victuals, and his bag of fuses dangled from his hand.

"The kitchen electric went out again, I'm afraid," he apologized, embarrassed. "Since these things need to go into the basement cooler, I thought I'd make one trip. Though I'll, um, be returning for the last desserts in a bit."

Hugh got the hint, and led me into Beth Ann and Acey's room, or as I now thought of it, Polly's room. The vanity lamp was still on, casting a soft glow.

Hugh shut the door, leaning back against it, in case anyone got the notion to barge in. He pulled me into a loose embrace. Think the romance began then? Ha! The first words out of his mouth were, "Do you think Evelyn's—okay?"

"You mean sane? Or a good match for your mom?"

"I mean, weird things are going on this weekend—someone's tampering with antacid, and the kitchen fuse box—"

"You think Evelyn's been rigging the electricity to go out?"

"I suppose you think the ghost is doing it?"

I did, but this wasn't how I wanted to broach the subject with Hugh. My hesitation doomed me.

He scowled. "You've been in contact with the—"

"No, not with the one who's blowing the fuses." Too late I saw the flaw in my stalling tactic.

"How many ghosts are there?"

"Just two. I think. Polly Carson—the one Beth Ann and Acey saw—I think she's sort of based in this room."

Hugh hugged me closer, all the while doing a wary survey of every corner.

I was tempted to point out the futility of the gesture to him, but said instead, "The other might be Elizabeth Carson—"

"Elizabeth? You mean Mom's right about her being here?"

"I don't know for sure. I haven't made, uh, meaningful contact." Funny how the English language has no words to express phantom conference calls, or at least, none that don't make me sound like a nutcase.

"But you're sure about Polly? You've contacted her?" *Violating your promise* was the unspoken end to his question.

I almost used the excuse that Beth Ann asked me to. Or that I had no choice, given the poisoning symptoms. But I remembered Acey's advice: if I intended to have and to hold Fitzhugh Lee for the rest of my life, then I'd best be honest about a promise I might not be able to keep.

So I started at the beginning and told Hugh everything about my Carson hauntings, not even editing out the parts about being kissed by strange men (and they sure don't get much stranger).

"Poison," he said at last, as if that was the only word he'd heard out of my entire chronicle.

"Right. Someone was poisoning John Brennan with mercury fumes and—"

"No, I mean you. *You're* being poisoned."

"No, I'm experiencing memories of poisoning symptoms." Hold the phone, I thought. Didn't those memories belong to Brennan? Yet the kisses were Elizabeth's, or a woman's, at any rate. *Three* ghosts?

Meanwhile, Hugh wasn't convinced. "You should leave. Go home. I'll tell Mom you aren't feeling well—"

I touched my fingertips to his lips to shut him up. "No way am I going to leave in the middle of your mother's Christmas dinner. Not when she put so much time and effort into it. And"—I took a deep breath, steeling myself, because I knew he wouldn't like the next part—"I *need* to stay. I need to get to the bottom of this ghost business. If I don't, I'll never be able to return to this house again. And I mean to come back, on January sixth for your mom's wedding. Then many, many holidays thereafter, as your wife."

He wasn't happy, but that last magic word got him to press his lips against my fingers, and with such emotion that I pushed myself up on my toes and pulled his neck down, to transfer the kiss to my mouth. When docking was complete, I let myself revel in the sensation a moment, then, fully aware of what I was doing, I closed my eyes and let down all my defenses.

Almost at once, I was thoroughly wrapped in what can only be described as a blanket of love, more pure and unconfined than I'd ever known, producing a wave of powerful euphoria. The feeling didn't come from Hugh, but he was a part of it. Polly was there and, in that instant, I felt another side of her, another dimension entirely. No, *more* than one dimension—all the love she had, but mixed with something darker. Something ominous.

Hugh and I gasped in unison. His eyes popped open a split second after mine. His expression was nothing less than awe.

"What was *that?!*" he asked, eyes wide.

"You felt it, too? Like a group hug? Only one of the huggers didn't have flesh-and-blood arms?"

His jaw dropped. "You mean . . . that was . . . I felt . . . ?"

"Yep. You just had your first spirit world encounter." I brought my hand around to close his jaw for him.

"Who was it?"

"Polly, but not the teenager Beth Ann and Acey saw. This Polly's already gone through motherhood. And grandmotherhood. And death." The presence I'd felt had definitely evolved past human existence. "What I think she was trying to tell us was how much she loved her husband, kids, and grandkids. And by extension, you."

An extension, I thought, which also covered Glad and all her children. That sense of foreboding I'd felt—did Polly mean it as a warning?

Acey's face came to mind, the way she'd laughed as she teased Horse about his Mylanta bottle, as she tried to keep a straight face while she swore her oath of innocence. All of a sudden, I saw a reason for her behavior. "Hugh!"

"What?!" Startled, he grasped my arms, looking like he thought I'd disappear before his eyes.

"Wait, let me think this through."

"Think *what* through?!"

"The protrip—whatever—in the antacid. I'm pretty sure I know who's responsible. Come on. We have to tell the others before anything else happens."

December 25, 1783—Mrs. Carson's House

MASTER THOMAS MUST HAVE been watching for me from the scullery window in order to meet me in the rear hall so promptly. "Mother says you should wait in her chamber, sir. I've laid a proper fire for you there. 'Tis only wanting a spark."

I hung my tricorn beside the front entrance, noting that the common room door was closed. I followed Tom into the room opposite, equal in size to Jim's and Riddick's above it, yet the placement of windows and doors made for an awkward sleeping space. The bed was set between and somewhat overlapping the front windows, so 'twas necessary to walk 'round it to the hearth.

Tom's "proper fire" was but one thin wedge of a log with twigs and dry leaves below. The lad set wick to it, teasing kindling with poker until the log caught, then with reluctance, he returned to his chores in the kitchen. I took a seat in the one chair, a low-back Windsor whose stain had gone black with age and whose arms wobbled 'neath the weight of my own. I fancied I might mend them with a few brads and a bit of sawdust paste.

Warming hands by the meager flame, I turned to face the bed—the marriage bed of Elizabeth and Thomas. I could picture her there upon the ticking, wearing naught but her shift, her hair free of her bonnet and let down about her shoulders, and in her eye, an allure no man could resist. The image brought heat to my bones as no hearthfire could. Not the heat of desire, rather, the heat of anger, that Thomas Carson should come through all the years of war, still whole and virile, to be put down by foul murder even as he prepared to reunite with his family.

"Sir, you may come in to dinner now." Polly, framed by the door jamb, bobbed a stiff curtsy. No smile graced her lips and her gaze took in the floorboards.

I stood, bowing. "May I escort you, mistress?"

"No, sir. I am to have my meal with my brother, in our room."

Reason, perhaps, for her mood. I was glad to hear it, though, for I had need to speak with Elizabeth alone this day. Sooner done, the better. Yet, I felt I should lighten Polly's temper before going. "A pity, mistress. I fear your loveliness and wit shall be quite lost on Master Tom."

My words brought her eyes from the floor. No delight danced in them, however, only a heartfelt ache.

I crossed the room to her in three strides. "What is it, Polly?" A notion came to me—I added in a whisper, "You haven't spoken of our—of what we found?"

"No, sir." She backed away a step into the hall, her voice a murmur. "I gave you my promise."

"What, then?"

"Please, sir, my mother awaits you."

"I would know what troubles you first."

She looked at me at last, her gaze defiant, her voice remaining soft but angry. "After you left today, before Mother returned, a Mr. Tyler came to the door. He'd heard tell of a man named Dunbar who in the taverns of Williamsburg was pleasing all men with his fiddle. So he'd come from Norfolk to seek you out."

"Seek me out?" I echoed, stunned.

"He'd been acquainted with a Mr. Virgil Ivey, the patron of Edward Dunbar, the dance master. And though Mr. Tyler hadn't been on familiar terms with Mr. Dunbar, he knew that his only son was named John, not Benjamin."

A half dozen lies came to me, in my defense, but I could not voice one of them to her face. Yet before any word at all could leave my tongue, the common room door opened and there stood Elizabeth, wearing her best shortgown, her hair held up prettily by comb and lace. "Polly—"

"I was about to bank the fire, Mother," the girl said in haste. "Pardon me, sir?"

I stepped into the hall to make room for her to pass, saying, "I fear I was blocking her progress, madam," as I bowed low and elegantly, turning my calf as forward as I dared without losing my balance.

Elizabeth read the gesture as I presumed she would, smiling, her daughter forgotten as her eyes met my own. She returned a slow curtsy, so beguiling I could envision her bare knees parting as they bent beneath her skirts. "Your dinner, sir, grows cold."

NINETEEN

When Hugh and I left Polly's room, Glad was just calling everyone in to the last course.

The dining room seemed dimmer this time, with an odd sideways glow emanating from the kitchen. The regular lights in that room were off, and I saw an orange extension cord snaking its way out of the dining room and through the pantry. The sideboard lamp had been moved, I surmised.

"What happened to the kitchen lights?" Miss Maggie asked.

"I'm down to four fuses," Evelyn explained, "so I'm saving them in case the stove or refrigerator go off again. Sorry, everyone. I'll have someone from Maintenance in first thing tomorrow. I promise."

"I don't like it," Miss Maggie muttered at my side, sending me a silent, worried question with her eyebrows.

I shrugged, though I was certain that prolific blowing of fuses was yet another phantom warning. I did a fast headcount, relieved to find everyone present, until I realized we were sitting down with thirteen once more. I shook off the tingles on my neck hair, reminding myself how Montellas tend to see omens in everything. Self-spooking was in my blood.

"Quickly"—Glad waved us to our seats—"before the ices melt." The "ices" were in the center of the table on a double-tiered silver tray. Ten small glass bowls each cradled a scoop of red or green sherbet garnished with a cherry and a mint leaf.

Circling this centerpiece, glittering in the candlelight, were parfait glasses, each layered in three shades of either yellow, orange, or red. Saucers of candied fruit, chocolates, and mints made an outer diamond. The table ends were anchored by sugar cookies and more ratafia, chocolate brown this time.

Even the card table sported a mini-arrangement of two parfaits, three sherbets, fruits, and mints. Over on the sideboard, the coffeemaker had been set up, along with an electric percolator, and a large ceramic teapot.

Delia claimed a place at the smaller table before Horse had a chance, telling him, "You sit with Magnolia. She prefers single men as dinner companions." Everyone laughed, to gloss over the tension. Delia's tone implied that if she sat next to her husband, she'd lose her appetite. Rich didn't meet her gaze.

"I apologize," Glad announced, "that we don't have enough syllabubs." She gestured to the parfaits. "We thought we'd have eleven for dinner, you see, and—"

"We hadn't more than twelve tall glasses, at any rate," Evelyn added.

Rich cleared his throat. "I was unexpected." He threw the barest glimpse over his shoulder at the card table, implying that his wife was to blame. "So I won't take one."

"Neither will I," Delia said, not to be outdone.

"No need, Delia. Sachi and I can share," Acey volunteered, wanting to annoy Rich.

"Thanks, but I shouldn't have more alcohol anyway, since I never got a chance to eat dinner." She glared at her husband's back, indicating this was his fault.

"I've made some without wine," Evelyn said. "The red ones have port in them, and the yellow are mead, but the orange ones are made with sweet cider."

We settled into passing and munching as Evelyn and Glad poured coffee and tea. I opted for a cider syllabub, thinking to keep my head clear. At some point I had to bring up the subject of Dr. Weisel's poisoning. Not great dinner conversation, and the cook in me couldn't ruin a meal. I assured myself that, while everyone was seated around the table, nothing else could happen.

I tasted the top layer of my syllabub—whipped cream flavored with cider and cinnamon and way too much sugar for my taste. Ditto the liquid cider layer beneath. The third layer was more sugar that had sunk to the bottom. Probably the wine versions were better, but remembering yesterday's black caps, also covered in sugar, I revised my image of America's founding fathers to include diabetes and bad teeth.

As the word "teeth" entered my head, Miss Maggie let out an exclamation. The candlelight enhanced her expression of shocked, puzzled surprise as she ran her tongue over her lower incisors. Her eyes met mine, cognizance dawned, and she shifted in her seat, closer to Horse. Then she nodded to herself, grinning with delight, as if she'd proven a theory of quantum physics.

"Magnolia?" Horse ventured, voicing the concern of everyone in the room.

"Oh, it's nothing." She smiled her assurance to all. "A problem with my bottom plate. One of the curses of getting old, you know, having teeth that chew on a delayed schedule."

I could believe this if I were sitting across the table from my Great-Uncle Rocco, whose upper partial regularly fell out during family dinners. Of course, he used to carry around a bag of potato chips, swearing that gnawing on them worked better than Super Polygrip. But Magnolia Shelby? I'd lived with her two months before I realized she no longer had her own chompers.

"This reminds me," Miss Maggie said, "of something I wanted to ask when we were talking about lead and mercury poisoning earlier. Is loose teeth one of the symptoms?"

Now I understood. When she moved closer to Horse, I was willing to bet she'd bumped her leg up against his, which made whatever sensation she'd felt in her mouth—loose teeth presumably—go away.

"In advanced cases," Rich replied. "Your friend's symptoms—had they progressed that far?"

"Oh, no. This was another case I recalled. Just wondered." Miss Maggie beamed at me. She'd felt a symptom of an eighteenth-century poisoning victim and she couldn't be more thrilled.

I, on the other hand, felt the bottom drop out of my stomach. Sure, like I told Hugh, when the symptoms hit me, I thought of them as memories, incapable of any real harm, other than possibly making me hurl in front of my future in-laws. With Miss Maggie, I couldn't take chances. She was ninety-one, after all, and frailer than she'd ever admit. And experiencing *advanced* symptoms.

Fright governing my motor responses, I stood, the linen napkin on my lap falling to the hardwood floor. "I . . . I need to . . ." All eyes were on me, and I didn't have a clue what to say. Start at the beginning, I told myself. "Last night, between dinner courses, I noticed Dr. Weisel. He looked like he had *agita*—that is, indigestion."

Eloquence isn't a skill I list on my resumé, but I took a deep breath and plunged on. "He went upstairs. When he came down, he had white goo on his nose, right where the top brim of a bottle would touch if he'd taken a swig of liquid antacid."

"That explains the antacid found in his digestive tract," Rich said impatiently. "So?"

"I think it also explains the protrip . . . protript . . ."

"Protriptyline," all the doctors said in unison.

"Right, protriptyline," I echoed, committing the word to my tongue muscles. "The drug was in the antacid. Specifically, in Horse's Mylanta."

"Mine?" Horse, with a mouthful of lime sherbet, voiced the question out of clenched lips, along with green drool.

"When was the last time you took a dose?" I asked him.

He swallowed his food. "A week ago tonight. Delia brought out this awesome mocha fudge cake when we all arrived at the shore house last Friday. Gave me heartburn for three hours, but it was worth it."

I turned to Foot. "Did *you* eat any?"

He shook his head. "Too much caffeine. Besides, I can't trust store-bought foods, not with my diet restrictions."

"I had some," Acey volunteered, "but I always take an *L. reuteri* supplement before I eat—it's a probiotic that aids in the digestion of carbs and lactose. So I suffered no ill effects—"

"Neither did I," Rich cut in, "and without benefit of Acey's snake oil and voodoo. Simply a matter of eating slowly and in moderation, and—"

"And not hogging down three helpings like Horse," Acey concluded.

"I only had two and a half," Horse protested.

"Pat's point is," Hugh said loudly, "that the protriptyline pills must have been crushed and added to Horse's antacid between when he took it last Friday and when Weisel took it yesterday."

Horse shook his head. "The bottle's been packed in my bag, in my apartment all week. If it happened last weekend, one of my siblings—Delia included—would be the guilty party, which I don't believe. Not even Acey's practical jokes are *that* nasty."

"So you're saying it happened here?" Hugh asked his brother. "Because if you eliminate family, only Miss Maggie, Evelyn, and Pat were here last night."

"Wait, I feel a deduction coming on." Acey stroked her chin with a look of pseudo-wisdom. "Pat knew Kevin before she met him here. Why would she want to poison him? Because he's her GYN, of course. That's reason enough. Heck, with a female judge, she'd get off scot-free."

Horse was giving me a LAG once-over, no doubt remembering that the birth control pills gave me a dandy motive.

"Nonsense." Glad put the coffeepot back in the maker. "Where would Pat or Magnolia or Ev get hold of a drug like that?"

"Ma's right." Acey had a rare frown on her lips. "Only a few of us in this room can write prescriptions."

"Sachi works in a drugstore," Horse mused.

Acey threw a mint at him. "She wasn't here last night, lobotomy-brain."

Glad sat down as Evelyn held her seat for her. "Good thing Williamsburg's apothecary doesn't stock antidepressants or you'd all be blaming Ev—"

Suddenly one of the electric candles in the front windows went out. Everyone jumped, but at least they shut up.

"The bulb must have died," Evelyn said, standing. "I'll fetch another—"

Glad touched his arm. "Get it later. We can eat by candlelight. Let's hear what Pat has to say first."

Evelyn resumed his seat. Glad nodded encouragement at me.

So, ignoring the slightly darker room, I turned to Foot. "Did you take any antacid last weekend?"

"Saturday night at bedtime and again Sunday, after lunch."

"Horse took his dose Friday night, and you had your first one about twenty-four hours later." I swung around to face the card table. "That means Acey probably switched the bottles during the day Saturday."

Her eyes opened wide, then she slapped the table. "Busted. Wow. You're better at this detective stuff than Scooby Doo."

"You switched them?" Foot wrinkled up his nose. "I've been taking Horse's antacid all week? After he drank out of the bottle. Oh, gross." He sounded just like his niece.

Acey roared with laughter. "I've been waiting for the right moment to tell you and get that reaction. Serves you right for picking on me all last Saturday. And if you insist on using the same brand as Horse, well, then—"

"His bottle's always so disgusting!" Foot looked like he might lose his dinner any moment.

"I cleaned it," Acey explained, "including removing the hair he'd left in the cap. You never would have taken it then. See Horse? I told you I didn't put anything *in* your bot—"

The other electric candle went out. We all stared at it a moment, as if that would make it come back on.

Evelyn shrugged in apology. "The bulbs were put in at the same time." As if that explained anything.

I was wondering if a certain ghost had found a new hobby that was more fun than blowing fuses.

Glad cleared her throat, attracting everyone's attention, including my own. "What you're saying, Pat, is that the drug was in Francis's antacid when Ann Carter switched bottles."

I nodded. "I think it was meant for Foot, because of the medication he takes. He'd more likely have a fatal reaction to the protriptyline."

"Ha! My bottle switching saved your damned life," Acey told Foot. "What do you think of that?"

"I think you should shut up so I can listen to Pat," her brother snapped.

Abruptly, I had everyone's rapt attention. The room grew so silent, I could hear the candlewicks hissing as they burned. Problem was, the silence enhanced the eeriness of the shadows.

I hurried on. "The protriptyline *could* have been introduced last weekend, but who would have done it? Acey wouldn't have switched bottles if she had. If Horse did it, then put the hair in his bottlecap to guard against mix-ups, the first thing he'd do when he saw the hair missing would be check the bottle contents. Oh, he might bring the bottle with him this weekend, to effect another switch, but he wouldn't put his out on the bathroom windowsill. Too dangerous."

I hoisted my water glass for a welcome gulp. "Rich claimed he found out Foot took antidepressants Sunday afternoon, after the antacid was spiked. He might have lied, but if he intended to kill his brother, why admit he knew at all? And Delia—"

"She didn't do it," Rich declared, with such passion he shocked everyone, including himself. Embarrassed, he added, "Delia couldn't get hold of the prescription."

Acey agreed. "They don't sell it on eBay."

"I didn't rule her out for that reason," I said. "For all I know, she knew of a way to fake prescriptions, or obtain a drug without one. But I can't see a motive. Acey said last night that none of you would inherit from Foot."

"Delia doesn't have a motive," Rich said firmly. "And neither does any of the rest of our family."

"That's not entirely true." Glad calmly stirred cream into her coffee. "Francis is upset that I sold my other house, and he wants me to leave this one, maybe even leave Ev. I also think my son believes I need to live in a retirement home or some such arrangement. Now, if he intends to take action on any of this, that gives me a motive, doesn't it? That is, if I were inclined to murder."

Her children were struck dumb by the notion, though after a half moment, Acey laughed and said, "You go, girl."

I agreed that Glad had a good motive. "But when was the last time you saw Foot?"

"Thanksgiving," Glad replied.

"And I guess you've taken antacid since?" I asked Foot.

He nodded. "Three, four times a week."

"So Glad had no opportunity." One candle in front of me flickered wildly, yet I felt no draft. I took another gulp of water. "The last doctor I went to in Pennsylvania, well, once or twice he had his front desk phone a prescription in to a drugstore for me. Foot, do you ever do that?"

"Certainly. Some of my patients would lose their scripts two minutes after walking out my door."

"Do you make the calls?"

His look implied that this was menial labor. "My receptionist does."

"And you've got two patients on protriptyline? One who claimed his ex-wife stole his pills recently? Was that prescription phoned in?"

Foot nodded, his face grave.

"What if someone overheard your receptionist make that call," I suggested, "then went to the drugstore to pick up the prescription before the patient got there?"

"Whoever picked it up would have had to sign for it," Sachi said. "At least, in my pharmacy."

"ID isn't required by Virginia law," Horse pointed out.

"Not yet," Sachi conceded.

"So, at most, signature only," Acey mused. "How hard would it be to sign 'Mrs.' and the name on the prescription? The patient sees that and blames his ex. His shrink"—she waved a hand at Foot—"thinks he's delusional and calls in another script for him. You're brilliant, Scooby. We should have thought of Irene in the first place—"

"Me?" Irene had her deer-caught-in-headlights look on.

"Well, the rest of us don't hang out in Foot's office, buddy-buddying around with his receptionist," Acey said.

"But I didn't know what medicine Francis was taking, let alone what other drug reacts with—"

"I told you I took MAO inhibitors," Foot said, giving his wife a LAG, "before we were married."

Irene nodded, patting his hand on the table. "I remember you mentioning that you took something, honey, but I didn't understand. It's not like I have a medical degree."

"Oh, good Lord!" Acey exclaimed. "You can't be *that* dumb."

"Foot," Horse cut in, "where do you store your pills at home?"

"In the cabinet by the kitchen sink."

"In the original prescription bottle?"

"Always. It's dangerous to store drugs any other way."

Acey slapped the table again. "She got the name of the drug off the bottle, then looked it up on the Internet. All the info she needed is online. No medical degree necessary, *honey*."

Every eye in the room was on Irene, except mine. Both candles on the table were now flickering, as were the ones on the mantel and beneath the glass on the card table, which shouldn't have been touched by a draft, even if I'd felt one, which I didn't. What I did feel was someone lurking just out of candle range. I placated my nerves by thinking that, on the upside, this meant we were no longer thirteen in the room.

"Don't be silly," Irene was protesting. "Why would I want to kill Francis? He's my husband. I love him." Said with such sincerity, with a lump-in-the-throat swallow before the last sentence, it was hard not to believe her.

"Duh!" That was Acey. I now knew where Beth Ann learned her inflection. "You'd kill him for his money, of course. Even if you can't contest what he's already got pigeonholed for cancer research, let's talk house, classic car, art collection, insurance—"

"Not life insurance," Rich broke in. "They won't pay for suicide and that's what it would look like, with the drug in Foot's system and the prescription issued by him."

"Not much of my other money either," Foot said. "I was smart enough this time to insist on a pre-nup."

"He got ripped off in his other divorces," Irene explained, smiling. "So if we split, I get zilch. Since we'll never split, I signed it willingly." She patted her hubby's hand again.

"Nothing if we divorce," Foot clarified, "and if either of us die, the remainder of the estate is to be divided in percentages equal to each of our prior year's earned income. I didn't include my investment income in the equation—that didn't seem fair. But my thinking was that if she died, her family couldn't claim half the house. And if I went first, well, more funds could go to research."

Irene turned to him, puzzlement all over her face, but she didn't say a word.

"You didn't understand that, did you, honey?" Acey cackled. "You don't have a math degree either, huh? Your—"

The hall lamp went off, and a quarter beat later, the lamp in the kitchen. I noticed the little red lights on the coffeemaker and percolator were also out. Just as Delia exclaimed, "Don't you people pay your electric bills?" all other ambient light, from the parlor and upstairs hall, went dark.

"Look!" Beth Ann jumped to her feet, pointing at the hearth right behind Miss Maggie. I didn't see anything, nor did I have a chance, because every candle was blown out at once, throwing the room into blackness.

After that everything happened in the same second. Foot shouted "Irene!" then Evelyn, "She's getting away!" and chairs were pushed back. I'm not sure whether I moved to follow, or in response to Beth Ann, but all of a sudden I felt myself falling.

The napkin, I had just enough time to remember. I must have slipped on it. Then my head banged against, I don't know, a chair leg maybe, and I hit the floor hard.

No, I realized. I was pushed, or tripped. And now I felt something—some*one*—on my back, holding me down. I heard my name called, but it was too late. The symptoms came back in an overwhelming wave: nausea, thirst, metal taste, loose teeth, and worst of all, what I supposed must be insanity—like I was on the very brink of a cliff in my mind. I felt I couldn't trust my senses or I'd lose my balance. Mental vertigo.

I heard something, too. Like a voice with no words. No, more like someone's thoughts. Someone's emotions. Anguish. A desperate plea for help.

The instinct to be still and listen made me stop fighting the symptoms. Yet, when I stopped fighting, they went away, even the feeling of being held down. I didn't get up, though. As if I'd made a promise to keep listening.

I heard a fire crackling in the big hearth. And smelled food. Daylight flooded the room. The furniture was sparse and old. The tablecloth was stained. Dinner was set out, in twenty small, mismatched bowls and plates, arranged symmetrically.

And there before me stood Mr. Dunbar. But I wasn't looking out of Polly's eyes. Not this time.

> *"Matrimony alters us mightely.*
> *I am afraid it alienates us from everyone else."*
>
> —from the diary of Lucinda Lee, 1787

December 25, 1783—At Dinner

WITH MY REPUTATION TO preserve, I left the dining room door standing open wide as we supped, however much, after our exchange of courtesies in the hall, I should have loved to bar the door and shutter the windows. I reminded myself that men were kept in closer attendance by the hope rather than the deed, and that, with patience, I might soon meet Benjamin Dunbar in a proper nuptial bed.

Still, I took pleasure in the feel of his fingers beneath my own as he led me to the table. I'd placed two chairs center, opposite, so we might be close as we spoke, and perhaps brush hands in passing food.

When we'd recited our grace and taken our seats, he remarked, "Madam, your table is quite extraordinary."

A compliment worded with care, I noted. My tablecloth was but common linen, yellowed with age, my plates of tin, and my bowls of Virginia red clay, turned and fired no farther afield than the potter's shop five blocks distant. And though I set out full twenty dishes in this course, the portions were trifling, containing no sack or cream, little meat or spice, and far less sugar than called for. "Thank you, Mr. Dunbar. Not as fine as to what you're accustomed, surely."

"These last seven years, madam, I've been accustomed only to army provisions, where a full meal might be a half gill of rice and a spoon of vinegar. I remember your Thomas once declaring that our rations of fat beef were so thin and transparent, he should make lanterns from them."

The mention of my late husband was unexpected, coming as I ladled pottage into a bowl. My hand shook.

Benjamin steadied the vessel from his side. "What is it, madam? Have I upset you with my talk of army victuals?"

"No, sir. You may speak of whatever you like." The stronger sex, I have found, are soonest won by an attentive ear, the more so if their discourse be pompous and dull. Though I was certain Benjamin could be neither.

He took the bowl from me. "Then, madam, I would speak to you of three men: John Brennan, Gilbert Underwood, and your husband."

"Tom?" My voice trembled as I said his name. "I am still much grieved to think of him, sir."

"As am I. We were not close—a lieutenant cannot consort with privates. Yet, had he survived the war, I believe he would have shed all pretense of rank and called me friend. So I should have been proud to call him." Benjamin set the bowl aside his plate, but did not eat. "But first I shall speak of Mr. Underwood, who retains the title 'Captain' as if 'twas his birthright, though he no longer drills with our militia."

"Washington is called 'General' yet," I noted, "and has retired to his home as well."

"General Washington earned his title. Gilbert Underwood did not. We who served under the captain were convinced he wore the uniform only to assure his recent foothold in genteel society."

"Have some of the stewed squab, Mr. Dunbar. It's quite good." I'd had to use mutton gravy in lieu of beef, bacon in lieu of anchovy, and but the wings and legs of one pigeon for meat, yet I thought the dish had turned out well.

"I've no doubt, madam. Allow me to serve you first." No smile attended his offer, yet his eye caught and held my own.

The blush of a young girl rose upon my cheeks. Averting my gaze, I lifted my plate to hide my confusion. "Thank you, sir."

Benjamin spooned the stew to each of us and, in like manner, began to fill his plate and my own with all the receipts of the table. "For myself, I thought Underwood arrogant and self-serving, and a poor leader of men. However, I have come to believe his blundering was a cunning act—that he was in truth in league with the Lobsterbacks, performing traitorous favors to be bartered when the British won the war and the king sent a new royal governor to Virginia."

"Surely, sir, you cannot make such an accusation of a gentleman of the captain's standing without some proof."

"Proof, madam, is what I lack. Yet our system of justice places more weight upon the testimony of a witness, and I believe witnesses exist. John Brennan was one such. Underwood paid him recompense for his silence under the guise of almsgiving."

Surprised, I dared raise my head once more. Benjamin's ardent gaze yet rested upon me.

Now he smiled, gesturing to my plate. "Please, madam, you must have the first taste of meat. I insist."

No man, not even Tom while we courted, had ever shown me such courtesy. Indeed, the most gentle of men seem to think food need enter their bodies as swift as smoke through a pipe, and only afford first taste to their social betters. "Sir, you do me honor."

"Then, madam, you shall have first taste of all."

My heart quickened, hoping his words extended to more than the fare of my table. Willing my eyes to convey that wish to him, I said softly, "I should like that, sir."

He took in a breath, slow, so that I let myself imagine in him a desire to kiss me then and there. I regretted placing the taller pottage bowl between us. A flat tray might have lent ease to the fulfillment of such desire.

Benjamin shifted his eye from me, politely, so that I might eat. "As I was saying, madam—"

"You were saying that Mr. Brennan was paid by Captain Underwood for his silence. Is that true?"

"So I believe. Furthermore, when the war began, the governing houses of Virginia sat here in Williamsburg. Next to the Congress, here were the most powerful men in America—"

"Some would say *before* Congress. The House of Burgesses themselves, certainly."

He smiled. "Precisely why the British would locate a spy in town, madam."

I'd brought a bite of the roast squab to my lips. Now I swallowed in haste to get my words out. "Spy, sir?"

Benjamin began to cut his food into smaller bits. "To spy upon the Virginia assemblies was, I believe, why Brennan settled here. His intelligence could have been conveyed to Tory couriers passing through."

"I—I suppose that's possible—"

"Yet Mr. Brennan remained here after the capitol moved. I can think of but two reasons he might do so." Benjamin took a taste of the roast bird from his portion, chewing before proceeding. "The British had already begun to wage war in the South. Perhaps their campaign for this part of Virginia was planned out, and they wanted a man in place, ready to bring intelligence between armies. Brennan traveled on occasion in those months before Yorktown, did he not?"

Nodding as I remembered that summer, my cheeks warmed once more. I hid the emotion by bending my head to spoon pottage from bowl to mouth.

"And after the surrender, madam?"

"After?"

Benjamin took up his spoon and sipped at the pottage. "The twenty-seventh of October, the day of your husband's death. Did Brennan travel then?"

"You've asked me before, Mr. Dunbar, when you first came to live here. My answer has not changed. Mr. Brennan was not away overnight. He did not speak of journeying, nor did he take so much as a haversack when he left the house early that morning. To the best of my knowledge, he was about town that day, selling his snuff—"

"But you did not see him," Benjamin said, with the air of a child reciting a rote lesson, "and he came in very late that night."

"He often did." I sampled the onion pie. The crust had come tough, and I'd not used enough eggs in the filling.

Benjamin set down his fork and once more looked directly at me. "Shall I tell you where Brennan was that day, madam? He was in our camp, poisoning your husband."

I drew in my breath, yet met his gaze. "I was told cramp colic."

"Aye, 'tis what the doctor thought. I had my suspicions when I spied Mr. Brennan here, yet recalled seeing him in camp on the twenty-seventh. Afterward, I found shavings of the poison in Thomas's canteen, and a lump of it where his tent stood. A certain root, a bit of which can kill a man within an hour. Today I learned that Brennan still carried a piece of that root about with him."

I was shocked all the more. "Did he mean to use the poison again?"

"To kill? More likely to remind those in league with him that he could ruin all, and so gain by blackmail."

I hit upon a solution. "Captain Underwood. Tom must have discovered his treachery, so the captain had him killed before—"

"Had him killed? Why should Brennan be so obliging?"

I glanced down at my table as I thought upon the matter. The stewed apples and Indian pudding now had a dull look from having gone cold. "Tom must have known also of Mr. Brennan's involvement."

"So Brennan went out of his way to procure rare poison?"

"No, not out of his way." I became more animated as I reasoned it out. "The British officers who lodged here—two had done duty in the Caribbean Sea. Either might have given Mr. Brennan the root."

Benjamin frowned, studying my face as he might a difficult passage of music. "A novel thought, madam. Here I'd presumed Brennan purchased the cassava from a sailor at the docks."

This simpler explanation had not occurred to me and I admitted it. "My fancy was taken by your talk of spies, sir."

His frown remained. "Still, while Underwood and Brennan may have conspired together to help the enemy, I'll warrant the captain had nothing to do with the actual poisoning of Lieutenant Carson."

"But if Tom knew of the treachery—"

"I think he did not. Brennan turned to murder, I believe, to forward his own plan, his true reason for remaining here when the capitol moved." Benjamin looked down at his plate, but his face now appeared bilious. "He was quite taken with you, madam. All the more so two years ago when we came to deliver the news of Thomas."

This time no blush came to my cheeks, but I did allow a faint laugh. "Mr. Brennan was taken by *every* woman, sir. Or more to the point, he thought us all taken by his spurious charm. I can assure you, Mr. Dunbar, I was never a fool for him."

"No, you would not be. No fool for any man, I'll wager. Do I guess right, Elizabeth?"

'Twas his first use of my given name and I thrilled to hear it. "I believe I could be, sir."

"But never before? Not for Thomas?"

My husband again! I did not want to speak of him, but of myself and Mr. Dunbar. "Yes, for Tom. As I've said, I still grieve to think of him. Yet, but for the letters he wrote and the short leave he was granted just before Yorktown—" I faltered, for the memory brought a pang to my heart. I'd spent as much of those few days as I could in Tom's arms. I dismissed the pain resolutely, and returned to the business at hand. "Otherwise, sir, I've lived as a widow these last six years. 'Tis my hope to marry again—soon."

Benjamin smiled at that, but merely said, "You have many suitors, madam."

"Suitors? They come not for me, Mr. Dunbar, but to court my house and land, offering little or nothing in return. All feel I should gladly hand over my property to gain a man in my bed, another mouth for my table, and more clothes for my mending basket." I regretted my words at once, thinking they might discourage. "Not that I require wealth or estate. I want prospects. For instance, I have heard that gentry will pay forty shillings or more for one subscription of music instruction. You need not have many students to live comfortably at that wage."

Benjamin's smile widened so, I felt he might propose at once. To my disappointment, he said, "I should let you see to your remove, madam."

"You've hardly eaten, sir."

"I save myself for your mince pies, madam." He stood and bowed with such grace, I regretted putting no meat in the tarts. "I shall tarry in your chambers once more, Mrs. Carson. No need to call young Tom—I shall see to the fire myself." His eyes, I fancied, conveyed a hope that one day he'd tarry in that room to kindle a different sort of flame.

I accompanied him as far as the hall, then summoned my children to the dining room, instructing them to clear the table. "Return the food to the pots. The large pail has clean water, so you may begin to wash the plates and bowls. Wash them well, for we shall need them all for the next course. I shall take two smaller pails and fetch fresh water—"

"I can do that, Mother," Thomas said, seeking an escape from kitchen chores, as was his wont.

"No, you would be too long about it, and I must visit the privy anyway. Make a quick, thorough job and you both may eat whatever you like from the first course." I took up the buckets and fairly ran for the back door.

The sun was gone from the yard, the breeze now fresh, placing a stinging chill upon my face and arms. I hurried to the well, leaving the pails beside it, then continued downhill toward the privy. At the door, I glanced back at the house. Seeing no one, I lifted my hems and dashed the short distance along the bank to Tom's tinshop, not stopping to breathe until I was safely out of sight on the far side of the building. Even so, I promptly unhooked the shutter and let myself in through the open window, cursing my full skirts for hindering my haste, yet I'd mastered the skill over the last few years, and so my clothes were neither torn nor soiled by the exercise.

The light from my window did not reach the darkest corners of the shop. No matter—I knew the place well. The tiny square room once held table, stool, and a round slice of tree trunk upon which Tom would hammer and punch his tin. The walls had boasted shelves of his work, ready for sale. When Tom went off to the army, I began to sell off his stock. After he'd been away more than a year, I'd sold all else save the tree trunk.

The room was always colder than outside. Indeed, when the creek first changed course and claimed the shop, I stored food here in summer. Yet water will bring rats, so I'd given up the practice. Now, before moving forward, I stamped upon the floorboards. An answering scuffle came from below, but not within the shop or cramped attic above. The poison I'd set out still kept the vermin at bay. However, I noticed that the boards themselves seemed to creak more as I crossed to the tree trunk near the east wall. The floor was beginning to rot from the water beneath.

The stump was knee-high and wide enough for me to stand upon. From it, I could reach the boards stretching over the low ceiling joists above. Here Tom had hinged a board to create a secret cache where he'd kept copies of documents and extra money in a small tin box he'd fashioned for the task. On my toes, I felt for the box and lifted it down. I'd spent the extra coin long ago, but the documents remained, along with the last four letters Tom had sent. I'd burned his others within a day of reading them, but kept these after his visit home, being all I had of him in his last months. Now I knew I must hide them beneath my stays and set flame to them before the next course.

The room grew suddenly dim. Startled, I nearly fell from my perch, for there at the window, blocking the light, stood Benjamin. He swung his legs over the sill before I could do more than jump down to the floor.

"I thought you'd come here, Elizabeth," he said, face shadowed, yet a hint of anger coloring his voice. "I searched the shop today after learning that this window had been propped open. I found no loose floorboards nor unmortared bricks in the hearth, but I am a fool, for the rafters did not occur to me." He held out his hand. "Your box, madam."

"No, sir. This is my property and the taking of it no less than theft."

"I shall have the contents before you'd destroy them. Long I've worked to find evidence of Thomas Carson's murderer. I'll not stand by and let you send it up a chimney flue."

He came forward, yet before he could touch the box, I wrapped my arms tight about it and turned from him. "Upon my word, sir, you'll find no such evidence here. Please, you must believe me."

"Believe a poisoner? For I already have proof of that. The logs from Brennan's room are beneath the refuse heap, where you placed them. Pockets drilled in them, containing quicksilver, had been plugged, cleverly, with pie crust. None of your lodgers, madam, have had daily access to both the firewood brought in to your hearth and your baking dough. Only you and your children. Would you have me accuse Polly or young Tom?"

"No, please." I kept my back to him, for he'd come no closer since I turned. Still, I kept a wary eye over my shoulder. "I only sought to drive Mr. Brennan from my home. I did not believe the breathing of quicksilver could bring lunacy, but—"

"You heard Dr. Riddick speak of the possibility?"

"Yes. 'Twas desperation drove me to try it. I knew not what else to do."

"So first you took Sam's powders and put them into Brennan's snuff pouch. When that was discovered and the lock affixed to Brennan's door, you began adding mercury to his logs." Benjamin crossed his arms over his chest in doubt. "As Brennan's landlady, why not simply *ask* him to leave?"

"He would not go. As you said, Mr. Dunbar, he was taken with me. When I did not return his attentions—'twas that jealousy that drove him to murder my husband."

"More than jealousy. With Thomas in his grave, Brennan could set about gaining your house and land, presuming you'd meet him at the altar to ensure his silence."

Bile rose into my throat. "Silence?"

"A women of your sensibilities, madam, concerned above all with rising in society, may have thought to gain material advantage by assisting the British. I believe you aided Brennan in his traitorous mission."

"Aided Brennan?" That brought a smile to my lips.

"He, in turn, killed Thomas *at your bidding*, for you would keep your husband from discovering your betrayal. You gave yourself away at dinner, madam, when you suggested that one of the Redcoats provided the poison. I did not mention 'cassava' before you spoke of the Caribbean. I presume, then, that the root was provided to you, not John Brennan. At what cost, I wonder?"

He could not understand. I'd saved my family and my home. And needed to do so again, now. "Your notion has holes, sir. I've gained no advantage, as you can see, and I did not marry Mr. Brennan."

"You turned him lunatic instead. You knew a madman would never be believed—"

"Do not give him the box, Mother!" Polly stood at the window, her hands clutching the sill, her face pale all over. "He lies. He has lied to us from the beginning."

"Mistress—" Benjamin turned toward her, struck to see her there.

I might have used the distraction, but I would not have my daughter involved in my troubles. "Polly! Return to the house at once!"

"No, Mother. I will not see my family destroyed."

There came a sound like shoes kicking the clapboards to the front of the south window, and a scuffling like a large rat scaling that side of the shop. I knew the source at once. "Thomas! Are you there?"

"Yes, Mother," came his voice through the wall, panting from the exertion. "I shall climb around to the door to help you."

"No!" I cried. "Go back! The wood is rotting—it might not hold—"

My son gave a cry. I heard his hands slap against the clapboards, then a splash. "Thomas!" The tin box with its damning letters fell to the floor forgotten as I ran for the door. The latch was rusted and the wood swollen with the damp, but I threw my body against the panels to loosen both, calling my son all the while. At last the latch lifted and the door swung in, and I rushed out upon the stoop which had become like a pier, surrounded by water and tall, brown reeds.

Yet no sooner was I clear of the door than the stoop gave way beneath my weight. I plunged down into the icy water, splintering boards catching at my skirts, shortgown, and hair. My spine caught the sill of the doorway, then my chin hit hard upon one of the stoop posts, snapping my head backwards. Blackness seemed to enshroud me, blinding my eyes. Still, I called to Thomas—called for someone to save him—until the weight of my sodden clothes dragged me under.

TWENTY

"Whoa! Quit kicking me!" Hugh's voice, directed at me.

How could I tell with my eyes closed? I just knew. I *was* kicking, so it made sense. Kicking because I couldn't move any other part of my body. I found, when I opened my eyes, that I was swaddled in a blanket while Hugh clutched me to his breast as he carried me out the kitchen door.

"Put her in my van," Delia called from behind. "Wait, let me clean the kids' junk out of the back seat."

"What's up?" I asked my bearer.

"You're going to the hospital."

"I am not!"

"Are, too," answered Horse, who appeared beside Hugh's shoulder. "You've got a concussion."

"Do not. I feel fine!"

"Well, *something* made you lose consciousness," Horse said. "A concussion may be the best-case scenario. Guess I should have had you checked for blood clots last night." He turned, yelling, "Come on, Rich! You've got the hospital privileges."

I needed a doctor to argue my case. "Where's Acey?"

"Helping with Irene," Hugh grunted, with a nod beyond the back gate.

"She didn't get away?"

He shook his head. "Her car was blocked in by Delia's van, so she tried running. Acey tackled her halfway up the hill and held on 'til Foot and Evelyn got there. They're waiting for the police now. You really feel all right?"

"I'm fine." I lowered my voice. "I was just—you know—Elizabeth this time."

His eyebrows went up, but he didn't comment because he'd arrived at Delia's van. She'd opened the back sliding door and was tossing school backpacks, football equipment, and empty soda cans into the last row of seats. "Rich'll take good care of you," she assured me. "He's a great doctor." Implying that he was only a rat at home.

"Go get checked out," Hugh said. "Find out what's making your legs hurt." Before I could protest further, he added, "I'll pay anything your health insurance doesn't cover."

"You will not."

"Will. I know that's why you don't want to go."

"We'll talk funding later," Miss Maggie said, coming up behind us. She was all wrapped up in her coat, scarf, hat, and gloves, and Beth Ann, zipping up her own jacket, was at her side. "You *did* bump your head, Pat. You're going."

I couldn't see more than her eyes, and in the dim light from the porch, not much of them, but I knew her desire to grill me about ghosts was at war with worry for my health. What made me give in, though, was seeing the same worry on Beth Ann's face, however much she tried to hide it with boredom.

Hugh piled me into a middle row seat of the van with Horse in attendance and Rich riding shotgun up next to his wife. Hugh, Miss Maggie, and Beth Ann followed in my Neon.

At least half of the next six hours were spent waiting around, shivering in a hospital gown with a sheet around my legs for warmth. The rest of the time I was assailed by vampires (who had to stab me in four places to suck out a measly two tubes of blood), had my brain and lungs scanned (inhaling argon feels like slow suffocation), my chest X-rayed, and something called a venus doppler, in which an ultrasound microphone was rubbed up and down my legs. It hurt like the Dickens. Inflammation, Horse and Rich surmised. I could have told them that.

Add to all this my mortification at not having done a primo job when last I shaved my legs (wintertime is pants season, after all).

Not a Christmas I'll ever forget.

* * *

"Now that you've seen the real eighteenth century, Pat, what do you think of this place?" Miss Maggie asked me the next morning after I had told her all about my session with Elizabeth.

We were sitting on a bench on Duke of Gloucester Street soaking up winter sunshine and enjoying a breakfast of hot cider and soft-pretzel-like rolls from the Raleigh Tavern Bake Shop. I was still sleepy—we hadn't gotten in until after midnight—but I didn't regret joining Miss Maggie for an early constitutional.

For one thing, though my legs still felt stiff and achy, it felt good to take a walk again. The upshot of my ER visit was no concussion—not even much of a bump, thanks to my thick Italian skull—and no clots. So the hospital kicked me out, saying they'd fax Rich the full blood and radiologic workups in a few days.

For another thing, I'd have been too antsy hanging around Glad's house. I couldn't sleep anyway, not after my vision the night before, and I couldn't find out more until Beth Ann and Acey awoke and I could get into Polly's room. Why Polly? Because I was certain Elizabeth had told me all she would. Or could. Why was I certain? Because I'd gone into the old part of the house alone this morning and—nothing. Not even under the mistletoe. I might add that, since my encounter last night, all electrical devices and connections had worked perfectly.

And, well, consider my answer to Miss Maggie. "Two days ago, when I tried to picture the colonial era here, something was missing. This morning, though, I felt it." Of course, I thought, my imagination was being stimulated by the cold, damp fog hanging low over the ground, and by the stillness. Only a few tourists were out and the living history guides, as they opened up buildings for the day, seemed to move on tiptoe, as if afraid of breaking the spell. Yes, there *was* a spell. But I couldn't explain it.

With Miss Maggie, I didn't have to. She simply nodded. "After dark, I swear history seeps out of the cracks of this place and swirls around until the crowds arrive the next day. Must have been what the Reverend Goodwin felt that gave him his dream of restoring the town, and what Rockefeller felt when he bought into the idea. I'm not sure either of them would be pleased by the theme park Williamsburg's become. Two-dimensional history, prettied up, entertaining maybe, but to my mind, not as interesting." She sipped her cider. "*There*'s the problem. The *human* side of history *isn't* pretty, yet if we're going to learn from it, so we can make better decisions in the future, that's the side we shouldn't forget."

Case in point: the version of Elizabeth Carson that Glad presented to the world compared with what I now knew. Still, no one wanted to hear bad things about ancestors, so there was no way I was telling the Lee family about their black sheep. I said as much to Miss Maggie.

"Never underestimate a woman who's kept hearth and home together all by herself."

"You mean Elizabeth? Or Glad?"

"You decide." Miss Maggie let out one of her throaty alto laughs. "Besides, Beth Ann'll want to be in on your next contact. Acey might, too."

And Hugh. I had to at least ask him.

* * *

The house was less crowded by noon. Delia had gone back to her parents and kids, with Rich right behind her in his Volvo, although he wore a cellular headset and was gabbing with someone at the hospital. Sachi had pointed her car for Richmond and a day of half-off-all-Christmas-items at her drugstore, but not before Glad had given her three big bags of leftovers and made her promise to return for Twelfth Night.

Evelyn left to spend the day at the Apothecary Shop. Glad, done up in her Betsy Ross outfit, had gone off to cover midday breaks at the Governor's Palace. Foot was at the jail.

"Irene's much more fascinating to Foot today," Acey said as the rest of us lunched on pumpkin soup and turkey sandwiches around the kitchen table, "now that he thinks she's psycho. He'll pay more attention to her as a patient than he ever did as a wife."

At the meal's conclusion, as the womenfolk were clearing the table, Horse declared his intention of watching football on TV the rest of the day and disappeared up the back stairway. With a wistful glance after him, Hugh hung around to help. When the dishwasher was all loaded, he asked me if I wanted to tour the historic area.

Leading him into the privacy of the pantry, I said, "You can watch football, but—" I told him what I planned seance-wise.

His face fell. "Aw, Pat—"

"I need to finish this." Though I didn't tell him why—that is, what I knew about Elizabeth. "You in?"

He heaved a sigh of disapproval.

I stood on tiptoe to put my arms around his neck. "Come on. Polly likes you, remember? And I promise you won't miss more than the pregame show. Maybe not even that."

He planted a provocative kiss on my lips, then checked to see if his sheer sex appeal had dissuaded me. Seeing it hadn't, he gave up. "I'm in."

Acey approved the seance, but declined to participate. "I'll keep Horse out of your hair for you and an eye out for Ma, in case she gets back early. Let me know what you find out."

So we gathered in Polly's room: me, Hugh and Beth Ann (who wouldn't be left out, however much her dad grumped about her inclusion), and Miss Maggie.

The latter wouldn't join our circle, maintaining, "You should always have an outside observer. I'll guard the door."

Father, daughter, and I settled on the bed, holding hands. A regular little family outing, I mused, then realized it was the first time I'd thought of us as a family, with me in the mom role. The notion must have spooked me, because when I closed my eyes, I was aware only of the ring on my finger and my blood vessels throbbing beneath it.

"Don't hold my hand so tight, Hugh," I said. His grip on my hand relaxed and the throbbing went away, but the ring seemed more of a presence than ever. I snapped my lids open.

"What's wrong?" Miss Maggie asked.

"It's not working. Wait." Taking back both my hands, I tugged on the ring. It slid easily off my finger. *Too* easily. Weird. "This is temporary," I assured Hugh, and asked Miss Maggie to hold the hardware for me, which she did.

We rejoined hands, I closed my eyes once more. Boom. I found myself entering the dining room. The sights and smells were all the same as when I'd been there with Elizabeth, including the food, still on the table.

This time, though, sunlight no longer came through the windows. Mr. Dunbar stood by the mantel, wearing a shirt that seemed too tight around his wide shoulders, tucked into white, much-stained long pants that flared out like bell-bottoms over his bare feet. The clothes he'd worn earlier were draped over the backs and seats of two chairs set close to the hearth.

The orange glow of the fire emphasized the sorrow on his face as he read the papers in his hands. Thomas Carson's last letters.

> *"now 1787 is Ended,*
> *it happy is if we are mended.*
> *God grant if not we may be."*

—from the diary of Martha Ballard, December 31, 1787

December 25, 1783—The Last Course

MR. DUNBAR LOOKED UP from his reading—yet I remembered his name could not be Dunbar. The man who stood before me, who'd so patiently taught me sweet music, was now a stranger. Tears welled in my eyes, but I blinked them away, willing anger to replace them. Yet that emotion would not come. I was too weary.

"How is your mother, mistress? And young Tom?"

"My brother is well. Dr. Riddick fed him a weak toddy of tea and whiskey, after which Tom fell asleep on a pallet I'd made up by the fire in mother's chamber. He refuses to leave her, for he blames himself for her injury."

"As do I, mistress. I heard the boards groan 'neath our feet as we talked. I should have guessed the danger and coaxed your mother out to solid ground."

"And I should have kept my brother here, clearing the table, instead of following you. Sir, Mother should not be alive at all, were it not for you pulling her from the marsh and sending me a-run to the hospital to call for the doctor."

Mr. Dunbar nodded, but spoke not of himself. "Never have I seen a man push water from lungs as he did. I thought sure Riddick would break your mother's ribs, yet she breathed again."

The speaking of his name seemed to conjure the man himself. Dr. Riddick, shirtsleeves rolled to his elbow, entered behind me.

My heart beat faster. "Doctor?"

"Do not distress yourself, mistress. I come in merely to steal a bite from the table, as I've had no sustenance all day."

"You'll find little meat," Mr. Dunbar said. "Sam and Jim arrived together not a half hour ago, cleansing the table of pottage and squab before I sent them off to the Eagle."

I told the doctor to help himself to what remained, and filled for him a bowl of mutton stew, still hot in its kettle on the fire. I would, I thought, need to provide him many meals ere he was paid for today's service.

"What of Mrs. Carson, sir?" Mr. Dunbar asked. "Has she awakened?"

Dr. Riddick lifted the plate of boiled potatoes, eating with his fingers, speaking around the morsels in his mouth. "One eye has opened thrice, and a corner of her mouth, as if she would speak, though no sound comes forth. She has a touch of palsy upon the right side of her face which I find worrisome." The doctor took a fistful of bread from the loaf and set it upon the plate. "You see, though Mrs. Carson's heart beat through her ordeal, her lungs ceased for quite a time. Many who survive this state do not live long after. We shall watch close tonight and the next several days." He spooned the entire serving of stewed apples atop the potatoes, then preceded to add samples of all the other foods to his plate. "As I've told Mistress Carson, her mother is a strong woman and I believe her chances excellent. Yet, though she lives, the possibility remains that she may never fully recover. Losses of movement and speech are not uncommon. Some regain these losses in time. Some do not."

"I shall nurse her, sir," I vowed, handing him the bowl of stew, "as long as she needs me and as best I'm able."

"I know you shall, mistress." Dr. Riddick, balancing plate upon bowl, took up a spoon. I poured small beer into a tankard for him and, hands full, he returned to Mother's bedside.

"Riddick speaks true, mistress," Mr. Dunbar said. "Your mother is strong."

"She does not appear so at the moment, sir. Her limbs lie still, as if—" The word "dead" almost parted my lips, but I could not say it, nor speak of Mother further. Instead I moved to the chair that held Mr. Dunbar's shirt and breeches, placing my hands upon linen and wool. "Your clothes are still wet, sir."

"They shall dry overnight. I hope. Mr. Brennan's spare shirt is tight and my soldiering trousers are no longer fit for public view." After a hesitation, he said, "Yet, perhaps they'd dry with greater dispatch should you give the fire new life—by adding these?" He offered the papers in his hand. "Sam and Jim did not see them. I told them that your mother met with an accident while trying to save your brother, who'd fallen in the marsh. No one need know if you destroy these."

"You—you would have me burn my father's letters, sir?"

"You knew of this tin box? Of what it held?" His tone accused, yet he kept his voice low, so the doctor would not hear.

I had no spirit to fight him. "I knew of the hiding place before Father left for war. When he'd gone, Mother would sometimes go to the shop late, when no one was about. I would hear her slip out and see a hooded lantern from my window. When the army came to Virginia, she frequented the spot each time she received one of Father's letters. Curiosity made me inspect the cache. I—I do not read well, sir. I did not understand—"

"You know what these letters imply, though, and thus did not want your mother to give them to me."

"Yes, sir. You said you thought Mr. Brennan a spy—" I blushed, admitting, "I stood in the hall and listened to your dinner talk with Mother."

"Go on, lass."

"As those letters say, Mr. Brennan did not spy upon the Virginia assemblies. Mother did. Or, at least, upon the couriers and clerks who stayed with us before the capitol moved."

"She wrote down what she learned and placed it in the cache, is that it? Then someone would come to retrieve the intelligence?"

"'Twas always gone within a day."

"Moreover, your father—" Mr. Dunbar let go a sigh, his eyes once more upon the missives in his hands. "I held Thomas Carson in highest regard. A fair, honest, God-fearing man."

"He was all those things, sir. But he was not a patriot."

"To think I suspected Underwood of that betrayal. 'Twas not the captain but your father who issued us false commands in battle. As he says here"—Mr. Dunbar tapped the letters with the back of his free hand—"Underwood gave no orders of his own, passing on those from above, letting his subordinates decide how to best accomplish the Commander's aims. Your father was never caught, for Underwood could not admit to his own failing. And Sergeant Lynch, also a traitor and trusted by Underwood, helped to hide the subterfuge. What did your father include with his letters that your mother left for Tory couriers? News of troop movements and strength?"

"Yes, when the war came to Virginia. Sometimes, those last months after Father visited, when I had the chance, I took the dispatches myself before their retrieval."

Mr. Dunbar's eyebrows rose in surprise and a sudden smile lit his face. "Did you? A brave girl you are. You may have saved all our skins."

"Not brave, sir, nor patriot, nor even loyalist like my parents. To save Father's skin was my only thought, for I was sure he'd die were the British to waylay our troops. Yet I could not prevent his death after all."

He came a step closer. "If you listened to our talk, you know your father was poisoned. Or did you know before this?"

I could not lie to him, so did not reply at all. In my manner though, he had his answer.

"You did know. Or suspected?"

"I knew, but not 'til after."

"Was I correct? John Brennan done the murder?"

I nodded. "You guessed right that he thought to gain our property by marrying Mother. He'd found out about her spying, and thought to force her to the altar that way, to keep him silent."

"Brennan was accomplished at blackmail. When he discovered your mother's treachery, he must have learned of Sergeant Lynch as well. The alms he collected at Underwood's door need not have come from the captain, but from Lynch himself. 'Twas why the sergeant shot him, I'll wager."

Mr. Dunbar came out of his musing to explain, "When Sam came in, he had news: the constable sent word to Richmond that Lynch should be arrested on sight. You see, Underwood, on showing off his rifles to his houseguests today, noticed that one had been discharged and not cleaned. Upon bullying all his servants, one old slave confessed that, from the kitchen, she'd seen Lynch leave through the house's rear door, gun in hand, then return after shots were fired. Why she didn't speak sooner—"

"She was afraid of Mr. Lynch, of course, and of the captain, who for all she knew might have sent his footman outside with the rifle. So until her master asked—"

Mr. Dunbar saw my reasoning and agreed. "And as far as Brennan's blackmail went, well, your mother did *not* meet him at the altar. To make his plan work, her husband had to die, yet once Brennan had done murder, your mother could employ blackmail of her own. Is that it, mistress? The last two years they had eyed each other like caged lions, each knowing the other's knowledge would bring hanging, until your mother could stand it no more and sent Brennan mad with quicksilver."

"Mother could not stand it, sir, because you came and she decided she would marry again."

Naught but the crackling of the fire could be heard the next moments. When Mr. Dunbar spoke anew, his voice had grown gentler. "I presumed that Brennan poisoned your father at your mother's bidding, because Thomas had discovered her betrayal. Yet here"—he waved the letters in his hand—"I find husband and wife in league together. But I cannot see Brennan killing Thomas on his own. 'Twas too much a risk and John Brennan too much a coward. And, as I said, I believe your mother procured the root. Mistress, do you know why your father was killed?"

"I—I shall speak no more of the matter, sir."

He came nearer still, his voice a whisper, pleading. "Please, mistress, I've labored two years for the truth. I must know. I promise you, no word shall go beyond this room. Brennan is dead, and your mother—" His eye strayed to the doorway. "I would not see her hanged even if she lives. I—I believe God doled out His own justice this day."

I was moved by his speech, yet— "Are you in earnest, sir, about burning those letters?"

He turned to the hearth and flung them upon the fire. We both watched as the papers were consumed, he retrieving any scrap that strayed from the flames, until all was ash.

I spoke at last. "When Father came home on leave that last time—seeing the capitol and much commerce gone from Williamsburg, and his shop ruined by the floods—he decided he would take his business elsewhere. Not Richmond, where a tinsmith would be one among many, but to the Shenandoah Valley or the Kentucky wilderness, where his craft would be needed. As soon as the war was over, he vowed, we would move west."

"I heard him speak of the wish," Mr. Dunbar commented. "So when Thomas furloughed out, your mother stood to lose this house, and what little proximity to gentry she still had."

"I heard her say she would never raise her children in a rude cabin, surrounded by savage Indians."

Mr. Dunbar reasoned out the rest. "She waited two months, likely praying that the war would take Thomas and save her home. When word of the surrender came, she could wait no longer, not knowing when he'd be furloughed. If her husband died here, she'd be suspect. Or worse, her children might be. For I believe, mistress, that all was done to protect you and young Tom."

My tears could not be held back then. "And what came of it? Tom and I orphaned. What protection is that?"

"Your Mother will live, mistress—"

"Even if she does, even if she recovers after a time, I must in the meanwhile run this house myself. And if she is never whole again—" The prospect frightened me so, I could not put words to my emotion.

"You shall not be alone." Mr. Dunbar seemed at a loss by my weeping and sought to assure me. "I shall help, mistress."

"I do not even know who you are, sir!" I shouted, ruing my outburst at once. We both glanced at the door, yet no one stirred in Mother's room.

He faced the fire once more, stirring embers with iron. "True, I am not Edward Dunbar's son, yet of those in Mr. Ivey's employ, he alone was as a father to me. He taught me to fiddle, though he did not approve when I worked out the chanteys I learned on the docks of Norfolk." A faint smile rose at the memory. "I was a lad of ten, with a brother of twelve, when we two were indentured to Mr. Ivey for our passage from England. Seven years each was the agreement, but Mr. Ivey was a cruel master and after only two years, my brother ran off. Indeed, I helped him do it."

Mr. Dunbar looked for my reaction thus far. I think he was encouraged that my tears had ceased. He leaned his shoulder against the hearth brick. "Mr. Ivey decided, and a magistrate agreed, that I should make up the five years owed him, raising my term to twelve years. I put in my first seven—likely I'd have done the rest, to protect my brother—however, when the rebellion broke out, Mr. Ivey decided to sail for England and take his house servants with him. Having no desire to find myself back where I'd begun, I ran off to join the army. I did not know if Mr. Ivey's agents would search for me, or if, when he sold off his property, any of his slaves and indentures were included. Regardless, I am not by law a free man, mistress. I cannot tell you my true name, for I would not have you need lie should Mr. Tyler or another like him return in search of me."

"Is it Michael?" I blurted out.

Taken aback by my bluntness, he warily shook his head.

I could not hide my disappointment. "'Twas your brother's name, then, and you are Habakkuk. You were wise, sir, to change it to Benjamin. I like that much more."

"Ben was the name my brother called me, so I knew I could answer to it—but, mistress, how do you know—?"

"Mr. Tyler left these." I undid the ribbon gathering my left sleeve and brought out two papers folded many times.

When he took them in hand, even before he'd fully unfolded them, he knew what they were. "Our indentures! Both mine and Michael's. But how—"

"Mr. Tyler said I should make particular mention of a scar he bore beneath one ear."

"Evans!" To me, he explained, "A comrade in servitude. He must have shaved his beard, else I'd have recognized him at Underwood's table last night."

"Best stoke the fire, Mr. Dunbar," I bid, pointing to the papers in his hand, "so you shall be dry indeed this night."

A smile lit his whole face. Tearing the indentures lengthwise, he fed the blaze once more. "I owe you much, mistress Polly. I said I'd help and I will. I can split wood, scrub floors, go to market, perhaps effect some repairs about your house. At Mr. Ivey's I was taught to clerk and I keep books quite well. Indeed, I hope to earn my bread among the new gentry doing just that. Which reminds me—where is my purse?" Setting the fire iron aside, he sought out his coat. "This very day, I shall begin paying my room and board."

He reached into a pocket, whereupon his expression changed to dismay and his hand brought forth not coin, but a white orb, soft and sodden. "Soap," he mumbled. "I'd bought as a gift, a small token for Christmas."

"For Mother?"

"No, mistress, for you." He seemed at once shy. "I thought you should enjoy it more than a few pence in your box."

He'd bought me a gift—'twas the only thought my mind could dwell on at first. Then I took in the sight of him, standing there with the slippery mass in his palm, and could not help but smile. "I can still enjoy it, sir." From the table, I took an empty plate and held it out to him.

As he set the soap upon the tin, he said, "I shall not wish you a Happy Christmas, mistress, for it has not been so, and I fear the New Year may bring more sorrow. Instead, I wish you comfort."

"And I to you, Mr.—" A notion came to me. "Have you searched for your brother, sir?"

"I've never had the chance. And where would I begin? Likely he also assumed a new name."

"Then perhaps, in case he searches for you, you should change yours back. You can still go by Ben, since he called you that, but—"

"Discard Dunbar and reclaim the family crest?" His voice was all jest, yet I sensed shame for humble beginnings.

"This is Virginia, sir, where all men are equal, regardless of their ancestry."

His smile broadened across his handsome face. "If *you* wish it, mistress Polly, I would go so far as to change my name to—Short-pockets. Benjamin Shortpockets. Nice ring to it."

I bit my lip to stem my laughter, lest the doctor should hear. "No, sir, I do not wish it."

"Greenshingles, then? Or, wait, what about Tornbritches? Most appropriate."

'Twas a moment before I could speak through my mirth. "Stop. I shall call you by your true name whether you like it or not—Mr. *Hawkins*."

Taking a step back, he bowed low. "Your pleasure, mistress, is my own."

TWENTY-ONE

Zela wasn't on duty at the King's Arms Sunday night, which was just as well because by then I had no more need to talk to her and every need to talk to Hugh.

Not that it was easy to begin. First, while we scanned menus, the Grand Illumination procession came down the street to light the cressets in front of the tavern. Since I'd walked along with it the night before, I didn't go outside, but the distraction didn't promote conversation.

Next our waiter, decked out in colonial duds yet carrying the kind of large plastic tray seen in any modern restaurant, kept showing up at our table to take our orders, tell us things like why the sugar was brown, and to ply us with homemade relishes, apple cheddar muffins, and Sally Lunn.

At last, Hugh's peanut soup came. I'd skipped that course, saving my appetite for the main meal, but when Hugh let me taste the soup, I went into such ecstasy, he put the bowl in the middle of the table so we could share.

"I still don't understand," he said, sotto voce. "Why is Polly haunting the Carson house?"

"Oh? You admit you believe in ghosts now?"

"Just answer the question."

"Polly vowed to nurse her mother as long as she was needed. Elizabeth's spirit never left the house—she's trapped, refusing to let go of all the bad memories from the two years before her accident. She makes herself relive the symptoms of Brennan's poisoning as a kind of penance, I suppose. She didn't see her husband die or I'm guessing she'd relive his symptoms as well." I wanted to use my forefinger to scoop up the last drops of soup, but controlled the urge. "She's not sane, Hugh—if that can be said about a ghost. Maybe she never was, or the brain damage she suffered that Christmas Day somehow permanently put her mind in a loop that even death couldn't break. So when Polly died, instead of reuniting with her husband and father, she stuck around to keep nursing her mother. I wish . . ."

Hugh frowned. "You wish what?"

"They're both still there, Hugh. Nothing I did this weekend changed that. All I did was find out their stories, not help them escape."

"Pat, don't even think—"

Our waiter appeared, taking bowl and soup spoons. When he moved on to the next table, I said, "Why do I have this bizarre talent, Hugh? I didn't ask for it. But if I have to live with it, I think I'm supposed to use it for more than just satisfying my curiosity. Polly and Elizabeth know someone's listening now. I'm like . . . like . . ."

"Their shrink?" He gave me a free smirk with the sarcasm.

"That's *exactly* it." I smirked back, but I was serious and he knew it. "I have an obligation."

"After dinner we'll be heading back to Bell Run, Pat—"

"We'll be back in a week and a half for your mom's wedding. After that, it wouldn't do you any harm to visit her once a month or so, would it? I'll want to spend time with my future mother-in-law, after all."

That made him smile.

I pressed my advantage. "Elizabeth will be an in-law, too. She's family. I can't *not* try."

The waiter showed up again with Hugh's Cornish hen and my game pie: bits of venison, rabbit, and duck, with carrots and pearl onions in a luscious dark brown gravy, all under a flaky crust. One bite (ooh, rosemary in the gravy!) and my eyes rolled in delight. Three bites later, I paused for air. "Well?"

"The Cornish hen's delicious."

"No, I meant about me working on Elizabeth. Maybe I can get her to dwell on pleasant memories, and to lay off the fusebox and making people sick."

He sighed, switching his fork to his left hand so he could drape his arm along the edge of the table, palm up, as an invitation. Hugh-ese for "okay."

I put my left hand in his, grinning at him. Yet, the gentle pressure of his fingers reminded me of the ring. Best to get this over with.

I took my hand back, sliding the ring off. Again, considering how tight it felt on my finger, it came off too easily. "I can't wear this."

He pursed his lips as he took it. "Because of Tanya?"

"Because of Beth Ann. It's hers. Or should be. Her mom would have wanted that, I think."

He looked at the ring with new interest, almost a LAG. "All right, I'll put it back in my safety deposit box for when she turns eighteen." Worming his arm beneath his pullover sweater, he slipped the ring into the breast pocket of his flannel shirt. "Want to shop for another next weekend?"

"Acey said I should ask you for Great-Aunt Mildred's."

He made a face. "You don't want that one. It's ugly."

A challenge I couldn't resist. Besides, after having an antique ring on my finger all weekend, the modern issues seemed boring by comparison. "At least let me see it."

He shrugged as he turned back to his food. "Whatever floats your boat, but I'll end up buying you one anyway. That is," he looked up, "if you still want to marry me?"

His grin said he was kidding. The insecurity was behind his eyes, where he thought I couldn't see it. "You aren't getting away that easy, Bub," I assured him. "But we *do* need to talk."

The puppy dog look came back, mixed with a dose of the universal male revulsion against "discussing the relationship." Could I tell him he wasn't over Tanya? That he'd been running from his grief all these years and had only now turned to face it?

This wasn't my theory but Beth Ann's, though she didn't know it. I'd had that talk with her. A short talk—neither of us wanted to be uncomfortable for more than ten minutes.

"Dad's been weird since you guys started going out," was her reaction. When asked "weird how?" she'd shrugged. "He mentions stuff he and mom used to do. Out of the blue. Then if I ask about her, he clams up again. And when we were coming home from

Grandmom's on Thanksgiving weekend, he stopped in Richmond and we visited Mom's grave. We *never* did that before."

I'd told her I thought it was a good sign. I hoped it was. Yet, I couldn't bring myself to discuss Tanya with Hugh. I needed to get to know her better myself first. *Paesan'* to *paesan'*.

Instead I brought up a more practical subject. "Your daughter wanted to know where we'd all live. She's afraid we'll leave Bell Run. I told her that wasn't an option for me."

"Nor for me," Hugh said. "I know the trailer's too small for the three of us, and I'm also not abandoning Miss Maggie. She likes to pretend she's independent, but she can't take care of that place by herself."

"She'd be heartbroken if we left." I remembered Miss Maggie's comment about her "own selfish motives"—in fact, I'd thought about it off and on since my early morning walk with her yesterday. "I think she wants to spend some time with me, Hugh, before I get married. I guess she thinks I'll get busy and won't have time later." No, I thought, *I* was afraid of that. "I'd like to take some little trips with her—let her show me around the historic sites in Virginia, however far she's able to travel."

He let out a belly laugh. "You'll end up in South America. Sure you could stand her singing that long?"

"I'll offer it up." I sobered again. "I've lived with her less than a year, Hugh, and she's been so good to me—"

"And you might not get the chance again—" He didn't mean because of marriage. He meant I might not have time because Miss Maggie was pushing ninety-two and nobody lives forever. We both had that scary thought in mind and neither of us could voice it.

He reached across the table and caressed my hand again. "Great idea, Pat. Miss Maggie would love traveling with you."

"Some trips could be the four of us," I suggested. "You and Beth Ann, too?"

He feigned horror. "Me travel with three women? You'd make me stop and ask directions."

"What makes you think you'd be driving?"

We bantered back and forth while we finished our meal, talking about vacations we could all take on spring break or after school let out for the summer.

When the waiter removed our plates and left us to decide about dessert, Hugh took my hand for the third time. "If I'm hearing right, you want to take this engagement slow?"

Part of me—no, two parts: heart and hormones—wanted to shout, "No! Let's get married tonight!" but I asked, "What do *you* want?"

"I want to hop a plane to Vegas right now." He'd read my mind, and the grip of his hand said he meant it. "But I guess slow is better. Not painfully slow, I hope?" His pseudo-evil leer surfaced.

"Not painful at all, Romeo."

We skipped dessert, opting for a moonlit walk through the historic area. Hugh was well-versed in all the dark corners conducive to necking. He led me to the chimney wall of a kitchen where they'd done living history baking that day. The bricks were still warm. With them at my back and him in front of me, I felt nice and cozy.

"I never took Tanya here," he said, as if handing me a gift.

"Yeah? What about every girl in your high school?"

"Quit being fussy." He kissed me in a way that proved he'd learned a thing or two since graduation. An avid student of the subject myself, I paid close attention to the lesson, even expressing a willingness to do extra credit.

But when our studies showed signs of going beyond the curriculum that night, I knew we had to discuss one more thing. I pushed on Hugh's shoulders. "Rich called this afternoon."

"You want to talk about my brother?" He paused to draw in a needed lungful of air, before adding incredulously, "Now?"

"Rich rushed the lab into doing my blood tests this weekend. He called with the results."

Unfortunately, that had the effect of a cool shower. Hugh straightened up, scared. "Well?"

First I reassured him. "I'm fine. Really. It's just that my blood showed a higher than normal tendency to clot. Rich says, given my family history, it's likely genetic, I guess sort of the opposite of hemophilia. He said I'm not anywhere near the danger zone, but I have to avoid anything that can aggravate it."

"Like birth control pills?"

"Right, and I—you see, my cousin Nicola almost lost her baby because of a blood clot, so I asked Rich—"

"You can't get pregnant," Hugh deduced.

"The problem is, I probably *can*. But I shouldn't. Not 'til I have more tests."

The thing about Hugh is, if you give him an opportunity to be a hero, he's there. He hates my playing with ghosts because he can't protect me, but by gum, he could protect me from pregnancy and swore he would, with an air of noble sacrifice that was almost Lancelot-esque.

I was trying not to laugh when he added, "What do you want to do about New Year's Eve?"

"Oh, right. Thursday night. I wanted to ask you—"

He hugged me closer, going all sensitive-guy on me. "If you don't want to take the risk before having tests, Pat, that's fine. Whenever you're ready."

The idiot. Couldn't he tell I was ready *now*? "It's not that. I just— I had this idea for New Year's Eve." I grinned up at him. "And you're gonna hate it."

NEW YEAR

"'I can cure the Itch, the Stitch, the Palsy, and Gout,'" Foot announces with all the slickness and bravado of a carnival barker. "'All pains within, all pains without. If this man has nineteen devils in him, I'll cast twenty out!'"

"My HMO doesn't cover that," says his patient. Miss Maggie, indeed bedeviled, is stretched out on her tartan recliner, eyes shut behind her thick reading glasses. One hand holds a plastic lily upright on her breast, the other clutches the play's script.

Foot nudges her with his reflex hammer. "I'll do the ad-libbing here."

One would presume her wounds are grievous, after fighting and slaying a three-headed dragon (played by Beth Ann and Rich's two youngest sons), then having a rubber-chicken-meteor fall out of the skies to bop her on the head (it missed—Horse's trajectory was off). Add Acey as Father Christmas and Rich's eldest, Bob, as the dress man (Hugh was right, Bob *is* a good actor), and I can see why this play's St. George needs an EMT.

It might not be the way Hugh and I planned to bring in the New Year, but it feels right. As predicted, he hated the idea at first. I told him I'd always spent December 31 at a family reunion, and since I'd be calling the Lees family soon enough, why not start a new tradition? Hugh said, "They won't come." I said, "Let's ask 'em." The upshot? Only Rich and Delia are absent tonight—they're using our hotel reservations. In fact, Rich accepted the offer like a man accepts a lifevest on a leaky ship. Hugh told his brother to leave beeper and cell phone at home. Now if only Delia didn't pack a laptop.

Anyway, here I stand beneath the archway of the living room in my home in Bell Run—standing in case I need to make a quick escape if I smell anything burning in the kitchen. My pork roast will go on the table not long after midnight, less than ten minutes away. Behind me stands Hugh, his arms circling my waist, his lips planting a smooch atop my head at intervals.

All evening I'd been resisting the urge to stare at the new hardware on my finger. Great-Aunt Mildred must have had Popeye forearms to wear this thing—it weighs a ton. The ring is truly ugly: a square of four tiny diamonds, imbedded in a double stripe of garnets that seem too blood red to be real, surrounded by too many scrolls of silver. Keeping the tarnish at bay will be a full-time job.

How could I say no to a ring with that much character? And it fits perfectly. The quote's the real clincher, though. No mushy Browning for Great-Aunt Mildred. She got Shakespeare.

"Wooed in haste . . . wed at leisure."

At my back, I feel Hugh laugh at the antics of his siblings, daughter, and nephews. He doesn't seem to be having regrets, but I look up at him anyway to be sure. He takes it as an invitation to kiss something besides my hair, which I don't mind at all.

"Hey, you two," Foot admonishes, "none of that. You're missing my best lines. Where was I? . . . 'Here I have a bottle of drops, made of lizard's milk and lollipops—'"

Acey: "What's the prescribing info on that?"

Horse: "Imagine the side effects."

Foot shakes the oversized brown bottle over Miss Maggie's prostrate form. "'A drop on her head,'" confetti pours out, "'and a drop on her heart,'" more of the same, "'Rise up, St. George, and play thy part.'"

Miss Maggie sits up, opening her eyes.

"No way!" Horse protests. "The quack doctor isn't supposed to bring the hero back to life."

Foot grins. "You write the play next year. In my version, the doctor works miracles." He cracks his knuckles for punctuation, then waves to his players. "Big finish."

Helping Miss Maggie off the recliner, they form a line. Noses in scripts, they recite in unison, "'God bless the master of this house,'" Miss Maggie takes a bow, "'likewise the mistress, too'" Bob curtseys, giggling daintily, "'and all the little children that round the table go,'" the kids bow, "We've had our fun, our play is done, we hope it brought you cheer,'" the rest of the cast bows, upstaging each other, "'We wish you all within this hall a joyful, glad New Year!'"

Thunderous applause. Okay, maybe not thunderous. Besides Hugh and myself, only Glad, Evelyn, Sachi, and a school friend of Beth Ann's make up the audience. But we're all enthusiastic.

"Two minutes to midnight!" Horse announces.

"Is not," Acey argues. "Your watch is fast."

"We should turn on TV and watch the ball drop," Bob suggests, pulling his dress over his head to reveal chinos and a long-sleeved tee from a production of *The Music Man* he'd done.

Miss Maggie lays down the law. "This is Virginia, not New York. We'll go by my watch." No one challenges her, of course. Four minutes later we're all wishing each other Happy New Year.

I go around bussing everyone on the cheek, deciding a little Italian-style affection won't do the Lees a bit of harm. All the teens blush up to their hairlines.

Foot seems horrified as I approach, but gives me a peck and a smile in return. He doesn't show it, but I know he's feeling down about Irene. When he arrived, he told us there's now a solid case against her. The pharmacist who'd sold her the protriptyline made a positive ID. Plus, tests on the remaining contents of the vanity bag showed the drug in a small bottle of mouthwash. Irene's fingerprints were on everything, but then, she's the wife, right? Thing was, the mouthwash had been a freebie given to Foot by a drug rep in his office Thursday morning. He'd shoved it into his jacket pocket, then stowed it in his shaving kit when he got to his mom's. Irene's prints *shouldn't* have been on that bottle, but they were. And we could all testify she'd been MIA while Foot was outside with Spade.

Not long after midnight, with Hugh and Beth Ann's help, dinner's served in the dining room. Fourteen of us sit down, mind you, which is why I'd had Beth Ann invite her friend. My mom didn't raise a dope.

Miss Maggie stands at the head of the table. For the occasion, she'd mixed up a family recipe wassail of sweet cider, orange slices, and spices, which will go great with the pork. We fill and pass out punch glasses, and she raises hers. "Each New Year's Eve when I was a kid, my grandfather would make us each declare a resolution at midnight before he'd propose a toast. My resolution is to be here next year."

Everyone laughs, but we're all praying the same thing.

"Anyone else?" Miss Maggie asks.

"I resolve to achieve inner serenity," Acey says, "and get Rich to acknowledge acupuncture as a viable therapy."

Evelyn raises his glass. "I'm going to keep up an e-mail correspondence with Spade, keep after him to take his meds. That is, when I'm not busy with my new wife." He and Glad smile at each other and I go all gooey inside.

Foot clears his throat. "I'm seeing one of my colleagues next week, to discuss therapy options. I've decided to wean myself off the damned antidepressants, if only so I can eat everything at dinner next Christmas."

Horse claps him on the shoulder and Acey applauds, saying, "I also resolve to make sure Foot keeps his resolution."

I don't say mine aloud, no doubt out of fear of failure. Besides, the list is too long, involving Hugh, Beth Ann, Miss Maggie, my family in Pennsylvania, Tanya, Elizabeth, Polly, and Bell Run. But I squeeze Hugh's hand beneath the tablecloth and he squeezes back, doing a Groucho Marx thing with his brows, so I know at least one of his resolutions is the same as mine.

When the room's quiet again, Miss Maggie lifts her glass a bit higher. "I can't resist a history lesson—"

We all moan in jest.

"And," she continues, louder, "since this last weekend put me in an eighteenth-century mood, I'm going to paraphrase Benjamin Franklin:

"'Be at War with your Vices,

At Peace with your Neighbors,

And let every New Year find you a better Person.'"

To which most of us respond with variations of "Hear, hear" or "I'll drink to that," except Acey, who says, "'God bless us, every one.' And Buddha bless us, too."

Then, we eat.

THE END

Read on for an excerpt from the
next Pat Montella Mystery by Elena Santangelo

Fear Itself

<small>COMING SOON FROM MIDNIGHT INK</small>

> *"We in America today are nearer to the final triumph over poverty than ever before in the history of any land. The poor-house is vanishing from among us."*
>
> —President Herbert Hoover, 1928

1933—East Main Street, Norristown, Pennsylvania

WHAT I RECALL OF the Depression was everyone saying we didn't have enough to eat. And they always said the coal had so many rocks in it we couldn't make it last a week. Bootleg coal was all we could afford—the small slaggy bits leftover after the good coal was shipped out. Though I didn't know any of that at the time. Only later, when I was older.

Do I remember feeling hungry? No more than usual. What I got to eat was how much I'd eaten every day as long as I could remember.

Same with feeling cold in the winter, I guess. I wore flannel underwear beneath my dress. Over it I wore a heavy sweater, with thick stockings below, hand-me-downs from some cousin or other, knit in better times by my grandmother. We all called her *Nonna*.

At night Aunt Gina would put a hot water bottle under the sheets of the bed I shared with my cousin Delphina. After we were tucked in, my aunt would throw the rug from the floor over us. We couldn't move from the weight. Then our cat would jump up to nestle between our feet and the hot water bottle. She'd lick her fur for maybe twenty minutes, making the whole bed rock. With the bottle, the rug, and the cat, we kept warm enough.

That's what a child remembers. Not the cold, but the way we kept warm. Not the hunger, but the days when we *didn't* eat macaroni for dinner. Or ate it, but with something besides beans or split peas or onions in tomato sauce. Sundays we had ravioli or once in a while Uncle Ennio brought home a chicken.

I can't picture the hand-me-downs we wore so much as when one of us got new clothes, like the brown oxford shoes Del put on when she started junior high early that year, and the white knickers Aunt Gina made my brother Salvatore for his First Holy Communion later in the spring.

It's the out-of-ordinary things that stick. That's why I remember that one week in 1933 so vividly. Roosevelt became our new president right after Lent started that week. We listened to him on the radio. But that was also the week a rich man got deathly ill on our front steps, and when I heard voices in a room with no people, and when our black cat Crisi helped me and Del uncover a secret best left alone.

ONE

February 26, Present Day
"Say *what?!*"

I was talking to a PC, to a laptop screen that seemed to float eerily atop the table in a kitchen otherwise illuminated by the glow stealing in from the hall behind me. I couldn't see wasting electricity by turning on the three-bulb overhead lamp when I didn't need it. The corners of the room were dark shadows, which some folks might think pretty spooky, given that the kitchen was in an 1870s farmhouse with a history of ghosts. Nope, the scariest thing in that room was the number on the screen—the hundred and thirty-two bucks Turbo Tax said I owed the government. Sent a chill up my spine, until that body part matched my nose, ears, and fingers, already cold from the draft coming through the north wall.

My "Say what?" was for the program's question about my car mileage deduction, which I couldn't seem to bend my brain around. I'd had similar reactions to the questions about accounting methods, 401K rollovers, and self-employment health insurance.

Most of my life I'd filled in a 1040EZ. Piece of cake. Those years when I had to deal with inheritance after my mom and dad died, I let H&R Block handle it. Since neither of my parents had written a will (superstitious Italians until the end), and since they *had* left a mortgage, car loan, medical bills, et cetera, I had to sell the house to pay everything, including the tax filer's fee. So I was back to an EZ the next time.

This past year, though, I'd been laid off, collected unemployment, and started a modest gardening business. The less money I made, it seemed, the more forms I was required to file.

Besides all that, I kept getting distracted by the gleam of the PC off the rock on my finger. My advice: never daydream about your wedding while you're doing taxes, especially if Turbo Tax says you owe a hundred and thirty-two bucks. It's depressing. I pictured myself feeding my guests Cornflakes. The food was my main concern. I didn't care about a gown, fancy hall, flowers, or a limo, but everyone *had* to rave about the food, and "everyone" meant several dozen aunts, uncles, and cousins on my side alone.

A hundred and thirty-two smackers. Didn't sound like much in this day and age, but I also had two big-ticket bills coming due before tax day in April: car insurance and health insurance.

I was hoping to start this year's gardening season soon—my clients' flower beds would need cleaning up, and the soil at Mrs. Tilden's ought to be turned over and fluffed up so I could get her turnips and radishes in by mid-March. (According to my family's age-old gardening traditions, root veggies *must* be sown March 19, St. Joseph's Day.) Thing was, the ground was too muddy to work, and we were still having hard frosts overnight, so the leaves protecting shrub roots were best left alone for now.

Chances were good that I'd be borrowing money from Miss Maggie again this coming month.

Last May, I moved to Virginia to live with Magnolia Shelby, a.k.a. Miss Maggie. She was ninety-one and claimed that it made sense for someone her age to have a live-in companion, so I didn't have to worry about room and board. For my part, the experience was rather like raising a two-year-old. Not that she was helpless—far from it— but she had the same sense of wonder and discovery as a tot. She could be just as stubborn, too.

We're not kin, yet somehow, since Fate threw us together, we've become a family, with her filling the void left by my mom and grandmother. She says I'm the granddaughter she never had. Sometimes, though, I feel more like her straight man. Or the Robin to her Batman.

As I sat in the kitchen, watching dollar signs swim dismally across my screen, she was in her parlor, which she called her "War Room" because it was also her office. She's a historian who takes old diaries and letters, annotates them, adds other pertinent data, and voila! puts out books that actually fascinate people like me who hated history in school. These books have made her fairly famous in history circles. Not bad for a woman who took up the career *after* retiring from teaching at age seventy.

Three days from now her revisions to her latest project were due back at her publisher's. That project was titled *No Borders From Above: The Vietnam War Letters of Louis Montella*. Lou was my brother, killed in the war, so the book was dear to my heart. I'd been doing my darndest to stay quiet and out of Miss Maggie's white hair all week.

So when the phone rang the next instant, I pounced. I assumed it was for me, anyway. Hopefully, my beloved, Hugh, was calling to commiserate after returning home from combat, that is, a field trip with his daughter's Cadette Girl Scout troop. They'd gone to a Sunday matinee of *CATS* up in D.C. I'd been invited, too, but I'd begged off. For one thing, we'd spent nearly every weekend together for the last two months—he and Beth Ann needed some bonding time without me. For another, the trip cost eighty dollars a person. Too rich for my blood. Oh, Hugh would have insisted on paying for me, I'm sure, but it's the principle of the thing. Girl Scout trips shouldn't cost so much that it's a hardship for some parents to send their daughters. So I was boycotting.

Anyway, figuring Hugh was on the other end of the jangling phone, hopefully wanting to schedule a little Sunday evening snuggle time, I snatched up the receiver and said, "You home?"

"Uh, actually no. I'm at Ma's." The voice was feminine, the inflections, pure Montella. "Where else would I be on a Sunday night?"

"Cella?" Why I asked, I don't know. I recognized not only my cousin's voice, but her attitude. After all, we'd spent most of our adolescence on the phone with each other. "What are you calling for?"

"Nice to hear your voice, too, Pat."

"That's not what I meant." I had to admit, it *was* good to hear her. Last January, right after I heard she and her husband Ronny had split up, I sent her a funny Hallmark card with a little note. Under my John Hancock, I wrote in my e-mail address (Miss Maggie set up one just for me, bless her). Cella dropped me a line the day she got it and we've been e-mailing every day since. Cheaper for both of us than long distance, plus we could say oodles more that way. So if she was calling, I knew something must be up. "What happened?"

"Uncle Rocco died."

"Oh." Not the worst case scenario, at least. Half expected. Great Uncle Rocco was—come to think of it, I wasn't sure how old he was.

"He was a hundred and two," Cella said, reading my mind the way she used to in high school, "and the last few years, he wasn't . . . well, you know."

"Longer than that. He's been talking to himself nonstop for ages." I had a vivid memory of my mom's wake—Great Uncle Rocco sitting alone in the third row at the funeral parlor, holding a spirited conversation with no one I could see. The memory creeped me out all over again.

"Rocco was *always* a talker" was Cella's explanation. "Just, after a while, we all stopped listening. His granddaughter should have put him in a nursing home sooner, where he would have had other people to talk to all the time. I think he got too used to talking to the walls. Got to thinking the walls were better company. They don't up and leave on you."

I wondered if she really meant her own hubby, but all I said was "It's sad. I always liked Uncle Rocco." And I had. His stories were the most entertaining. As the youngest of eight siblings, Rocco always got into mega-trouble growing up. Not that being an adult stopped him. He told us how during the Roaring Twenties he had, à la Cyrano de Bergerac, helped his brother Tonio woo the honest-to-Pete flapper who became my Great Aunt Benita. Or Uncle Rocco would talk about all of his get-rich-quick schemes during the Depression, or how he learned to fly airplanes in a hurry for World War II, even though he was older than all the guys in his outfit.

Even after he'd begun babbling to himself, I liked Uncle Rocco. "He had one of those easy smiles and a hug for everyone," I added to my eulogy.

Cella agreed. "Lots of charisma. Never heard a mean word out of his mouth."

"You can't say that about most people."

"Especially Beatrice."

Beatrice was Rocco's granddaughter. "Dad used to call her 'Miss Snooty.' She always thought she was better than the rest of the family from the day she was born." I stood to stretch my legs, then took the phone over to the sink so I could refill my tea mug.

"She still thinks so. Listen, Pat, I don't mean to cut you off, but Ma's giving me the eye. Gotta call my brothers yet."

"You called *me* before them?"

"What do you think? I *like* talking to you."

"Wait. Tell me when the funeral is."

"We don't know yet. Wednesday or Thursday. What? You coming up for it?"

I hadn't even been thinking in terms of choice. Montella funerals were like magnets that pulled us all home. Then again, when I thought of logistics—well, I'd just have to drive the distance. Couldn't afford a train ticket. The price of gas, though, would put a hole in my already Swiss-cheese pocket. But I said, "I have to. Rocco was the last of his generation. Dad would want me there. Can somebody put me up for a few days?"

"You kidding? I'll put you up myself."

"At your mom's?" Cella and her kids had moved back home after her split. I knew Aunt Lydia would take me in gladly, but there wasn't an extra bed in her place right now. I didn't relish sleeping on her couch. Aunt Lydia was a staunch believer in plastic slipcovers.

"No, no," Cella assured me. "I have a new place. It's a long story. I'll show you when you get here."

I pictured a small apartment, but at least Cella's couch would be comfy. We talked a half minute more, me saying I could get there Tuesday, her saying she'd e-mail me details tomorrow. I hit the off button on the phone.

"Heat up some water for me while you're at it," said a raspy voice across the room. Miss Maggie was standing beside the table, leaning on her hands, her nose almost touching the laptop screen as she scrutinized it.

Miss Maggie was dressed in yellow sweatpants and a matching heavy fleece top, the collar up to keep her neck warm. In the dim kitchen, it looked like an ominous glow-in-the-dark blob had swallowed her whole, leaving only her head sticking out.

"I thought you were working." Reaching for the kettle, I flicked on the stove's hood light to give us more illumination and make her look less sci-fi.

"Needed a break," Miss Maggie said, working the full-sized mouse we always plugged into the laptop—her arthritis and my patience couldn't deal with the fingertip torture device on the machine. "If I sit too long in the winter, I stiffen up so much, I can't move." She pulled her attention away from the screen, straightening as much as a woman with advanced osteoporosis could. "Make mine hot cocoa, Pat. Yours, too."

I didn't argue. Cocoa sounded perfect right then and, since it was Sunday, I was allowed to break my Lenten fast on chocolate.

Anyway, we stocked the fat-free kind, so not much guilt was involved. I retrieved the box from the pantry.

"I couldn't tell much from your side of the conversation," Miss Maggie continued as I filled the kettle, "but it sounds like you have a funeral to go to back home."

"I'll only be gone a few days." I explained about Great Uncle Rocco, giving his advanced age as an aside only. One did not imply a connection between age and death in front of someone who was in her nineties.

Miss Maggie expressed her sympathies first, then added, "You haven't been back to Norristown in almost a year. Be good for you to have a nice visit. I think we should stay at least through the weekend."

"We? You want to come? Not that it's a problem," I said hastily, hoping it wasn't. Miss Maggie could have Cella's couch and I could sleep on the floor. No big deal. "The family would love it. Aunt Sophie's been dying to meet you." For that matter, all my relatives were. They couldn't fathom an unrelated, non-Italian stranger more or less adopting me out of the blue. And truth to tell, I very much wanted Miss Maggie to meet them. "But, your revisions—"

"I can finish them tomorrow. All I have to do is stop wasting time cursing out my copyeditor every page. But I have to confess, I have an ulterior motive for wanting to go with you."

I poured a half-packet of cocoa into Miss Maggie's mug, in deference to the caffeine's effect on her blood pressure. "If it's that you want to eat gobs of Italian food all week, we're headed for the right place."

She rolled her eyes in anticipation of the ecstasy. Eating was a vocation of hers and Italian food, her favorite. "*Two* ulterior motives then. The other is that I've been wanting to visit . . . actually, while I was tracking you down, Pat, I read all about Montgomery Cemetery in Norristown—"

"Montgomery? Up in the West End? You want to go *there?*" I knew it well because Aunt Lydia and Uncle Gaet had lived only a block away for the first twenty years of my life. Cella and I weren't supposed to play inside the gates, but we did anyway. Montgomery was an old Victorian cemetery, no longer active, complete with ornate angel statues and tall obelisks. In recent years, the local historic society had been painstakingly restoring it.

"A slew of Civil War generals are buried there," Miss Maggie said, "including Winfield Scott Hancock."

Ah, I thought. A pilgrimage. After all, she *was* a historian. "Sure we'll go," I promised. "I'll even call the historical society when we get there to see if they have a map of the place." The kettle whistled and I poured out the water.

"Good. I'll pay your train ticket for that. You make the reservations and—"

"I was going to drive."

"Not recommended." Miss Maggie swung the laptop around so I could see the screen. She'd brought up the National Weather Service website. "Fixing to snow in Pennsylvania Tuesday and Wednesday. Maybe more for the weekend, too. March is coming in like a lion this year."

I brought our mugs over to the table and checked out the forecast. One of those Yankee clipper systems down from Canada, meeting moist air coming up the coast. Only three to five inches predicted, but not something I wanted to drive any distance in. And another possible storm behind it for Saturday.

ABOUT THE AUTHOR

ELENA SANTANGELO is the author of the Pat Montella mystery series, which includes Agatha Award finalist *By Blood Possessed*, published in both the United States and Japan, and *Hang My Head and Cry*. Also an award-winning short story writer, Elena's mystery and ghost tales have appeared American and Japanese periodicals such as *Alfred Hitchcock's Mystery Magazine*, and in the three *Death Knell* anthologies.

When she's not writing, Elena is an avid musician, singing with the Philadelphia Revels and Colonial Revelers, and composing choral music that has been published and performed throughout the country. She also occasionally helps the Pennsylvania State Museum dig up 4,000-year-old spear points.